LORD OF HER HEART

He kissed the tears from her cheeks. "I do love you, Aileanna, and I'm no' marryin' Moira. I willna' go through with the betrothal, no' now."

"Don't . . . don't lie to me. *Lust isn't love*—that's what you said, didn't you? I won't come second to anyone, Rory, not even your dead wife. I deserve more."

He gave her a slight shake. "Stop. Why will you no' try to understand? Aye, I desire you as I never have another, including Brianna. But I do love you, Aileanna, more than I should. And I canna' let you go. I willna' let you go."

"Did you just say you aren't marrying Moira?"

"Aye, 'tis what I said," he growled.

She hesitated then asked, "And you love me?" She lowered her eyes and her cheeks flushed. "As much as you loved your wife?"

"The love I feel for you is no' the same as my love for Brianna was. Canna' you understand that?"

"Aye, I can."

He blinked, then grinned. "I'll make a Scot of you yet, mo chridhe." His eyes darkened. "But now all I want is to make you mine . . ."

Lord
of the Isles

Debbie Mazzuca

ZEBRA BOOKS
KENSINGTON PUBLISHING CORP.
http://www.kensingtonbooks.com

ZEBRA BOOKS are published by

Kensington Publishing Corp.
119 West 40th Street
New York, NY 10018

All Kensington titles, imprints, and distributed lines are available at special quantity discounts for bulk purchases for sales promotion, premiums, fund-raising, educational, or institutional use.

Special book excerpts or customized printings can also be created to fit specific needs. For details, write or phone the office of the Kensington Special Sales Manager: Attn. Special Sales Department. Kensington Publishing Corp., 119 West 40th Street, New York, NY 10018. Phone: 1-800-221-2647.

Zebra and the Z logo Reg. U.S. Pat. & TM Off.

ISBN-13: 978-1-4201-1005-0
ISBN-10: 1-4201-1005-5

First Printing: April 2010

10 9 8 7 6 5 4 3 2 1

Printed in the United States of America

*This book is dedicated to the
memory of my father, Norm LeClair.
Not a day goes by that I don't think about you.
You are my hero, and always will be.*

Thanks . . .

To my amazing husband Perry, and our three incredible children, April, Jess, and Nic. Your love, encouragement, and support, mean the world to me. I love you very much.

To my mom, my sister, and brother, for their enthusiastic support. No one could ask for better cheerleaders. I love you.

To Ludvica, my adopted daughter, for being the best reader a writer could ever hope for.

To my friends and mentors in ORWA. I wouldn't have made it this far without you, especially Coreene, Vanessa, Teresa, and Joyce.

A special thanks to my dear friend and critique partner Lucy.

To my agent Pamela Hardy for believing in me, and making my dreams come true. You're the best!

To my editor John Scognamiglio for taking a chance on me, and for your patience while guiding me through the publishing process. You've been a pleasure to work with.

To my many family and friends. I can't name you all, but you have my deepest gratitude and love.

Chapter 1

The red hatchback came to a grinding stop at the bottom of a desolate gravel road, and the driver flipped off the meter. Wide-eyed, Ali stared at the back of the bald man's head. "You're kidding, right?"

The cabbie shrugged. His eyes meeting hers in the rear-view mirror. "I canna' make it up the hill, lass, on account of all the rain we've had. My car's too heavy you ken, but Dunvegan's just up the road a bit," he said in his thick brogue.

Ali leaned forward, peering past the rhythmic swipe of the windshield wipers to the mist-shrouded trees and the faint outline of a stone tower just beyond them, and released a resigned sigh. She shouldn't be surprised. Lately, where she was concerned, if something could go wrong, it did.

"Okay then, what do I owe you?" she asked as she dug her wallet from the bottom of her black leather satchel.

"Two hundred pounds," the older man answered as he opened the door and heaved himself off the front seat.

Ali let out a soft whistle before she followed after him, her low-heeled shoes sinking in the mud. "Can you give me a receipt, please?"

Her agent and best friend, Meg Lawson, had told her the magazine would pay all her expenses and Ali wasn't about to argue. It meant more money to go toward the hefty student loans she'd accumulated while going to medical school. And the sooner they were paid off the better. It was one of the reasons she'd agreed to take the modeling job in the first place. The money was great, and she'd get a chance to see some of Scotland—at the very least Skye, where the photo shoot was taking place. She just wouldn't think about why she had the time to take the job. If she did, she'd cry, and she'd done enough of that already.

"Aye." He lifted her luggage from the trunk and settled the strap of her carry-on over her shoulder. "I wish I could help with yer bags, lass, but I have a bum knee and wouldn't be much good to you."

"No problem." Ali managed a tight smile as she dragged the heavy suitcase around the back of the car, its wheels getting stuck in the mud. She thanked the man and shoved the receipt he handed her into her bag before heading out on what she hoped would be a short walk to Dunvegan Castle.

The trek was slow going, with the wheels of her suitcase getting stuck in every rut on the narrow, unpaved road. Her mud-splattered black shoes were waterlogged from the puddles she couldn't seem to avoid. In an attempt to save her jeans from ruin, she bent down and rolled them several inches above her ankles. She buttoned the navy blazer she wore over her white blouse—a blouse that had been crisp and clean when she left New York twelve hours earlier, but now was as limp and dirty as she was, or would be, after her little adventure.

Five minutes later she had to admit it wasn't so bad. The air was fragrant with the heady aroma of flowers, the misty rain warm and gentle on her face, and the scenery amazing. Some of the tension eased from her shoulders, and then she heard an ominous rumble, and a bolt of lightning crackled across the gloomy afternoon sky. Within seconds the clouds opened up and the rain came down in buckets. Ali shook her head and laughed. What else could she do—cry?

Rounding a bend in the road, a massive gray stone edifice came into view, and she felt an unexpected spurt of excitement. It looked like something out of a fairy tale with its majestic towers reaching toward the sky. Maybe Meg was right—the change of scenery would do her good.

Gripping the suitcase with two hands, she hauled it onto the pavers of the long driveway. The mud from the wheels on her suitcase splattered her legs, but at least it no longer felt like she was dragging a hundred-pound weight behind her. Hiking up the strap of her carry-on, she dashed toward the massive oak doors.

When she received no response to her first tentative knock she rapped harder, relieved when the door creaked open. She'd begun to think the place was deserted. A tall, elderly man stood framed in the doorway, staring at her, his bright blue eyes wide in his grizzled face, his mouth hanging open.

Ali didn't blame him. She could only imagine what she looked like with her long hair plastered to her head, and mascara no doubt running down her cheeks. "Hi, I'm Ali Graham." She offered her hand, but he didn't take it. Ali didn't think he even noticed—his gaze was riveted on her face.

Splat.

She glared up at the offending carved overhang from which the water had cascaded to land on her head, then back to the man blocking the entrance. "Uhmm, do you mind if I come in?" She didn't want to be rude, but she was drenched.

With a brief shake of his head the befuddled look left his eyes. "Sorry, lass, please . . . please come in." He ushered her into the warmth of the cavernous entrance.

Ali set down her bags on the slate floor and swiped her dripping hair from her face. She pulled her wet clothing from where it stuck to her body and shook it out. "It's really coming down out there," she said in an attempt to make conversation.

"Aye," he murmured, giving her an odd look before closing the door.

The intensity of his stare was beginning to give her the creeps. She wondered if she'd made a mistake coming inside—she was alone and didn't know this man from Adam. Not one to let things slide, Ali asked, "Is something wrong?"

"Sorry, lass, it's just that . . . och, you'll have to excuse an old man for his rudeness." He gave her an embarrassed smile. "I'm Duncan Macintosh, Dunvegan's caretaker. Who did you say you were?"

"Ali . . . Ali Graham. I have a reservation," she said, searching her bag for the elusive piece of paper. "Somewhere." Ali grimaced and pulled the sodden reservation from her jacket pocket. With a wry grin she handed it to him.

A frown creased his brow, and he looked from her to the paper. "Lass, you've come to the wrong place. It's Dunvegan Hotel you'd be looking for. You passed it a ways back."

She looked at the paper he handed back to her, the writing barely legible, but there it was, plain as day, Dunvegan Hotel. "I don't know how I could have been so stupid. Sorry for bothering you." Ali bent down to retrieve her bags from the puddle they'd left on the floor.

"It's no bother, Miss Graham. I was just about to have a spot of tea. You're welcome to join me if you'd like."

"Please . . . call me Ali, and a cup of tea sounds wonderful. Would you have something I could dry off with? I don't want to . . . oh, no." She groaned. "Look what I've done." The beautiful wool area rug beneath her feet was now marked with her muddy footprints. "I'm so sorry."

He chuckled. "It's seen worse. Don't fret. I'll get you some towels and then you can come by the fire and warm up. My wife is off on a wee shop, but when she returns with the car I'll take you over to the hotel. How does that sound?"

"Terrific."

With her jacket and mud-caked shoes disposed of, Ali followed Duncan. She gazed appreciatively at the wood-paneled room he led her into, noting its decorative ceilings with interest. The antique furniture was tasteful and inviting; muted greens and golds complemented the heavy crimson draperies and ornate cherrywood bookcases that ran the length of the drawing room.

"This place is amazing, Mr. Macintosh. You must love taking care of it."

"Och, now, Duncan will do just fine. And aye, it's a wonderful job I have," he said as he dragged a high-back chair closer to the fire and placed a forest green throw over its delicate embroidered fabric. "Sit down, lass. Dry off a bit and I'll get us our tea."

Ali sank gratefully into the chair, then leaned forward to warm her hands in front of the blazing fire. Its woodsy aroma reminded her of a damp day in fall, even though it was only the beginning of August.

Duncan reentered the room carrying a heavily laden silver tray. "Move that wee table over here, lass."

"That's quite a spread. I hope you didn't go to any trouble on my account, Duncan," she said as she placed the table between them.

The older man settled in the chair beside her. "No trouble at all." He smiled. Looking over the rim of the porcelain teacup, he asked, "What brings you to Skye, Ali?"

"I'm doing a photo shoot for *Vogue*. It's a magazine."

"I know of it. They requested permission a few months back to take photos here. So, you're a model, then?"

Ali laughed. "Actually, I'm a doctor, fourth-year resident. But my friend is an agent and every once in a while she passes a job my way. Helps pay the bills," she said, biting into a dainty sandwich.

"I thought you residents were a harried lot. Was it not difficult for you to get the time off?"

Ali choked and took a deep swallow of her tea before she answered, "Not really." Anxious to change the subject, she pointed to a tattered piece of silk encased in glass above the fireplace. "What's that?"

"Ah, that would be the fairy flag," he said, gazing at the box with reverence.

Intrigued, Ali asked, "Fairy flag?"

"Would you be wanting to hear the tale?"

"I'd love to. If you're sure you have the time."

"I always have time for this story, lass." He made himself comfortable; stretching out his long legs, he crossed them at the ankles.

"A long time ago, according to the legend, the Laird of the MacLeods fell in love with a fairy princess."

"Fairy princess? You mean like in storybooks?"

"Aye. Do you not believe in magic, Ali?"

She didn't. As far as she was concerned only children who had been loved and protected had the luxury to believe in magic and fairy tales. Not someone like her, who had been slapped with the harsh realities of life at an early age. But Duncan didn't need to know that.

"Of course." She smiled. "Now don't keep me in suspense, what happened next?"

He studied her with kind eyes, then went on with his story. "The two wished to wed, but the King of the Fairies refused to grant his permission. Noting his daughter's sorrow, he reluctantly relented, but on with one condition; after a year and a day she must return to the fairy realm.

"Within that year the happy couple were blessed with a bonny baby boy. Their time together went quickly, and too soon the heartbroken princess had no choice but to keep her promise to her father. As she tearfully left her husband and baby at the fairy bridge, she made the laird promise never to leave their son alone, or to allow him to cry. Even in the fairy realm, the sound of his sorrow would cause her great suffering," Duncan explained.

Flames shot up from the fire with a loud crackle and pop, and Duncan leaned over, taking a poker to the logs before continuing. "Their laird was grief stricken, and his clan, wanting to cheer him up, organized a celebration. The maid who had been left to mind the wee one could not resist the music and left the bairn alone while she went to watch the festivities. The baby started to cry, and hearing his cries, the fairy princess came back to comfort him. She wrapped him in her silk and was speaking to him in a lyrical voice when the maid returned. The princess kissed her son good-bye, then vanished.

"Years later, the lad came to his father with the story of his mother's visit, and repeated her instructions to him. If ever the clan was in danger, the laird was to wave the silk to call upon the fairies and their help. But the magic could only be summoned three times, and—"

Curiosity getting the better of her, Ali interrupted. "Has it . . . did the MacLeods ever raise the flag?"

"Aye, they did, back in 1570. The MacDonalds, an enemy to the MacLeods, attacked them. Severely outnumbered, the MacLeod unfurled the flag and its fairy magic. To this day no one knows for certain what happened, but the MacDonalds retreated. Some say it's because the fairies made the MacLeod's army swell, but others say something happened to the MacDonald's wife and daughter that day, drawing him from the field, leaving his army in disarray."

"Well, Duncan, that story alone was worth getting soaked for. Thank you."

"My pleasure." The older man glanced at her and seemed slightly embarrassed. "I don't know if you noticed, but I was a wee bit disconcerted when you first arrived."

Ali grinned. "Now that you mention it, I did."

Color bloomed in the man's heavily lined cheeks. "I should have said something. Come, I'll show you the reason."

Ali padded barefoot across the thick oriental carpet to the far end of the room where Duncan stood in front of a large gilt-framed portrait. He stepped aside and her jaw dropped. At first glance it was as though Ali stood in front of a mirror. The woman in the painting could have been her.

"That would be Brianna MacLeod, wife to Rory. He was laird in the latter part of the sixteenth century. The resemblance is uncanny, don't you think?"

"I do," she murmured, touching her wavy and still wet platinum blond hair. The woman in the portrait's long spiral curls were a burnished gold and caressed her delicate heart-shaped face. Her eyes were coffee colored, whereas Ali's were blue, but other than that, they could have been twins.

The man chuckled at her expression before turning back to the portrait. "She was a MacDonald. Their marriage brought an end to the families' long-standing feud, but they didn't have many years together before she died in childbirth."

"How sad," Ali said, drawn to the woman in the portrait. Although Brianna MacLeod radiated happiness in the painting, an almost palpable sense of sadness washed over Ali, and she took an unconscious step backward. She looked at Duncan to see if he felt the same thing, but he'd already moved away.

"And this is Rory, her husband." Duncan pointed proudly to the portrait on the other side of the large picture window.

For one moment, just as she turned away from Brianna's portrait, Ali sensed the coffee-colored eyes following her. She shook off the feeling. Dismissing the notion out of hand, she joined Duncan in front of the second portrait. Her uneasiness faded the instant she looked at the man in the painting. She sucked in an appreciative breath. Now *that* was a highland hunk.

Rory MacLeod was breathtaking. Wavy black hair accentuated high, chiseled cheekbones and a firm jaw. The sensual curve of his full mouth hinted at a man who laughed often. His green eyes glittered with a penetrating intelligence as he looked down his straight and aristocratic nose at her. He exuded power and strength. A man's man— no metrosexual there.

A sudden draft swirled around her bare feet and ankles. The cold air enveloped her in its icy embrace, causing goose bumps to form beneath her skin. Ali tried to contain the teeth-chattering shiver by wrapping her arms around herself.

"Och, and look at you, freezing in those wet clothes while I blather on. Come, I'll set you up in one of the rooms where you can change."

Ali nodded, unable to tear her gaze from Rory MacLeod, mesmerized by the powerful warrior he portrayed. She jumped when Duncan patted her shoulder. "Oh . . . sorry." With one last look at her handsome highlander, she followed the caretaker from the room.

"I'm going to give you a special treat." Duncan winked at her as he unhooked the red velvet rope that blocked the polished wooden staircase. "But you must promise never to tell."

"I promise." She smiled.

As they made their way up the curved staircase, Duncan relayed more of the MacLeod family's history, but Ali barely heard him, her mind filled with images of Rory and Brianna. She thought if she closed her eyes she would see them, young and in love, roaming the halls of Dunvegan Castle. Touching the wood-paneled walls, running her hand along the thick balustrade, Ali felt close to them, a part of their history. Hundreds of years ago they had walked these stairs; laid a hand on the same railing and walls.

Ali snorted, shaking her head at her whimsical musings. Totally out of character for her, she blamed it on jet lag.

"Here you go." Duncan opened the door with a flourish. "The laird's chambers."

Ali quirked a brow. "Are you sure, Duncan? I don't want to get you in trouble."

"Don't give it another thought. The present day laird doesn't sleep here, but Rory MacLeod once did. And after my behavior earlier, I thought it the least I can do."

"Please." Ali shook her head with a smile. "It was no big deal, but I'm not going to refuse. This is amazing," she said, stepping into the bedroom.

Duncan set her suitcase beside the four-poster bed. "It's chilly in here," he said as he crouched beside the stone fireplace across from the bed. "I'll get a fire going and leave you to freshen up. You can take a wee lie-down if you'd like, Ali. You're probably tired from your long journey. Afterwards you can join my wife and me for supper and then I'll take you over to the hotel, if you'd like."

"If you're sure it's no trouble I'd love to." Her gaze was drawn to the window and the breathtaking view. Dunvegan sat on top of a rocky hill with a rain-swept lake at its feet and cloud-draped hills beyond.

"There, you're all set, lass," Duncan pronounced, rubbing the soot from his palms onto the sides of his brown corduroy pants before heading for the door.

As soon as the door closed behind him, Ali stripped off her wet clothing. She laid them over the chintz-covered chair, but not before retrieving a white towel from the foot of the bed to protect the obviously expensive piece of furniture. Everything in the castle looked as though it belonged in a museum. Ali gave a rueful grin. It was a museum, and if she planned on using her paycheck to pay off her loan, she'd better not damage anything.

Settling her suitcase on the big bed with its opulent scarlet coverings and mounds of pillows, Ali flipped it open. She pulled out a long black T-shirt—her nightwear of choice— and slipped it over her still-damp head. Anxious to warm her chilled bones, Ali walked to the fireplace and sat on a small area rug in front of the roaring blaze. Tugging a brush through her hair, she studied the tapestry that took up most of the white plastered wall on the opposite side of the room. It depicted a battle in all its gruesome glory, and Ali was thankful she hadn't been born back then—an era when bloodshed was an everyday occurrence, and life, at least in her opinion, held little value.

The shiver that ran through her had nothing to do with the cold. Ali couldn't abide violence of any kind. She turned away from the tapestry, afraid she'd have nightmares if she didn't. Running her fingers through her hair and finding it dry, Ali walked to the bed and crawled beneath the crisp, cool sheets.

She sighed—heavenly.

Ali snuggled into the warmth that enveloped her and drifted off to sleep.

"Uhmm," she murmured when a heavy hand caressed her thigh. Sliding the stretchy fabric over her hips, the man kneaded her bottom, pressing her to his long, powerful body. Ali groaned. This was one dream she didn't want to wake up from. All she wanted to do was get rid of the material that bunched between her and the man in her dreams, Rory MacLeod. It seemed he had the same idea. He tugged the T-shirt over her head, and she lifted her arms to help him. Free from the confines of her nightshirt, she wrapped a leg over his, stroking the taut muscles beneath her hand.

A deep, husky voice whispered in her ear words she didn't understand, but she didn't care, not with his big hand cupping her breast. Ali arched her back, her body begging for more. She heard a low chuckle, and gasped when he squeezed her breast, tweaking the puckered nipple between strong, calloused fingers. She nuzzled his chest, inhaling his heady, masculine scent before she lifted her face for a kiss. His mouth closed over hers—hot, so very hot—and he swallowed her moan of pleasure. His tongue dueled with hers, exploring with a tenacity that left her weak with desire. She

quivered with anticipation when he trailed his fingers over
the heated flesh between her thighs, inching his way to her
moist core. Ali shuddered. She'd never had an erotic dream
before and was afraid to open her eyes, not wanting him or
his fingers to disappear. She didn't want to wake up, not
when it felt so good. She'd rather sleep forever.

He raised his mouth from hers. "Ah, Bree, my love, I've
missed you."

Ali stiffened. *What the hell did he just say?*

It was bad enough the men in her life wanted someone
else—what was wrong with her that she couldn't even sat-
isfy them in her dreams? Before she had a chance to mull
over her ineptitude with men, he took her nipple deep into
the heat of his mouth and suckled. Ali shifted, pressing her
breast to his lips, rocking her hips against the hard, banded
muscles of his thigh. She was close, so close. Rubbing
harder, faster, she anchored herself with a hand to his side.

Her dream lover cursed, loudly, and shoved her aside.

Ali blinked, and slowly turned her head. In the dim light
of the flickering candle she saw him: big, powerful, and
grimacing in pain. She scrunched her eyes shut and took a
steadying breath.

He wasn't real.

He couldn't be.

*It's just a dream, Ali. You were thinking about the man
before you went to sleep, that's all it is—an illusion.*

Ali opened her eyes one at a time. Biting the inside of
her lower lip, she pinched the big arm that lay on top of the
covers, jumping when a guttural curse exploded from his
lips. He was real, and he was in her bed.

Ali screamed and tried to scramble from the bed, tugging her entangled foot from the sheets.

Thud.

She fell onto the cold, hard floor.

Chapter 2

Ali didn't have time to contemplate the damage to her lower anatomy, not with the pounding of running feet coming closer. The last thing she wanted was to be caught bare assed on the floor by Duncan Macintosh. She scanned the room for somewhere to hide. Seeing no other choice, she scurried beneath the bed in time to hear the door crash open.

Beneath the heavy canopy of timber, she saw two men rush into the room. Duncan Macintosh was not one of them. Afraid if she could see them they'd see her, Ali shuffled farther into the shadows. The men spoke in hushed tones at the entrance of the room. Certain she was soon to be discovered, Ali felt around for her T-shirt. Relieved when her fingers came in contact with the stretchy fabric, she carefully pulled it toward her. Her muscles tightened as cold from the floor seeped into her skin.

Ali blinked, touching the hard surface beneath her, positive when Duncan had shown her into the room earlier the floor had been hardwood. She ducked her head to get a better look at the rest of the interior. Nothing looked the same, right down to the chocolate-brown comforter that had been scarlet.

How the hell had that happened?

"I'm no' dead yet, so you can stop with yer whisperin'," the man in the bed above her rasped.

Far from it, Ali thought, remembering the heat of his kiss, how his hands had caressed her bottom, bringing her . . . She shook the thought from her head before embarrassment consumed her, leaving a pile of ashes in her place. How could she have done *that* with a stranger? The men moved closer, their brown leather boots inches from her face.

Who are these people, and where's Duncan?

"You'd be all right then, Rory? We heard a scream and a loud crash. We thought you'd fallen from yer bed."

Rory? Oh, come on, this had to be some kind of a joke. Lying flat on her back, Ali wriggled into her T-shirt, smoothing it over her thighs.

"'Tis no' me you heard, but the lass." The bed creaked, a groan of pain accompanying his statement.

Ali stilled, frozen in place.

"There'd be no one aboot but you, lad."

"Rory, 'tis on account of yer wound. You must have imagined it."

"Nay, she was in my bed, of that I'm certain—willin' and eager."

Ali's face flamed. *Now, isn't he a gentleman. The big jerk.*

One of the men cleared his throat. "Mayhap 'twas one of the serving wenches."

"Nay, I thought 'twas Bree come to take me with her." The last was spoken so quietly Ali had to strain to hear what he said.

Someone cursed before saying, "You'll no' die, Rory. I'll no' allow it. 'Tis why I . . ." The man grunted as though he'd had the wind knocked out of him.

"I ken it wasna' Bree. The lass had the look of her, but bigger. Her breasts were full, and her arse . . ." His voice trailed off.

Ali groaned inwardly, deciding if this Rory person didn't soon shut up, she'd make sure he felt worse than he obviously did now.

"Nay, Rory, lie back," one of the men said before gasping, "Yer wound, 'tis reopened."

"I think she tried to finish me off."

Both men cursed at the same time Ali did. She'd had enough. It was her bed the man had crawled into—either that or he'd somehow managed to get her into his own, taking advantage of her while she slept. She ignored the little voice inside her head that said it would be a toss-up on who had taken advantage of whom. And now he seemed to be accusing her of trying to kill him.

Kill him? For God's sake!

It was too much, and Ali didn't plan on listening to any more of it, not without defending herself. With a closed fist, she whacked at the men's feet. "Get out of my way," she said, dragging herself from under the bed.

Two men dressed in old-fashioned attire—fitted suede pants tucked into their boots and white linen shirts—backed away from her with their mouths agape. The older one was tall and had a powerful build, his dark red hair threaded with silver, his brown eyes wide as he stared at her. The other man was much younger, his hair a golden brown, almost as handsome as the man from her dreams. He opened and closed his mouth, his gaze swiveling from Ali to his companion.

Hands on her hips, she turned to confront the man in the bed. "I didn't try to kill you . . . you big jerk, and what the hell were you doing in my bed in the . . ."

The rest of the question died on her lips. It was him—Rory MacLeod—the man in the portrait. She rubbed her eyes, but nothing changed. He was still there, in all his glorious perfection—except he was bleeding. A circle of crimson spread over the thick white linens pressed to his side.

"You're hurt," she gasped.

"Aye." Even in the dim light she could see the accusation in his emerald gaze.

Ali shook her head. "I didn't do it on purpose. I didn't know." She leaned over him to get a better look before being roughly jerked away. Strong hands restrained her, biting into the flesh of her upper arms.

She struggled to free herself from the younger man's grasp. "Let go of me. This man needs medical attention. I can help him—I'm a doctor."

"Let her go, Iain." The older man forcibly removed Iain's hands from her arms before dragging her to the other side of the room. Iain followed in their wake.

"Who are you?" the red-haired man growled, his expression fierce.

"Dr. Aileanna Graham, and there's no time for this. I told you, that man needs my help." She'd had to deal with over-protective family members before, but this was ridiculous.

"Where are you from?"

"New York." She rolled her eyes at the blank expression on the big man's face. "Look, this will have to wait or I swear to you he's going to bleed to death."

"How did you get in his chambers?" His manner had changed, no longer aggressive; there was an odd look in his eyes.

Ali let out a frustrated sigh. "I don't know. I fell asleep in another room, and then I found myself in bed with him." She jerked her chin toward the man named Rory, and heat suffused her cheeks. "So maybe the question isn't how I got in here, but who the hell put me in his bed, and why?" It was something she wanted to know, along with why they were dressed the way they were, and what this Rory person was doing here instead of at a hospital. But now was not the time for discussion.

Iain looked at the older man, a gleam of excitement in his eyes. "Fergus, they sent her."

"Quiet, lad," the other man snapped.

Ali crossed her arms over her chest. "I don't know what the two of you are talking about, or what's going on here, but I'm warning you, you'd better send for an ambulance. Your friend needs to be in a hospital, so I'd suggest you call 911 immediately."

Again with the blank stares.

Okay, so maybe it wasn't 911 in Scotland. "I don't care what number you call, but we have to get him to a hospital."

The man named Fergus shook his head slowly from side to side. "'Tis up to you, lass. There'd be no one else."

"I don't understand."

"There'd be no time to explain. See to our laird, if you please."

"Laird?"

"Aye. Laird MacLeod."

Lord Rory MacLeod, the clothes, the . . . no, she wouldn't go there. Not now. Whoever he was, he needed her help. With one last look at the men who watched her, their expressions bemused, she returned to her patient's bedside.

Rory MacLeod's look-alike reached out his big hand. Clamping it around her wrist, he jerked her toward him. "Who . . . who are you?" he rasped, the effort obviously costing him.

"Doctor Aileanna Graham." She pried his fingers from her wrist.

He opened his mouth to say something, but Ali silenced him with a firm, "Be quiet." She placed a finger to his lips when he tried to protest. "Shh," Ali said, trying not to think about how that particular set of lips had felt, pressed to hers.

She pushed aside her wayward thoughts and her professional persona slid into place. "Your questions can wait."

She laid her palm against the side of his face, then his forehead, relieved to find he didn't have a fever.

"Could you get Duncan for me?" she asked Iain, who was closest to the bed.

"Duncan?" the younger man asked, his brow furrowed. "There'd be no Duncan here."

Ali took in a deep, calming breath. Don't think about it. Do. Not. Think. About. It. "I need something to stop the bleeding. Can you bring me some fresh linen? And I'll need some more candles, or whatever it is you use for lighting."

"Aye." Iain shot a quick glance over his shoulder before heading for the door.

"And clean water and soap while you're at it," Ali called after him.

Sitting on the edge of the bed, she brought Rory's arm across her lap and wrapped her fingers around his thick wrist to check his pulse. She tried to ignore his intense gaze, fighting the urge to smooth the heavy lock of raven black hair from his forehead. Ali shook her head when Fergus tried to speak to her; without a watch she needed to concentrate. The older man didn't argue. Placing his hands behind his back, he rocked on his heels. Waiting patiently, his fierce expression softened when every so often he glanced at her patient.

Ali rose to her feet and lowered the comforter. Removing the makeshift bandage, she tried to mask her reaction to the deep, jagged gash in his side and the fresh gush of blood. She swallowed. The muscle in his jaw pulsated, sweat beaded on his brow, and his complexion turned chalky.

"I'm sorry," she murmured. "I have to examine the wound. I'll be as gentle as I can."

He gave a jerky nod.

"How did it happen?"

"In battle," he said between clenched teeth.

Battle? Ali assumed she must have misunderstood him.

Unless he meant they did reenactments of battles here. She had gone to one in Virginia, and even though she knew it wasn't real, she'd had to leave. "No, I mean, what did this to you?"

"A sword, lass," he explained, as though he spoke to a child.

A sword . . . in battle. "For God's sake, did you have to use the real thing? Honestly, that's about the stupidest thing I've ever heard of. A real sword." She shook her head while she palpitated his abdomen. Moving lower, Ali folded back the comforter to just below the top of his hipbone.

"Lass, I doona' think I can manage *that*." A weak smile tugged at the corner of his full, sensuous mouth.

Ali raised a brow. She couldn't believe the man had the strength to tease. The amount of blood he appeared to have lost should have rendered him unconscious. He cursed, glaring at her when she pressed her fingers inches from the wound. Ali staunched the flow with the clean side of the old bandage, and held the fabric to the candle on the bedside table. Examining it for signs of infection, she was relieved when she didn't see any. She sniffed at the cloth just to be sure.

A commotion at the bedroom door drew her attention. A gray-haired woman in a long puce gown followed Iain—who carried the buckets of water—into the room with an armful of white sheets, and a lantern dangling from her hand. When Ali came around the bed to retrieve the linens, the older woman drew in a shocked breath.

"Lass, yer naked," she exclaimed.

"Nay, Mrs. Mac, her dress may be odd, but she is no' naked. I would've noticed," her patient assured the older woman.

Ali looked down at her T-shirt. She didn't know what was so odd about it. But if she could have found her damn suitcase she would've changed. She might not be naked, but knowing she had nothing on underneath, that's pretty much how she felt.

She turned on him. "Shh, rest."

He rolled his eyes.

"Here, lass, put this around you. 'Tis no' decent what you have on." The woman retrieved a long length of red and black tartan and a thick black belt from the end of the bed. Wrapping the fabric around Ali, she fastened it at her waist with the belt. It fell well past her calves with one end draped over her shoulder. Mrs. Mac stepped back to view her handiwork. "'Twill have to do."

Ali clamped her mouth shut, knowing to protest would do her no good. A trace of humor glinted in her patient's eyes and she scowled at him. "Not a word out of you."

"I was only goin' to say my plaid is verra becomin' on you, lass."

She snorted. "I'm sure. Mrs. Mac, I need some alcohol to disinfect his wound. Unless you have some antiseptic on hand, it's the only thing I can think of."

"I doona' ken what ant . . . antiseptic is, lass, but I think I ken what you mean by alcohol." With that said, the woman set off.

Ali pressed her fingers to her temples, rubbing in a slow, circular motion. *Don't think, don't think.* She repeated the mantra in her head. She took a cloth and dipped it into one of the buckets, groaning when she saw the color. "I can't use this water. It's dirty."

"Nay, lass, 'tis fine." Fergus's brow furrowed.

"No, it's not fine," she snapped. "If any of this gets into his wound he risks infection. The water has to be boiled first." She glanced over at Rory, expecting him to say something, but his eyes were closed, and his breathing seemed shallow.

Ali cursed, ignoring the men's startled expressions.

"What's wrong? Is my brother gettin' worse?" Iain asked. A tremor threaded through the deep timbre of his voice.

Ali placed a comforting hand on his arm. "Look, I'm going to do everything I can to make sure he comes through this. We have a couple of things in our favor. First, as far as I can tell there's been no damage to any vital organs, and that's a very good thing. Second, I don't see any signs of infection and that's a big plus."

Iain smiled weakly. "Now I ken why the—"

The older man cleared his throat, interrupting the younger MacLeod. He shot him a silencing look. Ali raised a brow, but before she could ask Iain what he meant to say, Mrs. Mac returned. Ali thanked her, sniffing the contents of the earthenware pitcher. She choked on the fumes, her eyes watering. "That should work," she commented dryly.

The woman looked relieved. "And here'd be the soap you asked for."

Ali scrubbed her hands up to her elbows in the water from one of the buckets. "If any of you want to touch Rory you must wash your hands like I am, all right? We'll set this bucket aside for washing, but the water has to be changed often."

They stared at her like she was from another planet, which was exactly how she was beginning to feel.

Ali sighed. "You have to do as I say. We can't let his wound become infected."

"Mrs. Mac, the lass says the water has to be boiled before she'll use it," Fergus informed her.

"Och, well, she seems to ken what she's aboot. Come, Iain, help me with these. Fergus, you stay with the lass." The woman gave him a meaningful look, and Ali had the distinct impression they didn't trust her.

"What can I do, lass?" Fergus asked.

"At the moment the only thing we can do is try to control the bleeding. I'll wait until Iain returns and then I'll pour the alcohol into his wound to ward off infection. Hopefully the bleeding lessens. If it doesn't, well, we'll deal with that when the time comes." Rory sucked in a ragged breath and Ali stroked the thick waves of hair back from his face.

"I didna' ken you could be gentle, lass," he murmured.

She smiled down at him. "I can be very gentle, but only when my patient does as he's told."

"Ah, then, I promise to do whatever you want me to."

Ali had a sneaking suspicion Rory MacLeod's smooth tongue could be a very dangerous thing. "I'm glad to hear it. Now close your eyes and sleep."

"Aye," he murmured.

When Fergus called out to her, Ali drew her gaze reluctantly from Rory's beautiful face. He looked like a dark angel.

"Lass, I think you best have another look."

She pushed the woolen blankets lower.

"Can you no' leave a man some dignity?" Rory said as he watched her from beneath heavy-lidded eyes.

"You don't have to worry—you're decent. Besides, I'm a doctor, there's nothing you have that I haven't seen before."

The older man guffawed.

"I doona' think they're all the same, lass," her patient said, sounding disgruntled.

She shrugged. "If you've seen one, you've seen them all."

Rory's gaze narrowed on her. "Where do you hail from?"

"New—" she began before being interrupted.

"Rory Mor, do as the lass says and sleep. Yer questions will wait."

Ali removed the blood-soaked cloth. Replacing it with a fresh one, she applied pressure. Fergus caught her eye and shrugged. "He needs rest."

"Umhmm, he does," she agreed, raising a brow at the older man's continued scrutiny.

"Sorry, I didna' mean to stare, but 'tis uncanny how much you resemble the Lady Brianna, is all."

"So I've heard." *And seen,* Ali reminded herself.

"But only at first glance. There'd be differences."

Ali snorted. "I heard that, too."

"'Tis what you get for hidin' under my bed," Rory commented dryly.

A chuckle rumbled deep in Fergus's barrel chest.

Ali felt the color rise to her cheeks. "*You* are supposed to be sleeping."

"How am I to sleep with the two of you yammerin'? I need a drink."

"As soon as the water's been boiled I'll give you some."

"Water." He scowled. "I doona' want water. I want ale."

"'Tis no' a bad idea, lass. He'll need somethin' to make him sleep."

Ali looked at the blood seeping through the bandage. Sooner or later she would have to deal with it. If all they had was alcohol to knock him out, then she had little choice but to use it. Ali nodded. "All right."

She leaned over and adjusted the pillows behind Rory's back, careful not to jolt him. The plaid slipped from her shoulder, and she bit her lower lip. His warm breath heated the sensitive skin of her breasts through the thin fabric of her T-shirt. Her nipples tightened in response. Please let his eyes be closed, she silently prayed.

"'Tis no' fair to tease a dyin' man, lass," he said, his lips so close the material of her T-shirt rippled.

Oh, for God's sake. "You're not dying," she snapped, her tone more brusque than she intended. Ali stepped away, putting some distance between them.

"That's good to hear," Iain said, coming into the room with a mug in one hand and a bucket in the other. "And yer askin' fer ale—another good sign."

"Bloody hell, lass, you could have warned me you planned on gettin' rough," Rory growled when she placed the linens, as gently as she could, beneath his wounded side.

She grimaced and reached for the pitcher of alcohol on the bedside table. "Fergus and Iain, I'll need you to hold him down for me." Ali sighed when the three men glared at her. "I'm sorry, but I don't have a choice. I have to make sure there's no infection before closing the wound, and the only way to do that is to pour the alcohol on it. I won't lie to you," she told Rory. "It's going to burn."

Fergus and Iain tightened their hold on her patient as she carefully poured the amber liquid into the gaping wound. Ali clenched her teeth when Rory let out a string of expletives. Once she felt confident it was thoroughly cleansed, she returned the pitcher to the bedside table. "You can let him go. I'm finished."

For the last hour Ali had kept herself busy tearing the linens into strips while they plied Rory with alcohol. She turned to look at her patient, trying not to smile in response to his crooked grin. The man had the constitution of a horse. At this rate, they were going to have to hit him over the head to knock him out. The alcohol hadn't done any good. She pressed her palm to the side of his face, relieved there was still no sign of fever.

Tension knotted the back of her neck, and Ali rolled her shoulders in an attempt to ease the taut muscles. She knew the cause. She had been trying not to think about it, but she had no choice, something had to be done to stop the bleeding. She had been optimistic when the bleeding had subsided, but now a telltale circle of claret red appeared on the snowy white linen. He couldn't afford to lose any more blood.

"Lass, why doona' I bring you a wee drop of ale?" Mrs. Mac offered.

"Thank you, but I better not." She checked Rory's pulse, noting its steady rhythm.

"Will you be wantin' to wrap the wound now?" Iain asked.

"No," Ali said, unable to meet the younger man's gaze.

"But—" Iain started to protest.

"Ah, would you be stitchin' it then, lass?" Fergus interrupted him.

Ali shook her head. Clearing her throat, she said, "No, the wound is too wide, too deep. But he's lost too much blood and I can't let it go on any longer."

She felt Rory's gaze bore into her. "What is it yer plannin' on doin'?"

"I don't have a choice; the wound has to be cauterized." Ali's stomach lurched at the thought of what she had to do. "I'll have to seal the wound together. Burn it."

"I ken what you meant, lass," he commented dryly.

"Nay!" Iain shouted.

"Aye, lad." Fergus nodded. "The lass is right. I've seen it done before." He turned to Ali. "Do you think you can manage, because I ken I canna' do it."

"Yes, but not if he's awake," she admitted. Bile rose in her throat at the thought of him suffering, and her being the cause.

"Do it now," Rory ordered.

Ali's head jerked up. "I told you, I can't, not while you're awake. Just drink that damn stuff."

"It won't work, Aileanna," he said. Her name rolled off his tongue, his tone soothing.

Heat unfurled in her belly as though he caressed her.

"He speaks the truth, lass," the older man said, sympathy in his eyes.

"Get my sword, Fergus."

Ali's gaze flew to Rory. "No . . . no," she repeated when Fergus tried to press the weapon into her hand. "For God's sake, I can't. And certainly not with this. I can barely lift it," she protested.

Rory let out a ragged breath. "Give her my dirk."

Ali wrapped her arms around her waist, and shook her head. She was furious at what he wanted her to do. He was wide awake, for God's sake. She walked to the hearth and swiped a tear from her cheek. She heard Fergus coming toward her. Taking her hand, he placed the knife in her palm. He rubbed her shoulder and bent his head to her ear. "You can do it, lass. The fairies wouldna' have sent you if you couldna'.

"Yer the only one who can save him."

Chapter 3

Fairies. Only you can save him. The words echoed in Ali's head. She turned to gape at Fergus. "What the hell are you talking about?"

The big man shot a furtive glance over his shoulder before saying, "Hush, you canna' let the laird ken what I've told you."

"Know . . . know what? That you think I've been sent by fairies?" she hissed.

"Och, now, lass, doona' fash yerself," Fergus pleaded, keeping his voice low.

"I'm holding a knife, preparing to cauterize the wound of a man who is wide awake, and you're telling me I've been sent by fairies . . . fairies . . . for God's sake. And you expect me to stay calm?" She glared at him.

"Aye." He grimaced. "Please, lass, I promise I'll explain everythin' to you once 'tis over."

Ali's brain swirled with images and emotion, panic leading the way. She felt like she'd been tossed into another world where everything she knew didn't matter, and her confidence plummeted. She didn't trust her abilities, not here, not now. She wanted to run as far and as fast from Dunvegan as she could. Part of her hoped it was a nightmare and that she'd wake up, but she knew it wasn't. Just as she knew the man in the bed was real, and beautiful, and strong. So unlike anyone she'd ever met before. And she couldn't run away and leave him to bleed to death.

Ali glanced over her shoulder at Rory. His eyes locked with hers. He gave her a weak but encouraging smile, as though somehow he sensed her distress. She knew then she wasn't going to leave him—not yet.

"You have no choice, lass, it has to be done," he said quietly.

Ali gave him a brisk nod. He was right. Fairies aside, no one else was stepping up to volunteer for the job. The sooner it was done the better—for both of them. She thrust the knife into the flames, letting out a yelp of pain when the handle heated along with the blade.

"Fergus, did you no' wrap the hilt?" Rory growled.

Sheepishly, the older man shook his head and retrieved the knife. "Sorry, lass." He dug through a battered chest and found a piece of leather and a cloth to wrap around the metal shaft before reheating it over the flame.

After handing it to Ali, he went to stand behind Rory. She shook her head and pointed to where she wanted him. "I need you to hold the wound together while I sear it closed."

The man paled.

"Iain, it would be better if you sit behind your brother and hold him by his shoulders," she advised the younger MacLeod, whose mouth was set in a grim line. "Right about there, Fergus." She motioned once more to the side of the bed, grateful he would shield Rory's face from her line of sight. "Now press the edges together. No . . . no, I don't want to burn you. All right, much better." She tried to ignore Rory's agonized curse.

In an effort to center herself, Ali closed her eyes, only to find herself back in the operating room with a panicked

Drew, her supervisor and ex-boyfriend, yelling accusations at her, the equipment flatlining—a young mother dead.

"Lass, are you all right?" Fergus's tone was gruff with concern.

"Yes . . . yes, I'm fine." I will be. I have to be. *You didn't make the mistake,* the little voice in her head reminded her. Drew did. *You're a good doctor, no matter what he said.* Heat leeched from the red-hot steel blade to Ali's palm. A stinging reminder of where she was, and what she had to do.

Before she lost her nerve, Ali lowered the blade to the wound. The sizzling sound was quickly drowned out by Rory's shout of pain. His body jerked, then went still. Ali gagged as the smell of burnt flesh assaulted her nostrils. She pressed a fist to her mouth, and Fergus gently removed the knife from her trembling hand.

"Yer a brave lass," Mrs. Mac crooned, wrapping a comforting arm around Ali. "Come, I think you could use some lookin' after now." The woman gently guided her away from the bed.

"But . . . I . . ." she began to protest, looking to where Rory lay unconscious in the bed, his blue-black hair a sharp contrast to his paper white skin, his full sensuous lips pulled into a thin line of pain.

"Fergus and Iain will watch over him fer now. I've prepared a hot bath fer you and laid out a change of clothes."

There was nothing else she could do for him, other than pray the wound didn't become infected. If it did, Ali didn't know if she'd be able to save him. "Thank you." Exhausted, her muscles aching, Ali allowed herself to be led away.

Mrs. Mac opened the door to an adjoining room. "'Twas the Lady Brianna's. Come," she said when Ali hesitated in the doorway of a room twice the size of Rory's. The four-poster bed covered in maroon satin looked inviting, but it was the large wooden tub-like structure in front of a blazing fire that drew her in. She inhaled the lavender-scented water in an effort to alleviate the acrid smell that still invaded her senses. "Lovely." Ali sighed. Her gaze took in the pastoral tapestries that lined the walls and covered the floors. "What a beautiful room."

"Aye, the laird spared no expense when it came to his lady."

"He must have loved her very much." Ali tried to ignore the tightening in her chest when she stated the obvious.

"Aye, that he did," the older woman said. "He's had a hard time of it."

"When . . . when did she die?" Ali asked.

"'Tis been almost two years."

She hesitated before asking her next question. "How did she die?" Afraid she already knew the answer.

"In childbirth, lass." Mrs. Mac watched her closely.

Ali spun on her heel and headed for the door. "I'm sorry, but I really do have to talk to Fergus." She tried to get around the woman who now stood between her and the door.

Mrs. Mac shook her head, taking Ali's ice-cold hands in hers. "'Twill do you no good, lass. There's nothin' can be done aboot it now."

"Wh . . . what do you mean?"

"Yer bathwater is coolin'. I promise we'll answer all yer questions once you have a chance to freshen up."

"You know?"

"Aye, I ken what's happened." She nodded, sympathy in her gray-blue eyes. "I'll help with the laird while you bathe, and then we'll talk."

Goose bumps rose along Ali's arms and she shivered, noting the inviting warmth the steaming tub offered. "All right," she agreed, "but I won't be put off."

The woman nodded, then headed out the door.

Unbuckling the belt, Ali laid it on the floor along with the length of plaid. Shrugging out of her T-shirt, she stepped into the tub and slid down. She grimaced when her right hand hit the water, and turned her palm up. The outline of the knife's shaft was clearly visible. Slowly, she submerged it, sucking in a breath until the throbbing eased. She reached to take the bar of soap from the stool beside the tub and sniffed. Lavender—obviously Mrs. Mac thought the aromatic scent would calm her. Ali closed her eyes, letting the warmth seep through her knotted muscles and tried to do just that. But her thoughts were in turmoil. Rory MacLeod, the beautiful sixteenth-century laird, alive—at least she hoped he was— in the room next door.

It was unbelievable, inconceivable, and part of her refused to consider the possibility it was true, but the annoying little voice in her head kept flashing the evidence before her: the differences in the castle's interior from when she'd first arrived, no Duncan, no electric lights, no doctors, no medicines. And the most damning evidence of all—Rory MacLeod himself.

Fergus's words came to mind. *That's why the fairies brought you. You're the only one who can save him.*

Ali cursed and hopped out of the tub. Grabbing the towel off the stool, she rubbed herself vigorously. Fairy flag—it was that stupid fairy flag. Well, if the fairies had brought her here, they could damn well send her home.

She ran her fingers over the amethyst gown laid out on the bed, frowning when she lifted it to reveal what looked like a delicate white nightgown and a long ruffled skirt. She wondered which one Mrs. Mac wanted her to wear. Shoving them aside, she searched for a pair of panties and a bra.

There was a light tap on the connecting door, and Ali wrapped the towel around herself.

"'Tis only me, dear," Mrs. Mac said, coming into the room. "I thought you might have need of me. Here." The older woman held out the sheer, white nightgown. "The chemise goes on first."

Ali ducked her head, lifting one arm and then the other

to slip through the armholes before she released her grip on the towel.

Mrs. Mac tsked. "No need to be shy, lass."

"Sorry. I'm not used to someone helping me dress."

"Aye, well, there'd be a lot you'll have to get used to," the older woman chided, fastening the ruffled skirt at her waist.

Ali's response was muffled as Mrs. Mac pulled the gown over her head.

"Ye look verra bonny, lass. I didna' put out a corset fer you, but if you . . ." She prattled on, lacing the gown with brisk competence.

"Ahh, no, I'm fine." She barely got the words out of her mouth before Mrs. Mac nudged her toward the bed.

"Here are yer stockings and slippers."

"Are you sure whoever you got these from doesn't mind?" Ali asked, taking a seat on the edge of the bed. "They look like they've never been worn."

"They havena', the laird ordered them fer our lady. Spoiled her he did. Never wanted to give her father anythin' to complain aboot. Not many have gowns such as these. They were a gift fer after the bairn was born." She gave a sad sigh before she went on to explain, "'Tis why they're long enough fer you. I didna' have a chance to alter them fer her."

Ali didn't know what to say, so she concentrated on pulling up the stockings, wincing as the fabric scraped across her palm.

"What's wrong, lass?" The woman reached for Ali's hand. She tsked, and shook her head. "Fergus should have been the one to see to the wound, but I ken he couldna' do it. No' after the last time."

"The last time?"

"Aye, he tried to help Dougal, you see, doin' as you did fer our laird. Killed him instead," she said as she bent to roll on the stockings for Ali.

Ali's eyes widened. "Oh, ah . . . I'm sorry."

"Aye, well, these things happen, but at least our laird had you to care fer him." Stepping back she gave Ali the once-over. "Yer set now."

Ali got up from the bed, anxious to check on her patient. Not sure she was ready to have her suspicions confirmed. "Did Rory wake up when you were in his room?"

"Nay, but he seems to be restin' comfortably. Doona' fash yerself, lass. You can see to him once we've had our wee chat." Mrs. Mac opened the adjoining door and called out to Fergus and Iain, gesturing for them to come inside.

"I'd rather not leave him on his own. We can have this conversation in his room."

"Nay, we canna' do that. I have a lass sittin' with him. If need be, she'll call."

Fergus and Iain came into the room, looking ill at ease, unable to meet her eyes. Mrs. Mac closed the door behind them. "Sit, lass," she ordered.

Ali obeyed. The woman was bossy.

Iain rubbed the shadow along his jaw with the palm of his big hand, then lifted his eyes to hers. "Do you ken what happened?"

Ali chewed the inside of her lower lip, wondering if she dare risk the embarrassment of explaining exactly what it was she thought had happened. It was so far-fetched as to be laughable, but she wasn't laughing, and she needed to know what was going on.

"When your brother was wounded you thought he was going to die, so you raised the fairy flag, and *poof,* here I am." She tried to make light of it.

The three of them stared at her in stunned silence.

Oh, my God, they think I'm crazy.

Please, don't let anyone be recording this. Surreptitiously, she searched for cameras in the crevices of the gray stone walls.

"How did you ken?" Iain asked.

"Duncan Macintosh, Dunvegan's caretaker, he told me about the fairy flag when he took me on a tour of the castle this afternoon," she said absently, until she realized what Iain had asked. "What do you mean, how did I know? Are you trying to tell me that's what happened?"

"Aye." Iain grimaced.

She jumped off the bed. "Well, wave it again and send me back."

"We canna' do that. There's only one wish left," he explained, backing away as she strode toward him.

"I'm telling you to do it, now." She stabbed a finger into his broad chest.

"I'm sorry, lass, we canna'. We have to think of the clan," Fergus said quietly.

"What about me? You expect me to stay here, stuck in the sixteenth century, never to go home?" She choked back a sob, determined not to cry.

"Ah, lass, I didna' mean for this to happen. But I had no choice. I couldna' let my brother die."

"'Tis no' the lad's fault. He only raised the flag and the fairies did the rest."

Mrs. Mac, who had remained quiet the entire time, stepped forward. "Lass, do you have bairns you'd be leavin' behind?"

"If by bairns you mean children, then no, I don't."

"A man . . . a husband?"

Ali shook her head. She didn't, not for the last five months. And Drew Sanderson was one person she wouldn't miss. He was a lying, disloyal slimeball, who not only broke her heart; he did a good job destroying her reputation while he was at it.

"Mother, father . . . a family of any kind?"

"No," Ali snapped. She didn't need this woman to

remind her how little she had left behind. "But I have a friend and my career." Now that just sounded pathetic.

"You can make friends here, lass, and we're in need of a healer." The older woman gave her a sympathetic smile.

"No . . . no, I can't stay here. I won't." Ali's chest tightened, panic inching toward hysteria. "Don't you understand? I'm not like you. For God's sake, I'm from the twenty-first century!" She closed her eyes to keep from crying. Memories of her childhood crowded in on her. The images tormented her. The fear and rejection she'd felt, being shipped from one foster home to another after her mother's death, mirrored the emotions that now threatened to overwhelm her. "I can't," she whispered. "Please, please, just send me home."

Iain grabbed her by the arm. "Are you sayin' the fairies stole you from the future?" He didn't give her a chance to respond. "Fergus, can you believe it? She's from the future! Oh, Ali, there's so much I want to—"

"Quit yer blatherin', lad. Can you no' see the lass is havin' a hard time of it?" Fergus said, watching her with concern.

"Drink this, lass. Come on, there's a good girl." Mrs. Mac pressed a cup to her mouth.

Ali took a deep swallow. The liquid burned a path to her stomach, and her eyes watered. She swiped a hand across her mouth. "What the hell is that?"

"Uisge na beatha." Fergus grinned. "Not many a lass can stomach it."

"Why doona' you take a wee nap?" Mrs. Mac suggested, patting her shoulder.

Ali shook her head. "No, I'll go and sit with Rory." She'd see to her patient, and after she reassured herself he would be all right, she'd work on a plan to get out of this nightmare.

"Lass, you canna' tell my brother about the fairy flag."

"Why not? Maybe he'll agree to use the flag to send me home."

"Nay, I swear to you, he wouldna' do it. My brother puts the well-being of the clan above all else. 'Tis why he canna' find out. He'd kill me if he kent what I did."

"I'm sure he wouldn't, Iain." But the look on the faces of Mrs. Mac and Fergus reminded her she didn't know Rory MacLeod. The man was a warrior, very different from the men she knew. She'd been thrust into a time where brutality was an everyday occurrence. One more reason she had to find a way home. The fairy flag was the key, and if they weren't going to help her, she'd find it on her own.

"Aye, lass, if he didna' kill me, for truth he'd never forgive me, and I canna' live with that."

Ali sighed. How could she fault him when his only crime was that he loved his brother? She knew she wouldn't be able to make him suffer because of it. "I won't tell him, Iain, I promise. I know you were only trying to save him. It's not your fault those damn fairies picked me to do the honors."

A look of relief lightened Iain's handsome features. "You'll forgive me then?" he asked, taking ahold of her hand.

Ali nodded. "You, but not your fairies."

He pressed her hand to his lips. "Thank you," he murmured.

Mrs. Mac cuffed the back of his head. "There'll be none of that, Iain MacLeod."

"Can I no' kiss the lass's hand?"

The older woman folded her arms across her ample chest. "Nay, she'd no' be fer you, lad."

Iain frowned. "And who would you be thinkin' she's fer?"

Ali opened her mouth to protest, but before she could get a word out, the woman said, "The fairies sent her fer yer brother."

"Now just a—" Ali began.

Iain shook his head. "Mrs. Mac, you ken as well as anyone my brother will never take another. He loved only Brianna."

Mrs. Macpherson shrugged.

"Hello, I'm right here." Ali waved her hands at the two of them, annoyed to be treated like a prize up for grabs. "Just so we're all straight on this, I have no interest in Rory MacLeod, or any other man for that matter."

Fergus raised a bushy auburn brow. "You doona' like men, lass?"

"Oh, for God's sake," she grumbled in frustration. "Yes, I like men, but I'll choose one on my own, thank you very much." *Because you did such a good job the last time,* the little voice in her head said. "Now, if we're finished here, I'd like to look in on Rory." She walked toward the door.

"A moment, lass," Fergus called out to her.

Ali groaned. "I have a name, if any of you are interested. It's Ali."

A frown furrowed Mrs. Mac's brow. "'Tis an odd name, lass."

Ali rolled her eyes. "You can call me Aileanna if you'd prefer."

"Aileanna. 'Tis better."

She pressed her face into her hands, shaking her head before looking at Fergus. "What were you going to say?"

"We need a story, la . . . Ali, to explain where you've come from."

"Right. We wouldn't want to tell people the fairies sent me, now would we?"

"Aileanna, 'tis no' somethin' to make light of. Folks might think yer a witch, and that would be a verra dangerous thing," Mrs. Mac said, her expression serious.

"A witch?"

"Aye, and there's a priest in these parts who has stirred up some trouble of late. 'Tis why our healer left," the woman explained.

Ali rubbed her temples. *This just gets better and better.* "So, where am I supposed to have come from?"

"You said yer last name is Graham and I'm thinkin' the laird will have some memory of that. Do you ken any Graham that could slip us up, lad?" Fergus asked Iain.

"Nay, but I canna' say for certain Rory doesna'."

"We'll hope as no'." Fergus gave Ali an odd look. "I hate to say it, but I'm thinkin' we'll have to say she's English. It may goes a way to explainin' her strange way of speakin'."

"'Tis a shame, Fergus, but you have the way of it," Mrs. Mac agreed.

Ali frowned. "There's nothing strange about the way I speak, but what's the problem with saying I'm English?"

"We canna' abide the English, lass."

"We could say she's from the borders. Not so bad, aye?" Iain piped up.

Fergus nodded, rubbing a hand over the stubble on his chin. "Aye, and because of her healin' abilities, those bloody Fife adventurers kidnapped her to take her on to Lewis. But she escaped and we gave her shelter."

Mrs. Mac's eyes widened. "'Tis quite a tall tale to swallow."

"Can you think of somethin' better?" Fergus grumbled. "Nay."

"'Tis settled, and now I'll be off to get somethin' to eat," Iain said, heading for the door.

"I'll join you, lad. Doona' fret, Ali, we'll take good care of you," the older man promised.

"Thank you." Despite everything, Ali was touched by his offer.

"'Tis the truth, Ali. The clan is in yer debt fer savin' my brother. No one will say a word against you."

"That's good to hear."

After the men left, Mrs. Mac turned to her. "Go to the laird, Aileanna, and I'll bring you somethin' to eat."

"Thank you, but I'm not very hungry."

"A wee bit of broth, then. And, lass, though I'm sorry fer yer troubles I'm glad 'twas you the fairies brought to us."

Moisture gathered in Ali's eyes at the woman's kind words. Afraid she might cry, Ali nodded and opened the door to Rory's chambers.

When she entered the room, a young girl popped out of the chair beside the bed. Her mouth dropped open as Ali came closer. "My lady," she stammered, bobbing a curtsy.

Ali waved off the formality. "Please don't do that. I'm not a lady. I mean, I am a lady, just not the kind of lady you mean." She blew out an exasperated breath. It was obvious the girl didn't know what she was talking about. "Has Lord MacLeod awakened yet?"

"Nay," the young girl said, her eyes downcast.

"Well, thank you for watching over him. I'll sit with him now if you have somewhere else you need to be."

The girl bobbed another curtsy and scurried from the room with one last look at Ali.

Taking a seat on the hard wooden chair the girl had vacated, Ali looked at Rory. She smiled at the unruly wave of thick black hair that fell across his forehead, smoothing it from his face, pleased the skin beneath her hand was neither hot nor clammy. Without thinking, she allowed her fingers to trail along his cheekbones, to his strong jaw. He stirred. Guiltily she looked up, but his eyes remained closed. Long lashes rested against sun-bronzed skin, with no sign of his previous pallor. When her fingers grazed his full lips they twitched, curving into a smile. Butterflies quickened in her stomach.

Ali pulled her hand away, shaking her head at her foolishness. This was no time to be weaving fantasies about the man, no matter how beautiful he was. She needed to come up with a plan to get home. The sixteenth century was no place for her. Wearily she stood and eased back the bedding to get a better look at her handiwork. She winced. The wound was fiery red and swollen.

Her gaze wandered over his broad chest, the hard muscles beneath the taut skin of his belly. The man was in amazing condition. Muscles stiff, she lowered herself in the chair only to find Rory MacLeod looking at her. Or at least she thought he was, until she heard him say, "Brianna."

He reached out to stroke his long, calloused fingers along her cheek in a gentle caress. He smiled, then closed his eyes. His arm dropped back to the bed.

Ali groaned. She had to find that damn flag.

Chapter 4

"What are you doin' tiptoein' aboot, lad?" Rory grumbled. Gritting his teeth, he pulled himself upright in bed.

The young lad ducked his head. "Sorry, my laird, I didna' mean to disturb you."

"Disturb me?" Rory jerked his chin toward the light filtering into the room. "From the looks of it you've awakened me none too soon. Where are my brother and Fergus? Breakin' their fast, are they?"

"Nay," the lad said, shuffling from one foot to the other.

Rory let out an exasperated breath. "Connor, I canna' read minds, so you'd best tell me what's on yers."

"'Tis just that we've no' eaten, Laird MacLeod. No' since yester eve."

Rory frowned. "And why would that be?"

"Cook quit."

"Nay, lad, you must be mistaken. Cook wouldna' do that."

"'Tis the truth, my laird. He did."

Rory cursed. Swinging his legs over the edge of the bed, his muscles rebelled at the action. He stifled a groan at the wrenching pain in his side as he rose to his feet. Gingerly, he touched the site of his wound—the red, puckered flesh— and he thought of the woman who'd put it there. With the memory of her soft hands and their gentle touch on his heated skin, he felt himself harden. Sky blue eyes filled with concern, in a face as bonny as his wife's. He shook the image of her from his head. No matter that the lass had the look of Brianna; no one could take his wife's place. He was loyal to her memory. Swiving was one thing—a man had his needs—but love—nay, never again.

"Aye, Laird MacLeod." The lad bobbed his head, eyeing Rory's wound. "'Tis her that did it."

"Aye, lad, the lass made a fair job of it, she did."

"Nay . . . I mean aye, she did, but 'tis no' what I meant. 'Tis on account of Lady Aileanna that Cook quit."

"Nay, lad, she could no' have managed that. She was seein' to my needs yester eve."

Connor's mouth fell open; the tips of his ears pinked.

"Fer the love of God, 'tis no' those needs I was talkin' aboot. 'Twas my wound she saw to." Rory began to think the boy meant to drive him daft.

"But . . . but, my lord, 'tis been seven days since we carried ye home."

"Yer tellin' me I've been lyin' abed for seven days!" he bellowed, holding his side.

"Aye," the lad squeaked.

"Get the woman and bring her to me, Connor." Rory clenched his teeth as he reached for his plaid at the foot of the bed.

"She's seein' to the men that were injured. Mayhap ye should wait until—"

"Connor, you ken me well. I've given you an order, lad, and I expect it to be carried out. Bring the lady to me *now*."

The boy rushed headlong from the room, almost bowling over Iain and Fergus as they entered his chambers.

"What's got you riled, brother? We heard you bellow from down below," Iain asked after he'd righted the lad.

Rory folded his arms over his chest, eyeing the two

men. "Which one of you would care to explain how 'tis I've been abed fer seven days?"

The two men looked at each other, then shrugged.

"Why doona' I take a guess—would it be Lady Aileanna's doin'?"

"Aye, but 'twas fer yer own good, brother. You were restless, and she didna' want you to rip open yer wound."

"So you let her drug me? 'Tis too bad she didna' have the means to render me unconscious when she closed my wound." Anger reverberated in his voice and it had nothing to do with being awake when she had laid the blade to his side. Times were difficult, what with the MacDonald renewing the feud and King James sending the lowlanders to Lewis. It was no time for the clan's laird to be laid out flat, and by a lass he didna' ken.

Iain flushed under his scrutiny. "I brought the physician's notes to her, the one you had see to Brianna. 'Twas there she found the herbs listed."

"Now, lad—" Fergus began, then turned to the young maid who'd entered Rory's chambers. Her fiery red hair was tucked neatly beneath a cap. "Leave it on the table. That's a good lass." Fergus laid a hand on the girl's shoulder as she was about to leave. "Mari, this would be yer laird."

The girl bobbed a curtsy and gave Rory a shy smile.

He nodded, masking his shock when the lass looked at him, one eye blue, the other green. "Welcome to Dunvegan, Mari."

"Thank ye, my lord." She bobbed again, then looked to Fergus for direction.

He nodded, waiting until the girl left the room before he explained. "Her mother brought her to us on account of that bloody priest. He's been up to his tricks again, rantin' aboot the lass on account of her mismatched eyes and red hair. Claiming she's a witch, he is. He wanted to put her to the stake."

Rory sighed, lowering himself into the chair by the fire. "The last thing I'd be needin' right now is trouble with the Kirk, but if I hear he's put anyone to the stake on MacLeod land I'll send him to hell myself."

"Aye, I thought that's how you'd feel. I've sent a couple of men into the villages to keep an eye on him," Fergus informed him.

"Eat yer parritch, brother." Iain gestured to the bowl the lass had left, and pulled up a stool alongside him.

"And how is it I have parritch? I was under the impression Cook quit."

"Aye, he did, but I managed to smooth his ruffled feathers."

"And who would it be that ruffled his feathers in the first place—Lady Aileanna?" Rory asked, raising a brow.

"Aye, but—"

He interrupted his brother with a dismissive wave of his hand. "Just tell me what she did."

"'Twas more what she said." Iain glanced at him, then sighed. "She told Cook his kitchens were no better than a pigsty, and she was surprised he hadna' killed anyone as yet."

Rory snorted. It was something he himself had meant to do, and he wasn't at all certain that no one *had* died. But before he could admit as much, Connor returned.

"I thought I told you to bring Lady Aileanna to me."

"I tried, but the lady says she's busy and will come when she gets the chance." The lad, head bowed, twisted his hands in front of him.

"She will, will she?" Rory muttered, rising to his feet.

"And . . . and she said I was to tell you you'd better damn well be in bed when she does," Connor stammered, obviously quoting the lady verbatim.

Fergus covered a snort of laughter with a cough, shrugging when Rory shot him a quelling look.

"That'll be all, Connor."

"Rory, she's lookin' to the men who were wounded in

the battle with the MacDonald. There are a fair number of them."

"Yer quick to her defense, brother." Rory narrowed his gaze on Iain. The lad had a reputation with the ladies, and he wondered if he'd charmed his way into Lady Aileanna's affections—a thought that didn't sit well with Rory, not with the memory of her naked in his arms and her passionate response to his touch. Fists clenched at his sides, he reined in the spurt of jealousy. An emotion he had no right or reason to feel, he reminded himself.

"Nay." His brother gave an adamant shake of his head. "'Tis no' like that."

He ignored Iain. Lowering himself into the chair, he leaned back. "I appreciate the lass seein' to the men's care, but what I'd be needin' to ken is where she's from. Is there a chance she could be a spy sent by the MacDonald?"

Iain guffawed. "Brother, you'd think yer own mother a spy if she was alive."

Rory shrugged. "You canna' be too careful."

Fergus cleared his throat. "She's no spy, lad. She'd been kidnapped by those bloody lowlanders on the account of her healin' abilities, but she escaped. I found her when I went back to the battlegrounds lookin' fer our wounded."

Rory scrubbed his hands over his face, thinking on what Fergus told him.

"I thought I told you to stay in your bed."

He looked up. Aileanna Graham stood only a few feet from him, hands on her hips, more bonny than he remembered. The tops of her milky white breasts filled the square neckline of a gown the color of heather. Reluctantly, he pulled his gaze to her face. His hands twitched at the memory of how she'd felt in his arms.

Bloody hell, if he didna' get his heated thoughts under control they would all have a verra good idea what he was thinkin'.

His plaid would soon resemble a tent.

He cleared his throat. "Lass, in case you hadna' noticed, I am the laird. I listen to no one."

She arched a brow. "I know exactly who you are, Lord MacLeod. But you are also my patient, and until I decide you are no longer under my care, you *will* do as I say. Now get back into bed."

He folded his arms across his chest and glowered at her. "I'll no' get into bed. I've been in there long enough."

"I think I hear Mrs. Mac callin' fer me." Iain rose from the stool and headed for the door with Fergus fast on his heels.

"Fergus, Iain, I expect a full update on the army's condition before evenin' meal," he yelled, cursing when they shut the door firmly behind them without a word.

"That hurt, didn't it?" Without waiting for an answer, she leaned over and placed cool fingertips to his forehead.

Rory shook his head, not certain he'd get the words out. His mouth had gone dry. He licked his lips. She was so close he felt the heat of her body; the scent of lavender enveloped him.

"Let's get you into bed," she said, slipping her soft hand into his. "I want to make sure you haven't done any damage."

"I told you, lass, I'm no' gettin' back in that bed."

She sighed. "You're a stubborn man. Has anyone ever told you that?" Shaking her head, she knelt before him.

"Aye, often." He bit back a groan when she tugged at his belt.

"I'm sorry, did I hurt you?" Eyes the color of sapphires, awash with concern, met his.

"Nay," he muttered. Brushing her hands aside he undid his belt, dropping it to the floor.

She inched his plaid lower, exposing the wound, exploring with a firm yet gentle touch. Meeting his eyes, she lowered hers quickly, and he wondered if she could see the desire in his. He didna' doubt it was there. He wanted her with a need that surprised him. Closing his eyes, he imagined his wife, tiny and fragile, so slight and delicate. The memory of Brianna served to dampen his desire for the woman on her knees between his thighs.

"Are you all right?" she asked, the timbre of her voice low and husky. She cleared her throat. "Lord MacLeod?"

"I'm fine, lass," he said. "Are you finished with yer pokin'?"

"Yes." She patted his knee and rose to her feet. "I'm surprised at how well you've healed. It's quite amazing actually. You'll be as good as new in no time. Now, if you don't mind, I had better get back to your men." She retrieved his belt and handed it to him.

Rory adjusted his plaid. "I'd like a word with you first." He studied her, watching for a reaction.

"Oh." She smoothed her hands over her gown. Biting the inside of her cheek, she looked at him.

"Fergus tells me you were abducted by the lowlanders."

"Umhmm," she murmured, twisting the long length of her braided hair between her fingers.

"Does it trouble you to speak of it?"

"No."

"They didna' hurt you, did they?"

She shook her head, perfect white teeth worrying her full bottom lip.

"Lass, look at me." He stood up and tilted her chin, forcing her gaze to his. "You can tell me."

"No one hurt me."

He dropped his hand to his side. "How did you escape?"

"I . . . I don't remember." She dipped her head. "I think I must have hit my head."

Rory framed her face with his hands, searching her eyes. She sucked in a startled gasp when he ran his fingers through her hair, probing her scalp. Her braid came undone, and silken tresses slid between his fingers. "I canna' feel anythin'. Are you certain you hit yer head?"

She nodded, steadying herself with a palm pressed to his chest. He could stop; he had explored every inch of her head, but he didn't want to, not when she felt so good leaning against him. He inhaled her soft, sweet fragrance, barely resisting the urge to bury his face in the delicate column of her neck. With a concerted effort, he brought his hands to rest on her shoulders.

"Aileanna, you ken as laird to the MacLeod clan 'tis my duty to see to their protection."

She took a steadying breath, her breasts rising within the confines of her gown.

Pulling his gaze back to her face, he sighed. "Look at me, Aileanna."

She stiffened. Raising her chin, she took a step away from him. "I'm not a danger to you or your clan, Lord MacLeod, if that's what you're implying. In fact, quite the opposite. I think I've cared very well for all of you." A flash of temper flared in her eyes as she held his gaze.

"Aye, you have, and I thank you for that. I was remiss not to thank you earlier, but it seems someone decided to knock me out." He tilted his head, looking down at her.

She rolled her eyes. "So, Iain was right. He said you wouldn't be happy about that." She shrugged her shoulders. "I had no choice. You were thrashing about and other than tying you to the bedposts, which probably wouldn't have worked anyhow, it was my only option." Her gaze traveled the length of his body, a delicate flush of pink tinting her cheeks.

"No man likes to be drugged, lass, especially a man responsible for others."

She gave an unladylike snort. "And what do you think you could have done in the condition you were in?"

"More than most," he answered truthfully.

"Right—king of the castle and all that."

He narrowed his gaze on her. "Yer speech is verra strange, lass."

"So is yours," she grumbled, a stubborn set to her chin. "Are you finished with me now?"

"You said you were a Graham?"

"I did. What of it?"

"There's no need to get prickly, lass."

"I'm not prickly," she snapped. "I'm just tired of being treated as though I've done something wrong. I haven't."

"Which Graham?" He fought back a smile, finding her temper amusing.

"I'm from the borders," she said through clenched teeth, stabbing her finger into his chest.

He wrapped his fingers around hers. "Now—" he began, frowning when he saw the raised welt on the palm of her hand. "What's this?"

She tried to pull her hand from his. "Nothing."

Rory tightened his hold on her. "'Tis from the dirk, isna' it?"

"Yes. Now will you please let me go?"

Holding her gaze with his, he pressed her palm to his lips, trailing light kisses along the reddened mark. "I'm sorry you were hurt while you cared fer me."

She swallowed, shaking her head slowly from side to side. "It was nothing compared to what I did to you." Her voice had gone soft and breathy.

"Ah, but you meant to save me, Aileanna, no' hurt me," he said into her palm.

"Umhmm." Her eyes fluttered closed.

He tugged her closer, pressing himself against her lush curves. "Aileanna, what were you doin' in my bed that night?" he whispered in her ear before lowering his lips to her neck.

"Sleeping," she murmured. A soft moan of pleasure

escaped from her parted lips. She tilted her head back, granting him access to a creamy expanse of skin.

With a low chuckle, he accepted her invitation. Bending his head, he kissed his way across the top of her full breasts, delving beneath the gown's fabric with his tongue.

He tugged her neckline lower, ignoring the sound of the cloth tearing. He freed her breasts to his hungry gaze. Lust pounded in his veins.

"Nay, you weren't sleeping, lass." He tweaked her nipple between his fingers before taking it into his mouth.

"Dreaming . . . I thought I was dreaming." She moaned.

Rory cupped her breasts, kneading, squeezing, watching the play of emotions on her angelic face. "'Twas no dream, lass. 'Tis no dream now," he said against her lips.

He'd slowly maneuvered them toward the bed and carefully lowered Aileanna onto the mattress. Her eyes sprang open and she gasped, tugging at the bodice of her gown. He eased himself onto the bed. Lying down beside her, he stopped the frantic movements of her hands, pulling her against him when she struggled to sit up.

"Calm yerself, Aileanna." He stroked the hair from her face.

"We . . . we can't do this," she stammered.

"Why? We've done it before," he reminded her, trailing his finger along the soft swell of her breasts. He didn't want to talk. All he wanted to do was feel her, warm and willing, beneath him.

She shivered, stilling his hand with hers.

"I told you, I thought I was dreaming that night. And you . . . you thought I was your wife."

Rory didn't stop her when she struggled to rise from the bed. She was right. He had thought she was Brianna, but not now. He knew who she was, and he wanted her more than he thought he'd ever want a woman again. He scrubbed his hands over his face. Bloody hell, what was wrong with him? What had Aileanna Graham done to him?

"Did I . . . did I hurt you?" She stood at the end of the bed, clutching the front of her gown, her hair spilling over her shoulders in wild abandon.

"Nay." He winced as he sat up.

"Good." She gave a brisk nod of her head, then turned to walk away.

"Where are you goin', Aileanna?"

"To my room." She hesitated, her hand on the latch to the room that adjoined his. His wife's room. She looked at him over her shoulder. "It's where I've been staying. Mrs. Mac put me in there. If you'd prefer, I can take a room elsewhere."

He stood, adjusting his plaid. "Nay, that'll be fine, lass. Aileanna, I'm—"

She shook her head, closing the door firmly behind her.

Rory cursed. He ignored the burning pain in his side as he wrenched the door to his chambers open. He barely acknowledged the greetings of his men gathered at the bottom of the staircase as he made his way to the study. Once inside, he rummaged through the desk for a piece of parchment and his quill. Finding what he required, he sat down to compose a letter to Angus Graham inquiring into the identity of one Aileanna Graham.

Chapter 5

Ali rested her forehead against the rough wood-planked door, softly cursing the man on the other side and her reaction to him. His tender kisses and heated caresses had turned her into a quivering mass of boneless desire. Her brain had stopped working, and she was lucky he hadn't prodded further with his questions. She slapped a hand to the door, pretending it was his broad, muscular, and totally gorgeous chest.

Typical man; seducing her with his tempting kisses only to get the answers he wanted. It would serve him right if she told him the truth. But Ali couldn't, not without breaking her promise to Iain, and his only crime was that he loved his brother. She envied them that.

No, she wouldn't reveal his secret. She'd find the fairy flag on her own and no one would be the wiser. *Until the MacLeods are in danger and need the fairies' help,* the annoying voice in her head reminded her. Ali grimaced at the thought of the MacLeods' suffering because of what she planned to do. But it couldn't be helped. She had to find a way home. *To what? Charges that could ruin your career, and all because a man you thought you loved made a mistake that cost a young mother her life and left you to take the blame,* the voice in her head taunted. *A man who professed to love you while he slept with how many other women?* All right, so her personal and professional lives were a mess. But at least she'd be back where she belonged.

Belong? When have you ever belonged, Aileanna Graham?

"Would you just shut up," Ali muttered.

"My lady?"

Ali whirled around to face Mari, who hesitated in the doorway to her room, a wary expression on the young maid's face. "Ah, hi. I didn't hear you come in."

The young girl dipped her head. "I'm sorry, my lady. I didna' mean to disturb ye."

Ali waved off her apology, hoping Mari hadn't been there long enough to witness her hitting the door and talking to herself. "You didn't." She smiled in an attempt to ease the young girl's discomfort.

Mrs. Macpherson had persuaded Ali to take Mari on as her maid. She'd resisted at first; she didn't have any idea what she was supposed to do with a lady's maid and didn't plan on being here long enough to find out. But the older woman was nothing if not tenacious. And Ali had given in, once Mrs. Mac explained that because of Mari's appearance, and the clan's superstitious tendencies, the girl would have a difficult time of it if she didn't. Ali knew how it felt to be on the outside looking in, and she wasn't about to allow Mari to suffer the same fate. Not if she could help it.

"Come in, Mari. Is Mrs. Mac looking for me?"

"Nay, she said to tell ye the last of the men have been seen to and ye can have yerself a wee rest."

"Well, I don't know about taking a nap." She wouldn't. Now was the perfect opportunity to search the castle. Too busy during the last week seeing to the men of Dunvegan, Ali hadn't had a chance to look for the fairy flag. With

Mrs. Mac occupied, and Rory MacLeod tucked away in his room, she could search at her leisure.

"My lady, what have ye done?"

Ali followed the direction of Mari's stricken gaze. "Ah, this?" She touched the tear in her gown. Her face flushed, remembering who put it there. "I caught it on . . . on the chair when I was seeing to Lord MacLeod. Do you know how to sew, Mari?"

"Aye, my lady. I'll take care of it fer ye. I'll find ye another gown," the girl said. She bent over the trunk and pulled out a gown of robin's egg blue. "'Twill look bonny on ye, my lady." Mari held up the dress, a wistful expression on her young face.

Ali's heart clenched. She couldn't help but notice the sharp contrast between the beautiful gown Mari held out to her, and the threadbare brown woolen dress the girl wore.

"I don't know, I think the color would be perfect on you, Mari. Why don't you try it on?"

Mari gasped. "Nay, my lady. I canna' do that. 'Tis no' right."

"Don't be silly. Mrs. Mac said you're my maid, so there's no reason you can't wear what I want you to."

"'Tis verra kind of ye, my lady, but 'tis no' my place."

Ali took the dress from the girl's trembling fingers. "Let's just see . . ." She frowned. "I guess I'm quite a bit taller than you, and . . ." Looking at Mari's slight frame, she remembered the comments about how tiny the laird's wife had been. "I have an idea. I'll be right back."

Returning after a brief conversation with Mrs. Mac, Ali smiled at Mari. "Well, it's all settled. Mrs. Mac has agreed, so no argument from you."

The girl watched her warily from where she knelt rearranging the contents of the trunk.

Ali opened the wardrobe and pulled out a lemon yellow gown, holding it up for Mari. "Come and try it on."

The girl hesitated before rising to her feet. "Are ye certain?"

"Of course I am."

Mari looked at Ali; moisture clung to the girl's auburn-tipped lashes as she gently caressed the fabric. "'Tis bonny, my lady," she whispered reverently.

"It is. You'll look beautiful, Mari. The color will show off your gorgeous red hair."

Mari lowered her hand, shaking her head. "I doona' think I can accept it, my lady, but I thank ye fer yer kindness."

"Don't be silly—of course you can. Mrs. Mac said it was fine."

"Aye, but folk might think I doona' ken my place."

Ali blew out a frustrated breath. "Who cares what anyone else thinks?"

"I do, my lady," she said softly.

"I'm sorry, Mari, of course you do. I understand how you feel." And she did, only too well. "I shouldn't have pushed."

"I ken what yer tryin' to do, and I appreciate it. 'Tis just with my eyes and my hair, I stick out enough as 'tis."

"You're very pretty, Mari. You'll always stand out from the others."

The young girl giggled. "Yer verra funny, my lady. Pretty." She repeated the word and laughed again, shaking her head.

"It's true, Mari, whether you believe me or not. Now, I want you to take the dress and try it on later, when you're on your own. Maybe you'll change your mind. No arguments." She wagged her finger at the girl, placing the gown in her arms despite her protests.

Mari looked up at Ali with a shy smile. "My lady, once ye've changed gowns ye must let me see to yer hair. 'Tis a bit of a fright if ye doona' mind me sayin'."

Ali shrugged, self-consciously touching her head. "I forgot to comb it after—" She let the rest of her sentence drop. It's not like she could say *after the laird ran his fingers through my hair* to the girl.

With her young maid's help, Ali changed into the robin's egg blue gown. Her poking and prodding complete, Mari held out a chair for Ali. She took a seat and Mari began combing the tangles from Ali's hair.

"Sorry," she apologized when Ali cried out, the comb catching on another knot.

When all the tangles were combed through, Ali leaned back in the chair. "Mari, do you like it here?"

"Aye, my lady, 'tis blessed I am to be yer maid."

Ali snorted. "I'm sure."

"'Tis true. Yer verra kind to me."

"Thank you, but I've been worried you might be missing your mother."

"My mam's verra busy with the others. There are eleven in my family, my lady."

Eleven. Ali shuddered. "What about friends?"

"I doona' have friends. I'm too busy helpin' me mam."

"You'll have time to make friends here at Dunvegan. You'd like that, wouldn't you?" Ali asked, turning sideways in the chair to look at Mari.

"Aye." The girl sighed, a wistful expression on her face.

Ali reached back and patted her hand. "I'm going to make sure you do." And she meant it. Something about the young girl touched her deeply. Perhaps Mari reminded Ali of herself a long time ago, a time when she wished someone had been there for her. She promised herself before she left Dunvegan, she'd see that Mari was safe and happy.

"Mrs. Macpherson and Fergus have been verra kind— the laird, too."

"You met Lord MacLeod?"

"Aye. He's the bonniest man I ever did see." The girl sighed.

Ali wrinkled her nose. "I guess."

"You doona' think he's bonny, my lady?"

"Aye." Oh, for God's sake, now she was starting to talk like them. "I mean, yes, he's very handsome. But you know, Mari, it's more than good looks that make a man."

"I ken it well, my lady, but everyone kens the laird is a good man. He's kind and generous, and verra powerful. No one man can take our laird down."

Ali snorted. "Well, someone almost did."

"Are ye talkin' aboot his wound? 'Twas five against one, my lady—no' a fair fight."

Five . . . one man against five. Ali didn't know why she was surprised, not when she thought of his rippling muscles and the strength of his hands—hands that could crush a man, or bring a woman to the edge with a gentle caress.

Ali's stomach clenched at the memory, and she shot out of the chair. "Okay, perfect, that's wonderful, Mari." She tossed her hair over her shoulder, unwilling to continue the conversation about Rory MacLeod's many attributes any further. "Thank you. Now I'd better see if Mrs. Mac needs me for anything. Would you like to spend some time outside? It's a lovely day."

"Thank ye, my lady, but I'll see to yer gown."

"All right."

Standing in the long narrow corridor outside her room, Ali contemplated her best course of action. Deciding to begin one floor at a time, she headed for the stairs and almost collided with the laird himself when he slammed out of his chambers.

"Lady Aileanna, I'm sorry." He reached out to steady her.

"No harm done." She took a step backward, putting some distance between them. "You know, Lord MacLeod, just because you're feeling better doesn't mean you should resume your daily activities right away."

He arched a brow; the corner of his mouth twitched. "And what do you consider my daily activities, lass?"

She waved her hand. "Oh, I don't know—laird things."

"Laird things?" He grinned. "I'll keep that in mind, Aileanna."

He walked down the curved staircase beside her, matching his long stride with hers. "'Tis a verra bonny gown you have on, my lady. As bonny as the one you wore this morn."

Ali stopped and stared at him. "I can't believe you just said that. It is not very gentlemanly of you to remind me of this morning," she muttered.

He leaned into her. His heated breath fanned her cheek. "I'm no' a gentleman, Aileanna."

"You're telling me," she huffed. Anxious to get away from him, she fairly flew down the stairs, catching her foot on the underskirt of her gown.

"Lass, be careful you don—" His hand shot out, and he grabbed her before she tumbled headlong down the stairs.

"Thank you," Ali murmured, feeling her cheeks flush. "I'm fine. You can let me go." She tried to pull away from him, but he held her firmly against his chest.

"Mayhap I doona' want to, lass." Heat flared in moss green eyes that ensnared her.

The sound of raised voices broke the spell, and she jerked her gaze from his. "Let me go."

Laughter rumbled in his chest. "Aye, I will, lass, as soon as you tell me where 'tis you'd be goin'."

Ali's eyes widened, panic inching its way up her chest at the thought he knew what she was up to. "Why? I didn't realize I was your prisoner, Lord MacLeod."

He arched a brow. "Yer my guest, Aileanna, and as such, under my protection. I only meant to suggest as yer unfamiliar with the lay of the land, Connor should accompany you. I would do it myself but I have things I must attend to."

"No," she blurted out. "I mean, thank you, but I won't wander."

"See that you don't, Aileanna." His voice held a warning,

and Ali didn't want to think what he'd do to her if he knew what she planned.

She felt his gaze follow her as they parted company at the bottom of the stairs.

Two hours later, Ali abandoned her search. She'd managed to investigate only three rooms, spending most of her time in the drawing room where the flag had resided in her time. She searched every nook and cranny, but to no avail. It didn't help that Mrs. Mac kept popping in and out, and if not her, Connor seemed to show up at the most inopportune times.

Frustrated, Ali closed the door of the drawing room with a little more force than she intended.

"There you are, lass. I've been lookin' fer you. Dinner is bein' served." Mrs. Macpherson gestured for her to follow.

Ali's stomach grumbled. She was starving, but after witnessing the filth of the kitchens, she'd been unable to eat anything for the past few days other than the freshly baked bread.

She stepped aside to allow the servants to pass into the dining hall. Their arms were laden with heavy trays containing steaming platters. The smell of roasted meats made Ali's nostrils twitch. She followed Mrs. Mac into the cavernous room lined with long wooden tables. Torches lit the interior, casting a golden hue on the tartan banners that hung from the gray stone walls between the narrow windows. The room was crowded—at least twenty people hunkered down at each table, mostly men, and the servants scurried about trying to accommodate them all at once. At the table on the raised dais, she spotted Rory. He came to his feet when he saw her. The loud chatter quieted as the diners watched her walk by. Their curiosity was one of the reasons she'd taken to eating her meals in her chambers.

"Mrs. Mac, maybe it's better if I eat in my room," Ali suggested, growing more uncomfortable by the minute.

"Och, no, the laird wanted you to join him and so you shall."

"Of course, we wouldn't want to upset his lordship."

Mrs. Macpherson shook her head, making her now familiar tsking sound.

"I'm glad you've joined us, lass," Rory said when Ali reached them, indicating the vacant chair to his left, beside Iain.

"I didn't think I had a choice," she muttered, nodding at Iain, Fergus, and Connor as she took her seat.

"Ah, still prickly I see."

Before she could respond, two platters were placed on the table in front of her. She eyed them with trepidation; fish of some sort on one, lamb on the other. Relieved when a basket of fresh bread was placed to her left, she smiled at the girl who put it there.

"Thank you."

The girl bobbed her head.

"You canna' live on bread alone, Aileanna," Rory said, with a hint of amusement in the low rumble of his voice. "Cook took yer suggestions to heart. I've checked on the kitchens myself. 'Tis safe to eat."

Even if that was the case, Ali wasn't sure she could. She didn't know how. Not without a fork or a knife to cut the meat. There was only a spoon beside her wooden plate. She glanced surreptitiously down the tables to see how everyone else was managing. Iain, obviously aware of the problem, took his dirk and sliced off some mutton for her. Everyone was so busy eating they no longer watched her, and she took a tentative bite.

"So, Aileanna, did you find what you were lookin' for?"

Ali choked on the piece of meat and both Rory and Iain pounded her back simultaneously.

"I'm all right," she managed, knowing if they didn't

stop with their forceful slaps, she wouldn't be. She took a deep swallow of wine from the goblet in front of her.

Clearing her throat, she said, "I wasn't looking for anything in particular, Lord MacLeod. I just wanted to see more of Dunvegan, since I've spent most of my time caring for your men."

"Did it meet with yer approval?" Goblet in hand, he swirled the liquid, looking at her over the rim.

"Yes, it's lovely." She bent over her plate, pretending to be absorbed with her meal, ignoring the suspicious look Fergus shot at her across the table and the one she felt coming from Iain. Ali had a sneaking suspicion she would be watched closely from now on.

She drained her wine.

Rory refilled it for her. "I'm sorry I didna' have the time to show you aboot myself."

She shrugged. "You were busy."

"Aye, and I've learned, thanks to you, Aileanna, that my men fared much better than I anticipated."

"Aye, and next time we meet the MacDonald, we'll be ready for the sneaky old bastard," Iain said. Men all along the tables heard his comment and pounded their fists against the scarred wood. A loud chorus of *ayes* filled the room.

Ali couldn't believe what she was hearing. "Please, tell me you aren't serious. My God, you were almost killed. Several of your men died." An image of a battlefield like the one she'd seen on the tapestry the day she arrived flashed before her. Her stomach lurched at the thought of Rory in the midst of that slaughter.

He shrugged. "'Tis the way of it, lass. We have no choice."

"Of course you do. You always have a choice. Wasn't your wife a MacDonald?"

Iain nudged her foot beneath the table, and she nudged him back. She wasn't about to keep quiet. It was too important. She had to find a way to make Rory see reason—to stop the senseless loss of life.

"Aye." Rory's expression turned fierce. Gone was the teasing man of earlier, replaced by someone she wouldn't want to meet in a dark alley, or anywhere else for that matter.

"Are the men you fight with not related to her, can't—?"

"'Tis her father."

"You both loved the same woman. Surely there's a way to settle your differences without bloodshed."

"'Tis none of yer concern." His tone was dismissive.

"You're right, it's not," she said, pushing back from the table. "Please, give Cook my compliments. Good night."

Rory looked ready to say something, but instead he stood and offered her his arm. "I'll see you to yer room, Aileanna."

"I can manage." She brushed past him, her attention drawn to a flurry of activity at the far end of the hall. Several men surrounded a big, fair-haired man, pounding his back. Ali caught a glimpse of his face when the crowd parted and noted his coloring—the man was purple.

"Stop that," she called out. Lifting her skirts, she rushed toward them. When she reached the man, she wrapped her arms around him. Making a fist, Ali placed her other hand over it and gave a quick upward thrust to his abdomen, repeating the motion five times. On the last thrust, a small bone shot out of his mouth and landed in the goblet of the man across from him.

"Thank ye, thank ye, my lady," he gasped. "I couldna' breathe."

Ali patted his arm. "That's what happens when you're about to choke to death. Next time you might not want to swallow the bone along with the meat."

"Aye," he said sheepishly, to the amusement of his friends.

"It seems I'll be forever in yer debt where my men are concerned, Lady Aileanna." Rory took her arm, grabbed a torch from the wall, and led her from the hall.

"Here, give me that." She reached for the torch. "I wouldn't want to take you away from your battle plans."

Rory sighed, the grim lines of his face softening in the dim light. "Aileanna—" He stopped. A commotion at the castle's entrance drew his attention. The two men who entered were covered in grime and armed to the teeth. Rory indicated they were to wait, then stepped back into the hall and called for Connor. When the lad appeared he said, "Take Lady Aileanna to her room."

Just like that she was dismissed, and more annoyed than she knew was reasonable. After all, hadn't she been the one to tell him she didn't want him to see her to her room? *Ah, but when you looked at that towering mountain of a man, and his beautiful green eyes, all you could think of was how his mouth would feel kissing you good-night,* the little voice in her head said. Ali didn't bother issuing an objection. The stupid little voice was right.

"Thank you, Connor," Ali said when they came to her room. The hall was damp and cold, and she was unable to contain a shiver.

"I can see to yer fire, my lady," he offered with a shy smile.

"I'd appreciate that. I'm not very good at it." She wasn't. On her second day at Dunvegan—if not for Fergus and Mrs. Macpherson coming to her rescue—she would've died from smoke inhalation after her first attempt.

Ali opened the door to her chambers to find her young maid scouring the floor, a bucket of soapy water at her side. "Mari, what are you doing working at this hour? Have you had anything to eat?"

"Nay, but I will, my lady. I didna' realize the time, is all," the girl said, averting her eyes from Connor, who appeared to be doing the same.

"Connor, have you met Mari?"

His cheeks turned bright red. A lock of reddish brown hair fell across his forehead. "Aye . . . nay."

"Mari, have you met Connor?"

The girl shook her head. Her face flushed the same color as her hair.

Ali held back a laugh. "Connor, Mari. Mari, Connor."

They gave each other a brief nod, but while Connor busied himself with the fire, Ali saw him glance every so often in Mari's direction. And Mari peeked at him whenever she thought he wasn't looking.

"Connor, when you're finished here would you mind taking Mari to get something to eat? She's new to Dunvegan."

"Nay, my lady, 'tis fine, I . . ." Mari began to protest.

With a sidelong look at Mari, Connor said, "Aye, my lady, I will."

The young maid glared at her, and Ali suppressed a laugh, happy to see her spurt of temper. When Connor wasn't looking, Ali mouthed *He's very cute.* Mari's expression didn't change, but Ali thought she saw her lips twitch.

Ali shut her eyes to the early morning sunlight streaming through the open drapes on her window and snuggled deeper into the comfort of her feather bed. Now that was something she'd miss. *Hah, you'll miss that beautiful hunk of a man next door,* the voice in her head chimed in. Ali buried her head beneath the pillow. That wasn't something she wanted to think about.

"My lady?"

Ali removed the pillow from her head and blinked. "Oh, Mari, sorry, I didn't see you there. I—" She sat up and stared at her maid. The girl stood before her, resplendent in the bright yellow gown, twisting her hands in front of her.

"Mari, you look wonderful." Noting the girl's frightened expression, she said, "Something's the matter. What is it?"

"He's here, my lady." Her eyes filled with tears.

Ali got out of bed and pulled the trembling girl into her arms. "Who's here?"

"The priest. The one who wanted to put me to the stake."

Ali rubbed her maid's back, remembering what Mrs. Mac had told her the day she brought Mari to her. Knowing what she did, Ali could well imagine the young girl's terror. "Shh, now, how do you know he's here?"

"The maids were talkin' aboot it. The laird's men brought him in yester eve."

"Did they say why?"

"Aye, he's demanding an audience with the laird." The last of her words came out on a sob.

"Don't worry, Mari. Lord MacLeod won't let anyone hurt you, and neither will I. You trust me, don't you?"

"Aye, my lady." She sniffed, wiping her eyes with the back of her hand.

"You'll stay in my room. I'll find you some mending and you can sit by the fire for the day. How does that sound?"

"Verra good."

"I have to check on Mrs. Chisholm, but after that I'll come back and sit with you. I'll talk to Lord MacLeod as soon as I get dressed." Ali didn't trust herself to confront the priest, not with the look of terror he'd put on Mari's face. She was afraid she'd put him to the stake herself.

"He's not here, my lady."

"What do you mean, he's not here?"

"He and his men are trainin' in the glen this morn. He's to meet with the priest later."

"Training?"

"Aye, for battle."

"For God's sake, does the man have no brains? He was on

death's door less than a week ago and now he's running—"
She cursed.

Mari clapped a hand over her mouth, her eyes wide as
saucers.

Ali grimaced. "Don't repeat that."

There was a sharp rap on the door to her chambers and
Mari jumped.

"'Tis only me, my lady," Mrs. Mac said, peeking around
the door. Stepping into the room, the older woman's eyes
widened. "Och, now, would you look at that." She smiled at
Mari. "You look bonny, lass."

"Thank ye." Mari bobbed her head shyly.

Mrs. Macpherson squinted, looking at the girl more
closely. "Ah, I see you've heard."

"About the priest? Yes. I've told Mari to stay in my room
until I can speak to Lord MacLeod. Which I gather won't
be for some time since the fool's off playing war games
with his men."

"Lady Aileanna, 'tis no way to speak of yer laird," the
older woman chided.

Ali curled her lip. "He's not my laird."

Mrs. Macpherson gave her an odd look before bustling
about the room, setting out Ali's toilette. "I'm goin' to the
village, but the laird has left Connor to see to you, my lady."

Spy on her more likely, Ali thought. "I have to check on
Mrs. Chisholm, but other than that I'll be staying with Mari."

"Aye, Maureen's time is drawin' near. I'll leave you to get
aboot my business. Remember, my lady, if you need anythin', yer to ask Connor." Mrs. Macpherson leveled a pointed
look at her before closing the door.

Leaving Ali in no doubt the older woman knew exactly
what she was up to.

Chapter 6

On the short walk back from Mrs. Chisholm's with Connor, Ali savored the warmth of sunshine on her face. With her days spent caring for the wounded, she'd had little time to take advantage of the beautiful scenery Dunvegan's grounds provided. She inhaled the salty tang of sea air and knew if it wasn't for Mari, shut up in her room, frightened and alone, Ali would have been unable to resist the urge to scramble over the rocky banks to the aquamarine loch where the gulls now played. The birds' noisy serenade faded into the distance as they came closer to Dunvegan and another sound—a low, ominous chant—reverberated through the air.

Ali stood at the center of the well-worn path, straining to make out the words. "Connor, do you hear that?"

"Nay, I . . . aye, my lady." His expression tensed.

The sound seemed to be coming from the inner courtyard of the castle. "What are they saying?"

"Witch."

Mari.

A feeling of dread tightened in Ali's chest. She grabbed the boy's arm. "Connor, you have to get Lord MacLeod. Now!" Not waiting for a response, she took off at a run, cursing when she stumbled on the loose stones beneath her slippered feet. Unable to get enough traction, she bent down and yanked off the impractical shoes.

Connor was looking at her as though she'd lost her mind. "I canna' do that. I'm to look after ye, my lady," he said, following close on her heels.

Frustrated at his unwillingness to go against his laird's directive, Ali bit back a curse, but she had no time to waste arguing with him. She heard the plaintive wail of a young girl and her heart pounded in her ears. Her throat tightened, making breathing painful as she raced toward the courtyard, past the men lining the walls.

Several young children and three serving girls were gathered in a circle, hurling rocks. A faint, pitiful cry was drowned out by their abusive taunts. A short, middle-aged man in voluminous gray robes encouraged them from the sidelines.

"Why aren't the men doing anything?" she yelled at Connor over her shoulder.

"'Tis on account of the priest. They willna' stand against him," he panted, trying to keep up with her.

When a young boy bent down to retrieve more rocks, Ali saw a flash of yellow. "Oh, dear God," she groaned. "Connor, you have to get Lord MacLeod," she begged, unable to contain the sob that bubbled up in her throat.

"'Tis Mari," he croaked. Without further pressure from Ali, he tore from the courtyard in the opposite direction.

"Stop it!" she cried, grabbing a young boy by the scruff of his neck as he resupplied his cache of ammunition.

He looked up at Ali, and his mouth dropped. He released the edges of his grubby white shirt and the rocks tumbled to the ground. Ali shoved aside the children to reach Mari, who was crouched low to the ground, an arm raised to protect her face. Her beautiful gown was in tatters, leaving her half naked, her arms and chest smeared with dirt and blood.

"Mari," Ali whispered, dropping to her knees beside her.

She heard a whizzing sound, then a rock bounced off Ali's shoulder and grazed her cheek in a stinging blow. She turned to face the crowd that seemed to have doubled in size, like a dark, sinister shadow closing in on them.

Furious, she rose to her feet and stared them down. "Throw one more of those rocks and you'll answer to your laird. Do you hear me?" Ali prayed she was right and Rory would be as angry with what they'd done as she was. There was a rhythmic thud as one by one the rocks were released from their grimy fingers.

"Nay . . . nay, they answer to no one save their Lord our God."

Ali whirled on the speaker. The slight man was all but swallowed up by his gray robes. A thick wooden cross hung around his scrawny neck. A neck Ali was tempted to wring. His pasty white face was pulled into a mask of hate while his black eyes blazed with self-righteous recrimination.

She took a step toward him, trembling with rage. "Their God tells them to do this?" She waved a hand at Mari. "To stone an innocent child to death?"

"She is no' innocent. The devil's spawn is what she is. Look at her," he screeched, reaching for Mari.

Ali put herself between them. The man was a raving lunatic, but he held sway over those gathered at her back— a crowd she knew he could fan into an angry mob with his words. Afraid she would be unable to keep them at bay much longer, Ali backed away before turning to help Mari to her feet. She wrapped an arm around the young girl's waist to keep her upright. The priest's bony fingers dug into Ali's injured shoulder and she bit back a groan of pain. "Get your hands off me," she growled low in her throat.

Before she could stop him, he wrenched the cap from Mari's hair. The force of the motion jerked the young girl's head back and she whimpered in pain, a look of terror on her face.

"Tell me ye doona' see it now, the devil's mark—red hair and eyes of two colors." Spittle ran down his weak chin, and his eyes bulged.

"Don't touch her," Ali yelled. Pulling Mari out of his reach, she put up a hand to stop him from coming any closer. He took a step toward them, and his foot caught on the edge of his robe. The crowd gasped when he stumbled, falling to the ground with a resounding thud.

"Yer my witnesses," he cried from where he lay prone on the cobblestones, pointing a gnarled finger at Ali. "She struck me down in defense of a witch. In the name of the Lord, my Father, I demand ye seize them both."

Panic threatened to overwhelm her, but Ali forced it down with a vengeance. Fighting to keep Mari close to her side, she pushed past the menacing faces, but it was too late. The crowd came at them as one, sinking their claws into their exposed flesh, tearing at their clothes, their hair.

"No, stop! You have to stop!" she cried when someone wrenched Mari from her arms.

A man loomed over her and everyone else, hauling her to his chest. It was the blond giant she'd saved from choking the night before, but from the look on his face she wasn't sure if he was friend or foe. He wrenched Mari free from two serving girls before he dragged Ali and her maid along with him. Their feet barely touched the ground. "Doona' fret. All will be well once the laird comes," he reassured them quietly. To the crowd he shouted, "Our laird will hear of the priest's charges upon his return."

Helped to his feet, the priest brushed off his robes and bellowed his demands after them. "See you lock them away like the criminals they are. Justice will be served this day."

"Aye," the man-at-arms muttered. Under his breath he said to Ali, "Emotions run high. 'Twill be safer and appease the old buzzard if I put ye in the dungeons. But doona' fret, my lady, I'll see to yer care myself."

"Thank you," she murmured, trying with difficulty to keep up with his long strides. Her feet ached, and she left a trail of bloody footprints on the unforgiving stone. But Mari's condition was worse. She was limp as a rag doll; the man-at-arms all but carried her.

As though sensing Ali's concern, he reassured her. "As soon as we're out of their line of sight I'll carry her, my lady."

Ali appreciated his kindness, but she couldn't help but feel it had come too late.

Mari could've died. With the thought, Ali's temper flared. "I can't believe Lord MacLeod would allow his men to stand back while a child was being abused on his land."

With a furtive glance over his shoulder, he scooped Mari into his arms and turned to Ali. "He wouldna' allow it, my lady."

"But the guards on the wall never did anything and you—"

"I wasna' here. I had returned to have my wound tended to when I came upon the mob."

"Oh, I'm sorry, I didn't know." Brow furrowed, she searched for his injury and found the place on his arm where blood stained the fabric just below his shoulder. "Are you sure you can manage?"

"'Tis no' but a scratch." He crossed the slate floor, past the hall, barking orders at the servants who darted out of his way. "Bring whatever Lady Aileanna will need to see to the wee lass." He unhooked a lantern from the wall beside a heavy wooden door and handed it to Ali. The thick oak creaked as he opened it and gestured for her to take the lead.

"Step carefully," he advised.

She did as he suggested, easing her way down the rough-hewn stone steps. Cool, musty air enveloped her at the foot of the stairs, and she was unable to suppress the shiver that skittered down her spine. He nudged her forward from behind and something brushed the bottom of her gown. Ali screamed, nearly dropping the lantern. "What . . . what was that?" she croaked.

"Rats," he murmured. "I'll send for the cats. The laird should be on his way."

Ali nodded. She sure as hell hoped so, for both her and Mari's sake. The man-at-arms propped the girl against his side while he retrieved a key from a heavy iron ring. The barred metal door clanged open, and his mouth flattened as he ushered them inside the four-by-four-foot cell. He gently placed Mari on a rusty old cot.

The girl hadn't made a sound and Ali was afraid she was in shock. "I'll need some blankets . . ."

"Callum. I'll see to it, my lady. I willna' be long."

Ali sat beside Mari, trying to ignore the grating sound of the key turning in the lock. She cupped the girl's face between her hands and looked into her eyes. "I won't let anyone else hurt you, Mari. I promise."

The young girl shuddered. A strangled sob escaped her pale lips, and she threw herself into Ali's arms.

"There . . . there, it will be all right." Ali patted her back, relieved at least to get some sort of reaction from her. She pulled away and rested her hands on Mari's shoulders. "Let's have a better look at you."

Mari tugged self-consciously at the tattered remnants of her beautiful gown. Ali came to her feet. Lifting the bottom of her own gown, she tugged the ruffled underskirt down and stepped out of it, careful not to get any blood on the snowy white flounces.

Mari gasped. "My lady, what are ye doin'?"

"Well, in case Callum has abandoned us, I won't have you sitting around half naked when Lord MacLeod arrives."

"Do ye think he'll come?"

"Of course I do. And when he does, it'll be that psychopathic priest who's down here, not us."

Mari shook her head. "Nay, 'twill no' happen."

Ali shrugged. "We'll see," she said as she ripped the underskirt in half and draped it over Mari's shoulders. "Now, do you think you've broken anything?" She knelt on the cold, damp floor, carefully running her hands over Mari's legs.

Mari drew the shawl closed with hands that were scraped raw. "Nay, I hurt is all," she whimpered.

Ali blinked back tears and hugged Mari to her chest, knowing the young girl hurt as deeply in her heart as she did in her body. Ali vowed the priest would pay for what he'd done. Somehow she'd make sure of it.

"I'll have to wait until Callum comes back before I can see to your cuts." Scanning the dimly lit dungeon, she was thankful the lantern provided as little light as it did. She could hear the unmistakable sound of rats scurrying in the dark corners. Ali pushed herself to her feet and took a seat beside Mari. She pulled the young girl into a tight embrace and leaned against the wall. She tried to ignore the slimy dampness that seeped through the fabric of her gown.

Ali longed for the comfort and safety of her cozy apartment, the chance to curl up on her couch with a good book and a cup of coffee after a long, hot shower. She swallowed a heartfelt moan. If only she'd found that damn fairy flag. *But then you wouldn't have been there to protect Mari,* the voice in her head reminded her. Ali shuddered, not wanting to think about what might have happened if she hadn't been there to intervene.

The sound of feet thudding on the floor above their heads and a familiar deep voice issuing orders caused Ali's heart to quicken. She squeezed Mari's hand. "It'll be all right now."

She heard the door leading to the dungeon crash open and the thunder of footsteps on the stone steps. And then he was there, standing in front of her, big and powerful. His raven black hair was slicked back from his handsome face. His white shirt was open almost to his waist. Sweat beaded on his sun-bronzed chest. She drew her eyes back to his face, to where a muscle pulsated in his clenched jaw.

"Open the bloody door," he shouted over his shoulder.

From amongst the men crowded behind Rory—Fergus, Iain, and Connor included—Callum stepped forward and ducked his head. He fumbled with the key as he tried to fit it into the lock. Ali wanted to tell Rory not to be angry at the blond giant. If not for him, she didn't know what would have happened to her and Mari. But the look in Rory's eyes when they met hers stopped her cold. Anger reverberated from him as he strode into the cell, and Ali shrank away from him.

He crouched in front of Mari and quickly took in her condition. "Let's get you out of here." He tucked the lacy fabric around her. Brow furrowed, he slanted a look at Ali, and something flickered in his piercing green eyes. He reached out and skimmed his knuckle along Ali's cheek. "Yer all right?" he asked, his voice gruff.

Their eyes locked, oblivious to anyone else in the room. Her throat went dry, and she was unable to draw her gaze from his.

Rory quickly lowered his hand to his side, resisting the urge to take Aileanna into his arms, to run his hands over her soft, sweet-smelling skin and see how badly she had been injured.

He scooped Mari into his arms and strode from the cell. He caught Iain's eye and jerked his head toward Aileanna. Iain nodded and along with Fergus, escorted her from the cell, each taking a firm hold of her. Rory wasn't certain if he did it to protect her, or the priest. Both Connor and Callum had told him how she'd leaped into the fray in order to protect the young maid, without regard for her own safety. His admiration for her only served to inflame the desire he tried so hard to deny.

But it would be difficult to defend her against the priest's charges if she went after him again, and Rory had no doubt that was exactly what would happen if the two crossed paths before he could intervene. He understood her anger. He'd been hard-pressed when he encountered the man not to beat him to a bloody pulp.

Mari stiffened in his arms when the bellows of the priest, coming from the tower above them, reached her ears. "Shh, he canna' hurt you, Mari. I willna' allow it," he soothed the young girl. She seemed to relax, but his words didn't have the same effect on the woman cursing behind him.

He shook his head. Aileanna Graham was like no woman he'd ever known—more of a warrior than many of his own men. He only wished she hadn't seen fit to strike the priest. She'd put Rory in an unenviable position. He had to find a way for all to save face. Somehow he would prove Mari was no witch, but was at a loss as to what to do with Aileanna. The priest demanded she be lashed, or at the very least sent to a nunnery to atone for her sins.

For a brief moment Rory had been tempted to send her away. After all, he still had his suspicions where she was concerned, and the well-being of his clan was his first priority. But if he was honest, he'd admit what disturbed him most was her ability to stir him in a way no other woman had, not since he'd lost Brianna. Her resemblance to his wife was uncanny, and at first he was able to put his desire for her down to that, but no longer. Aileanna was as different from Brianna as night was to day.

He glanced over his shoulder and caught the angry flash in her blue eyes and the stubborn set of her chin as she argued with Iain and Fergus.

"Aileanna," he said firmly. She looked up at him, a challenge in her expression. "You'll have yer say, but no' until you've calmed yerself."

"Calm? You expect me to be calm after what that . . . that," she sputtered.

Rory sighed. "You'll see to Mari and yerself, and then we'll talk."

Before she could say anything else Mrs. Mac hurried toward them, a hand pressed to her mouth. "You poor wee thing. What have they done to you? When I get me hands on that lot I'll—"

Rory rolled his eyes. *God save me from vengeful women.* "Mrs. Mac, you will let me deal with the matter and help Lady Aileanna see to Mari." He ignored her exasperated harrumph and continued up the stairs. When he reached the landing, he called down to his man-at-arms. "Callum, you'll stand guard outside Lady Aileanna's room." The big man nodded, a smile lightening his rough-hewn features.

Rory knew his choice was a good one. Callum had withstood the brunt of his anger when he'd informed Rory that he'd placed Aileanna and Mari in the dungeons. Callum had meant to protect the women, but when Rory had seen them huddled together in the cell it was all he could do to keep his hands from the big man's throat.

"As will I, my lord," Connor said, coming up behind him. The lad's ears pinked at Rory's perusal. Connor had been beside himself when he reached Rory on the field. He sensed the boy's concern had been not only for Aileanna, but for the young maid as well. Rory nodded his assent.

Once he saw Mari settled and did his best to reassure her there was nothing for her to fear, he took his leave. He hadn't realized Aileanna followed him until she stopped him with a tentative touch to his arm.

"You won't let him hurt her, will you?"

"Nay, Aileanna, he willna' harm either you or Mari ever again." He couldn't stop himself. He stroked her bruised cheek with a gentle caress.

"Thank you." Her heated breath whispered across his palm. He dropped his hand. Clenching his fist, he gathered what little control he had left.

Chapter 7

White-hot pain lanced through Rory's side as he shrugged into the clean linen. He clenched his teeth, determined his brother would not witness his discomfort. Taking a slow, shallow breath, he rode it out.

"What?" he rasped at the look of concern on Iain's face.

"You canna' hide it from me, Rory. I ken yer wound is troublin' you. I'll get Aileanna." His brother rose from where he sat by the fire and made to leave Rory's chamber.

"Nay, she's seein' to Mari. Leave it be, Iain." The last thing he wanted was to feel those soft, gentle hands of hers touching his bare skin, or her sharp tongue cursing him for being a fool. She'd be right. He shouldn't have gone with his men. It was too soon. But he hadn't had a choice. The MacDonald, knowing Rory had been wounded, would press his advantage. Ever since his year of mourning his daughter had passed, the old man had been relentless.

Belting his plaid, Rory took the mug of whiskey Iain held out to him and shot the amber liquid back. He eased himself into the chair opposite his brother and sucked in a harsh breath as his side rebelled. "Did you get the answers I asked fer?"

"Nay, they all closed up tighter than clams on a sea

bed." His brother's voice was laced with frustration. "'Tis no' helpin' matters that the priest hasna' stopped rantin' since you placed him in the tower. Truth be told, my head will explode if I have to listen to him much longer and 'tis no' helpin' our cause."

"Yer right. Best I deal with this now. I wanted to give Aileanna and the lass some time, but 'tis no' playin' out as I hoped." He sighed wearily and placed the mug on the table at his side. "Has Fergus returned with the sheriff?"

"No' that I ken. Mayhap 'tis no' a bad thing, Rory. 'Tis yer word that is law, no' his."

"Aye. Be that as it may, I've heard he's put a stop to the priest on two separate occasions these past months while we fought the MacDonald. He's a fair man fer all that he was appointed by James."

Iain snorted in disgust at the mention of the king. "Aye, and 'tis James who stirred up this hornet's nest."

"Aye, well, we'll deal with it as best we can, brother. Now, give me some time before you bring Aileanna and Mari to the hall. 'Twould be best if you stand by them— Callum and Connor as well."

His brother gave him a knowing look. "Ah, so you think Aileanna might cause a spot of trouble, do you?"

Rory's mouth twisted in a grin. "Aye, I'm certain of it. Mind you keep yer hand at the ready to cover that mouth of hers."

Iain waggled his brows and rose from the chair. "I can think of another much more enjoyable way to cover that delectable mouth of hers."

"Hold yer tongue, Iain," he growled, his body's response to his brother's words primal.

Iain's eyes widened. "You want her." He let out a low whistle. "After Brianna, I didna' think—"

Rory stiffened, his body as taut as a freshly strung bow. "Leave it be."

"Nay, I willna'!" his brother all but shouted at him. "If you want Aileanna only to warm yer bed, Rory, doona' do it. The lass deserves better."

He narrowed his gaze on his brother. "I am laird, Iain, no' you, and 'twould be best if you remembered that." But Iain was right. Aileanna was not the kind of woman for a quick tumble. She was a lady, although not like any lady he'd ever known. Her beauty alone set her above the rest, but it was her courage, her strength that intrigued him beyond measure. And a tumble was all he could offer her. Never again would he give his heart to another. The cost was too high.

The door rattled on its hinges as he slammed from his chambers before he said something he'd regret. He gave Callum and Connor a curt nod. "You both will accompany Lady Aileanna and Mari to the hall when the time comes. Be prepared for trouble."

"Aye," they responded as one, purposefully avoiding his gaze.

Bloody hell, he cursed beneath his breath. They'd heard his exchange with Iain. He opened his mouth to say something, then closed it. What could he say? His gaze drawn to the door they guarded, he could only hope Aileanna hadn't heard them, too.

The priest's voice broke through his thoughts, preaching the dangers of hell and damnation. He pinched the bridge of his nose, almost wishing he battled the MacDonald instead of dealing with what was to come. "Connor, tell the men to bring the priest to the hall." He shot the order over his shoulder as he made his way below, scattering the servants gathered at the base of the stairs with an impatient wave of his hand.

He looked up in time to see Fergus stride into the keep empty-handed. "I take it the good sheriff was nowhere to be found."

Fergus raised a bushy brow. "Yer no' surprised?"

"Nay, but what of Mari's mother?"

The big man shook his head. "Too terrified of the priest to stand in defense of her daughter."

Rory scrubbed a hand along his jaw. "I canna' say I blame her. At least she thought to bring Mari here when he threatened her the first time."

"Aye, and Lady Aileanna will stand up fer her."

"Aye, and that's what worries me," he commented dryly. A commotion from behind him drew his attention. The priest, slapping at his guard's hands, barreled toward them. With his robes billowing behind him he looked like an overgrown carrion crow come to feed. The man cuffed one of the guards that tried to restrain him. "Laird MacLeod . . . my laird, do ye no' hear me?"

"I wish I didna'," Rory muttered under his breath.

Fergus snorted, clasping his big hands behind his back as he stared down his oft-broken nose at the twitching bundle of fury that stood before them.

"Laird MacLeod, if ye will release the woman and the girl into my care ye'll be done with the matter."

"And what is it you're plannin' on doin' with them?"

The priest cleared his throat. "There will be a trial, of that ye can be certain." His beady eyes darted toward the entrance of the hall.

"Ah, I see. And do you plan on usin' torture durin' this so-called trial?"

The man gave an indifferent shrug of his birdlike shoulders. "'Tis necessary at times, ye understand."

"I understand only too well, and you should understand this." He leaned toward the man. "They are under my protection. You came onto my lands and almost killed that child. The only reason yer no' locked in my dungeon is on account of my clan and the fact they hold you in some regard. Fer that reason, and that reason alone, I'll allow you to state yer case."

"Ye canna' stand against the Kirk, Laird MacLeod, and well ye ken it."

"Yer new to the Isles, Father, or you'd already ken I've stood against the Kirk before when it comes to those under my protection. And I'll do so again if need be."

"But . . . but . . ."

Rory jerked his head at his men, leaving the priest to protest until he was blue in the face. "Take him to the hall."

Fergus followed behind at a leisurely pace. Tilting his head, he took a look into the grand hall and let out a low whistle. "'Tis packed to the rafters."

Rory rolled his eyes. He wasn't surprised. Superstition ran deep amongst his people. They would be crying for the young maid's death as loudly as the bloody priest. They were slow in giving their acceptance, and Aileanna and Mari had not been around long enough to earn it. "'Tis time, Fergus. See to the women."

"Aye." Fergus clapped a heavy hand on Rory's shoulder. "All will be well, lad. They respect you. No one will doubt the wisdom of yer decision once you render it."

"We'll soon see." He hoped Fergus was right. The problem was not in making the judgment, but in seeing that his clan saw the truth of it.

He made his way into the hall. A warm, musky scent assaulted his senses. Bodies packed twenty deep lined the walls. It took time to reach the dais in front of the room as those around him clamored for his attention.

Looking out over his clan, the mantle of responsibility settled over his shoulders. His father had entrusted them to his care. They were as much his legacy as the land and the riches that went with his title—maybe more so. Every decision he'd made since assuming his role as laird had been for the good of his clan. His marriage to Brianna had been one such decision. Their union brought peace and stability to his people, but with her death, they were once more mired in the constant turmoil of war. His thoughts turned to Aileanna and her eloquent plea for peace. It was as though she assumed he took pleasure in the battle, but that was far from the truth. She didn't understand.

How could she?

She was a woman.

As though his thoughts conjured her up, she stood in the entrance to the hall, her bonny face pale. The somber color of her simple gown didn't help, but the choice had been a good one. She looked prim and proper, with the collar buttoned up to her throat and the cap hiding the bounty of her long, flaxen hair. Although, when Rory looked at her, all he could see was the outline of her voluptuous curves and wisps of hair that escaped the tight confines of her cap to caress the delicate beauty of her face.

From where he sat, he sensed her vulnerability. She was strong, but he could feel her fear, see it in the way she twisted her hands. She wasn't daft. She had good reason to be afraid.

Eyes lowered, she took a cautious step forward. The tenor of the room changed. All conversation halted, and a menacing silence resonated in the hall. Aileanna flushed, and Rory noted the rapid rise and fall of her chest. If he could, he would go to her and offer his reassurance, but that would be a foolish move on his part.

Rory's hand came to rest on his dirk. His muscles coiled with tension, ready to spring into action if the need arose. He would protect her even if it meant one of his own would die. He'd let no harm come to Aileanna. Iain, Fergus, Connor, and even Mrs. Mac would do the same. He could see it in the grim determination on their faces.

Aileanna cast a sidelong glance at the young maid who now entered the hall behind them. The wee lass would move no farther, frozen in place by fear. Tears streamed down her pale cheeks. Connor and Mrs. Mac tried to nudge her forward. Even though he imagined their words were ones of reassurance, they did no good. It was only when Aileanna took Mari's hand in hers and whispered in her ear did the lass gather the courage to move forward.

Aileanna squared her shoulders and looked out over the crowd as though she dared them to do or say anything against the young girl at her side. She'd swallowed her own fears in defense of Mari.

Rory felt a surge of admiration well within him. There was no denying it; Aileanna Graham was an amazing woman, and he was drawn to her like he'd been to no other. But he refused to act on those feelings. She was under his protection, nothing more. For both their sakes he had to keep his distance.

The priest, surrounded by members of his flock, was only now becoming aware of the women's presence. The priest's chest puffed out like a rooster, and Rory knew he was getting ready for his tirade. He caught the man's eye and shot him a fierce look. It was a look Rory had perfected over a decade of being laird. He had Fergus to thank for the ability. Since the death of his own father, the older man had stepped aptly into the roll of surrogate. Rory trusted him like no other, and seeing him sit at Aileanna's side brought him a measure of calm.

A buzz of excitement hummed in the air as those gathered anticipated what was to come. Rory cleared his throat to gain their attention. "The first charge to be dealt with is the charge of witchcraft brought against the young maid, Mari." Out of the corner of his eye he spied Aileanna draw the wee lass closer. And he would have to be blind not to have seen the aggrieved look she shot him. What did she expect? As laird he had no choice. "Who has evidence to support this charge?"

The priest leapt to his feet. "I do."

Brow quirked, Rory regarded him evenly. "I would imagine so, since yer the one to bring the charge against the child. Are there no others?"

"Aye," a voice shouted from the back. The rotund figure of the cook pushed his way to the front of the room and pointed to the lass cowering beside Aileanna. "Three of my chickens died fer no reason the day after she arrived."

He heard Aileanna's undignified snort. "He probably fed them the slop I insisted he throw away," she muttered.

Both Fergus and Iain barely managed to suppress their mirth at her comment. He shot the lot of them a foreboding look. "Cook, was the lass anywhere nearby when the chickens died?"

"Nay, but—" the man sputtered.

"Did you no' have several chickens die a few months past?"

"Aye, but—"

Rory gave a dismissive wave of his hand. "Are there no others?" He noted some movement at the back, and for their benefit hardened his tone as he added, "Think twice before you cast aspersions on the girl. I will demand evidence of yer charge; if there is none, I will assume you cast it for no other reason than malice and will no' look kindly on the one who does."

The priest's eyes darted from left to right, scanning the crowd. He appeared to be trying to cajole the woman beside him to come forward, but she shook her head, eyes downcast.

He glared at her, then came to his feet in a show of bluster. "Laird MacLeod, as the Kirk's authority in these matters no other witness is required," he began self-importantly. "My evidence alone should be enough to convict the lass."

Rory raised a brow, tilting his head. "And yer evidence is?"

"She carries the mark of the devil's handmaiden. Her hair is red, her eyes mismatched."

"Oh, come on." Aileanna shot to her feet, shaking off Fergus's restraining hand. "Genetics is what it is. Look around you. What about him, or her?" She pointed out a redheaded man and woman on either side of the hall who were doing their best to duck behind those who stood in front of them.

The priest pointed at Mari, trembling with frustrated rage. "'Tis no' only the hair. 'Tis the eyes that damn her the most."

"A condition called heterochromia is what is responsible for Mari's eyes. It's because she has either too much pigment or lack of it in her iris."

Rory didn't know what she was saying, but he did know it was not her place to say it. His brother was to defend Mari. He skewered Iain with an angry glare. Iain shrugged his shoulders helplessly. "Lady Aileanna, you will sit!"

"This is a farce, and I can't believe you're allowing it."

"Sit down. Now," Rory growled from between clenched teeth. The bloody woman would undermine him in front of his clan if he was not careful.

"Harrumph." She sat back down on the bench, folding her arms across her bountiful chest, and gave him a damning look.

The priest sneered at her, and Rory expelled a sigh of relief when Iain grabbed her before she went after the man. His brother leaned over and quietly spoke to her before rising to his feet.

Iain held out his hand to the wee lass. "Mari, come here, please."

Aileanna urged her to her feet.

Noting the curled fist at his brother's side, Rory hid a smile of satisfaction behind his hand. Iain turned the girl to face the gathered crowd and looked directly at the priest. "Correct me if I'm wrong, but 'tis my understandin' that no one who is possessed of the devil would be able to come in contact with a cross, and if it was metal it would surely burn them."

"Well, aye, but—" The priest's eyes widened when Iain removed a silver cross from his hand and placed it around the lass's neck. For added effect, he had her bring it to her lips.

"I would say that's all the evidence we need. But perhaps we should simply ask Mari." Rory raised his voice to be heard above the din of voices in the hall. "Are you a witch, lass?"

"Nay." She shook her head vehemently.

"In league with the devil?"

"Nay, my laird."

"Thank you, Mari, you may take yer seat."

Iain guided her back to the bench and Aileanna wrapped Mari in her arms while the lass sobbed quietly. Rory met her gaze above Mari's head. The smile curving her soft pink lips and the look of gratitude in her sapphire eyes stoked the flame of desire that had simmered inside of him since the moment she'd walked into the hall.

Determined to dampen the fire that threatened to engulf him, he tried to draw forth an image of Brianna, but all he managed to conjure of her was an intangible wisp of memory. Guilt ate at him. He was beginning to forget, and all because of her, the woman who sat in front of him. He'd made a promise on Brianna's deathbed that no other would take her place. He'd meant it then, as he did now. Rory turned his attention from her to the priest.

The man was scarlet with pent-up fury. "What of her?" He pointed a gnarled finger at Aileanna. "I demand she be punished or I shall go to the king."

Rory leaned forward. "Do you threaten me, Priest?"

"Nay . . . nay, but ye must—"

"What I must do is get at the truth."

Mrs. Mac relieved Aileanna of the burden of Mari. The woman looked like she prepared for battle.

God help him.

"She struck me down. There are witnesses."

"None who have come forward," Rory commented dryly.

"Surely ye jest."

"Yer callin' me a liar, are you?" Rory kept his voice quiet, dangerously so.

"Nay, but—"

"There's only one person who is lying and that is you." Once again, Aileanna was on her feet, ducking beneath Fergus's outstretched arm she crossed to the priest before anyone could stop her, and grabbed the hem of his gown. "He caught his foot . . . see, right there." She pointed to the tear at the bottom of his robes. A tear the priest was doing his best to conceal. "That's why he fell. I didn't push him. Although I was tempted to." She said the last under her breath.

Rory jerked his head at some of his men to take up their positions amongst the crowd, afraid the excited chatter would soon turn ugly.

"Blasphemy. Laird MacLeod, I demand this woman be made to pay fer her sins."

"Be quiet. Lady Aileanna, are you sayin' you didna' push the priest?"

She gave a curt nod. "I didn't. He fell because he'd worked himself into a frenzy and his robes are too long." She turned her head and gave the priest a look of condemnation. "Perhaps God was punishing him for encouraging others to harm an innocent child."

Bloody hell. She surely would be the death of him. The priest looked about to have an apoplexy. The crowd was stunned into silence.

"Someone must have been a witness to this."

"Aye, Laird MacLeod, it is as Lady Aileanna says." Callum, the blond giant, lied through his teeth. He flushed under Rory's scrutiny.

"Lady Aileanna speaks the truth, my lord," Mari bravely added.

From the back, Rory saw a flash of movement. Janet Cameron pushed her son forward. The lad was all of about eight. "Ye tell yer laird what ye told me," she admonished him.

The boy stumbled toward the front of the hall.

"What's yer name, lad?"

"Jamie. Jamie Cameron," he mumbled, glancing back at his mother, who glared at him, arms crossed over her heaving chest.

Rory closed his eyes at the memory of the battle where the lad's da had lost his life. He released a weary sigh. Cameron had fought hard and died honorably earlier that year. He gentled his voice. "And what is it you have to tell me, young Jamie?"

"The lady didna' trip the priest. She held her hand like so." He demonstrated the defensive posture with his own wee hand. "To protect the maid, and then he fell." He lowered his head, casting a sidelong glance at Mari. He let out a pained breath, and once again looked over his shoulder at his mother. She jerked her head toward Mari. He shuffled his feet, then directed his full attention to the lass. "I'm sorry fer throwin' the rocks at ye."

The young maid's eyes widened. She flushed, then smiled at the boy. "Thank ye," she said, blinking back tears.

Rory noted Aileanna swipe at her own cheek, then squeeze Mari's hand.

"Jamie, yer a verra brave lad to come forward. Just like yer father, and I willna forget it. Yer mother's done a fine job with you, lad. When yer old enough, I'd be as honored to have you fight at my side as I was to have yer father." The boy beamed at his words.

Out of the corner of his eye Rory saw Robert Chisholm

come forward and whisper something in Aileanna's ear. She started to rise, then looked at Rory. He nodded when he realized Maureen's time must have come. Anytime a woman of Dunvegan was about to deliver, Rory battled his fears, praying no other would suffer as he had. He was thankful Maureen would have Aileanna to see to her. His gaze followed them as they left the hall.

"What . . . ye canna' mean to let her get away with this?"

"Were you no' listenin'?"

"But I am a man of God."

"Aye, but that didna' stop you from trippin' over yer own two feet." He ignored the snickers his words drew and continued. "In the future I would suggest you be verra careful before you bring charges against another. Yer welcome to join us fer the evenin' meal, and then my men will see you to wherever it is you travel."

The priest dropped onto the bench with a thump, no longer surrounded by supporters. He looked around him and turned back to Rory. "I have matters elsewhere that require my attention. I shall leave now."

"My men will be ready to escort you shortly."

Ali laid the bundled baby into his mother's arms. "He's beautiful, Maureen, and very healthy." The look of pure joy on the woman's face wiped away Ali's exhaustion.

"Thank ye, Lady Aileanna. Thank ye fer all ye've done."

Ali smiled and patted Maureen Chisholm's arm. "I didn't do a thing. You were the one who did all the work."

"I was verra scared and ye took my fears away. I'll no' forget ye fer that."

"It was my pleasure. Now I think his father's waited long enough, don't you? I'll tell him to come in and I'll see you first thing in the morning. Get some rest."

As the door to the tiny thatched cottage squeaked open,

two men straightened from where they leaned against an old, battered oak tree. A half moon hung overhead, casting a glimmer of light on the men's shadowed faces. Her heartbeat quickened at the sight of Rory, her body's response to him immediate. She tried to ignore the implications, to pretend her reaction was no different than any woman's would be to a man as powerful and as gorgeous as the Laird of Dunvegan. But she didn't need the voice in her head to tell her she was full of it.

Everything she'd witnessed in the hall earlier that day had proven to her beyond a shadow of a doubt that this was one man worthy of not only a woman's love, but her respect as well. His strength of character, the fairness of his judgment—although she'd doubted it in the beginning—and the depth of loyalty he garnered from his clan all bore witness to that. She envied Brianna MacLeod more than she cared to admit. Envied the love they had shared—a love worthy of a romance novel, and she should know—she'd read enough of them.

One day, if she was lucky enough to find her own hero, he'd be a very tarnished version of Rory MacLeod. They didn't make men like him anymore. Drew Sanderson, her slimeball of an ex-boyfriend, was proof of that. The man was nothing like Rory, nor were any of the others she'd dated before him. And that said a lot about what her love life would be like once she got back to the twenty-first century.

She shoved her thoughts aside and took a step toward Robert Chisholm. "Your wife and son are waiting for you." A big grin creased his craggy face.

Rory clapped a hand on his friend's back. "Go to Maureen and the bairn. I'll see you on the morrow."

"Aye, I'll do that." Robert clasped Ali's hands with his. "I canna' thank ye enough, Lady Aileanna."

"There's no need. Your wife did all the work. He's

lovely, and they're both doing well," she reassured the proud father. "I told Maureen I'd stop by in the morning, so I'll see you then." A cry that sounded like a little lamb came from within the cottage and they laughed. "I think your son is impatient to meet you."

With one more squeeze of her hands, Robert released her, ducking his head before entering the cottage.

A breeze wafted off the loch, rustling the trees, tugging at the cap on Ali's head. She scratched beneath the stupid piece of fabric Mrs. Mac had insisted she wear. Damp and hot, her head itched after the hours she'd spent closed up in the cottage with the blazing fire Robert had insisted upon. The smoky scent of peat clung to her clothes.

She heard Rory's chuckle rumble deep in his chest and looked over to where he stood watching her. "I'm surprised yer still wearin' the cap. I didna' think 'twas one of yer favorites."

She snorted. "It's not, but Mrs. Mac didn't give me much choice in the matter."

Rory pushed away from the tree and seemed to hesitate before he came to her side. He looked down at her. "You can take it off, Aileanna. The priest is gone," he said quietly.

"Thank God. Mari will be relieved." She grimaced, pulling out the pins that dug into her scalp.

"Aye, and you?" He lifted his hand as though to help her, but then let it drop to his side.

"Of course. The man is crazy." The cap finally free, she tugged it from her head. "Uhmm, that feels so good," she murmured, closing her eyes as she combed her fingers through her hair. When she opened them, she saw that Rory watched her with a pained expression on his face.

She frowned. "Is something wrong?"

"Nay . . . nay. I'll see you home." His tone was gruff.

"Oh, I didn't . . . you didn't have to come for me. It's light enough to make my way back on my own."

"You were no' the only reason I came, Aileanna." Her name rolled off his tongue in a low, smooth rumble that caused her toes to curl. "I thought I should be here fer Robert, in case . . ." He closed his mouth, his lips drawn in a thin, tight line. Tilting his head back, he squinted up at the stars that twinkled overhead.

It took a moment for Ali to realize what he meant, and when she did her heart ached for him. "Oh, Rory." She squeezed his arm. "Maureen and the baby are fine. They were at very low risk for anything to go wrong."

His eyes searched her face, and then he shrugged. "I ken it."

"I'm sure it's difficult for you. Would it help to talk about it?"

"Nay, it willna' do any good. I canna' bring her back."

"No, but sometimes talking can help." Her voice trailed off. His beautiful face was set in hard, razor-sharp edges. She thought she'd pushed too far and was surprised when his deep voice filled the silence.

"'Twas my fault. I should never have allowed her to get with child in the first place. She was too fragile, too small."

"Rory, don't blame yourself. Women of all shapes and sizes have babies all the time. Sometimes these things just happen, and it doesn't matter whether a woman is delicate or not."

"Nay, Brianna was no' like you. She—"

Ali couldn't help but feel a pinch of hurt at his words. "Yes, I know, you've mentioned that before." It was difficult being compared to his wife and found wanting. A woman he loved even now. Not that it should bother her. She didn't love him, didn't want him to love her. She smothered the little voice in her head before it could call her a liar and make her face things she had no intention of facing.

He raised a brow; the corner of his mouth twitched. "Nay, you misunderstand me, Aileanna. Yer strong and healthy. Brianna never was. She wanted to give me a bairn and I couldna' refuse her. I should have. I had a physician come from Edinburgh, but he could do nothin'. 'Twas her heart that gave way. Neither she nor the bairn had a chance."

Ali blinked back the moisture that gathered in her eyes. Even after two years, his pain was palpable. It lay thick and heavy between them. She cleared the emotion from her throat. "I'm sorry."

"Come." He held out his hand. "You'll catch a chill."

She hesitated before placing her hand into the warmth of his. He captured her fingers in his firm grip. They were rough and calloused, and she remembered how they felt skimming over her body when he'd caressed her that first night. *When he thought you were his wife,* she reminded herself. A poor substitute for the woman he adored. Preoccupied, she forgot to pay attention as they walked along the path to Dunvegan and stepped on a sharp-edged rock that pierced her slippers and her still-sore feet.

She stifled a cry of pain. Rory, as though sensing her distress, turned to look at her. "It's nothing. I'm fine . . . go." She jerked her head in the direction of the castle.

He cursed under his breath when he noticed her limping. "Yer a stubborn one, Aileanna Graham. Enough," he said as she tried to push past him and continue down the path. With little effort, he reached over and scooped her into his arms.

"No, Rory, put me down. You'll hurt yourself." She twisted in his arms, but it only caused him to tighten his hold on her. His hand brushed the underside of her breast, and the hard muscle of his arms flexed just below her bottom. He was more of a man than she'd ever known, and she wanted him. And he wanted his wife.

"You willna' hurt me, Aileanna." His voice was husky, his breath hot against her ear.

Maybe not, but she knew, without a doubt, he could hurt her.

Chapter 8

The air whooshed from Ali's lungs when Rory dumped her unceremoniously onto her bed with a muttered curse. "Did you have to cause such a bloody commotion down below?" He glowered at her, hands on his hips, his hair and clothes dripping with ale. He smelled like a brewery.

"Me? It wasn't me who caused a scene—it was you. There was no reason to carry me once we arrived home. I didn't know the girl was behind me when I tried to get out of your arms." Truly, she hadn't meant to kick the maid carrying the full jug of ale, and certainly hadn't meant for it to land on Rory's head. Remembering his stunned expression, the helpless giggle she could no longer contain turned into an all-out belly laugh. Ali fell back onto the satin comforter, clutching her sides.

Rory leaned over, bracing a hand on either side of her head. The muscles in his arms rippled beneath the fine lawn of his white shirt. His emerald eyes gleamed with amusement, and the corner of his mouth twitched. "I think you ken exactly what you were doin', Aileanna. You doona' take orders well, lass."

His gaze fastened on her mouth and the laughter died in her throat. The feel of his thick, powerful legs pressed between her thighs sent a surge of heat to her core. She curled her fingers into the starched fabric of her gown, resisting the urge to trace his full, sensuous lips, and the shadow that darkened his jaw.

Slowly he drew his gaze to hers. How easily he ensnared her with his powerful body and the heat of desire she saw there, desire that mirrored her own. She wondered if he knew how easily she'd succumb to his passion. How she longed to feel his mouth on hers, his fingers stroking between her thighs. She swallowed a frustrated groan when he pulled away.

Without a word, he crouched before her.

"Uhmm, Rory, what . . . what are you doing?" she stammered, pushing herself into an upright position. She fisted her hands into the maroon comforter.

He didn't look at her. Instead, he bent his head, his long fingers leaving a heated trail along her too-sensitive skin as, inch by inch, he rolled the stocking down her left leg. She winced as he gently tugged the silk from where the blood adhered the fabric to the sole of her foot.

Encircling her ankle in a firm grip, he examined her foot, then raised his eyes to meet hers. "Yer a healer, lass. You shoulda' taken care of this."

Did he expect a response? She could barely think, let alone speak, as he turned his attention to her other leg. Her eyelids fluttered closed, and she bit her lower lip to keep from begging him for more.

Ali slowly lifted her lids when he removed the other stocking. From the look he gave her, she could tell he had watched her the entire time, had seen the play of emotions on her face, and knew what she wanted from him. And all he'd done was see to her needs with gentleness and consideration. She felt the color rush to her cheeks. How stupid could she be?

He stood, abruptly turning away from her. "I'll send Mrs.

Mac to see to you. Mari needs time to heal before resumin' her duties."

Ali blinked, startled by the underlying anger she heard in his voice. "Of course, I didn't expect her—" She might as well have saved her breath. Her words ricocheted off the barrier of the oak door he slammed between them.

Ali pressed her fingers to her temples. She had to leave Dunvegan before she made a bigger fool of herself than she already had. Not that her powerful attraction to their laird—an attraction that wasn't returned—was her only reason for finding the flag—far from it. She wanted to go home. To the life she left behind.

The man destroyed her equilibrium, her common sense. He was every woman's ideal of a dream lover, and that was the problem. She was living a dream, or as today had proven—a nightmare. The fairy flag was her only way out, away from Rory and the pain of wanting more from him than he was willing to give.

She rose to her feet and grimaced.

"Och, now, sit yerself down," Mrs. Mac said as she bustled into the room, linens draped over one arm, a pail of steaming water looped over the other. She set the pail onto the slate floor and water sloshed over the rim. "So what did you do to put the laird in such a temper?"

Ali shrugged. "Nothing." She hadn't. It wasn't like she'd asked him to make love to her. And now that she thought about it, she doubted he even knew what his heated touch had done to her.

Mrs. Mac gave her a considering look. "'Tis probably his wound botherin' him. Iain spoke of it earlier."

"He never said anything." He'd been in pain and now she'd made it worse. Ali shot a nervous glance at the adjoining door. "I should check on him." She pushed off the bed and rose on her heels to protect her sore feet.

"Nay." Mrs. Mac gave her a gentle nudge, forcing her to

sit back down. "Iain has already suggested he let you tend him, but he refused."

"Oh." Once again she felt the heat rise to her face. He didn't want her anywhere near him. Aware of what he could do to her with just a look, a touch, she thought maybe it was for the best.

"Och, now, doona' fash yerself, lass. He doesna' doubt yer abilities. 'Tis on account he doesna' like to be fussed over is all."

Ali returned her attention to Mrs. Mac and waved off her explanation. "That's fine. I understand how he feels." She raised a brow to make her point.

"Och, yer two of a kind." She held out the linens to Ali. "If you doona' need me I'll see to Mari."

"Why? What's happened?" Gingerly, Ali hopped off the bed.

Mrs. Mac shook her head. Steel gray curls bounced as she pointed to Ali's feet. "If you doona' stay off those fer a while, they'll never heal. As fer Mari, there's nothin' time and a little kindness willna' cure."

"Of course, I'll do whatever I can. I still can't believe what they did to her. I don't think it's something I'll ever forget." She shuddered. Mari was the one reason she'd delayed her search for the flag. She had to be sure her maid would be all right before she left.

"I'm thinkin' we should be a mite careful with the type of kindness we give her from now on."

Ali's gaze narrowed on Mrs. Mac, certain the woman held something back. "What do you mean?"

Mrs. Mac released a weary sigh. "I'm hearin' the lasses turned her over to the priest on account of the yellow gown. They thought she was reachin' above her station and were a wee bit jealous."

Ali pressed a hand to her mouth to stifle her cry of dismay. "It's my fault. Everything she suffered was because of me." Remembering the scene in the courtyard, bile rose in Ali's throat. She felt dizzy, overcome with guilt. "My God, look at what I've done. I can't stay here any longer, Mrs. Mac. Please, you have to help me," she pleaded.

The older woman patted her shoulder. "Hush now. You ken I canna' do that, Lady Aileanna."

"Lady!" Her voice rose to a hysterical pitch. "I'm no lady. You know who I am. I don't belong here. I never know what to do, what to say, and now look—someone almost died because of it." Mari. Sweet, innocent Mari had nearly died because of her.

The connecting door flew open and Rory stood framed within it, filling the entryway with his broad shoulders. "What the bloody hell is goin' on in here?"

Mrs. Mac quickly placed herself between the two of them. "There's nothin' goin' on, my laird. Lady Aileanna is a mite overwrought is all." She waved him off. "No need to trouble yerself. I'll see to her." Mrs. Mac sent a pleading look over her shoulder to Ali when Rory strode toward them like a panther stalking his prey.

Ali could barely raise the effort to care. All she wanted to do was crawl in the bed, bury her head, and pray the nightmare would end. She'd wake up in New York and everything would be okay. *Other than the malpractice suit and the fact you could lose your job, you're right—everything will be just peachy,* the voice in her head jeered.

Ali didn't think she could take much more. What had she done to deserve this? Waves of despair threatened to drown her and her anguish broke free. Body-quaking sobs racked through her body.

Rory tried to step around Mrs. Mac to reach Aileanna, but the woman placed herself in front of him, putting her hands up. "Nay, 'tis no' proper. I'll see to her." Determination marked her stance.

He moved to the left and once more Mrs. Mac blocked

his advance. Rory growled in frustration, lifting her bodily out of his way. "I doona' give a damn if 'tis proper or no'."

Before he could take the crying woman into his arms, Mrs. Mac whispered urgently in her ear. Whatever she said caused Aileanna's sobs to intensify. Rory drew her toward him. He was at a loss as to what had broken the woman he cradled in his arms. She hadn't shed a tear during her ordeal with the priest. Yet now, she soaked his tunic with her tears.

"Leave us be," he ordered Mrs. Mac, ignoring her dire warnings as she closed the door behind her with a resounding click.

"Shh." Rory stroked hair the color of moonbeams from her bonny face. His fingers combed through the silken tresses he'd denied himself the pleasure of touching earlier, for fear he'd be unable to stop himself from going further. Lifting her into his arms, he carried her to the bed. Unwilling to release her, he sat with her on his lap, all the while trying to quiet her with words of comfort.

Her gown had worked its way over her thigh, revealing long, shapely, bare legs. She was pure temptation; the reason he'd left her to Mrs. Mac's care. The memory of her heavy-lidded, passion-filled eyes sent a bolt of heat to his shaft, and it jerked against the soft curve of her behind. She shifted, and the friction made him throb.

"All right now. You will tell me what has upset you, Aileanna," he said, his voice gruff with pent-up frustration.

"I wan . . . I want to go home," she sobbed.

Rory buried his face in her honeysuckle-scented hair. "Aye, Aileanna, we'll find a way to get you home." It was a decision he'd come to only moments before he'd walked from her room. So why now did he feel a hollow, empty ache at the thought of her leaving Dunvegan? She sniffed and wiped the moisture from her cheeks. Rory patted the far end of the bed and found the linens he saw there earlier. He handed the cloth to her.

"Thank you," she said, her voice hoarse.

"Is that why yer cryin', Aileanna? You miss yer home?"

"No . . . yes." She hiccupped.

Rory held her chin with his thumb and forefinger, forcing her to look at him. Eyes the color of the loch after a storm met his. "Which is it, lass?" With tenderness, he stroked his knuckles over her tearstained cheek.

"It was my fault, Rory. Oh, God, I didn't know."

"Aileanna, I doona' ken what yer talkin' aboot."

"Mari." She clutched at his shirt. "Don't you see? It was my fault the girls gave her to the priest." She burrowed her face into his neck, sniffing back fresh tears.

"No, I doona' understand, Aileanna. Tell me."

She murmured her answer into his neck. The feel of her soft lips moving against his skin and the warmth of her breath fanned the flame of his desire. He bit back a groan.

"Aileanna, sit up, lass. I canna' make out what yer tryin' to tell me." He held her upright with a firm grip on her forearms.

"I . . . I didn't mean to do anything wrong. I just thought it would be nice if Mari had something pretty to wear." She looked at him from beneath long lashes spiked together with tears. "Mrs. Mac said it was all right, but that was why . . . that was why the girls gave her to that madman. They were jealous, and it was all my fault. Oh, my God, I can't believe what I've done."

He framed her face with his hands and brushed away the moisture with his thumbs. "You were bein' kind, Aileanna, that's all. And when Mari needed you most you were there fer her. Yer braver than any woman I've ever known, and Mari is lucky to have yer friendship."

The vulnerability he saw in her eyes was his undoing, and when she appeared ready to argue the point, he lowered her onto the bed and covered her mouth with his. He swallowed her startled gasp. Taking advantage, he swept his tongue past her lowered defenses.

She whimpered, encircling his neck with her arms, her tongue matching his stroke for stroke. Rory groaned. Her passionate response was all he hoped for. He had thought he imagined it that first night with her in his bed, thought he'd been hallucinating with the pain, but feeling her now beneath him, he knew it wasn't so. She was everything he remembered: giving, sensual, and responsive.

It was nothing like it had been with Brianna. Because his wife had been so delicate, so very fragile, the few times they'd made love Rory had been reluctant to unleash the full strength of his desire. With Aileanna there would be no need to hold back.

He deepened the kiss, making love to her with his mouth. She arched her back, her lush curves pressed full against him, and his fierce hunger for her drove the guilt from his mind. Lifting his mouth from hers, he pressed a kiss to her eyes, the curve of her cheek, and the corner of her lips; trailed kisses along the delicate line of her jaw while he worked at the buttons of her gown in an effort to get to the slender elegance of her neck.

He kissed every inch of pearly white flesh exposed with each button he opened. She speared her fingers through his hair, drawing his mouth back to hers. Her kiss was hot and wet. He plundered her mouth, taking everything she offered and more—losing himself, forgetting everything but Aileanna and how he wanted her, needed her. The words echoed in his head, need her . . . need her. Like an icy bucket of water they cooled his desire. As though sensing his retreat, Aileanna stiffened beneath him.

"Did I hurt you?" she asked. Her concern was obvious, and she gently brushed her fingertips over the heated flesh near his wound.

Rory rolled onto his side and brought her hand to his lips, taking the excuse she offered him. "'Twill be fine."

Her brow furrowed and she drew away from him, touching his forehead, his cheek, before she began to prod near his wound. "No, it won't, not if you don't take better care of yourself."

He took a firm hold of her wrist to stop those insistent fingers of hers from traveling lower. Without interference from his head, his body readily responded to her. "Speakin' of wounds, I take it Mrs. Mac didna' have a chance to see to yers."

She gave him a questioning look, then slowly pulled herself up from the bed, turning away from him, but not before he saw the hurt in her eyes. "Please, don't worry about me. I can take care of myself."

She sat on the edge of the mattress, stiffening when he laid a hand upon her shoulder. "I'm sorry, Aileanna, it's just—"

She released a heavy sigh. "It's because this is your wife's room, isn't it?"

Rory groaned. Stomach churning, he rose from the bed. Bloody hell, he'd nearly taken another woman in his wife's chambers. He couldn't think straight around Aileanna. With an effort conceived of desperation, he hardened his resolve and his heart, doing his best to ignore the compassion he saw in her tear-swollen eyes. Eyes he could easily lose himself in.

Knowing the danger she posed, he forced himself to say, "I ken you wish to return to yer kin but have no memory of them, so I took the liberty of makin' an inquiry on yer behalf to Angus Graham. If anyone will have the answers, 'twill be him. I expect word shortly."

Aileanna looked startled. "Why . . . why did you do that?" She smoothed her hand over her gown, avoiding his gaze.

Rory frowned. Unsure why, her response gave him pause. "Is there somethin' yer no' tellin' me, Aileanna?"

She shook her head, eyes averted. "No."

With his fingers beneath her chin he forced her gaze to his. "Aileanna, I'm warnin' you—doona' keep anythin' from me."

He'd made her angry. The stubborn jut of her chin gave her away, as did the temper that brought out the midnight blue of her eyes. He'd seen it before—both passion and anger turned them that same shade of violet blue. If it wasn't a matter of importance, he would've laughed.

She stood up to him, closing what little distance there was between them. "Don't you threaten me, Rory MacLeod, just because you feel guilty for wanting me, because for a few minutes you forgot your precious Brianna." Tears and fury glittered in her eyes. "It was only lust. It happens. But don't worry, it'll never happen again. Now, I'd appreciate it if you'd leave my room. As Mrs. Mac said, it isn't proper." She turned away from him, wrapping her arms around her waist.

He'd made a mess of it, but she was right.

It was only lust.

Chapter 9

Ali sat huddled with Fergus and Iain at a table in the hall, picking at the big bowl of porridge in front of her. She grimaced as she tried to swallow the mouthful without a swig of ale. It was difficult to get past her modern-day sensibilities, and ale at eight in the morning was one of them, even if it was watered down.

"Is somethin' wrong with yer parritch?" Iain asked.

She held up her spoon. The oats stuck like glue no matter how hard she tried to shake them off. "You can't convince me Cook isn't doing his best to kill me."

Both men guffawed. Ali smiled, a little surprised that she could. After last night, she didn't think she'd ever smile again. Learning Mari had been handed over to the priest because of her had devastated Ali. And her response to Rory's heated kisses only made matters worse. She'd almost convinced herself he wanted her as much as she wanted him. But men only cared about one thing. She thought she could do the same, but her heart always managed to get in the way. With her dating history, she was surprised she'd been so gullible. *Most of them weren't worth wasting that precious emotion on, but this one . . .* Leave it to the little voice in her head to reappear now.

Fergus studied her from beneath his bushy brows. "Is somethin' amiss, lass?"

More than I can tell you. She took a furtive look around the room. None of those gathered at the other tables appeared to pay them any attention, but she lowered her voice just the same. "Did either of you know that Rory wrote to someone named Angus Graham to ask about me?"

"Oh, sweet Jesu', I'd forgotten all aboot Angus." Iain rubbed a hand over his clean-shaven jaw. "What are we to do now, Fergus?"

The big man shrugged. "Waylay any messengers that come to Dunvegan."

Iain tapped his spoon on the side of the wooden bowl. "Yer better at sneakin' aboot than me, so I'll leave it to you."

Fergus nodded, then gave Ali a long, considering look. "Mrs. Mac says yer verra upset aboot the wee lass. Holdin' yerself to blame."

Ali blinked away the sting from behind her eyes. She *was* to blame, no matter what any of them said, and they couldn't convince her otherwise. She shoved a spoonful of porridge into her mouth to avoid arguing with him.

Fergus wagged his wooden spoon at her from across the table. "I'll hear no more of that nonsense. You've done more good than harm, lass, and you remember that."

Iain shot her a look of concern. "I ken 'twas a terrible day fer you, Ali. They'll no' all be like that."

She tried to swallow past the thick lump in her throat, but it was no use. Grabbing her mug, she gulped down a mouthful of ale. "That's comforting," she choked out.

She studied the two men who sat across from her while they ate. Ali wished she could think of another way to find out where the fairy flag was hidden, but knew there was none. Using her wiles on Fergus would be next to useless, but Iain was another matter. A handsome man, charming to the extreme, he'd made it clear that given the slightest bit of encouragement he would jump at it—or her.

"Iain, would you walk with me to the Chisholms' this morning? I promised to check in on Maureen and the baby, and after . . ." She let her voice trail off and hoped the events of yesterday would make her little act as a distressed female believable. Trying her best to come across as helpless, she didn't realize Rory had joined them until she heard the scrape of his chair as he dragged it back from the table.

"I thought you meant to miss breakin' yer fast. Is yer wound actin' up?"

"Nay, I didna' have a chance to speak with Callum and rectified the matter this morn." Rory directed his answer to Fergus, but his gaze lingered on Ali. "Good morn, Aileanna," he said quietly.

She gave him a cool nod, but kept her gaze trained on Iain, who looked from her to his brother before answering. "Aye, Ali, 'twill be my pleasure."

"Thank you. I appreciate it, Iain."

Rory eyed her over the rim of his mug. "And what does my brother have the pleasure of helpin' you with, Aileanna?" Although asked pleasantly enough, there was no mistaking the edge of steel beneath his question.

"He's agreed to accompany me to the Chisholms'." She poked at the oats with her spoon.

Iain, as though he felt it necessary to explain, added, "After yesterday Ali is understandably nervous to be on her own."

Rory quirked a brow in her direction. "Is that so?" He kept his gaze trained on her while he took a mouthful of porridge.

Ali cursed Iain's unerring need to explain his actions to his brother. She hoped he hadn't triggered Rory's suspicions. He was one man she wouldn't be able to fool. And the one man that for the life of her she couldn't keep her eyes off of. Fascinated despite herself, she watched the movement of the powerful muscles in his throat as he drank his ale. With a concerted effort, she dragged her gaze away, wishing, not for the first time, he'd been cursed with some deformity. He was too damn gorgeous for his own good—and hers. "If you'll excuse me, I'll meet you in the courtyard in a few minutes, Iain. Fergus, Lord MacLeod." She nodded in their direction.

"Aileanna—" Rory paused, waiting for her to acknowledge that he'd spoken to her.

She sighed and turned to face him. Her knuckles whitened as she gripped the back of her chair.

The corner of his mouth twitched and amusement glinted in his eyes as he looked at her. "You'll be ridin' to the Chisholms'."

Ride? Her brow furrowed. Good God, he wanted her to ride a horse. "Thank you, but I'd prefer to walk."

"Nay. You'll ride."

What the hell was she supposed to say? Was there a woman in this godforsaken time that wouldn't be perfectly at ease in the saddle? "I . . . I can't ride. I'm allergic."

"Allergic? I've never heard of the word." He narrowed his gaze on her.

Damn, she'd done it now. She glared at Fergus and Iain. It was their fault she was in this predicament. But did they come to her rescue? No, of course not. "Horses make me sneeze."

"'Tis all in yer head," he scoffed. "A horse canna' make you sneeze. And you will ride, Aileanna, or you will no' go to the Chisholms'. Yer feet are no' yet healed."

She leaned across her chair to glare at him. "You can't tell me what to do, Rory MacLeod, and don't you forget it."

He sat back, arms folded across his broad chest, his eyes

locked onto hers. "Yer wrong, Aileanna. I can, and I will. Now, if yer scared of ridin' a horse, that I would understand."

"Of course I'm not scared." She waved her hand offhandedly.

"Good. I'll meet you at the stables after I've eaten."

"No . . . no, I'm not going with you. I'm going with Iain." She silently pleaded with Iain to intervene. His answer— a helpless shrug of his shoulders.

"If you plan on goin' to the Chisholms' you'll meet me at the stables." That said, Rory went back to eating.

Her fingers itched to dump the mug of ale on his arrogant head.

Head bent, he glanced at her from the corner of his eye. "I wouldna' try it, Aileanna. You wouldna' like the consequences."

"Achoo, achoo." Aileanna sneezed again and again. She stood just inside the stable door, as far from the horses as she could get. Sunlight played in her unbound hair, turning it to burnished gold. None too gently, she rubbed her eyes and nose. "I told you I have allergies. Do you believe me now?" She sniffed dramatically.

Rory pushed away from the rough-hewn boards of the stable wall where he'd watched her put on her wee show. "Nay." He brought his face within inches of hers and tapped his finger on the tip of her reddened nose. "I doona' believe you, Aileanna, but you'd do well on the stage, lass."

Her eyes widened as she stared at him in disbelief. "You can't be serious. Look at my nose, my eyes." She pointed at each of the parts she referred to.

"Aye, and if I rubbed at mine as much as you, they'd be the same."

"You're insufferable." She tossed her hair and turned to walk away.

"Oh, no, you doona' get away that easily." He grabbed her by the arm and tugged her toward him. "What, no sneezes? *Achoo.*" He mimicked her dainty sneeze, unable to keep the laughter from his voice.

Her mouth dropped. She punched him in the arm, making him laugh harder than he had in a long time. "You'll have to do better than that if—" He took hold of the hands she'd balled into fists before she could follow through with her threat. "Now, why canna' you just admit yer afraid?"

Aileanna struggled to free herself. She tugged her hands from his at the same time he let go. She stumbled and fell with a resounding thud onto the hard-packed, hay-strewn ground. He reached down to help her and she slapped his hand away, glaring up at him.

"I didna' do it on purpose, Aileanna," he said, biting back a smile.

Her eyes flashed deep violet. "Hah, as if I believe that!" She sat there and shook out the dirt from her dark blue gown.

He crouched at her side. "Let me help you."

"No, I think you've helped enough." She squinted up at him. "And don't you dare laugh at me."

He grinned. "Come now, you must admit yer wee performance was funny."

She dipped her head, lips curved in a slight smile. He helped her to her feet and brushed off the back of her gown. His movements were light and brisk so as not to touch the rounded curves of her delectable behind.

"Thank you," she murmured and took a step away from him.

"Will you tell me now why you willna' admit yer fears, Aileanna?"

She shrugged. "Why should I? I think you've been

entertained enough for one day." Her attention was drawn to Lucifer, his black stallion—a beast of a horse that even now pawed the ground in his stall.

"No one is without fears, Aileanna. I wouldna' laugh at yers."

She tipped her head to look at him, her eyes taking his measure. "I doubt you have ever been afraid of anything, Rory MacLeod."

She was wrong. He was afraid of her and what she made him feel. She awakened emotions he thought he'd buried with Brianna. He cleared his throat. "Come." He motioned for her to follow him. "Doona' worry, I'll choose a docile mount for you."

She moved across the hay-strewn floor with a discernible limp. Her gaze widened as she scanned the horses, a look of relief when they lit on the last stall. "I'll take that one." She pointed to the white filly.

Rory choked on his laughter. "Nay, Aileanna, she's no' fully grown."

Hands on her hips, she rounded on him. "Are you saying I'm too big for her?"

"Nay, only that she's too small for you. Why doona' you wait outside and I'll bring yer mount to you." Having decided on the horse for her, he thought it best if they met outside the close confines of the stables. Aileanna left without an argument while Rory retrieved her mount.

"Come, girl, 'tis time to meet yer lady." The honey-colored mare shot him a baleful look and went back to her oats. Anyone else would be offended if he suggested old Bessie be their mount. Most could walk faster than the mare, but it was all Aileanna required for now and, Rory surmised, all she could handle.

Rory saddled the horse and brought her out to where Aileanna waited.

"What's her name?" Aileanna asked, keeping herself well away from the horse.

"Bessie. Aileanna, she willna' bite. Come closer."

She gave him a disgruntled look before she took a cautious step forward. "Nice horsie." Aileanna held out her hand in the direction of the horse's muzzle. Bessie gave a disdainful snort and Aileanna jumped away.

Rory sighed. "We doona' have all day, lass."

"This was your idea." She sucked in what sounded like a panicked breath when he grabbed her around the waist and lifted her onto the saddle. "You could've warned me," she snapped, her nails biting into his shoulders.

He eased himself away from her hold. "Now take your left leg and put it around the pommel." She swung her leg over the horse, and now sat astride, giving him and anyone else who happened to wander by a tantalizing view of a bare and shapely leg. *Bloody hell.* "Aileanna, 'tis no' how a lady sits a horse." He patted the horn. "Now bring your leg back over this."

"No, I'll fall off. I like it better this way."

"'Tis no' proper you showin'—" He ran his hand through his hair, then gestured at her leg.

Aileanna huffed out a breath. "It doesn't matter. No one else will see."

She might think it fine for him to see her naked flesh. After all, he'd seen his fair share of her satiny smooth skin of late. But it did not aid in his intention to keep his hands or his thoughts off of her. Nor for that matter had his brilliant suggestion that she meet *him* at the stables. He had yet to figure out why he'd made the offer in the first place.

"I willna' let you fall. Now, do as I say." His hand at her waist, he tried to ignore the heat of her skin beneath his fingers. He watched as she complied with his order, all the while muttering under her breath.

When Rory lightly slapped her hindquarters, Bessie began to saunter across the courtyard while Rory walked alongside. Aileanna sat frozen in the saddle.

He gave her knee a squeeze of reassurance. "Now, that was no' so bad, was it?" he asked as they made their way out of the courtyard and onto the tree-lined path.

The reins clutched in her white-knuckled grip, she muttered, "I'll tell you once she gets going."

"This is aboot as fast as it gets with Bessie."

"Oh." Her lips curved into a wide smile that took Rory's breath away.

Bessie stopped short and lowered her head. "Wha . . . what is she doing now?"

Rory laughed. "Eatin'."

Aileanna wrinkled her nose. "I think I could've walked faster to the Chisholms'."

"Aye." He grinned. "But then you'd hurt yer feet."

He saw the tension ease from her shoulders as she inhaled deeply of the heather-scented air. "It's so beautiful here." Her gaze wandered over their surroundings.

"Aye, verra bonny." But it wasn't the scenery he referred to. Not the shimmering loch the golden eagle soared above, or the Cuillens in the distance, wreathed in mist. For him, their attraction dimmed in comparison to the woman at his side.

"I'd love to take a walk over there." She shifted carefully in the saddle, pointing toward the loch. "It looks so peaceful. I imagine heaven would be a little like that." She gave him a shy smile; a becoming flush bloomed in her cheeks. "That sounded silly, didn't it?"

"Nay." He returned her smile. "When yer feet have healed I'll take you there, Aileanna. 'Tis where I go when I need to think."

She studied him for a long moment before she said, "It

must be difficult to be responsible for all of this. To have so many depend upon you."

Rory shrugged. "Nay, 'tis what I was raised to do." He paused and stroked Bessie's mane. "I only wish it were no' necessary to fight to hold on to what is ours."

"Is that what your feud with the MacDonalds is about?"

"Aye, and now the king draws us into yet another battle."

She frowned. "What other battle?"

"You doona' remember, lass? The adventurers who kidnapped you, they're bound for Lewis—and my cousin Aidan will need our help to hold them back."

"Of course, I'd forgotten." She turned away.

He narrowed his gaze upon her, but before he could question her further, he heard his brother call out. Iain's deep voice scattered the birds that moments before chirped happily in the branches overhead.

His brother scrambled up the path toward them. He chuckled when he saw Aileanna's mount. "No wonder I had no difficulty catchin' up to you." He gave Bessie a pat and smiled up at Aileanna.

Rory tamped down his annoyance at the interruption. "What is it?"

Iain gave him a questioning look, then shrugged. "A messenger arrived. We're receivin' guests." He handed Rory a rolled parchment.

The paper crackled as Rory unraveled it. He scanned the missive. With a troubled sigh he looked out over the loch. "See Lady Aileanna to the Chisholms' fer me, Iain." His tone was brusque as he stalked off toward the castle without a backward glance.

Rory crumpled the parchment and cursed under his breath. His cousin Aidan now rode to Dunvegan accompanied by Moira and Cyril MacLean. He knew Aidan wanted to assure himself that when the time came Rory would aid him in his fight against the adventurers. Rory couldn't refuse him, but with the ongoing feud against the MacDonald, he'd be hard-pressed to provide the men his cousin required. An alliance with the MacLeans would be the answer, and Aidan knew it as well as Rory did. The MacLeans had the men they needed, but their price was steep.

They wanted a match between Rory and Moira MacLean.

Chapter 10

"Mrs. Mac. I can't breathe," Ali protested. The corset sucked in her waist several inches smaller than it had the right to be, crushing her ribs in the effort. Her breasts pushed up to ungodly proportions.

"Hush with yer complainin'. I'll no' have that viper ensnarin' my laird," the older woman muttered under her breath while she gave the laces at Ali's back another firm tug.

Light-headed, Ali wrapped her fingers around the wooden post of the bed. "What viper? And what does it have to do with you stuffing me into this thing?"

"Lady MacLean . . . Lady." She harrumphed. "Did you no' ken they'd arrived?"

"Iain said something—" The rest of her response ended up buried beneath layers of plum colored satin. Arms flailing, Ali pushed her way out, determined to get an answer from Mrs. Mac. The woman hadn't given her a moment's peace since she'd returned from the Chisholms'.

Iain had mentioned the MacLeans and his cousin in an attempt to excuse his brother's abrupt departure and manner. He needn't have bothered. Ali was growing accustomed to the Laird of Dunvegan's domineering behavior. Although she had to admit she had enjoyed their time together before Iain appeared on the scene and had been sorry to see it end, it was for the best. The more time she spent with the man the more she came to admire him, and that was not a good thing, especially when she had every intention of finding the fairy flag.

Not that her time with Iain had proven productive in that area. She hadn't managed to find out anything about the clan's revered treasure. She ignored the dull ache in her chest. No matter how she felt about Rory, any relationship between them was doomed. She didn't belong here, and if she had any doubts before, what happened to Mari put an end to them.

Freed of the voluminous fabric, Ali tugged at the low, squared neckline her breasts threatened to pop out of. "You can't tell me this is considered acceptable." She faced Mrs. Mac and pointed to her chest. "If you so much as catch a glimpse of my ankles you have a fit, for God's sake, but this . . . this is okay?" she said in a low, aggravated voice. Even though she'd prefer to shout the words, she couldn't risk being overheard, and truthfully, she didn't think the straitjacket posing as underclothes would allow anything above a whisper.

Mrs. Mac had the nerve to grin. "Aye, 'tis acceptable, and I'm certain my laird will think it verra acceptable indeed."

Ali's gaze narrowed on her torturer. "What are you up to?"

"Sit." With a firm hold on Ali's shoulders, Mrs. Mac guided her none too gently onto the most uncomfortable wooden stool Ali had ever sat on. The corset didn't help; her posture was perfect, and it was painful.

"Ouch," Ali cried as Mrs. Mac tugged a comb through her hair. She glared at the woman over her shoulder. "You can fuss with me all you want, but I'm not leaving this room until you tell me what's going on."

"'Tis as I was sayin'. That woman wants nothin' more

than to get her claws into my laird, and I will no' stand fer her bein' Dunvegan's lady. Fer all her fancy ways she's a viper, just like I said."

"Marry? You think she wants to marry Rory?" Ali stared at the dying embers in the fireplace as she absorbed what Mrs. Mac was saying.

"Think, nay. I ken 'tis what she wants. She's always wanted him. When he married Lady Brianna the woman flew into a rage that lasted fer weeks, from what I've been told."

Ali worked the words past the tightness in her throat. "But I didn't think Rory would marry again. He's still in love with his wife."

"Och, well, that mon would do whatever he had to for his clan, and a match between the MacLeans and the MacLeods would serve us well. Most would welcome the union, but no' I. It would be a disaster. He's too good fer the likes of her. He deserves better. His whole life he's sacrificed fer the clan, and 'tis aboot time he put himself first, if you ask me."

"I'm sure he'll do what's best for everyone." Ali twisted her hands in her lap like her heart twisted in her chest, leaving a dull and familiar ache. It felt the same as when she found out about Drew and all the women he'd been unfaithful with. But it was unfair to compare Rory to Drew. She and Rory hadn't exchanged words of love, or made a commitment. They'd shared nothing more than heated kisses. Yet, no matter what her head said, in her heart she felt betrayed.

"Aye, well, then she'd be it. But you mark my words, no good will come of it. She'll be a hard taskmaster. Dunvegan will no' be the same."

The thought of Rory married to someone else was beyond painful. And at that moment, Ali realized she'd fallen a little bit in love with the man, despite that she couldn't compete with his dead wife, or win his clan's acceptance. *For the love of God, you're not from the same century.*

Ali cleared the emotion from her throat. "I'm sure it's difficult for you to think of anyone else taking Lady Brianna's place."

"Doona' get me wrong, Lady Brianna was a sweet lass, but she never assumed the role of lady to Dunvegan. You ken she was no' strong, but what you may no' ken is she was verra shy and left the runnin' of the keep to me. The clan loved her fer it. Nay, 'twill no' be the same with the other one. I warrant we'll feel the lash of her tongue, if no' her hand as well."

Ali stiffened. "You aren't implying she'd hit you?"

"Och, aye, she has the reputation fer it."

"There's no way Ro . . . Lord MacLeod would ever allow that to happen, so you have nothing to worry about."

"She's a sneaky one, she is. I warrant the men doona' see that side of her. She'd keep it well hidden."

"I'm beginning to think this will be an interesting evening."

"Aye, 'twill be that. And you be careful, Lady Aileanna. She willna' take kindly to yer presence. Be wary of the lass."

"I doubt—" A light tap on the door to her chambers drew Ali from their conversation. "Come in," she called out, surprised when Mari crossed the threshold. "Mari, it's so good to see you up and around. Mrs. Mac, give me a minute, please." Ali reached back and stilled the older woman's hand before she gave her attention to her young maid. Other than bruises that would take some time to heal, Ali was pleased how well Mari looked after her ordeal, but she couldn't completely brush aside her concern. "Is everything all right?"

"Aye, my lady." Mari offered Ali a hesitant smile and tilted her head to the door. "Connor thought it best I come to ye." The young girl blushed prettily.

With a rustle of silks, Ali went quickly to her side. "Why? What's happened?"

"Lady Aileanna, you mustna' worry so." She patted Ali's arm.

"I'm sorry, it's just . . . well, you know. But there must be some reason Connor sent you to me, and please don't tell me it has anything to do with my hair."

"Nay, but it might be best if it did." Mari smiled and reached up to pat a strand into place.

"Och, now, I'm doin' the best I can. Sit back down here, Lady Aileanna, and Mari will tell us what's brought her here." Mrs. Mac waved her over with the comb. "Hurry on, or you'll miss the evenin' meal."

Once seated, Ali gave the girl a pointed look. "Mari?"

"'Tis Lady MacLean is all. She's lookin' fer a maid to tend to her needs."

"'Tis a canny lad our Connor is. You have enough bruises without her addin' to them. But why the woman didna' bring her own help is beyond me."

"Oh, but she did, only from what I hear tell the maid ran off on the trek here."

"You see, Lady Aileanna, 'tis as I said," Mrs. Mac huffed.

"Well, I can tell you right now she won't get away with that type of behavior while she's at Dunvegan. If Ror— Lord MacLeod doesn't deal with her, I will."

Mrs. Mac and Mari exchanged what looked to be a conspiratorial smile, and Ali narrowed her gaze on them. "What?"

Rory tried to focus on the woman at his side, but Aileanna's husky laugh coming from the far end of the table captured his attention. From the moment she'd entered the hall, he'd found himself unable to ignore her. The curve of her long neck beneath the elegant upsweep of her hair, and the creamy swell of her breasts filling the neck-line of her beautiful gown, all conspired against him.

"Yer brother seems much enamored of Lady Aileanna." Moira MacLean nodded in the direction of the two. An impish grin curved her tinted lips.

"They're friends," he said, his tone more gruff than he intended. The muscle in his jaw twitched at the sight of Aileanna's hand on his brother's sleeve, their heads bent toward each other. He tightened his grip on the pewter mug before he brought it to his lips, taking a deep swallow.

An elegant brow lifted at his response, her fawn colored eyes intent. "I thought she was his betrothed, yet I've seen no sign of her chaperone, Rory. 'Tis no' proper to have a woman under yer roof without her kin."

"She was injured when the adventurers kidnapped her and has no memory of her kin. Fer the moment she's under my protection, Moira. I await word from Angus Graham."

Aidan, who sat on his left, halted his conversation with Fergus. "Ye didna' mention that earlier, Rory. Are ye certain she's no' a spy?" His cousin Aidan, who arrived late to the hall, had yet to meet Aileanna and now leaned back in his chair to cast a suspicious look her way.

Rory had kept introductions to a minimum, commenting little on Aileanna's presence even when he and his cousin had shut themselves away most of the day to strategize. He hadn't realized it had been intentional, but obviously it had been, and Moira's comments of impropriety reminded him why.

"You've only just arrived, Aidan, and we had other matters to discuss. Rest assured, Lady Aileanna is no spy."

Moira walked her fingers along Rory's arm and tilted her head to gaze up at him. Her nut brown hair brushed his shoulder. "And what would those matters be?"

Her brother Cyril, seated to her right, laughed, saving Rory from answering. Rory wasn't about to be pushed into the union. Even though he knew the match had merit, something held him back, and he was beginning to fear that something was at the moment chatting up his brother.

"Ye must excuse my sister, Rory. She has never been known fer her patience." Cyril patted her hand with an indulgent smile.

"Cyril." Moira pouted prettily. "Ye wouldna' want Rory to think me spoiled, now would ye?"

"Doona' fret, Moira, that wouldna' happen," Rory reassured her, looking up in time to catch Aileanna's stormy blue gaze upon him. Their eyes locked before she turned her back on him. It was then Rory noted Moira had entwined her fingers with his.

He heard his cousin's sharp intake of breath. "Sweet Jesu', she has the look of Brianna." His mouth gaped. "Are ye certain she has no' turned yer head because of it, cousin? Mayhap ye should let me question her."

Before Rory could respond, Fergus cut in. "'Tis I who found the lass, Aidan, and if it wasna' for her, our laird would be dead."

Aidan's head swiveled between Rory and Fergus. "Ye were wounded and ye didna' tell me?"

Rory shot Fergus a look of reproach. "'Twas nothin', I'm fine now."

"Oh my, Rory, ye were wounded?" Moira clasped a hand to the slight curve of her breast and blinked back tears. "I could swoon at the thought," she said breathlessly, the color draining from her face.

"Doona' distress yerself, Moira. I'm fine." He laid a comforting hand on her shoulder.

Cyril held a mug of ale to his sister's lips. "There . . . there, love, take a sip. She's a wee bit emotional," her brother confided to Rory while he stroked the curls from his sister's face.

Aileanna's gaze fell on them. With a roll of her eyes she

shared a laugh with his brother. A small measure of anger flared in Rory at her reaction. He didn't think it fair she condemn the lass on account of her tender feelings. Most women did not have Aileanna's strength. "Lady Aileanna, Lady MacLean is feelin' faint. Mayhap you could see to her."

She passed a cursory glance over Moira before she returned her gaze to his. "I'm sure she'll be just fine. Besides, you're doing such a good job, I wouldn't want to interfere." She dropped her eyes meaningfully to where his hand laid on Moira's back.

Moira rewarded him with a wan smile. "She's right, Rory. I'm feelin' much improved. Ye have a calming touch."

"Mayhap it would be best if ye retire for the evenin', Moira. 'Twas a long ride and yer a bit peaked," her brother commiserated.

She nodded. Peeking at Rory from beneath her long lashes, she placed a dainty hand upon his arm. "Would it be too much to ask fer ye to see me to my room?"

"'Twould be my pleasure." Rory offered his arm.

Moira politely bid the table and those gathered in the hall good eve. Rory could feel the scrutiny of the many eyes upon his back as he left the hall. His clan was hopeful that he'd agree to the match and give them a fighting chance against the MacDonald. And Aileanna, he wondered, what was it he'd see in her eyes? More than curious, he glanced over his shoulder, but her gaze did not follow him. She was too busy listening to some tale his brother told.

He cursed under his breath.

"Did ye say somethin', Rory?" Moira enquired sweetly.

"Nay." He looked down at the petite brunette at his side. She reminded him of Brianna in her nature, but she had her health and wouldn't take to her bed as his wife had. The match would benefit his clan, of that he had no doubt, and they all but begged him to comply. It would be no hardship on his part. She was bonny and would know his expectations, not question him or demand more than he was willing to give.

Then why had he not yet signed his name to the contract?

They climbed the stairs in companionable silence until they reached the upper hall and his rooms. Moira stopped in front of his chamber door and ran her finger along its smooth planes. "This is yer chambers, Rory, is it no'?"

Something in the look she gave him made him uncomfortable and he scrubbed a hand along the stubble on his jaw. "Aye." He all but croaked the word out.

She closed the distance between them and dropped her voice. "Would ye no' like to show me yer rooms, Rory?" She pressed her palm to his chest.

He gently removed her hand and said, "Nay, 'tis no' proper, Moira."

"Then place me in the room adjoinin' ye and no one would have to ken. 'Twould be good fer us to spend some private time together, doona' ye think?"

"I canna' do that. Lady Aileanna already occupies the room."

"The room beside yers—*she* resides there?" Her voice grew shrill, her face pinched.

"Aye. It grows late, Moira. I'll see you to yer chambers," he said, his words clipped.

"Ye had best remove her from that room, Rory MacLeod, or I will no' allow my brother to sign the betrothal papers. I willna' have ye sleepin' with yer leman while I'm under the same roof."

Rory bit back a sharp response until he got his anger under control. He took a firm hold of her elbow and guided her none too gently down the dimly lit corridor. As they were about to round the corner, he heard the rustle of silks and the resounding click of a door in the direction from whence they'd come. He knew who it was without looking and had no doubt she'd heard what Moira said.

He came to an abrupt halt outside of Moira's chambers and brought her around to face him. "Lady Aileanna is a *lady,* and I remind you to remember that. She saved my life and those of my clan. And, Moira, the papers have no' been drawn up yet. It hasna' been that long since I buried my wife and I'm no' even certain I wish to take another."

Her face crumpled. "I'm sorry, Rory." She clasped his hand between hers, bringing it to her breast. "Please, forgive me."

He felt the soft, heated skin beneath his hand, the quickening of her heartbeat, and abruptly disengaged himself from her grasp. "'Tis forgotten. Good sleep, Lady Moira. I will see you on the morrow." His tone was curt. He couldn't get away from her fast enough, angry at what she accused Aileanna of being, and what it would do to her reputation if Moira chose to spread her tales. The decision Moira now forced him to make fueled his anger.

Once inside his chambers Rory hesitated before he strode to the door that adjoined the two rooms. He heard a crash. The wood shuddered beneath his hand. He wrenched it open, his gaze drawn to the overturned trunk and the brightly colored gowns that spilled onto the floor. Aileanna stood by the bed with her back to him.

"Aileanna?"

She put up a hand and shook her head.

Rory ignored her request and reached for her. "Aileanna, what were you doin'? Are you hurt?"

Beneath his hand her shoulder stiffened. She took a step away, then turned. Violet eyes looked up at him. "I'm doing as your bride-to-be demanded. I was going to take the gowns, and then I realized they're not mine to take—nothing is." She looked at the candle beside the bed and blinked her eyes.

"Aileanna." He brushed his knuckles along her cheek.

"Don't . . . don't touch me," she cried out in a strangled voice. "Please, don't."

Rory dropped his hand. "The gowns are yers. Anythin' you want from this room is yers." He took a deep breath. "But 'tis best you take another room, Aileanna. I willna' have yer reputation besmirched. I hadna' considered the consequences, and I should have."

"I'm sure it is for the best, and of course you wouldn't want to jeopardize the match with the MacLeans."

He scrubbed his hands over his face. "I have no' made up my mind on the matter, Aileanna. No' yet."

"But in the end we both know what you'll do, Rory. You always do what's best for the clan, and so you should." She knelt on the floor and gathered the gowns to her chest before she rose unsteadily to her feet. With her head held high she left the room.

Chapter 11

Anger overrode her humiliation as Ali watched the young mother hurry into the cottage, her sickly infant clutched to her chest. "I don't understand why she won't let me look at the baby, Callum. I'm sure I could find some way to help him." She glanced back at the blond man who shadowed her as she went unsuccessfully from one cottage to the next, checking on those Mrs. Mac had asked her to look in on. Not one of them had allowed her anywhere near them. You would think she carried the plague.

Her childhood insecurities resurfaced. Feelings of being unwanted, of not belonging, taunted her. She thought she'd overcome them, put them behind her, but coming to Dunvegan had forced her to contend with them once more. Her hard-won armor was slipping, allowing the pointed barbs to pierce her self-confidence and a heart battered more times than she cared to remember.

Callum appeared sympathetic. "'Twill take time is all, Lady Aileanna."

"That baby may not have time." She took his hand as he helped her over a fallen log. "Does this have anything to do with the priest?"

"Nay, 'tis on account they doona' ken ye, and mayhap—" He hesitated, looking decidedly uncomfortable.

"Callum, I'm sure whatever you say can't hurt my feelings anymore than they already have been." *Good Lord, why did I feel the need to blurt that out?*

He looked toward Dunvegan. Only the tower remained visible above the soaring pines. "In the hall this morn Lady MacLean questioned yer loyalties. She said as how ye were a spy sent by the MacDonald to turn the men's heads, gettin' them to spill their plans with yer bonny looks. Her voice carried loud enough fer all to hear."

Ali cursed under her breath. She should have gone down to breakfast instead of putting her new rooms to right. At least she could have defended herself. Then again, she would have had to face Rory and Moira MacLean. And if she was honest, Ali would admit that was the real reason she'd stayed to putter in her chambers.

"But Ro—Lord MacLeod must have come to my defense. He knows—"

Callum interrupted her. "'Twas Fergus and Iain who sought to protect ye, my lady. I thought they did a fair job mind ye, but it seems some of the clan chose to believe Lady Moira." He shrugged apologetically.

"I'm thankful they at least tried." Fergus and Iain—but not Rory. He actually thought she was a spy, out to harm his beloved clan. Despite the heat, she shivered. "What about you, Callum—do you think I'm a spy?"

"Nay, my lady, yer speech and ways are a mite strange, but I doona' think ye'd bring us harm," he said with a gentle look on his face.

She tilted her head to look up at him. "Is that why you accompany me instead of Connor?"

"Aye, Lord MacLeod was concerned fer yer safety after Lady Moira's—"

"If he was so concerned with my safety, why didn't *he*

defend me?" Her anger flared as she pictured Rory sitting silently by while his betrothed maligned her character to everyone gathered in the hall.

Callum winced. "Lady MacLean was verra upset that ye meant to bring harm to the laird and he was busy comfortin' her."

Ali snorted. "I'm sure he was."

"But doona' fear, my lady, Fergus willna' allow anyone to speak against ye in his presence." The big man smiled. "He's verra protective of ye, as is the laird's brother."

"That's something to be thankful for at least." Her head jerked up at the sound of a sharp crack and the rustle of branches. Callum shoved her behind him and drew his sword.

Peering around his bulky frame, Ali scanned the cluster of trees. If that little witch got her killed because of her stupid accusations, she'd make her life hell. *And how are you going to do that?* the voice in her head snorted. *You'll be dead.*

"Oh, be quiet," Ali muttered.

"Shh, my lady," Callum admonished, his eyes fixed on their surroundings.

"There's nothing out there," she whispered, just as a streak of brown darted amongst the pines.

"Halt," her protector growled. "Show yerself."

Out from behind a tree stepped the young boy who'd stood up for Ali and Mari the other day in the hall. "What are ye doin' so far from home, Jamie Cameron?" Callum resheathed his sword; the tension in his stance eased.

"I'm goin' to the glen to train with the laird."

"I doona' think so, laddie. Yer mother willna' be allowin' that, I'm certain."

Ali heard the rumble of laughter in the big man's words as she stepped from behind him.

"I doona' care." With his bottom lip thrust out, the

young boy began to march in the direction from where they'd come.

For a man his size, Callum was quick. He had Jamie by the collar before he'd ventured more than a foot. "Aye, ye will. I ken yer mother well, laddie, and if she catches ye anywhere near the glen, she'll tan yer hide."

Jamie glared at Callum, a mutinous expression on his freckled face.

"Save yer wee looks. They'll do no good on me. Now, come with me and Lady Aileanna. I'll see ye home." Callum nudged him onto the trail ahead of them. The boy grumbled, kicking at any stone that happened to be in his way.

"How is it ye got away from yer mother in the first place? I hear she's been keepin' a tight rein on ye these days."

The boy shrugged. "She's helpin' in the kitchens. They're busy preparin' fer the big feast Lady MacLean has ordered."

"I imagine they'll be needin' extra hands. 'Twill be as hot as Hades in the kitchens this day." Callum shook his head, muttering under his breath.

"I don't suggest you kick that one, Jamie. You'll break your toe," Ali advised absently as the boy drew back his foot to strike a rock the size of a watermelon. "Is there a special reason for the feast, Callum?" Ali asked, keeping her voice as casual as she could despite the tension building inside her.

"The MacLeans are expectin' some of their kin to arrive at Dunvegan this day. 'Tis said they're bringin' word of the adventurers, but I'm thinkin' there's more to it than that."

"Oh, I thought maybe it was a . . . a wedding feast," Ali said, the relief in her voice obvious; unable to deny, at least to herself, that she didn't want Rory to marry Moira MacLean. And it had nothing to do with her wanting him, Ali reassured herself. She just couldn't imagine him being happy with that woman.

"Nay, but I fear 'twill no' be long before 'tis."

"Why . . . why would you say that?" Ali grabbed ahold of Callum's arm as she stumbled over the same rock she'd warned Jamie about and cursed inwardly.

Callum shrugged as they came to the clearing. With no trees to shield them from the sun, the searing rays beat down upon them. "The laird has no choice, my lady. He has to make a decision verra soon. 'Twas all the talk in the hall this morn."

"Was that before or after the discussion of me being a spy?"

Callum chuckled. "'Twas after." Shaking his head, he clapped a big hand on Jamie's shoulder as the boy picked up his pace. "Nay, yer no' gettin' off that easy, laddie. 'Tis to yer mother ye go."

The boy wiggled out from beneath Callum's hand and stomped through the wildflowers, pulling the heads off those he didn't manage to tromp.

Ali picked a bellflower that managed to escape Jamie's wrath and sniffed its fragrant petals. She twirled the flower between her fingers, then returned her attention to Callum, who kept a close eye on the boy.

"Are you happy about the match between the MacLeans and the MacLeods, Callum?"

"Fer the clan, aye. Fer the man, nay."

Ali pushed her hair back from where it lay plastered to her cheek. "Why?"

He gave her a long, considering look. "I ken we're in need of the men the match would provide, but I doona' think 'tis fair our laird should sacrifice a chance at happiness."

"You don't think he'll be happy with Lady MacLean?"

Callum cocked his head to study her. "Nay, I ken there's another who interests him. One who would be a true partner to him."

"Really." Ali cleared her throat. "I didn't think Lord MacLeod would ever love again."

He grinned. "I think you ken well enough, my lady. I'm no' blind." Callum didn't give Ali a chance to respond—not that she could. He'd struck her dumb. You could knock her over with a feather. What had she done to make him think she was in love with Rory? She must have misunderstood. He couldn't possibly mean to imply Rory was in love with her.

Rattled by his comment, she stumbled through the long grass after him until they were within a few feet of the kitchens. The heavy oak door flung open at their approach. A woman Ali recognized as Jamie's mother came into view, her face flushed, her gray gown flattened to her body. She leaned against the wall for support. As though only then becoming aware of them, she squinted past the sweat rolling off her forehead.

"Jamie Cameron, what have ye gone and done now?" Wearily she pushed herself off the stone wall, wiping her sleeve across her brow.

Callum placed a steadying hand beneath the woman's elbow. "Doona' fash yerself, Janet. We met up with him on the path is all."

Janet looked from her son to Callum. The boy, who had paled at his mother's question, now beamed at the blond giant as though he was his savior. Which Ali was fairly certain he was. Janet Cameron might be small, but the woman seemed fierce. Callum gave Jamie a furtive wink. The young boy winked back, but his mother caught him, and no matter how many times he blinked to cover it up— the game was over.

"Nay . . . nay." Janet shook her head, dark spiral curls escaping from beneath her white cap. "I'll have the truth, Callum." She rounded on him, her chest heaving.

The big man held out his hands in surrender. "Janet, 'twas nothin'. The lad wanted to go to the glen is all."

"Oh, that's all, is it? He only wanted to go to the glen and play at makin' war with the rest of ye fools. Is it no' bad enough I've lost his da, now I'm to lose him, too," the woman said on a broken sob, burying her face in her hands.

"Hush, Janet. I'll no' let anythin' happen to wee Jamie. I promise ye that."

Callum awkwardly patted her on the back while her young son looked on. Jamie's face was beet red, his hands balled into small fists at his sides. Ali could see he tried his best not to cry, and her heart went out to him.

Janet pulled away from Callum and brought her grease-spattered apron to her face and wiped at her tears. "I'm sorry, my lady. I'm tired is all."

"Please, don't apologize. I understand how you feel, really I do. Not about your loss by any means, but your sentiments." She took a hesitant step toward Janet and squeezed her arm, steeling herself for the rebuff she was sure would follow, but none did.

Janet patted her hand in return. "Thank ye," she said quietly. "Now 'tis back to the kitchens fer me. Her lady-ship has ordered a feast and a feast there'll be, even if it kills us," she remarked dryly. "And, Jamie, me lad, ye best be right here when next I take a wee rest."

"Janet, you're exhausted. Go home with Jamie and I'll help Cook in the kitchens."

The three of them looked at Ali as if she'd grown two heads. She grimaced. "What?" Glancing toward the kitchens, she lowered her voice. "Do you really think Cook would try to kill me if I go in there?"

Janet and Callum shared a laugh. "Nay, but 'tis no' right ye bein' in the kitchens, ye bein' a lady and all."

Ali cut her off with a wave of her hand. "For the moment, I think it's the best place for me." It was true. Ali knew if she went anywhere near Moira MacLean she'd tell the woman exactly what she thought of her, and none of it was good.

She waved good-bye to Jamie and Janet, and finally to Callum. It took five attempts before she was able to reassure him that she really did want to work in the kitchens. And no, she wasn't suffering from heat stroke. And yes, she was sure she'd be safe enough—unless you included Cook and his kitchen knife.

Upon opening the kitchen door a blast of hot, humid air sucked Ali's breath from her. She grabbed hold of the doorframe before venturing down the three stone steps into the kitchen. The sweltering heat and smoke-laden air caused her eyes to sting.

Cook sat on a stool, slouched over the heavily scored wooden table. He turned his head to look at Ali, his face gray, his lips parched. "Dear Lord, I doona' ken what I did to deserve this much punishment in one day." His words were slurred.

Ali ignored his comment and hurried to his side. She removed the knife from his hand. "Have you had anything to drink?"

"Nay." He shook his head, eyes drooping.

Ali knelt at his side, pulling his lower lid down. "Come on," she said, tugging him to his feet. "You have to get out of here before you drop dead."

"Nay." He tried to fight her off, but was too weak. "We are no' done preparin' the feast." He waved limply at the two open flames where four young girls tended to a huge cauldron and a spit that held a pig. They didn't look as though they fared much better than Cook. She tightened her hold on the man and nudged him forward. "Girls, you come, too. Out you go," Ali said as she managed to get him up the last step.

The young maids exchanged worried glances. Their hands twisted in their aprons. It was then Ali recognized three of the four. They were the girls that had abused Mari in the courtyard. Ali tamped down her anger. It was the first time she'd seen them since that day. Mrs. Mac had assured her they'd been punished, and Ali guessed this was it.

"But, my lady, there is still much to do," said a girl Ali didn't recognize.

"Well, you won't be getting it done if you pass out, now will you? Come on." She waved them up the steps. "We have to get you out of this heat and get some fluids into you."

Once outside, Ali lowered Cook to the ground and propped him against the outside wall of the kitchens. The girls stumbled into the bright sunlight and sank down alongside him. Ali went back in and stirred what looked to be a thick stew. She wrinkled her nose at the pig on the spit. She cranked the handle, but barely managed to get it halfway around.

A low cackle from behind her startled Ali and she jumped. A stooped old woman, her face as wrinkled as a prune, appeared at her side. "I'm sorry, I didn't know anyone else was here," Ali apologized.

"Ye canna' do it yerself, lass." The woman placed gnarled hands over Ali's and between the two of them they managed a full turn of the spit.

Beads of sweat dripped from Ali's forehead and she lifted her arm to wipe it from her face. "Has any of the water been boiled or heated? I have to get Cook to drink something."

"Aye." The woman pointed to an iron pot that hung toward the back of the flames.

"Thank you. You should get out of this heat, too, at least for a little while," Ali suggested as she carried the pot to the table, her hands wrapped in linens. Although, despite her age, Ali thought the old woman looked in better condition than the rest of them.

"Nay, I'm good, lass. I've no' been here long." She gave Ali a gap-toothed smile.

"I'll be back in a few minutes to help," Ali said as she filled the last of the mugs. "I just have to get them to drink this and find some way to cool them off."

"There's a well at the back of the kitchens. Throw a big bucket on Cook. It should do the trick." Cackling, the woman walked to the other end of the room, well away from the open flames.

Ali managed to get the mugs to her patients without spilling more than a few drops. The girls drank greedily. She held the mug to Cook's mouth, trying to get him to drink, but had little success. "Girls, you make him drink, slowly though, and I'll get some water from the well."

"I can help ye, my lady," the petite girl with the curly brown hair offered.

Ali noted her flushed cheeks. "As long as you think you're up to it."

"Aye, I've been workin' in the kitchens fer a long time. This day's worse than most, but I'm more accustomed to it than the other girls."

"Thank you . . ."

"Katrina, my lady."

With Katrina's help Ali wet down Cook, the girls, and unintentionally herself. They helped to settle Cook beneath the big oak tree she'd spotted not far from the well. The girls insisted they were fine and accompanied her back to the kitchen. In companionable silence, Ali and the young girls, along with the old woman, worked together. Ali was regulated to more of a fetch-and-carry position, which suited her just fine. Their assumption that her lack of knowledge was a result of her being a lady worked in Ali's favor.

Drenched with perspiration and splattered with grease, her cornflower blue gown hung on her like a rag. Ali sank onto a stool and surveyed the three trestle tables that groaned under the weight of the food. "That's it, ladies. There's enough here to feed an army."

"But . . . but, my lady," one of the girls sputtered, "Lady MacLean will no' be pleased. 'Tis no' all of her menu."

"Katrina, you said you've worked in the kitchens a long time. Is this enough food to feed the numbers they're expecting?"

"Aye, more than enough."

"But Lady MacLean wants it special." The other girl was clearly upset, winding her apron around her fingers.

Ali sighed. With a hand to her back, she rose to her feet. "You leave Lady MacLean to me." She heard a familiar cackle from the back of the room and smiled. Removing the apron one of the girls had given her, she set it on the stool. "You've all done a wonderful job, and I'm sure it's a meal Lord MacLeod will be proud to serve his guests. I'm going to head back to the keep now. Leave Cook to sleep for a bit longer, but if he takes a turn for the worse, come and get me."

"My lady," Katrina called out as Ali went to leave. "Thank ye fer all yer help. 'Tis no' often a lady would lower herself to aid the likes of us."

Ali's throat tightened, and she swallowed past the ball of emotion. "It was my pleasure and, Katrina, in no way did I lower myself. Don't ever think that."

"Lady Aileanna, have a care around Lady MacLean," the old woman advised, her pale blue eyes piercing even from across the dimly lit room. "Laird MacLean as well. The two of them have it in fer ye. I'll do what I can to help ye, lass, but it would be best if ye had a care." Having said her piece, the old woman slipped out through a back entrance Ali hadn't noticed before.

"Who . . . who is that?" Ali asked, turning to the girls.

"'Tis old lady Cameron. She holds sway over much of the clan. A good one to have in yer corner with what—" Katrina began before she clapped a hand over her mouth.

The frame of the door creaked when Ali leaned against

it. "Obviously *Lady* MacLean's accusations have spread far and wide."

"We doona' believe them, Lady Aileanna, and we'll tell as many who will listen," Katrina promised. The other girls chimed in their agreement.

"Thank you. Now why don't you all go out and sit under the tree with Cook for a bit."

The four of them smiled, but it seemed they chose to ignore her suggestion as they busied themselves with one task after another. Ali left them, her protest dying on her lips. She might object to their being treated like slave labor, but it was obvious they didn't feel the same. They were proud to provide for their clan, and it wasn't Ali's place to disabuse them. She wouldn't, but she was going to make damn sure their efforts were appreciated.

Exhausted, Ali barely managed to shove the heavy doors to the keep open. The air in the cavernous entrance was decidedly cooler than the kitchens—a welcome relief. She lifted her hair to shake out some of the dampness and noticed the gleaming floors and the high sheen of the wood paneling.

Ali rolled her eyes—Moira MacLean. She wondered how Mrs. Mac and Mari had fared. Hopefully they'd had the good sense to hide out in her room. Two serving girls smiled wanly at her greeting. Just as she was about to take the stairs to her room, she heard Mari cry out.

Ali rushed into the great hall, following her young maid's panicked cry.

Mrs. Mac swayed on top of a very tall wooden stool, broom in hand. "For God's sake, Mrs. Mac, what are you doing up there?" Ali called out as she hurried across the room.

Ali reached her side and steadied the makeshift ladder. "You get down from there, right now."

"Och, I'm fine. I've only one more of the banners to clean," Mrs. Mac protested in a tired voice.

Ali took the broom from her and handed it to Mari. "I'll do it. I'm taller than you are. Come on, off you get."

Mrs. Mac sighed. "'Tis a bossy one you are," she said, climbing down from her perch.

Ali reached out to steady her. "Look at the two of you. You're exhausted."

"You doona' look much better yerself, my lady. I didna' think her highness would put you to work as well." Mrs. Mac raised a brow.

"She didn't. It's a long story," Ali said as she carefully climbed to the top of the stool, steadying herself with a hand on the stone wall. "And where is her *ladyship?*"

"She'd be havin' her toilette seen to," Mari said, handing her the broom.

Ali beat the long banner. Clouds of dust billowed in the air, making her cough. "Is that right?" She seethed as she pounded the cloth with renewed vigor.

The continuous loud thwack of the wooden broom hitting stone drowned out the sound of the men returning home. It was why when Rory's deep voice called out to her, Ali, who was lost in her own thoughts, forgot where she was and jumped. Losing her footing, she grabbed hold of the edge of the banner. The stool toppled over, leaving Ali to swing precariously above the floor. The panicked cries of Mari and Mrs. Mac drowned out everyone but Rory.

Rory's heart slammed in his chest at the sight of Aileanna clinging to his clan's colors. "Bloody hell, lass," he yelled, positioning himself beneath her. "What are you doin'?"

"What does it look like?" She glared down at him, her eyes flashing.

"Let go and I'll catch you." He held up his arms, widening his stance.

"No." She jerked her head in the direction of the stool. "Just put it back up."

He sighed. "Aileanna, 'tis broken. Now do as I say and let

go." Rory didn't have to cajole her further. The fabric gave way with a loud rip, and whether she liked it or not, Aileanna landed with a whoosh in his arms. If he could go by the look in her stormy blue eyes, she didn't like it one bit.

"Rory, yer back," a voice of pure femininity called out breathlessly. When Rory turned with Aileanna in his arms, Moira's sweet smile of welcome faltered. A degree of iciness frosted her manner. "What goes on here?"

He had barely set Aileanna on her feet when she strode toward Moira. "What's going on here is everyone's practically killing themselves catering to your every whim. Do you have any idea what you've done? Do you?" Aileanna cried, her voice shrill, an accusatory finger wagging in Moira's pale face.

Rory grabbed her arm. "That will be enough, Aileanna."

She whirled on him, jabbing her finger in his chest. "Will it? Is it enough that she practically killed Cook demanding a meal fit for a king, and in this heat?" Her chest heaved, and white-hot anger radiated off her.

Moira sobbed into her hands and her delicate shoulders trembled. "Oh, Rory, I didna' ken. I only meant to make ye proud."

He looked from one woman to the other. Aileanna's rage was barely contained. "You will apologize to Lady Moira, Aileanna." It was not right her going off on Moira like she did. The MacLeans were guests in his home, and Moira had obviously meant no harm.

Aileanna narrowed her gaze on him. She picked up the broom from the floor and slammed it into his chest. "If you want an apology, do it yourself. And while you're at it, you might want to do the rest of her bidding. That way you may have some servants left by morning."

"Aileanna, you will come back here and apologize," he roared to her retreating back.

"Stuff it," she yelled at him as she marched up the stairs.

Chapter 12

"Stuff it. She told me to stuff it. Do you ken the meanin' of that?" Rory asked Fergus, who stood across from where he sat at his desk in the relative quiet of his study.

His old friend shrugged, a glint of amusement in his eyes. "I take it to mean she's a wee bit fashed with you."

"With me? The woman is daft, goin' off on poor Moira like she did."

Fergus crossed his arms over his chest and raised a bushy brow. Rory threw up his hands in disgust. "You canna' mean to defend her. She goes too far. Even you who are bewitched by the lass have to admit 'tis so."

"Aileanna's a healer, lad, and was angry at the state of yer help. Did you no' take note of the look of her? I'd say she fared no better than the rest."

Rory leaned his elbows on his desk and rubbed his temples—he had. She'd been wet and filthy, a bedraggled mess, signs of weariness visible on her pale, drawn face. He had been concerned about her, more than he cared to admit, but before he could question her, Moira had entered the hall and Aileanna sprang into action like a crazed woman.

"What the hell went on here?"

"Doona' ask me, lad. Have you forgotten . . . I was with you?"

Rory glared, in no mood for humor. "Callum!" he roared. Despite the closed door, he had no doubt the man was close enough to hear him.

Callum entered and shut the door on the curious faces gathered outside. "You called, my laird." He fought back a grin.

"'Tis no time for jokes, Callum. Now, tell me what went on to put Aileanna in such a state."

The big man held Rory's gaze. "She tried to see to some of the clan and they shunned her. Wouldna' let her near them on account of Lady MacLean's accusations in the hall this morn. I ken she was hurt by it, though she didna' say much."

A stab of guilt twisted in Rory's gut at the thought she suffered on account of him. If he had not been busy placating Moira, he would have defended Aileanna himself and not left it to Fergus and Iain. The clan had obviously taken his silence to mean he concurred with Moira's accusations. Moira's sweetness reminded him more of his late wife than Aileanna, who so closely resembled her physically, and he found himself trying to protect Moira as he had failed to protect Brianna.

He cleared his throat. "And that was it?"

Callum shrugged. "We met up with wee Jamie, takin' himself off to join ye in the glen he was."

Rory grunted. "Janet would no' be pleased."

"Nay, she wasna'. She'd been helpin' Cook in the kitchens and Lady Aileanna offered to take her place so she could tend to the lad."

Rory stared at the man, certain he misunderstood him. "You canna' mean to say she worked in the kitchens."

"I ken it was what she intended on doin'. But I'm no' certain Cook would let her past the door."

"I'm certain he wouldna'. Fergus send Iain to speak with Cook. He has a way with the mon."

"I'll see to him myself. Iain is busy seein' to Aileanna."

The muscle in Rory's jaw pulsated. His hands clenched into fists. The thought of his brother comforting Aileanna brought him to the edge of his control. Both men eyed him expectantly, as though they awaited an outburst, but he refused to give them the satisfaction. He denied them the confirmation that she'd gotten under his skin, into his heart. He knew that's what they thought. Fergus had said as much.

When Fergus opened the door to leave, Cyril and his cousin pushed past him. Fergus shot Rory a questioning look and he shook his head. Well aware of what Cyril wanted, Rory thought it best Fergus was out of earshot.

"Rory, what do ye intend to do with that . . . that woman?" Cyril demanded, waving his hands in a dramatic fashion.

"Doona' worry, I'll deal with Aileanna in my own way. Now if you have nothin' further to add, I need to speak to my housekeeper. Callum, tell Mrs. Mac I'd like to have a word with her." Callum gave him a curt nod and went to do his bidding, leveling Cyril with a cold, hard stare before he left the study.

"Well . . . well, I never." The man puffed up like a peacock. "Yer household is in sore need of discipline if ye ask me."

Rory reclined in his chair and folded his arms across his chest. "I didna'. Aidan, you look to be gearin' up to give me a piece of yer mind. Why doona' you get if off yer chest?"

"Nay, cousin, sittin' back and enjoyin' the wee show is all." Aidan leaned against the book-lined shelf and grinned. "I hope Lady Aileanna will be joinin' us fer the evenin' meal. The lass is verra entertainin' and has an interestin' way with words. Stuff it—is that what she told ye to do?"

Before Rory could respond, Cyril hotly interrupted. "Ye

canna' mean to have that woman join us this eve, Rory. 'T-would be most upsettin' to poor Moira."

"I'm sorry fer that, Cyril, but I fear I doona' have much choice. If I did, several members of my household will see I pay fer the slight."

His cousin guffawed. "I never thought I'd see the day the great Rory Mor was brought low by a woman."

Rory stifled his response when Mrs. Mac entered his study, drying her hands on her apron. It didn't take much to note her displeasure upon seeing Cyril there.

"Cyril, Aidan, I'll speak with you later." He dismissed the two men.

They had barely left the room when Mrs. Mac said, "You'd best get on with it. I have much to see to with all the guests aboot to arrive."

"I'm sorry, Mrs. Mac. I didna' ken the invitation had been extended until it was too late. I think Moira—" Rory stopped himself, well aware Moira MacLean was not one of Mrs. Mac's favorites. He thought it best not to tell her Moira had assumed by this time the betrothal would be as good as done, and thought to celebrate with her kin this eve. Rory didn't have the heart to deny her, but still, he would not commit to making the announcement and had spent most of his time on the field, avoiding Cyril.

For some reason his cousin had kept his pestering to a minimum, but every so often Rory had sensed Aidan watching him. They'd been close as boys. Aidan had fostered with them in his youth, and Rory thought him as much a brother as Iain.

"What is it yer wantin' to ken?" she asked, wiping the back of her hand across her forehead.

"What was Aileanna doin' in the hall?"

"Cleanin' the banner in my stead."

"And why were you cleanin' the bloody thing in the first place?"

"'Tis what her *ladyship* demanded. Wantin' the keep all shiny fer her kin. Showin' off what she's marryin' into."

"Mrs. Mac, I doona' think—"

"Och, well, I ken that." She looked down her nose at him.

Rory kneaded the muscles at the back of his neck, looking up when Fergus reentered the study. "Did Cook allow her in his kitchens?"

"He didna' exactly let her—"

Rory threw up his hands. "You see, 'tis as I thought. I kent Callum must have been mistaken."

"Nay, you didna' give me a chance to finish. The kitchens were like a bloody inferno and the lass got them out of there. Cook was in a bad way. He's still no' himself. I've sent him to his bed, but doona' worry, the lasses have it under control. There's food enough for an army. You'll no' be disappointed." The censure in the look Fergus gave him irked Rory, and the one Mrs. Mac added to it didn't help.

"I ken what the two of you are thinkin', but yer no' bein' fair to Lady MacLean. She'd no' hurt a fly. She only meant to please me."

Mrs. Mac grumbled something about stupid men and left the room without so much as a by-your-leave.

Rory stood abruptly and his chair scraped across the floor, punctuating the tense silence between Rory and his old friend.

"Just so you ken, the lasses were singin' Aileanna's praises. She worked alongside them fer most of the day. I gather old lady Cameron was there as well. I ran across a few of the men she tore a strip off when they dared to say a word against Aileanna. It seems our lady has another protector." A wide grin split Fergus's face.

Rory tamped down a surge of pride for Aileanna and what she'd done. It was admirable; she was an incredible woman, but it did not give her the right to go on as she had in the hall, ranting at Moira, and worse, taking him to task in front of his men and guests.

"Where are you goin', lad?" Fergus questioned him as he left the study.

"To speak to Lady Aileanna," he shot over his shoulder as he took the stairs two at a time, unwilling to consider his need to go to her.

His brother descended the staircase as Rory ascended, and Iain grabbed hold of his arm. "You'll no' upset her, Rory. She's exhausted."

Rory shook off his hand and leaned toward him. "I will do as I see fit, brother. And no' you, nor anyone else will tell me otherwise."

His brother thumped him in the middle of the chest with his finger. "Doona' do it, Rory, or you will answer to me." Iain didn't back down as he so often did in their confrontations, and it surprised and angered Rory.

His brother had all but declared Aileanna his, and Rory, who remained in control at all times, even in the heat of battle, felt the thin rein he held on his temper snap. He saw red. His blood boiled. He grabbed Iain's hand and shoved him hard against the wall.

The pounding of feet on the stairs penetrated the veil of rage that filmed his eyes. Fergus grabbed hold of the arm he drew back to pummel his brother with, and Aidan wedged himself between them, his eyes glinting with amusement. "'Tis quite the show yer puttin' on fer yer guests, cousins, but might I suggest we take this up at another time. And I must insist ye let me partake in the sport. 'Tis been a long time since I've gone a round with the two of ye."

Rory broke free of Fergus and lowered his hand, his fist clenching and unclenching at his side. Aidan clapped a heavy hand on his shoulder. "Mayhap 'twould be best if ye saw to the lass after ye've had time—" His cousin met Rory's gaze and he shrugged. "And mayhap no'."

Iain tried to shove Aidan aside, but their cousin held firm. "Rory!" his brother shouted over his cousin's shoulder.

Aidan shook his head, turning to pin Iain in place. "Doona' be a fool, lad. Come, leave yer brother be and have some ale with me."

Rory didn't wait for Iain's response. He ignored the excited chatter below and brushed past the two maids who gaped at him as he strode down the corridor toward Aileanna's room.

Mrs. Mac had informed him last eve she'd set Aileanna up in his mother's chambers, a room Rory hadn't entered in years. His parents' suite in the east wing of the keep held bittersweet memories for him, and he'd wondered at the time if Mrs. Mac had taken some perverse pleasure in placing her there.

Rory leaned against the wall outside Aileanna's room, allowing the coolness of the stone to calm the raw emotion that warred within him. He'd almost convinced himself his cousin was right and he should confront Aileanna at a later time. But the iron handle was already beneath his hand, and he eased the door open before he could stop himself.

Stepping across the threshold, his jaw dropped. His breath stuttered in his chest at the sight that greeted him, and he couldn't move. His gaze riveted on Aileanna in her bath. Her lush curves, full, milky white breasts and satiny smooth skin glistened. If he was a gentleman he'd leave, but he'd warned her before he wasn't, not with her. He couldn't pull his eyes from her dusky rose nipples, her narrow waist, or the gentle curve of her rounded hip, even if he wanted to. He was enchanted, bewitched. She drew her long, slender legs toward her as she washed her hair beneath the water.

He should leave before she saw him. Before he could no longer contain the raging heat unfurling in his belly and kneel at her side to take those jutting nipples into his mouth. Cup her breasts in his hands, knead them, taste every sweet inch of her.

His cock throbbed in the tight confines of his trews, begging to be released, to drive into her. He had to get out of there, but as he turned to go the door inexplicably slammed closed. Aileanna emerged from beneath the water, eyes squeezed shut. Her long hair formed a curtain over her breasts; only her nipples peeked through, pebbled, primed for his attention.

"Oh, thank goodness, Mari, I've got soap in my eyes. Hand me a towel, please."

Rory couldn't help himself. He was drawn to her, a pull too great to deny, like a raging thirst needing to be quenched.

She rose from the tub and stood but a breath away, so beautiful, so ripe. He could touch her if he dared. Trail his finger alongside the bead of water that dripped from the tip of a rosy bud over her flat stomach to rest in the silky curls at the juncture of her thighs. His fingers itched to stroke her there, to dip inside her moist velvet heat and make her moan in pleasure. Soft sounds he had heard her murmur once before, and had never forgotten. His breathing grew ragged, and his hand hovered above his stiff cock.

She reached out blindly and Rory picked up the toweling from the floor and placed it in her outstretched hand. "Thank you," she said as she brought it to her face. "Tell me, has his highness stopped his ranting and raving?" Her words were muffled behind the toweling.

"He has," he said, his voice thick and low.

Ali squealed. Her feet slipped as she tried to leap from the tub holding the towel in front of her. The soap blurred her vision, but she didn't need her sight to know it was him. His deep smooth voice, his clean masculine scent, and the tingle of awareness she always felt whenever he was in the same room left her with no doubt it was Rory.

Big hands, calloused and strong, gripped her upper

arms to steady her. "Let go." She pounded on his chest as he hauled her from the tub.

"Shh, lass, you doona' want to draw a crowd." His heated breath caressed her ear.

"Why? Because they'd find out their laird spies on women while they bathe?" Her face flamed with the knowledge he'd watched her. The huge bulge pressed tight against her stomach told her so.

"How . . . how long were you standing there?"

Rory exhaled a shaky breath. "Too long. Give me a moment, Aileanna, and I will apologize as I should." He didn't let her go. He took several long, deep breaths and then released her. Taking a step back from her, he ran his fingers through his wavy black hair.

"Close your eyes," she demanded. He locked his gaze with hers, and Ali's fingers tightened on the towel that barely covered her naked, damp body from the hunger that glittered in his heavy-lidded gaze.

"Please," she groaned, afraid if he looked at her like that much longer she'd forget her earlier anger and drop the towel. Give in to the desire to feel his rough hands caress her naked flesh.

With determination she pushed the image aside, reminding herself of the apology he'd demanded of her earlier, of the risk he took with her safety by not defending her against Moira MacLean's accusations, and most damning of all— the fact he intended to marry that woman. No matter how much she wanted him, it would never be enough. She would be nothing more than a means to slake his desire.

Ali padded across the floor to the foot of the bed and slipped the delicate chemise she'd laid out before her bath over her head. She wrapped her arms around her waist and turned to face him. Her cheeks heated. "I asked you to close your eyes. Damn you, Rory. For once couldn't you behave like a gentleman?"

"I told you, I'm no gentleman, lass." His voice was rough and he took a step toward her. "Sweet Jesu' but yer beautiful, Aileanna. I—"

"No . . . no, don't say anything else. Please, just leave." She held up her hand to keep him at bay, her knees weakening at the look he raked her body with, well aware the fine white fabric did little to conceal her from him. With a jerky nod of his head he turned away and strode toward the door.

She cleared her throat. "Rory, what was it you wanted?"

He leaned his forehead against the door and said, "I doona' remember."

Chapter 13

Moira's incessant chatter came to an abrupt end and Rory breathed a sigh of relief, until he saw what drew her attention from him. It was Aileanna, preparing to take her seat by his brother. The image of her in her bath as she rose from the water with pearls of moisture beaded on her luminescent skin, her lush curves, stirred his desire as fiercely as it had only hours before. He pulled his gaze from her and drew a deep swallow of his ale in an effort to quench his growing lust.

"Lady Aileanna, ye will take a seat at one of the other tables. My kin will be requirin' that one." Moira gave an imperious wave of her bejeweled hand. The hard edge in her usually sweet tone took Rory aback as much as the request.

Iain rose stiffly from his chair and gallantly offered Aileanna his arm. He led her from the dais, her cheeks stained a bright pink. His brother glared at him. Seconds later, he heard Fergus mutter under his breath before his chair scraped across the floor and he too strode from the table.

"Oh my, I didna' mean for Iain and Fergus to leave as well. I just couldna' constitute that woman sitting there as though it was her God given right, after what she said to me." Moira's tinted lips pinched into a thin line. Her gaze narrowed to where Iain seated Aileanna; then he and Fergus each took a place beside her. "I hope ye didna' mind, Rory." Patting his hand, she batted her lashes at him.

"I do mind, Moira. 'Tis no' yer right to decide who is seated at *my* table and who is no'." Anger reverberated in his voice, and it took everything he had not to ask her to leave. To shout from the rafters that there would be no union—his clan be damned. But he couldn't do it; his loyalty, his sense of responsibility was too deeply ingrained.

Moira squeezed her eyes shut and a solitary tear trickled down her cheek. "I've made ye angry. I didna' mean to upset ye, Rory, but ye must understand my reasons. I canna' believe ye expect me to have her at the same table after what she said." Her hand fluttered to her chest. "'Tis too much for me to abide." Her brother handed her a handkerchief and she dabbed at her eyes, sniffling.

"Doona' worry, pet, I'm certain the last thing Rory would want is to have ye upset." Cyril who sat on the other side of his sister looked at Rory over her bowed head and jerked his chin in her direction as though he expected him to offer her some measure of comfort, but he couldn't bring himself to do it. He grew tired of pandering to her tender sensibilities.

He brought the goblet to his lips, studying Aileanna over the rim. As though she sensed his perusal, she looked at him and held his gaze with hers. Strong and defiant, Aileanna would bend to no one, but she was mistaken if she thought he did not know that beneath her beautiful, tough exterior lay a heart that could be broken as easily as anyone else's. Rory offered her a silent salute with his goblet. Her mouth curved in a slight smile, and she tipped her own in his direction.

"Rory, my aunt was askin' ye a question," Moira chided him.

"I'm sorry, what was that, my lady?" He leaned forward and addressed the sharp-nosed female who sat beside Cyril.

"I was just wonderin', Lord MacLeod, if the weddin' will take place before Michaelmas. I have a verra busy social calendar and—"

Rory was quick to cut her off. "I think settin' a date is premature considerin' yer niece and I are no' betrothed as yet."

"But . . . but I thought—" the older woman sputtered, looking askance at her niece. "Moira, ye said—"

Moira, face flushed, rounded on him. "How could ye . . . how could ye do this to me, Rory? Cyril, ye must speak to him. I willna' be treated in such a manner."

Her brother tugged at the collar of his tunic. "Ah, Rory . . . I think mayhap ye owe Moira an apology."

Rory sighed heavily. "The meal is bein' served, Cyril. I doona' ken aboot you, but I'm starvin'. We'll discuss the matter later."

"Good . . . good. See, poppet, all will be well. Dry yer eyes now, that's a good lass."

Rory thanked one of the serving girls who placed a platter of pork in front of him. He turned at his cousin's snort of laughter. "Got yerself in a fix now, cousin. 'Twill be interestin' watchin' ye maneuver yer way out of this one."

"There's no way out of it, Aidan, and you ken it as well as I. We need their men." Rory kept his voice low so only his cousin would hear him. Not that Moira who sat beside him paid him any mind. At the moment she was too busy being coddled by her brother. Rory began to think the man would join them in their marriage bed given his druthers.

Aidan rubbed his forehead. "I will be the first to admit things would go easier if we were tied to the MacLeans, but I'll no' have ye sacrifice yerself to obtain it. I didna' ken ye had no interest in the lass, Rory. And if I had thought there was another, I wouldna' have pressed fer the match as I did."

"There is no other," Rory said. As though to make a liar

of him, his eyes sought out Aileanna, who conversed with one of the serving girls. He smiled as the two of them shared a laugh.

"Of course no', I can see that." Aidan grinned. "Ye make a poor liar, Rory." He brought his ale to his lips, shaking his head. "I'd no' give up on that one so easily if I were ye." He tipped his chin in Aileanna's direction. "Like the highlands, she is. Wild and passionate, strong and brave. Like us. She'd be yer match, Rory Mor. Mark my words."

His cousin's sentiments rang true, and a dull ache built in his chest. Aidan spoke as though Rory had a choice. But if he did not do everything in his power to provide all they needed to battle the MacDonald and the adventurers, his clan's blood would stain the ground and turn the waters red. And that he could not live with.

"How much ale have you imbibed? Was it no' you who accused her of bein' a spy?"

"Nay." His cousin waved him off. "She's no more a spy than ye or me."

Moira tugged on his sleeve to gain his attention and Aidan waggled his brows at him. "I've missed ye, cousin. I'd forgotten how amusin' life is at Dunvegan."

"I'm glad we're keepin' you entertained," Rory drawled as he turned to the woman at his side. "What is it, Moira?"

She looked surprised by his tone. "I . . . I only thought mayhap ye have a toast to make."

"Aye, I'll do that now." He banged his empty goblet on the table to gain the crowd's attention and rose to his feet. "'Tis time fer a toast, my friends." Rory noted the smiles that greeted his words and the knot in his gut tightened. They expected an announcement he was not yet prepared to deliver. His gaze shifted to Aileanna, and her face paled as she stared up at him. If she wanted him as much as he did her, and his eventual decision would hurt her, it would tear him apart. He closed his mind to the thought, unwilling to entertain the idea.

"First, a toast to Cook and the lasses who provided us with such a fine meal." Metal clanged and cheers resonated through the hall, but all Rory could see was Aileanna smiling at him, a beautiful wide smile that could bring a man to his knees.

"And to Mrs. Mac and the lasses fer all their hard work. The keep is a-shinin' thanks to you ladies." Rory was tempted to include Aileanna for all that she'd done, but didn't think he could cope with Moira's hysterics if he did. And there were those who would condemn Aileanna for her actions, and she'd suffered enough for one day.

Cyril cleared his throat. The third time he did so, Rory turned to offer him a drink, but the man once again jerked his head toward his sister. *Oh, for the love of God.* "And to Lady MacLean, who did such a fine job overseein' everythin'." The crowd hesitated before breaking into their cheers, obviously expecting more. Rory sat down heavily, his duty done for the night.

Moira's aunt leaned across her nephew in an attempt to catch his eye. "Laird MacLeod . . . Laird MacLeod." She raised her voice when Rory continued to ignore her.

He sighed and turned his attention to her.

"With all my niece has accomplished, ye must think she'd make a fine lady of Dunvegan."

"I'm certain she would." He offered the woman a tight smile, leaning back in his chair so Mrs. Mac could refill his mug. Bending over him, she tipped the pitcher and the ale splashed into his lap.

Mrs. Mac clapped a hand to her mouth.

Rory cursed.

She tsked. "Och, now, look what I've gone and done. 'Tis sorry I am, my laird. My only excuse bein' I'm a wee bit tired." She fought back a smile.

His cousin was having a mighty fine laugh at his expense, as were Iain, Fergus, and Aileanna. Rory grabbed the linen before Mrs. Mac could dab at his lap. "I can see to it on my own, thank you," he said while he tried to sop up the ale.

"You doona' have to be fashed, Laird MacLeod. I was only tryin' to help." She sniffed and walked away, head held high.

"I'm certain you were," Rory muttered under his breath.

"Rory, ye shouldna' allow yer help to speak to ye that manner. When I . . ."

Moira let the last of her statement trail off, and Rory wasn't about to follow up on it. He'd had enough of emotional women for one day.

A full moon shone down from the clear night sky. The luminous ball lit Ali's way along the path Callum had told her led to the loch. She glanced over her shoulder. In the distance, lights twinkled at Dunvegan, giving the castle a fairy-tale appeal, but at the moment Ali didn't care; she was simply glad her absence had gone unnoticed. As she came closer to the loch the sweet cloverlike scent was replaced by the salty tang of sea air. A cool breeze drifted off the water to lift the hair from her shoulders. A deep sense of peace washed over Ali, and she quickened her pace, eager to sit at the water's edge, to be lulled by the gentle ebb and flow of the tide.

Following the moon's path, Ali paid little attention until a hulking shadow rose up from beside the rocky outcrop that lined the loch, dark and menacing, like the monsters from her childhood nightmares. A panicked scream curdled in her throat, but before she could let it loose, a familiar voice said, "Aileanna, what are you doin', lass?"

She let out a relieved sigh. "Rory?" She squinted, and he stepped from the shadows. His hair was as dark as the night sky and his face as beautiful. More like a fairy-tale prince than a monster.

Rory looked up at her, his white linen shirt billowing in the breeze, dark brown suede pants molded to his thick, muscular thighs. "Let me help you." He placed his hands at her waist and lifted her easily over the rocks to his side. His gaze focused on her, he said, "You didna' answer my question, Aileanna. What is it yer doin' down here on yer own?"

She shrugged. "It was noisy and hot, and I wanted to go somewhere quiet." Realizing she had invaded his privacy, she grimaced. "I'm sorry, that's why you're here, isn't it? And now I've disturbed you. I'll just—"

"Nay, 'tis all right. And I did promise to bring you here, but as I remember it was to be after yer feet healed." He raised a brow.

"They're as good as new." She lifted her foot and smiled at him.

The corner of his mouth twitched, and his gaze softened. "The stones are not as smooth here. Why doona' you let me carry you? 'Tis just beyond the bend where I mean to take you."

Moonlight shimmering over the loch and the man of her dreams were a lethal combination. Afraid if he took her in his arms she'd never be able to let him go, Ali shook her head. "I'm fine."

"Give me yer hand at least," he said quietly.

Ali hesitated, then slid her hand into the warmth of his. She drew her gaze from their entwined fingers and met his.

"I'm glad you came, Aileanna. There's somethin' I wanted to talk to you aboot."

"Oh no," she groaned. "Can't we call a truce, just for one night? You won't yell at me, and I won't yell at you."

Rory laughed and squeezed her hand. "Aye, a truce, but first you must let me apologize to you fer this afternoon. Sit here," he said, leading her to a big, smooth-faced rock.

"Thank you." She smiled at him as he sat down beside her. "To tell you the truth, I really couldn't understand how you expected me to apologize to that woman in the first place. I know you're going to marry her, but after what she did—" Ali shook her head. "It surprised me, it really did. You always seemed fair, but this time . . ." At his silence she looked at him. "What?" she asked when she spied his incredulous expression.

"Aileanna, 'twas no' what I was apologizin' fer. 'Twas fer later, when I—" He cleared his throat. "Interrupted yer bath."

Ali felt the heat rise to her face at the memory.

He looked down at his hands and shrugged his broad shoulders. "I ken there's no excuse, but you took my breath away, and I'm thinkin' my brains as well. Yer a verra bonny woman, Aileanna, and I canna' deny I've wanted you from the first time I saw you."

"Only because I remind you of your wife." She forced the words past the lump in her throat.

"Mayhap in the beginning, but no longer."

"Why are you telling me this now? Nothing can come of it." Her heart hammered in her chest. Could it? What if he told her he loved her, that he wanted her to be his wife and not Moira? Would she agree? No matter how hard she'd tried not to fall in love with this man, she had. He was everything she wanted. But could she stay here, in a time where she didn't belong? *Yes, yes, yes,* the little voice in her head shouted. Lifting her eyes to his, seeing the tenderness there, she knew she had to try. To give them a chance. If she didn't, she'd regret it for the rest of her life.

He ran his knuckles along her cheek. "I ken that, but I need you to ken that I wish things were different. I have to do this fer the clan, Aileanna. Too many lives depend on the union."

Ali felt like crawling under the rock. How could she have been so foolish as to allow herself a glimmer of hope? Rory was too loyal, too honorable to do anything other than what he had decided to do, and it was one of the reasons she loved him. She struggled to keep her emotions in check and looked away so he would not see how painful his words were for her to hear.

It was a cruel twist of fate that had brought her into his life. If only she had been born in this time, in this place, then his clan would accept her. And maybe she would have had family connections that would have made her as much an asset to him as Moira.

With a gentle touch of his fingers to her cheek, he forced her to look at him. "The last thing I want is to hurt you, Aileanna. I wish there was a way I didna' have to." He looked deep in her eyes. "Mayhap it would be best if we went back."

She placed her hand over his fingers. "Not yet. Please." If this was to be their only time together, she needed to make it last.

He kissed the top of her head and wrapped her in his powerful arms. "All right. This night will be ours, but only tonight. You understand I canna' put it off any longer, Aileanna. On the morrow I must sign the papers."

She wanted to rage at him, to cry out at the unfairness of it, but she couldn't. In her heart, she knew it was what he had to do. She wouldn't want him to risk the lives of his clan because of her, to have him live with that on his conscience for the rest of his life. He would never forgive her, and she would never forgive herself.

Ali snuggled into the warmth of his embrace and nodded, unable to speak, to control the hot tears that slid down her cheeks.

Rory groaned. "Nay, Aileanna, yell at me, anythin' but yer tears, lass."

"I'm not crying," she said, her words muffled against his chest. "I'm tough, Rory MacLeod. I don't cry."

He tilted her head back and captured a teardrop on his

fingertip. "Be strong, mo chridhe, fer me. I canna' bear yer tears."

Ali gave him a watery smile and wiped her eyes. "I'll try." There was so much more she wanted to say to him, but the words wouldn't come. Her heart ached, and she needed to put some distance between them if only to gain a semblance of her self-control. She lifted his arm from her chest and pressed a kiss to his palm.

"Where are you goin'?" he asked when she stood up.

"Over here," Ali said as she walked to the water's edge. She removed her slippers and dipped her toes into the foam that rolled onto the pebble-lined shore. Lifting the hem of her gown, she trailed her foot through the froth in a circular pattern.

Rory embraced her from behind, pressing her back to his chest. "That's how I'll remember you, Aileanna. Playin' in the loch with moonbeams in yer hair. I'll no' forget you, lass. Till the day I die, you'll hold a piece of my heart."

Chapter 14

As they neared the edge of the clearing and Dunvegan loomed before them, Rory stopped. They could go no farther without being seen and he needed to touch her, look into her eyes one more time before he said good-bye. It had been the hardest thing he'd ever done, not to kiss her lips, to find a soft place to lay her down and love her like he wanted to. But he knew if he did, he'd never be able to let her go, and he would not dishonor Moira, or Aileanna, by lying with her

He brought their entwined hands to his lips, and kissed her palm. She looked up at him, moisture gathered in her eyes, and he framed her face. "You promised."

She attempted a smile, but her bottom lip quivered and she caught it between her perfect white teeth. "I didn't . . . didn't think it would be this hard."

He groaned, and pulled her against him, burying his face in her silky hair, breathing her in as though to keep some part of her with him. "Doona' be angry, lass, but I pray Angus sends word soon. I canna' bear to think you suffer because of what I must do."

She tipped her head back and placed two fingers on his lips. "Don't worry, Rory, I won't be here much longer. And if this is to be our good-bye, there's something I have to ask you to do for me. I need you to make me a promise."

"What is it, Aileanna? I would give you whatever you want, you must ken that."

"There's only one thing I want, but you and I both know it can't happen. We weren't meant to be." She gave him a sad smile. "But there is something you can do for me that will make it easier for me to leave."

"What would that be?"

Her gaze was intent as she held his. "You have to promise me, if anyone comes to you with a complaint against Moira, you'll listen. And that you won't give her control over Dunvegan when you're away from home. She—"

"I ken Mrs. Mac and Fergus have their reservations, but you doona' ken her, Aileanna. She means well. She but tries to please me."

Her skepticism was evident in the look she gave him. "Please, just give me your promise. You're a man of your word, and all I ask is you give it to me on this."

He sighed, shaking his head. "Aye . . . aye, I will do as you ask."

The sound of men's voices in the courtyard drew his attention and he said, "'Tis time, mo chridhe."

She reached up on the tips of her toes to brush her soft lips over his. "Good-bye, Rory. Be happy and stay well," she said against his mouth.

He threaded his fingers through her long hair to cradle her head and gaze into her beautiful blue eyes. Rory had never wanted anything as badly as he wanted Aileanna. He yearned to deepen the gentle kiss, ravage her mouth and mark her as his, but he couldn't, not without causing both of them more heartache.

"Good-bye, mo chridhe."

With difficulty he stepped away from her, and together they crossed the courtyard. The night was still, the men's voices fading off into the distance, the only sound the clicking of Aileanna's heels as they struck the stone. He reached out to assist her on the steps, but she shook her head without looking at him. As he pushed the doors open the ache in his chest grew, and he hoped all were abed. His hopes were dashed when Mrs. Mac, Fergus, and Iain rushed into the entranceway, followed by Cyril, Moira, and Aidan, who gave him a knowing look.

"Och, now, Lady Aileanna, you've been cryin'. What has that big oaf done to you?" Mrs. Mac cried, scowling at him. She drew Aileanna into her protective embrace.

Fergus and Iain took a threatening step toward him.

"No more than she deserves, I'd imagine," Moira said, smiling like a cat that'd swallowed a wee warbler. "And ye willna' speak to yer laird in that manner, Mrs. Macpherson."

Rory was about to intervene, not wanting the tension to escalate, but Mrs. Mac didn't give him a chance. "Och, and I'll speak to him any way I please. I've been doin' so since he was in nappies, and you'll no' be tellin' me different."

Moira's incensed gaze shot to Mrs. Mac and Aileanna, and then back to Rory, as though she waited for him to explain, or at least intercede on her behalf, but it was Aileanna who took it upon herself to defuse the situation.

Once she managed to extricate herself from Mrs. Mac, she said, "I was out for a walk and tripped. Lord MacLeod came to my rescue, nothing more. Now if you don't mind, I'd like to go to bed."

"Good sleep, Aileanna," Rory said to her retreating back. He clenched his hands at his sides lest he reach out to her.

Her eyes met his over her shoulder. "To you, too, Lord MacLeod. To you, too." Her voice was low and husky.

Mrs. Mac sniffed. "My apologies, Laird MacLeod, and my thanks fer yer assistin' *my* lady." She turned on her heel and hurried after Aileanna.

Fergus's and Iain's thunderous expressions relaxed, but the MacLeans were none too pleasant to look upon.

"Ye were alone with . . . that woman?" Moira shrieked.

"Now, poppet, he came to her rescue is all," her brother soothed. Giving Rory a pointed look over her head, he added, "I'm certain my sister will no' be so sensitive once the papers have been signed."

"'Twill be done on the morrow. Now if you will excuse me, I wish to retire fer the evenin'." Ignoring Fergus, Iain, and his cousin's looks of astonishment, he walked away without another word.

Ali's muscles strained and burned as she and Connor, under Mrs. Mac's unrelenting supervision, moved another piece of heavy furniture. They deposited the trunk beneath the floral tapestry the older woman had appropriated from another room. Ali straightened and kneaded her lower back. "Are we done now?"

"Och, you doona' need to be so prickly, my lady. Doona' you think yer chambers look bonny?"

"Fit for a princess." They were. Mrs. Mac had determined Ali's new accommodations would be better than the ones she'd been forced to leave, and Ali didn't have the heart to tell her it wasn't necessary. She wouldn't be there much longer. She couldn't be, not after last night.

"Or lady of the keep." Mrs. Mac smiled smugly.

Ali's eyes widened. "Are you telling me we've been breaking our backs readying the room for Lady MacLean?"

Mrs. Mac rolled her eyes. "Nay."

Ali sighed. "Mrs. Mac, he's marrying her whether you like it or not. They're signing the papers today."

"Curious thing, that. The papers have gone missin'."

Wide-eyed, Ali watched as the older woman sauntered toward the door, a self-satisfied smile on her lips. She shook her head. No matter what Mrs. Mac had done, the union would go ahead. Rory would not let anything stand in the way of him protecting his clan.

"Connor, I'll send Mari up so you doona' need to go lookin' fer her. She was givin' me a hand with the other rooms," Mrs. Mac said as she closed the door behind her.

Connor bent over the trunk, making a show of rearranging it, his ears pink. "I wasna' lookin' fer her. I doona' ken why Mrs. Mac said such a thin'," he muttered in a disgruntled voice.

Ali bit back a smile. "I'm sure Mrs. Mac knows that, but, Connor, I'm glad you're watching out for Mari. You've been a good friend to her." Knowing Mari was well looked after made it easier for Ali to leave, and leaving must now be her only focus. She couldn't remain at Dunvegan any longer. If she did, her heart would never recover. *At the rate you're going, you might not have much of a choice,* the voice in her head reminded her.

Ali sat down heavily on the edge of the four-poster bed. It was true. She hadn't gotten any information about the location of the fairy flag from Iain. Not that she'd pushed very hard. Mrs. Mac had been only too happy to inform her that Rory and Iain had almost come to blows over her. Ali was resigned to find another way. She wouldn't cause a rift between the brothers. What she needed was someone who wouldn't suspect what she was up to.

A resounding thud caused the mattress to bounce.

"Connor, what on earth—" Connor—of course. "Here, let me help you." She hopped off the bed and righted the small table he'd knocked over.

Patting a chair, she said, "Come and have a rest." Ali pulled up a stool and sat across from him. "You're a big help, Connor. Lord MacLeod must be glad to have you with him."

The boy shrugged. "I suppose."

"I'm sure he is. How long have you been at Dunvegan?"

He furrowed his brow. "Since I was a wee lad, a verra long time."

"You have a lot of responsibility for someone so young. Lord MacLeod places a great deal of trust in you."

"I'm no' so young, my lady. I'm sixteen."

She grinned. "You're right, you're very old." Pausing, Ali concentrated on pulling her features into a pensive expression.

"My lady, are ye no' feelin' well?"

Obviously her acting skills needed work. "I'm just a little concerned is all."

"Aboot what? Mayhap I can be of some help." He leaned toward her. Elbows propped on his knees, he regarded her with heartwarming sincerity.

Ali choked back a sob. There was so much she would miss when she left. "Maybe you can, but you must promise not to tell anyone of my suspicions."

He nodded.

"You know about the fairy flag, don't you?" She held her breath.

His eyes widened. "Aye, ye ken aboot the flag?"

"Of course, Ro—Lord MacLeod told me all about it. And that's what concerns me, Connor. I think Lady MacLean knows about the flag as well and means to use it as a way to force Lord MacLeod into the union."

"I doona' think she needs much to force his hand. As I hear it the papers will be signed this day."

Damn.

"But the papers are missing, and she might get desperate. I'm sure that's what she was doing when she had everyone cleaning the keep from top to bottom yesterday. She was searching for the flag, Connor. I'm sure of it."

"She'll no' find it. She wouldna' enter the laird's chambers without his permission. Besides, 'tis well concealed. The wall—" He clamped his mouth shut.

Bingo.

Ali rose from the chair, anxious to begin her search. She schooled her features. "That's a relief. I should've known Lord MacLeod would do everything he could to protect the flag. I've kept you long enough, Connor. You've been a great help. Thank you."

"'Twas no' a problem, my lady, I—"

The door squeaked open and they both turned to see Mari, one foot over the threshold, frantically motioning for someone to follow her. "Ye must let my lady see to ye," she urged.

Ali frowned. "What's going on, Mari?" She moved toward the door and gasped when Mari gently guided one of the serving girls into the room, bloody linens pressed to her face. It was one of the girls Ali had worked with in the kitchens. One of the three that had attacked Mari. "Good Lord, what happened? Bring her here," Ali said, holding out a chair. Connor took hold of the girl's arm and helped her to sit.

"Tilt your head—that's it." Ali carefully removed the blood-soaked linens and sucked in a ragged breath. A deep, six-inch gash sliced from just above her brow to her cheekbone, barely missing her eye.

Mari twisted her blood-spattered apron in her hands. "I had her press the linens to the wound like you did fer me, my lady."

Ali reached over to squeeze Mari's arm. "You did exactly right," she reassured her. "Now I'll need a bucket of water, and make sure you boil it. And the herbs I used to keep Lord MacLeod asleep, I'll need those, too. Connor, you remember the ones I mean?" At his affirmative nod, she continued. "A needle and thread and some of that . . . Uisge na beatha, I think Fergus called it. Anyway, ask Mrs. Mac. She'll know what I'm talking about."

"Nay!" The girl gave a strangled cry. "No one can ken. She'll kill me."

"Shh, now." Ali patted her shoulder. "No one is going to kill you. Mari, what's going on?"

"'Tis Lady MacLean who done it. She told Ina she'd kill her if she said anythin'. Told her to see to it on her own, but I made her come to ye. I said as how ye would protect her."

Ali's hands balled into fists, and she had to take a calming breath before she said or did something she'd regret. Crouching beside the girl, she took her hands in hers. "Ina, we're going to take care of your cut, and for now no one will know, but Lady MacLean can't be allowed to get away with this. Whatever I do, I promise you won't suffer because of it."

"Ye didna' see her eyes, my lady. She looked crazed."

"I can imagine." Ali stood up and removed the linen, relieved to see the bleeding had slowed. "Do you know what set her off?"

"Aye, the papers were missin' from Lord MacLeod's study and she was in a rage, castin' blame on us fer cleanin' near his desk."

Dear God, do you know what you've gotten yourself into, Rory? Leaving him was hard enough, but knowing what his life would be like made it that much more difficult. But maybe he wouldn't care. He'd have the men to help fight his battles. He'd have done his duty.

Once Ali finished stitching Ina's cut, with Connor and Mari's help she settled the girl into her bed despite her groggy protests. "Mari and Connor will stay with you while you rest. I won't be long."

"My lady, please take care. I doona' want her to harm ye," Ina pleaded.

"You don't have to worry about me, Ina, but I can't say the same for Lady MacLean."

Mari giggled behind her hand, and Connor gave a snort of laughter. "Give it to her good, my lady."

"I plan on it, Connor. Now do either of you know where I might find her ladyship?"

"Mrs. Mac was grumblin' as to how she had to show her the gardens. They'd be to the back of the keep, my lady," Connor informed her.

Ali descended the stairs, avoiding the servants who scurried about as best she could, afraid someone would question her as to what she was about. She bowed her head and hurried past Rory's study. As she did, she heard voices raised in anger, and recognized two of them as Rory's and Cyril's. *Good,* she thought, grateful the men were occupied. It was time Moira MacLean got what was coming to her. Mrs. Mac had been right from the beginning. Men didn't see clearly when it came to the woman.

Hurrying out the doors of the keep, she spotted Fergus. Trying not to attract his attention, Ali lowered her head and strode to the opposite side of the castle.

"Aileanna." Fergus waved to her from across the courtyard. "Where are you off to in such a hurry?"

"The gardens." She smiled and kept on walking.

"Hold up there, lass," he said, closing the distance between them. "Aileanna, mayhap it would be best if you were to see the gardens at another time." He took hold of her elbow and turned her back toward the entrance of the castle.

She shook his hand off. "Fergus, don't be silly. It's a beautiful day to visit the gardens. I hoped to find a small patch where I could add some of the plants I'd read about in the book Iain lent me. Actually he read it to me, too. Remember, the one the physician from Edinburgh wrote? Where I found the herbs to drug Rory—well, not drug him, but you know what I mean." She waved her hand.

He narrowed his gaze and crossed his arms. "What are you up to?"

"I don't know what you're talking about."

"Yer ramblin', lass. You do it when you have somethin' to hide. Now tell me."

"No, and you can't stop me. *Omph,*" she grunted when he flipped her over his shoulder and marched determinedly toward the keep.

With a cry of outrage, Ali pounded on his back.

"Stop yer caterwaulin'. You were goin' to make trouble with Moira MacLean, and doona' deny it. I can see it on yer face. And if you do, Rory will have yer head."

She kicked her feet. "You don't understand." He whacked her soundly on her bottom. "Ouch, Fergus, that hurt," she cried.

"Then stop yer kickin', lass. Those parts I'm a mite fond of," he said as he pushed open the doors to the keep.

"Bloody hell, Fergus. What's goin' on here? Put Aileanna down."

"Nay, I think it would be best if I lock her in her room and let her cool down fer a wee bit."

"Like hell you will. Put me down." She slapped him on the back and gave him another kick for good measure.

"Eh, Fergus, watch yer bollocks, mon." Someone laughed, and Ali was certain it was Rory's cousin.

Whack.

"Fergus!" she yelped, covering her behind.

"That's enough." Big hands locked on her waist and hauled her from Fergus's shoulder to set her upright. "Now one of you will tell me what is the meanin' of this?"

Ali glared at Fergus, who glared right back at her. She pushed the hair from her face with an angry swipe of her hand and met Rory's unamused gaze.

"I'm waitin'." He crossed his arms over his broad chest,

showing no sign of what had passed between them the night before.

"Ali, what happened? You have blood on yer gown?" Iain asked, concern in his voice as he pushed past his brother.

Rory's gaze racked over her as though he searched for a wound.

"It's not mine." She stepped around Iain. "You made me a promise, Rory, and I'm holding you to it. I have a complaint against Moira that must be addressed."

"What is it that yer sayin' aboot my sister?" Cyril cried in a high-pitched voice.

"She threw a goblet at Ina, one of the serving girls. She needed stitches and was lucky she didn't lose her eye. *Lady* MacLean threatened to kill her if she went to anyone about it."

Cyril looked from her to Rory. "'Tis no' but an accident. Yer jealous and tryin' to make trouble fer my sister is all."

Her gaze locked onto Rory's. The muscle in his clenched jaw pulsated. "You promised."

"Aye," he grunted, drawing his attention away from her at the sound of Moira's and Mrs. Mac's voices headed in their direction. He jerked his chin, and Fergus and Iain took hold of her arms.

"No!" she cried, struggling to free herself. "If you don't do something about this, I'll never forgive you."

The object of her fury came to stand beside her brother, looking the picture of innocence in her pretty pink gown. Mrs. Mac, who trailed behind, cast a startled glance at Ali.

"What's goin' on, Rory?" Moira asked in a soft, gentle voice.

"Cut the crap, lady. Everyone knows what you've done. And if you so much as touch a hair on one of those girls' heads again, you'll answer to me," Ali yelled over her shoulder as Fergus and Iain dragged her toward the stairs.

Ali craned her neck in an attempt to see over Iain's shoulder. She was determined to catch Rory's eye before she was dragged away, but he turned his back on her, ordering Moira and her brother to his study. Ali had the satisfaction of seeing Moira's mouth drop. Aidan caught Ali's eye, and gave her a reassuring wink.

"Ali, he'll take care of it. I'll add my promise to his. She'll no' harm another," Iain said, angrier than she'd ever seen him. "I canna' believe he's goin' through with the betrothal."

"I thought you wanted the match."

"Nay, Aileanna, I want to see my brother happy. 'Tis all I've ever wanted."

Ali listened to every footfall, every creak in the hall outside Rory's room. She timed her search of his chambers to when they'd be dining in the hall. Mrs. Mac had unhappily informed her that a new agreement was being drawn up and would be signed after the evening meal. With luck, Ali figured she had several hours to look for the flag. But there had been several delays before she had the chance to sneak unseen from her room.

Mari and Connor had come to check on her and report on Ina's progress; Fergus, to apologize for smacking her behind, although he informed her it was well deserved; and Iain, to share what had taken place between his brother and Moira. He said Rory told Moira in no uncertain terms how he felt about his servants being abused, and accident or not, he would not constitute it happening again. And although she'd be lady of Dunvegan—Iain had shuddered as he said the words—Mrs. Mac would see to the staff and oversee the keep much as she did before.

Ali had tearfully thanked him, saying a silent good-bye as she had to all of them. No one commented on her tears, and Ali figured they assumed she grieved because Rory was going through with the betrothal. They were right, but her tears were for them, too. They'd become the family she never had.

Ali sniffed and wiped the moisture from her cheek. She kept her gaze averted from the bed, but the memories refused to be kept at bay. Rory's hand on her naked body, his mouth on hers—him lying there wounded and in pain, but still managing to tease. Every little detail of their time together flashed before her. How could she leave . . . how could she not? It was only when Ali relegated all she stood to lose to the recesses of her mind that she had the strength to move ahead with her search.

The wall. He said the wall.

She placed both palms alongside the doorframe and slowly worked her way around the room. It seemed like hours had passed. Her arms ached from stretching and pressing every inch of the walls, stone and paneling alike. Painstakingly she checked for signs of wear. Knowing she had little time left, and half the room still to explore, she had all but given up. Then the panel creaked beneath her palm. She tapped lightly—it was hollow.

She was tempted to use the knife she wore strapped to her thigh—the one Callum had given her—but was afraid to damage the wood. A tremor of nervous excitement ran through her as she slid her nails along the edge. The wall moved. Her heartbeat echoed in her ears as inch by inch she worked it open. Behind the panel she discovered a closet-like space. On the dusty floor sat a black trunk. Ali knelt beside it, closing her eyes when it squeaked open, her nerves scraped raw, every sound magnified a hundred times.

Slowly she opened her eyes. On top lay the cream colored square of silk. Her search was over, and she didn't know whether to laugh or cry. She clutched the flag to her chest. Aware she didn't have much time, she began to push the panel back into place, but it was stuck. Ali leaned her shoulder into it. With a long, drawn-out creak, it shuddered closed.

A deep voice rumbled over her. "What are you doin', Aileanna?"

Chapter 15

"Aileanna, I asked you a question. What are you doin'?" Rory hesitated, slowly closing the door behind him, not sure he could withstand the temptation of being alone with her. He had come to his chambers for a moment's peace before he put his name to the agreement. Aileanna's accusations against Moira had not helped matters, nor did her entreaty that he hold true to his promise. His head still ached from Moira's hysterics in his study, and her constant attentions in the hall.

Aileanna turned toward him, her face flushed, hair in disarray, and a look of panic in her bonny blue eyes. Wariness crept over him. He noted her hands behind her back and unwillingly his gaze went to the hidden chambers. A dull, knife-like pain twisted in his gut. The wooden panel had been tampered with, the seal at the top broken. All evidence pointed to Aileanna, and anger raged within him.

She was a spy.

She betrayed him.

Moira and Cyril had been right all along. Ruthlessly, he shoved aside a niggling of doubt. "What do you have behind yer back?" He kept all emotion from his voice.

"Nothing." Her eyes searched his and her smile faltered.

"I didn't mean to disturb you. I . . . I lost my ring." She carefully showed him her right hand, leaving the left behind her back. "On the night you were wounded. I . . . I thought it might be here."

"Show me both of yer hands, Aileanna." He closed the distance between them in three long strides, but did not come close enough to touch her, afraid of what he'd do if he did.

"I—" She bowed her head and choked back a sob. "Please believe me, it's not what you think, Rory," she pleaded, bringing her hand from behind her back to reveal the flag, clutched in her fist.

Her betrayal felt like a blow, fast and hard to his gut, and Rory sucked in a pained breath. "You will give it to me now," he grated between clenched teeth, holding out his hand.

With a look of anguish on her bonny face, she said, "I can't. I'm sorry, but I can't." She held the flag tight to her chest, covering the silk with both of her hands.

"Never before have I hurt a woman, Aileanna, but if you doona' give me the flag, I make no promises I won't."

Her eyes darted to the door and he grabbed her. His fingers bit into the delicate bones of her wrists. She cried out, and her knees buckled.

"Drop it," he said harshly.

Her hands opened and the flag slipped to nestle in the deep valley of her breasts.

He jerked her hands behind her back and encircled her wrists with one hand while he retrieved the flag with the other. "They chose you well, mo chridhe," he rasped against her ear, feeling the heat of her skin beneath the silk. His breathing grew ragged and his fingers lingered, stroking the tops of her full and heaving breasts. "How far would you have gone, Aileanna?" He shoved his hand into the bodice of her gown and rolled her nipple roughly between his thumb and finger.

"Rory, no, it's not what you think." She gasped when he kneaded and squeezed her breast.

"Yer a spy. Doona' try to deny it, and before this night is out you will tell me all," he ground out.

She leaned her head against his shoulder in an attempt to look back at him, her chest heaving. "Rory, you have to believe me, I'm not a spy. I can't tell you anything."

He dragged his hand from her breast. Letting go of her wrists, he threw her onto the bed. She fell face first, and the mattress bounced and squeaked from the force of her landing. He was on top of her before she could catch her breath. Flipping her onto her back, he straddled her, anchoring her arms over her head.

"Please, don't do this. I know what it looks like, but it's not . . . it's not what you think." She struggled, her hips arched beneath him, and despite his anger, his disgust with himself and with her, his cock hardened. With her hair spread across the dark brown coverlet, the rapid rise and fall of her voluptuous breasts, she was pure temptation.

"Aye, they knew what they were doin' when they sent you, lass. They would ken I wouldna' be able to resist you." He spat the words at her.

"Why won't you listen to me? I'm not a spy. I know you're angry, but please, just think. Why would I save you and your men's lives, if I was?" A lone tear slid across her cheek and into her hair.

He tried not to consider her words in the same way he tried to ignore his lingering doubts, to forget about her loyalty to those who were close to him, her fierce protectiveness. Like her actions at the loch, she had all but convinced him she cared for him as much as he cared for her, but now he knew she but played him for a fool.

"Then why, Aileanna, why did you steal the flag?"

"I wasn't stealing it. I only wanted to—" She shook her head, eyes closed. "I can't, Rory. I made a promise."

"Even to save yerself?"

Her eyes blinked open. "You wouldn't kill me. I thought you loved me," she whispered.

"Love, Aileanna? Nay, yer mistaken. I spoke of lust and desire. And only that because you reminded me of Brianna. But you canna' hold a candle to her." His laughter was cruel, his words intended to wound her as deeply as she wounded him.

Her head jerked as though he'd slapped her. Color leached from her face. "What . . . what are you going to do with me?"

He saw the fear in her eyes along with the pain his words caused, but he hardened his heart against it and lowered his face to hers. "Mayhap I should take what you so readily offered that first night I was too weak to accept." Before she could turn her head he captured her mouth with his, forcing his tongue past her lips, ravaging her, devouring her. She twisted beneath him and he ground his cock into her. She bit his tongue. He wrenched his lips from hers. The metallic taste of blood filled his mouth.

"If you take me now, Rory MacLeod, it will be rape," she panted, her face flushed, her eyes the same shade of violet as her gown.

Her words penetrated his lust-addled brain, past the anger and the pain, and stopped him cold. He flung himself away from her and strode to the door. He ripped it open, nearly tearing it from the hinges. "Byron and Cedric!" He bellowed for his men-at-arms. Rory leaned against the doorframe for support, watching as Aidan, Fergus, and Iain pounded up the staircase after the men.

"What's the matter, Rory?" his brother asked, moving Byron and Cedric aside. Rory stepped back, allowing his brother a clear view of Aileanna, her knees tucked to her chin as she sat huddled at the head of the bed.

Iain grabbed his arm. "Sweet Jesu', what have you done to her? If you've harmed her, I swear to God—"

Rory slammed him against the wall, fisting his hand in Iain's tunic. "'Tis no' I. She's a spy . . . a thief. I caught her attempting to steal the fairy flag."

His brother's eyes shot to Aileanna and he shook Rory off to make his way to her side. "Why, Aileanna?"

Slowly she lifted her head from her knees. Holding his brother's gaze, she shook her head.

Rory almost felt sorry for Iain, for the hurt he saw in his eyes. "What will you do with her?" his brother asked, dragging his gaze from hers.

"Put her under guard in the tower until she talks."

Iain helped her from the bed, and Rory noted the change in her. She no longer looked haunted, beaten down. She held her head high and walked by him with a haughty grace that caused him to add, "She'll have no food or drink until she does."

She held his gaze, her mouth swollen from his kiss.

He jerked his head and the guards took hold of her. Mrs. Mac, Connor, Fergus, and Iain watched her being led away. They all wore the same expression of betrayal. Her attempt to steal the clan's treasure was nothing compared to what she'd done to their hearts.

"Byron, Cedric, hold. I have one question mayhap you *will* answer, Aileanna Graham, if that is who you are."

She raised her eyes to his.

"Who betrayed the clan? How did you ken where the fairy flag was?"

"No one betrayed you," she said wearily. "I've been looking for the flag since the night I arrived. Your room was the last one I had to check, and I'd been searching it for days. The boards sounded hollow when I tapped on them. That's the only way I knew where it was."

Rory heard a feminine gasp at his back. "I told ye, Rory, I told ye. I knew she was a spy." Moira clapped her hands gleefully. When she reached his side, she placed a proprietary hand on his arm. "Ye willna' be so high and mighty when ye feel the lash open the skin on yer back," she taunted Aileanna.

"Moira, that will be enough," Rory ordered. His stomach roiled at the image of Aileanna's porcelain white skin flayed to a bloody pulp. He watched as the men led her toward the tower, back straight, head held high.

"Rory . . . Rory." Moira plucked at his sleeve. "Cyril tells me ye have no' signed the papers as yet. Shall we retire to the study and do so now?"

"Nay, I have much to deal with, Moira. Mayhap 'twould be best if you and yer kin left until I have had sufficient time to deal with the matter at hand. Aidan will see you to Duart. I'll send a messenger when I'm of a mind to sign the papers." Rory knew he should just sign the agreement and get it over with instead of leaving it to hang over his head, but at the moment he had no desire to deal with it, or the MacLeans. Moira's comments to Aileanna chilled him to the marrow. No matter her guilt, it was not something one would expect a woman to say to another. Rory had known Moira for a long time, but he was beginning to question if he truly knew her at all.

Ali smoothed her finger over the dagger Callum had insisted she wear strapped to her thigh on the morning Moira MacLean had turned the clan against her. She wedged the blade between the iron bar of the window and the spot right below it where the stone had weakened. It was boring, tedious work. She had to be quiet and make sure she swept the stone dust under the narrow cot. Locked away for two days now, Rory's only compromise had been to allow her water.

He had come yesterday morning to try to make her talk, but she hadn't uttered a single word. She'd lain on the cot with her back to him. He didn't touch her, questioning her in a tightly controlled voice. The only emotion he revealed was when, after what seemed like hours, he'd stormed from the tower, cursing the MacDonalds.

Ali blinked, trying to keep the tears at bay. She couldn't cry anymore. He believed she was a spy—that she betrayed him—and that wouldn't change. She saw it in the way he looked at her. Heard it in the words he'd spat at her, words she wished she could forget. Felt it in the way he had touched her. She'd thought she'd been hurt before, but it was nothing compared to this.

Ali listened to the dull scrape of the blade as she chiseled her way to freedom. Two of the bars were loose; only three remained. She didn't know where she would go, but she knew she couldn't remain at Dunvegan. The looks of betrayal from Mrs. Mac, Fergus, Iain, and Connor would be too much to bear.

And Rory—well, she couldn't think of him without her heart breaking into little pieces. Telling him the truth wasn't an option. She wouldn't betray the others any more than she already had. But no way in hell was she going to let anyone torture her. The thought of leaving Rory was no longer as difficult as it had once been. He didn't love her. He felt nothing for her now but disgust.

At the sound of heavy footfalls on the wooden staircase that led to the tower, Ali carefully dislodged the dagger. Grabbing a piece of linen, she swept the powder under the bed, then tucked both the cloth and the blade beneath the thin mattress. She heard the guards mutter something before they turned the key in the lock and the door creaked open. Iain entered, his face drawn. He carried a tray with a piece of bread and a mug of what she assumed was water.

"I thought your brother planned to starve me."

Iain shook his head. "Why did you do it, Ali?" he asked, joining her on the bed. He set the tray down beside him and offered her the chunk of bread. She politely refused, accepting the water instead. "Yer no' plannin' on starvin' yerself, are you?"

Ali smiled. "Of course not." But she didn't plan on making it easy on Rory either. Let him suffer thinking she starved herself. *But he'd only suffer if he cared,* the little voice in her head said, *and he's already told you he doesn't.*

"You still havena' told me—why, Ali?"

She stared at the water in her cup. "You did boil this, didn't you?" she asked, taking a deep swallow.

Iain sighed. "Aye. 'Tis because my brother's marryin' Moira, isna' it? 'Tis what both Fergus and Mrs. Mac believe."

Ali nodded. It was the truth. Emotion knotted her throat. "Do you think they can ever forgive me?"

Iain squeezed her hand. "Aye, we were hurt'is all. We thought you'd come to care a little fer us and your life at Dunvegan."

Ali placed the cup on the tray and smoothed her hands over her gown. Her gaze shot to Iain, praying he didn't notice the white dust that coated the dusky pink silk. He didn't. She wouldn't have been so lucky had it been Rory. "I did. I do. It wasn't an easy decision, Iain, and I'm sorry I disappointed all of you. I really am."

"I canna' fault you, and I thank you fer no' tellin' my brother the truth. My only regret is it cost you dearly. But doona' worry. Fergus and I are thinkin' on a way to convince Rory yer no' a spy." He gave her a weak smile. "The wee tale you told Connor might be of some use if we can convince my brother you meant to protect the flag from Moira."

Ali groaned. "What did Rory do to him?"

"Nothin'. The lad was feelin' guilty and went to Fergus. He's blamin' himself fer you bein' held in the tower."

"Iain, you have to tell him not to feel bad. I just would have found someone else to tell me."

Iain grimaced, then patted her knee. "I'd best go. Rory is no' fit to live with these days. If I stay longer than my allotted time, he'll have my head."

Ali raised a brow. "Sounds like he and Moira will make a charming pair."

Iain gave her an odd smile. "The MacLeans are no longer here. The signing of the papers has been put aside for now."

Ali tamped down a sense of hope. Nothing could come of it. Not now. "Thank you for coming." She chewed on her lower lip, then asked, "Iain, would you be able to get me some linens? It gets cold at night."

He ran his hand through his tawny brown hair. "Sweet Jesu', what have I done to you, Ali? I should just tell him the truth. You should no' be locked away up here."

She stood beside him and patted his arm. "It will all work out, Iain, you'll see."

He frowned. "Yer no' plannin' anythin', are you, Ali?"

"Of course not." She lowered her eyes, unable to look at him when she lied, wishing she didn't have to. "I'll leave that to you and Fergus." They didn't have a chance where Rory was concerned, and she wouldn't allow herself to be locked away for however long it suited him. The only one she could depend on was herself: a lesson she'd learned repeatedly growing up, and one she should've remembered.

"Good. We'll no' let you down," he said, leaving with a promise to send Mari to her with the linens.

In the early morning hours on the fourth day of her imprisonment, Ali wiggled the last of the bars free. Her time before the keep came to life was limited, and she had to hurry, no matter how tired she was. She lifted the rope of linens from the chair and knelt on the cold, hard floor, winding the rope through the bedframe. As quietly as she could, she dragged the bed beneath the window, stopping every few minutes to listen to the rhythmic snoring of the guards stationed outside the door. With a silent prayer, she dropped the makeshift rope over the edge of the casement.

Standing on the mattress, she lifted first one leg and then the other over the ledge. She closed her eyes. The second rope dug into her stomach as she lay in the window, the wind whipping the gown around her legs. She gritted her teeth and began her careful descent down the sheer face of the gray stone wall. Her foot slipped, and she swallowed a panicked cry. Despite the chill in the air, sweat beaded on her forehead.

Tightening her grip, she lowered herself several more feet until she came to the knot that warned the rope was about to end. Carefully, one hand over the other, she twisted until she faced outward. The wind lifted her damp hair, cooling her flushed face. She forced herself not to look down at the yawning, twelve-foot gap, knowing she had to get over it if she was to land on the slanted roof of the empty guards' room.

She kicked off the wall to swing in midair, slamming back into the unforgiving stone. Ali groaned, but there was no time to waste moaning over the dull throb in her back. She'd spent the last few days watching the guards' routine and knew there wasn't a moment to spare before the next one came on shift.

A sense of desperation played havoc with her courage. She pushed it aside and used the last of her strength to give one final push. Legs flailing, she dropped with a dull thud to the roof below. Her knees scraped on the rough tiles, shredding her gown. She tried to grab hold of the peaked roofline, but missed, and slid down the roof. Crying out in frustration, she kicked her feet until the toe of her shoe dug into a crevice between the tiles. Ali sucked in a breath and dove for the chimney, wrapping her arms around it. She stifled a startled cry when a large blackbird dive-bombed her and she waved a hand to shoo it away.

Ali pulled herself up until she sat tucked securely between the roof and chimney. Battered fingers trembling, she unraveled the linen rope from her waist. She threw it around one side of the chimney and grabbed it as it came around the other, tying a knot she prayed would hold.

Once more she descended. With only a few more feet to freedom, she began to relax. A door slammed and Ali froze, clinging to the rope, her feet dangled high above the ground. She held her breath, slowly releasing it when no one and no other sound followed. With the rope wound between her legs, she lowered herself farther. Her head jerked up when she heard a slow tearing sound. Panicked, she looked down at the twelve-foot drop. The rope shredded. She fell to the ground with no hope of breaking her fall.

Thud.

Ali moaned, scrambling awkwardly to her feet. She stifled a cry of pain when she put weight on her right foot. She tried to rotate her ankle; it wasn't broken, but she wouldn't get far on her own. She wrinkled her nose. Bessie.

She scanned the deserted courtyard, then hobbled toward the stables. Mauve and pink streaked the azure sky and Ali quickened her pace, anxious to put some distance between her and Dunvegan before the sun came up.

"How did she come by a dagger?" Rory bellowed, yanking on the linen rope that hung outside the window.

Callum shuffled from one foot to the other, his face flushed. "'Twas me, Laird MacLeod. I gave it to her on the day Lady MacLean accused her of bein' a spy."

"Bloody hell," Rory cursed, tossing the rope to the floor. He ran his hand through his hair. She would be the death of him. But despite his anger, he couldn't help but admire her bravery, her ingenuity. The woman was amazing. Too bad she was a spy.

He lifted his gaze from the cot and met the look of condemnation in the eyes of Mrs. Mac, Fergus, and Iain. His temper flared. "Doona' give me that look. 'Twas no' because of me she did this."

"Nay? It was no' her who locked herself in the tower and half starved herself to death."

"In case you've forgotten, brother, the woman's a spy. And I didna' starve her. She was just too stubborn to eat."

Byron and Cedric entered the room, shamefaced. "There's no sign of her, my laird, but the lads in the stable say old Bessie is missin'."

He met his brother's gaze and they both let out a shout of laughter. Relief surged through Rory. He would get her back, but more importantly, she wasn't hurt. It had been his worst fear when he'd been called to the tower. The guards had said nothing, simply pointed to the barless window. Rory fully expected to see her broken body lying on the ground below, and nothing had prepared him for the terror he felt. No matter that she betrayed him; he still had not managed to purge her from his heart. "'Twill no' be difficult pickin' up her trail if she's even made it off Dunvegan land."

"I'll bring her home," Fergus and Iain offered in unison.

"Nay, I'll go."

He strode from the room, leveling his brother with a hard stare when Iain called out to him, "You willna' hurt her, Rory."

Rory picked up Aileanna's trail easily enough once he realized she had not headed to MacDonald land after all. He assumed whoever she was in contact with must have arranged a meeting place closer to Dunvegan. Coming upon horse and rider in the glen, he eased back on the reins. Hidden within a cluster of pines, he patted the black's powerful neck. "We'll stay and watch for a bit, Lucifer. See who the lass meets up with."

He bit back a smile when she delicately tapped the mare's flanks. Bessie didn't budge. Holding on to Bessie's mane, Aileanna bounced up and down several times. The horse snorted, and she threw up her arms in frustration. Rory watched in amusement as she awkwardly slid from the mare. But his amusement faded when he saw her hobble forward to cajole her horse. She'd been hurt. He dug his heels in Lucifer's sides and left the shelter of the pines.

Each time Aileanna urged the horse on with a tentative pat to her flank, Bessie would take a step back. The lass lost more ground than she gained. She gave a muffled groan and sunk to the heather-covered ground, drawing her knees to her chest. Bessie nudged her, nickering.

"Don't try to be nice now—it won't work," he heard her grumble.

"You shouldna' be fashed with her. She made it much farther than I expected she would," Rory commented dryly.

"You!" she gasped, turning to look up at him. "How did you find me?"

"'Twas no' hard." He dismounted and came to stand over her. "I've come to take you back to Dunvegan."

A hopeful light appeared in her eyes. "You believe me now?"

"That yer no' a spy? Nay, I doona' believe that." He wished he could.

"Then I'm not going anywhere with you." She lowered her forehead to her knees.

"And where would you be plannin' on goin', lass?"

"I don't know." She mumbled the words into her gown.

"Then you might as well come home with me," he said quietly. She was exhausted, beaten down, and it bothered him more than it should.

"Why? So you can lock me away again, starve me, torture me?" Her voice was weak, but angry.

He shook his head. "You've no' been starved or tortured."

She snorted and tossed her head.

"You sound like yer horse."

She narrowed her gaze on him. "Go away."

He ignored her, leaning over to scoop her into his arms. She gave an affronted cry and struggled, kicking her feet. "Ouch." Tears sprang to her eyes.

"Be still, Aileanna. You'll only cause yerself more pain, and I'll no' let you go." He placed her on Lucifer's back. "Doona' move. He's no' as tame as Bessie," he warned her as he put the bridle he'd brought with him onto Bessie.

Swinging himself onto his horse, he wrapped an arm around her and felt her stiffen. They traveled in silence, and she slowly relaxed against him. Rory battled his body's response to her, fought the urge to bury his face in her heather-scented, silky hair, to fill his hands with the weight of her full breasts. Even reminding himself of her betrayal was of little help, and he hoped she did not feel him harden beneath the curve of her behind. Upon hearing the soft sounds of her snoring, he gave a relieved chuckle.

Rory took the long way back to Dunvegan in an attempt to avoid as many of the clan as he could. Anger against Aileanna ran high. Only the morning before he had been confronted by an angry mob seeking vengeance. Old lady Cameron had been quick to shout them down. To Rory's surprise, Cook and several of the serving girls, along with Janet, Jamie, and the Chisholms came to Aileanna's defense, giving him and the others the same tall tale Fergus and Iain tried to feed him.

Obviously awaiting his return, Mrs. Mac, Fergus, Iain, and Connor hurried toward him as he entered the courtyard.

"What have you done to her?" Iain cried out.

"Nothin', brother. She hurt her foot in her attempt to

escape is all, and obviously exhausted herself while she was at it," Rory commented wryly when she remained asleep in his arms despite the commotion.

Iain reached for her and Rory carefully handed her down to him. Dismounting, he said, "I'll take her now."

"Nay, I will—"

"You will give her to me now," Rory grated out.

His brother looked down into her sleeping face, and shook his head. "You canna' put her back in the tower, Rory. I willna' allow it."

"'Tis my decision, Iain, no' yers," he said, reaching for her.

"You doona' understand, brother, you . . ." Iain shook his head and looked at him, a pained expression on his face. "I canna' let her suffer any longer. I have somethin' I must tell you, Rory, and I pray you will be able to forgive me."

Chapter 16

Fairies. The fairies brought her—for you. To save you.

"Bloody hell," Rory muttered under his breath. "What have you done, Iain?" But he knew what his brother had done. Desperate to save him, he'd waved the flag without thought to the consequences.

At first Rory had been tempted not to believe him, to think the wild tale was just another attempt to get him to believe in Aileanna's innocence, to keep her from the tower. One look at Fergus's and Mrs. Mac's faces convinced him it was no story Iain concocted, but the truth.

With the toe of his boot he nudged the peat into the mouth of the flame. A shower of sparks followed with a loud crackle and pop. He glanced over his shoulder from where he sat by the fire to look at Aileanna. Hours had passed, and still she slept in his bed, beneath the mountain of covers Mrs. Mac had piled on top of her.

Rory pressed his fingers to his temples. What was he to do with her? A woman snatched from her own time to save him. He allowed himself a slight smile. It went a long way in explaining the strange way she had of speaking and behaving. But how would she feel when he told her he could not send her home? That he must sacrifice her desires for the good of the clan. He would not use the last wish. One day it might mean the difference to the clan's survival. Surely she would understand.

He heard the rustle of bedding and turned to see Aileanna sitting up, looking down at her nightclothes. Through the dim light of the candles he saw her scowl at him.

"You have a lot of nerve," she sputtered.

Rory eased himself from the chair and walked toward the bed, suppressing a smile. "I didna' disrobe you, lass. 'Twas Mrs. Mac who saw to you," he assured her, unable to keep an image of him slowly stripping each layer of clothing from her, revealing her naked flesh, from playing out in his mind.

Aileanna clutched the sheets to her chest, and croaked, "Why . . . why have you put me in your room and not the tower?"

Rory lifted the pitcher from the bedside table and poured her a cup of water, offering it to her. "And before you ask, 'twas boiled."

Her fingers brushed his when she took the cup. "You didn't answer me," she said, eyeing him over the rim.

"I ken who you are, Aileanna."

She choked on a mouthful of water, but was quick to recover. "Oh, you've heard from Angus then. What did he tell you? Obviously something to make you believe I'm not a spy, or I'd still be locked away."

He retrieved the cup and set it on the table before he turned back to her. "Nay, that would be Iain's doin'."

"Iain." She shot a panicked look around the room. "Where . . . where is he?"

Rory sat on the edge of the bed and brushed a strand of hair from her pale cheek. "I ken everything, Aileanna. Iain confessed."

"Did you hurt him, because if you did I'll—"

He shook his head, unhappy with her willingness to believe the worst of him. "No matter what you think of me, Aileanna, you must ken I would no' hurt my brother." He lifted her hand to examine the damage she'd done in her escape from the tower. "I appreciate the lengths to which you went to protect him. I only wish you would've told me before I—"

"You what, tortured me . . . starved me?"

Rory let out an exasperated sigh. "You ken I didna' torture or starve you, Aileanna, but I ken I hurt you, and fer that I'm sorry."

She bowed her head and her cheeks pinked.

He tipped her chin, forcing her to look at him. In the candlelight her eyes, awash with tears, shimmered. Rory sucked in an anguished breath. "I didna' mean what I said. I was angry and hurt that you betrayed me, and I lashed out at you. 'Tis no' somethin' I'm proud of. All I ask is that you understand where the words came from and accept my apology."

Ali tilted her head and looked up at the ceiling, blinking back tears. When her emotions were under some semblance of control, she forced herself to ask him, "Now that you know, will you use the flag to send me home?" Her head was spinning, not sure what she hoped his answer would be. What she really wanted to know, but was too afraid to ask, was if he'd meant it when he denied his love for her. Did she compare as poorly to his wife as he suggested? Even now, repeating his words in her head caused fresh tears to spring to her eyes. She couldn't bear to ask him the questions for fear she would be humiliated again, and her heart couldn't stand the rejection.

"Doona' you think you could be happy here at Dunvegan?"

How could he ask her that after what had gone on between them? Nothing had changed. He still meant to marry Moira. The sheets pooled at her waist as she wiped the moisture from her cheeks with the backs of her hands.

He smoothed the hair from her face with his fingers, then trailed them down her arms. Her nipples tightened, and she groaned inwardly when they puckered against the thin fabric of her shift. How was she supposed to think clearly with him so close? With him touching her?

"How . . . how could I be happy here? They all think I'm a thief, and if that's not bad enough, a witch."

He continued to stroke her arms, as though he knew what he did to her. Goose bumps formed beneath her heated skin. Her nipples ached, and her breasts grew heavy and full.

His eyes softened. "Doona' worry. I will find a way to make them believe in yer innocence without tellin' the truth."

Her heart raced, and she shook her head. She couldn't do it, not with how things stood between them. He felt nothing for her, and her feelings for him were too strong. "No, I can't stay. I want to go home."

He gave her a pained smile. "Aileanna, if I use the last wish to return you to yer home, I leave the clan vulnerable. We are in difficult times. I may have need of the fairies' magic. Can you no' understand?"

"Oh, I understand all right. You expect me to sacrifice my happiness for the good of your clan." She flung the words at him.

"There was a time when I thought you could be happy here, Aileanna," he said quietly. "Will you no' try?"

She flopped back onto the mound of pillows. "It doesn't look like I have much of a choice, now do I?"

"Do you have kin you leave behind?"

"No, there's no one," Ali admitted unhappily. "My mother died when I was seven, and none of the foster homes I was sent to ever worked out." She wouldn't tell him Dunvegan had become more of a home to her than any she had ever known growing up.

He lifted her hand to his lips and pressed a kiss to her palm, murmuring, "I'm sorry you suffered, and I doona' mean to make you suffer further, but I canna' send you back."

"You can . . . but you won't."

He stood at the side of the bed and looked down at her. "Mayhap you'll feel better once you have something to eat. I'll have Mrs. Mac fix you a plate."

She was starved. But she wasn't a man, and if he thought he'd soften her up by feeding her, he was sadly mistaken.

"Aileanna." He gave her a pointed look, his hand on the handle of the door. "The flag is no longer in my room, but even if it was, lass, it would do you no good. The magic only works if a MacLeod waves the flag."

"You'd think someone could've told me that before," she muttered.

She heard his husky laughter as he left the room and threw a pillow, hitting the back of the door instead of him.

Ali swung her legs over the edge of the bed and cursed. Her foot—she'd forgotten. She brought the candle from the bedside table and held it so she could examine her leg, noticing her bloodied fingers as she did. Her ankle was swollen to twice its size. She blew out a frustrated breath. It was obvious she wouldn't be going anywhere anytime soon. At the end of Rory's bed she noted the linens piled on the battered wooden trunk. Unable to reach them, she grabbed ahold of the carved wooden post and groaned; every muscle ached, protesting the movement. Gritting her teeth, she hopped on one foot, then bent down to pick up the piece of cloth.

Back in the comfort of Rory's big bed, Ali dipped the fabric in the pitcher of water. Wringing it out, she wrapped it around her ankle and propped her foot on a pillow. Anxious to inspect her injuries, she hiked the chemise to her thighs to check on her knees. Obviously Mrs. Mac had cleaned her up as well as changed her. Only a small amount of dried blood was visible on her skinned knees.

Her stomach grumbled as she dabbed at the scrapes with the other cloth. Maybe she would feel better if she had something to eat, especially if it was Mrs. Mac or Mari who kept her company instead of Rory.

Looking up at the sound of metal clanging against metal, she saw Rory, framed in the door. The flickering light from the torches in the hall cast him in shadows— a hardened warrior, the man she'd fallen hopelessly in love with, a man who tore her heart from her chest and flung it aside. She was too tired, too vulnerable to deal with him.

"Thank you, you can leave it over there." She pointed to the table that stood by the fireplace.

Rory hesitated before coming into the room, and she quickly realized what held his attention. Hastily, she pushed the shift over her knees.

He cleared his throat. "I doona' think 'tis a good idea fer you to be walkin' aboot," he said, jerking his head in the direction of her foot.

"No, it'll be fine. I'll—" She sent her eyes heavenward when he ignored her and strode to the bed. "Do you ever listen to what anyone says?"

"Nay." He smiled. "You ken I'm right, Aileanna. Yer in no condition to be leavin' the bed."

"I did just fine, thank you very much." She gestured to her foot. "I really do appreciate you bringing me something to eat, but you can—"

The bed creaked under his weight when he sat beside her. He took the bowl and set it on his lap, dipping a wooden spoon into what looked like stew with dark gravy.

Ali's eyes widened. "What do you think you're doing?"

"I'm feedin' you. Look at yer hands, lass. They're a mess. You'll no' be able to do it on your own." He brought the spoon to her mouth.

Glaring at him, she shook her head and pressed her lips together.

He frowned. "I doona' think I've met anyone as stubborn as you."

"I'm . . . ugh—" The second her mouth opened, he shoved the spoon inside.

"Yer a verra messy eater," he said as he dabbed at her chin with the edge of the linen.

"I wouldn't be if . . . Oh, my God, you are the most infuriating man I've ever met," she cried when he managed to get another spoonful into her mouth.

"You canna' win with me, so be a good lass and eat yer dinner."

Five minutes later, Rory gave her a satisfied smile. "There, that wasna hard," he said as she finished the last of the stew.

"It was good. Thank you," she admitted grudgingly as he returned the bowl and spoon to the bedside table. "Now if you don't mind, I'd like to get some sleep."

"Aye, I'll leave you be in a moment. Mrs. Mac sent some salve fer yer bruises and to take the ache from yer muscles."

Ali narrowed her gaze on the small pot he held in his big hand, recognizing the scent of fragrant herbs with a hint of animal fat as a formula she and Mrs. Mac had recently come up with. They had been combining their knowledge of herbs to create medicines for the clan, but it was difficult with no refrigeration, and the concoctions had to be made almost daily. "If you think I'm going to let you put that on me, you have a few screws loose."

Rory raised a brow at her. "Aidan was right—yer speech is verra interestin', but at least I ken why. Now, be a good lass and turn on yer side."

Ali crossed her arms over her chest and scowled at him. "You can't honestly expect me to believe Mrs. Mac suggested *you* were to put that on me."

He grinned. "Aye, she did. You canna' do it yerself, Aileanna. You have open wounds on yer hands. It will sting."

"I'm tough." She motioned for him to give her the pot of cream.

His gaze softened. "Aye, you've told me that before."

She closed her eyes, damning the tears that threatened at the memory of when she'd said those exact words to him.

"Let me do this fer you. I promise, I'll be gentle."

That's what she was afraid of. "It's all right. Mrs. Mac can do it for me."

"They're all abed, lass," he murmured, scooping a small amount of cream onto his fingers. Despite her protests he began to massage it into her arm. His hands were warm and strong. Holding the strap of her shift aside he worked his way from the top of her shoulder, down to her wrist. Carefully he lifted her hand and brought it into the light from the candle, his fingers tracing the bones. "The other night I hurt you when I grabbed you here." He brought her hand to his lips and pressed a tender kiss to the inside of her wrist, his eyes never leaving hers.

Her mouth went dry and she didn't dare speak—she didn't think she could. Her heart hammered in her chest. He lowered her hand and scooped more of the salve onto his fingers to massage the other arm in a slow, sensual motion. Her eyes fluttered closed, his gentle touch a form of exquisite torture. She wanted to feel those powerful hands all over her. He pressed his lips to her other wrist and murmured an apology.

She prayed he was finished as much as she prayed he'd just begun. Rory leaned over and lifted her hair away from her shoulders. "Roll on yer side, mo chridhe." His words came out deep and gravelly against her ear. She couldn't protest—it felt too good. He skimmed a knuckle along her cheek and down her arm. The bed creaked when he stood and gently cradled her foot with his hand while he urged her onto her side with the other. Placing another pillow between her calves, he propped her injured foot on top.

The weight of his body settled in behind her as the mattress dipped. His fingers worked at the delicate buttons at the back of her shift. Before she realized what he had done, the fabric drifted apart and the whole of her back was exposed to him. She felt naked and vulnerable, and she'd promised never to let herself feel that way with him again.

"Shh, 'tis all right, mo chridhe. I willna' hurt you."

She gave a short, bitter laugh, wincing as she rolled over to face him. Ali pressed her hands to his chest in an attempt to push him away. "No, I won't let you do this to me. Not again. Do you remember what you said to me, Rory? Because I know I'll never forget."

He cupped her face between his roughened palms. "Aye, I remember. I was angry, angrier than I've ever been before. Can you no' understand what I felt?"

"What about me? I loved you. You're marrying another woman and I have to let you go, and not because I want to, but because I have no choice. Those damn fairies didn't give me a choice and neither did you."

He kissed the tears from her cheeks. "I do love you, Aileanna, and I'm no' marryin' Moira. I willna' go through with the betrothal, no' now."

"Don't . . . don't lie to me. *Lust isn't love*—that's what you said, didn't you? I won't come second to anyone, Rory, not even your dead wife. I deserve more."

He gave her a slight shake. "Stop. Why will you no' try to understand? Aye, I desire you as I never have another, including Brianna. But I do love you, Aileanna, more than I should. And I canna' let you go. I willna' let you go." A hard edge crept into his deep voice.

His words penetrated the anger and the hurt. She searched his face. "Did you just say you aren't marrying Moira?"

"Aye, 'tis what I said," he growled.

She hesitated before she asked, "And you love me?" She lowered her eyes and her cheeks flushed. "As much as you loved your wife?" Her voice was whisper soft.

"The love I feel fer you is no' the same as my love fer Brianna. How can it be when yer no' the same woman? Canna' you understand that?" He was angry now. She could hear it in his voice.

"Aye, I can."

He blinked, then grinned. "I'll make a Scot of you yet, mo chridhe." His eyes darkened. "But now all I want is to make you mine."

Chapter 17

Rory's low, gravelly voice, and the heated words he whispered against her ear, triggered a frisson of desire that left Ali weak and trembling. Heavy-lidded, passion-filled emerald eyes sought hers before he lowered his mouth. But the fierceness of his kiss brought with it the unwanted memories of the last time he had her at his mercy.

As though sensing her withdrawal, he drew back, his gaze searching. "What is it, mo chridhe?"

She shook her head and tangled her fingers in his thick black hair, forcing his mouth to hers in an attempt to push the memories aside, and the words he'd earlier tried to explain away.

"Nay, Aileanna, you will tell me what it is," he said, refusing to let her coax him back to passion.

Ali's hand fell to her side, and she lay back amongst the pillows. Catching her lower lip between her teeth, she scanned the dimly lit room. "I keep thinking about the other night, and what you said to me. I—"

"I apologized, Aileanna, fer my words and actions." Frustration laced Rory's voice.

She swallowed hard and lifted her gaze to his. "I know, but I'm having a difficult time getting past it. I still don't understand why you didn't believe me." Torn between the desire to be embraced by the heat of his powerful body and needing distance from it, she carefully rolled to her side.

"Mayhap because you had the flag in yer hands, and you didna' tell me the truth."

"And you know why." The pillow muffled her voice.

"Aye." He lifted the heavy fall of her hair and pressed a tender kiss to her neck. "I do. There's no more I can say to you, Aileanna, other than I'm sorry. Mayhap 'tis too soon." The thin strap of the shift slipped from her shoulder, and his hot mouth moved down the curve of her neck to taste her there. "I want you, mo chridhe, but I'll wait."

His body tight to hers, she could feel the evidence of his desire, big and hard, pressed to the back of her thigh. Her breath shuddered as he emblazoned a fiery path of kisses along her spine. The feel of his tongue dipping into the two dimples at the small of her back made her squirm.

The shift gaped wider, and the strap slid farther down her arm. With a practiced hand, he slipped his fingers beneath the thin fabric, trailing them along the curve of her waist to her hip. "Do you want me to stop?" His deep voice vibrated against her heated flesh.

Ali's breathing quickened, desire unfurling in her belly. "Yes . . . no, don't stop," she whimpered as his long fingers tweaked her puckered nipple.

Rory gently rolled her to her back, amusement glinted in his green eyes, and his mouth lifted at the corner in a knowing grin. "Are you certain?" he asked as he lowered the flimsy material inch by torturous inch, exposing her breasts fully to his gaze. He devoured her with a heated look as he laved first one nipple and then the other. She arched her back, pressing her breasts to his lips, wanting him to suckle her deep into his hot, wet mouth.

His laugh was low and husky. "That brings back a memory of the first time you were in my bed, mo chridhe."

Irritation penetrated the passion-filled haze that engulfed her. When she glared at him, he laughed harder. "If you were any kind of gentleman, Rory MacLeod, you wouldn't remind me of that night, especially since you now know how it came about."

"Aileanna, have I no' told you I'm no gentleman when it comes to you. And I'm thinkin' I should thank the fairies fer deliverin' you to me naked."

"That wasn't the fairies' doing, it was yours. You had my T-shirt off of me the minute I landed in your bed." Heat tingled between her thighs at the memory, at the feel of him beside her.

"T-shirt? I doona' ken what that is, but I ken I want you naked in my bed now." Propping himself on an elbow, he skimmed his hand to the edge of her shift and slowly worked it over her hips, her breasts. She helped him as she had that first night, her arms trembling with eagerness as she raised them over her head. When she lay naked before him, he sucked in an appreciative breath.

Ali's cheeks heated as his intense gaze raked over her, and she tugged at the sheets to cover herself.

He stopped her. "Nay, let me look at you." He stroked his big, strong hand over her breasts to her belly, the heat of his palm searing her to her core, fanning her desire.

She had to see him—all of him—and ran her fingers along the front of his shirt. "It's your turn now," she murmured as she tugged at the laces, revealing his broad, powerfully muscled chest. Trailing a finger along the puckered line of his scar, she lowered her head and pressed her lips to the mark she'd left on him. The banded muscles of his stomach contracted beneath her gentle kiss.

"Aileanna," he groaned as her fingers moved lower to the thick bulge in his pants. "Are you certain yer no' too sore? What aboot yer foot?"

Concentrating on freeing him from the confines of his

pants, she barely registered his concern. Only when he took her hand to press her palm to his lips did she look up. He drew away from her to sit on the edge of the bed.

She groaned in frustration. "What are you doing?"

Rory laughed as he tugged off his boots, dropping them to the floor. "I'm no' leavin' you, lass, of that you can be certain. I thought I might make a faster go of sheddin' my clothes is all." He stood, towering over her, the flickering flame of the candle accentuating the chiseled planes of his face. Rory looked terrifyingly big and powerful as he shrugged out of his shirt and tossed it onto the trunk at the end of the bed.

Mesmerized, she watched as he peeled off his pants. He was huge and hard, and her experience was limited. It had been important for her to wait until the right man came along. She thought she had. There had been only Drew, but he was nothing compared to Rory. She regretted not having waited, because the only man who would ever be right for her stood before her now in all his rugged, naked glory.

Entranced by his beauty, Ali couldn't pull her eyes away, not until she heard a low rumble of laughter. She lifted her gaze to his, and his emerald eyes gleamed with amusement. Ali grabbed a pillow and threw it at him. "You're so full of yourself."

Laughing, Rory caught the pillow, then lay down at her side, his amusement fading as he crushed her soft body to his. His cock, pressed to the curve of her belly, throbbed. He shuddered when her long, delicate fingers encircled him. "Careful, lass, or this willna' last long."

"No?" She smiled, sliding her hand along his shaft.

"Nay." Rory could barely rasp the word out before he slanted his mouth over her soft pliant lips. He filled her mouth with his tongue. Teasing, tasting, he kissed her with a growing urgency. He struggled to hold back his need to take her, to claim her with one savage thrust.

Ali increased her rhythmic stroking of his cock, and he groaned, certain he would spill his seed like an untried lad if she continued. He stilled her hand, nudging her thighs apart with his knee. She whimpered. He raised his head, concerned by the soft, desperate sound. "Did I hurt you, Aileanna?"

Passion-glazed violet eyes focused on him. "No . . . no, I want . . . I need you to touch me."

"You want me to touch you, mo chridhe, like this?" He stroked the silky curls at the juncture of her thighs.

She raised her hips. "Yes," she moaned. "More."

Her passionate response enflamed his desire. Aileanna was everything and more than he had imagined. He watched the play of emotions on her beautiful face as he stroked her moist core, dipping his fingers into her velvet heat, the desire to taste every glorious inch of her lithe body outweighed by his all-consuming need to be inside her, to make her his.

She writhed beneath him. "Rory, now, please," she gasped.

Carefully he entered her, his restraint causing the muscles of his arms to quiver in protest as he held himself above her. Her eyes slid closed, her head tipped back, and soft moans of pleasure escaped her parted lips when he thrust inside. At the sound of her wanton cries his cock swelled even more. He filled her to the hilt, savoring the feel of her inner muscles tightening around him.

He moved inside her tight, wet sheath with slow, deep thrusts. The wanton look upon her face, her lush curves and puckered nipples rubbing against his chest, brought him to the edge of his control. No longer able to take it slow and easy like he wanted, he plunged in and out of her, hard and fast. Certain he could withstand it no longer, he reached between them and touched her swollen nub, stroking. She bucked beneath him, crying out at the same time he found his release and filled her with his seed.

Rory smothered her cries with his mouth, deepening the kiss as he rolled carefully to his side, shifting his weight from her body. His cock jerked inside her and he cupped her firm behind with his hands, pressing her against him to thrust one last time. "The next time we'll take it slow, mo chridhe," he murmured against her lips, brushing her tangled hair from her face. She snuggled into his chest, and nodded her assent. "I doona' think I will ever get enough of you, Aileanna. You've bewitched me." Something inside of him froze at the truth of the words that slipped unbidden past his lips.

Fear skirted the edge of his consciousness. The depth of emotion he felt for her was dangerous. He needed to temper his desire for her, control his love, or all would be lost. He would not allow himself to become consumed by her as his father had been by his mother, at the expense of all else. It would bring nothing but heartache, possibly death. And because of Aileanna, Rory had already put the clan at risk.

But he had told her the truth. There would be no union with the MacLeans. Thrust into his world through no fault of her own, Aileanna was now his responsibility. He owed her his life, and would marry her to make up for all she had lost.

"You might not want to say that too loud, Rory, or you'll have that priest after me again." Her throaty, contented laugh jerked him out of his unwelcome musings.

Absently he kissed the tip of her nose. "Nay, I'll let no one harm you, Aileanna." Sliding his cock from her heated clasp, he ignored the sense of loss when he pulled away from her. "'Tis time for you to rest."

"Where are you going?" she murmured sleepily, reaching out to him when he rose from the bed.

"'Tis best if yer no' found in my chambers come morn, at least until the betrothal is announced."

Ali blinked. "What did you just say?" Her gaze focused on his face as she gathered the tangled sheets to her chest.

He glanced up as he pulled on his pants, addressing her as though she were a child. "The betrothal, Aileanna. Until 'tis announced, it would be best if you slept in yer own room."

Ali's heart thumped painfully against her rib cage. She clutched the sheets tighter. "Who . . . whose betrothal?"

Rory quirked a brow. He gave her a puzzled look, then tossed her the crumpled shift from the floor. "Ours. Did you no' think I would marry you, after this?" He tipped his head toward the bed.

"No, since you didn't ask and I didn't say yes," she sputtered, pulling the nightgown over her head with jerky movements. Her chest constricted with the painful realization that he only wanted to marry her because she'd slept with him. And he didn't even have the decency to propose, tell her he loved her, get down on his knee and offer her a ring. Oh no, his lordship simply assumed she would be thrilled to marry him. That she would bow to his commands like everyone else. Angry tears clogged her throat.

"'Tis because of me you find yerself here, Aileanna. Yer my responsibility now, and I will do right by you."

"Oh, I see. You feel responsible for me because the fairies sent me to save your life, and because you refuse to send me back you've decided you have to marry me. Does that about cover it?" The suffocating tightness swirled higher in her chest. Beyond hurt, she was devastated. He would marry her, but not because he loved her. Ali couldn't bear to be just another responsibility to him, like everyone else in his clan. She wanted to be someone he could turn to in times of trouble, someone for him to lean on. She wanted all of him—heart, body, and soul.

"Aye," he responded warily.

She flung back the covers and swung her legs over the edge of the mattress. With a tight grip on the post, she awkwardly came to her feet.

Rory stepped in front of her, his brow creased with concern. "What has gotten into you, Aileanna? You seem angry, lass."

"Angry? You think I'm angry?" She tried to shove him out of her way, but the man was built like his damn mountains and didn't budge.

He crossed his arms over his bare chest, muscles rippling beneath his golden skin. "You will tell me what has you in such a temper."

"You." She poked the middle of his chest with her finger, blinking back tears. "I'm not marrying you, Rory MacLeod. Not now, not ever."

He frowned. "I doona' understand you, Aileanna. Mayhap yer tired and we should talk aboot this on the morrow."

"No, there's no need. I've made up my mind. I'm not marrying you."

"Did you no' tell me you loved me? Did we no' just make love?"

"What does that have to do with anything?" she ground out between clenched teeth. The pain in her foot was now as intense as the pain in her heart.

"I doona' ken how things work in yer time, lass, but in mine, when a woman and a man make love, speak words of love, they wed."

"Is that right? So the only person you ever made love to besides me was Brianna?" She'd heard all about his prowess with the ladies, whether she had wanted to or not. For some ridiculous reason his clansmen were as proud of their laird's reputation in the bedroom as on the battlefield.

The man was a legend. *Let's see him talk himself out of this one,* she thought.

"'Tis no' the point," he grumbled. "I bedded you, I'll wed you."

Ali's hand clenched into a fist, itching to strike the arrogant look from his face. "In my time, it doesn't matter, so you're off the hook. Marry Moira MacLean. I know you, Rory MacLeod. It's killing you to give up on a union you think will save your clan. Just do it. I don't have anything to offer you."

He shuttered the emotion in his eyes, and Ali's stomach lurched. She was right. He'd marry her, but at what cost? He'd resent her. She would be the reason there could be no alliance between the MacLeans and the MacLeods.

"There will be no union with the MacLeans. You and I will wed. 'Tis the end of the discussion." He lifted her easily into his arms and strode to the door, jaw set.

Ali wanted to fight him, to leap from his arms, but he was too strong, and she was too sore, too tired, too devastated by the turn of events.

Once they were inside her chambers and Rory had placed her carefully on the bed, he looked down at her, running his fingers through his hair. "I doona' understand you, Aileanna, but I tell you we will wed." She could hear the steel in his voice.

"No . . . we won't." Ali thumped her pillow and turned her back to him.

"Yer bloody stubborn, lass," he grumbled. She heard his frustrated sigh as he padded across the floor. There was a clunk, like he threw something, and then the sound of the fire roaring to life. The smoky smell of peat permeated the room.

The bed dipped when he sat at her side. He stroked her back and she was barely able to contain her shiver at his gentle touch. "Will you no' tell me why yer fashed, Aileanna?"

She shook her head, misery twisting her insides.

Rory blew out a ragged breath. He leaned over her to kiss her forehead. "We'll talk on the morrow, Aileanna, but mark my words. You will be my wife."

Chapter 18

Arms crossed, Ali watched from the bed while Mrs. Mac flitted about her room, doing her best to ignore her. Unable to bear the frigid silence any longer, Ali asked, "Are you never going to speak to me again?"

Mrs. Mac avoided meeting her eyes. Hands on her well-rounded hips, she surveyed the room. "Och, now, I'm busy is all."

"I'm sorry if I hurt your feelings, Mrs. Mac. I didn't know what else to do," she offered quietly.

The older woman nodded. "I ken how you felt, but 'twas hard you tryin' to leave without a good-bye. I . . . we thought you cared for us a wee bit, you ken."

"I do, and I don't think any of you understand how hard it was for me to think of leaving you all." Ali blinked back tears at the memory of just how difficult it had been. None of them knew how much they'd come to mean to her.

"Och, well, yer here for good now. All will be as it should be," Mrs. Mac stated succinctly.

Ali narrowed her gaze on her. "What's that supposed to mean?" If Mrs. Mac thought she was marrying Rory anytime soon, Ali planned on setting her straight.

"'Tis like I said. The fairies meant you fer our laird, and 'tis how it will be. He'll no' marry Moira MacLean now."

"He's no' marrying me either. I mean not . . . I'm not marrying him—no matter what he thinks."

A wide grin split Mrs. Mac's lined face. "Ah, so he came to his senses and asked, did he?"

"No." Ali scowled. "He didn't ask—he told me. But I won't marry him, Mrs. Mac, so you can wipe that silly grin off your face." She flung back the covers in an attempt to get out of bed.

"Och, no you don't. Yer to stay in bed. You need yer rest. 'Tis what the laird has ordered."

"He's the bossiest, most aggravating man I've ever met," Ali said, flopping onto the pillows.

"Aye, he is, but he'll make you a good husband, of that I'm certain."

"Yes, if all you want is someone to protect and take care of you."

Mrs. Mac frowned, making herself comfortable on the side of the bed. "You doona' want someone to look out fer you?"

"Of course I do, but he only wants to marry me because of those damn fairies. He feels responsible for me, guilty about what happened. But in the end he'll resent me, Mrs. Mac, for his not being able to marry Moira. The welfare of the clan is more important to him than anything else."

"Ah, I see the way of it. You want his love, to hold his heart."

"Aye—oh for God's sake, yes, that's what I want."

Mrs. Mac stood and gave a reassuring pat to Ali's leg. "Take it from a woman who kens the lad well—he loves you, Lady Aileanna, of that I'm certain. I ken what yer sayin', but you'll see, everythin' has a way of workin' itself out."

Ali wanted to believe Mrs. Mac, she really did. She knew Rory loved her, but not enough. He only wanted to marry her out of a sense of obligation, and for her that was no reason.

"If yer wantin' a bath, I'll have Connor get started on it. Och, I almost forgot to tell you—Mari and Connor ken about the fairies and who you'd be."

Ali's eyes widened. "How? Who told them?"

"'Twas no' that someone told them exactly. When the laird brought you to his room they followed us in, worryin' aboot you, they were. They overheard Iain tryin' to explain to the laird what happened. No one realized they were there until it was too late. But doona' fash yerself, they'll no' be tellin' anyone. They ken it would be dangerous fer you if word got out."

Mrs. Mac, Connor, and Mari stared at her in open-mouthed astonishment. Face flushed, Ali blew out an exasperated breath. So maybe she'd let her temper get the better of her, but she couldn't stand being in bed any longer. Or to listen to the three of them insist she had to follow the laird's orders. She wasn't dying, she had a sprained ankle for God's sake, and it felt much better, at least good enough for her to go out and get a breath of fresh air.

"The laird will be none too pleased with you, Lady Aileanna," Mrs. Mac warned as Ali hobbled toward her chamber door.

"I'm sure I'll hear about it." If Ali was honest, she'd admit at least some of her anger was due to the fact Rory hadn't bothered to check on her himself. It was late afternoon and the man hadn't come near her. Yesterday he'd made love to her, told her they would marry, and yet today he couldn't spare her a single minute of his time. Just thinking about it made her mad.

"He's a wee bit busy, so mayhap you'll be lucky and he'll no' ken what yer aboot."

Ali harrumphed. "Busy playing his war games, is he?"

"'Tis no game, or won't be. Laird Aidan arrived back early this morn from escortin' the MacLeans home. He brought word the MacDonalds are on the move. The laird's been shut in his study most of the morn, and the men are gatherin' in the hall." At this point Mrs. Mac avoided her eyes, and Ali's heart pinched.

"They're going to pressure him to marry Moira, aren't they?" She wasn't prepared for the wave of utter despair that washed over her. No matter that she had told him to go through with the betrothal herself, she didn't think she could bear it if he did.

"Aye, some do, but he willna' do it. He's promised himself to you, and he'd no' go back on his word."

"And when men die in the battle, I'll be the one they blame." There was no way around it; she lost either way.

The three of them looked at one another, obviously unable to dispute the truth of what she said. When she opened the door, Ali was met by the sound of men's voices raised in anger. Taking a steadying breath, she limped from the room.

"If you have yer mind set, my lady, Connor will accompany you. Mari, we must see to Laird Aidan's room. He'll be here for a wee while I'm thinkin'."

Ali closed her hand over the smooth wood of the banister and Connor took a light hold of her arm as they slowly made their way down the stairs.

"Why will ye no' just wed Lady MacLean?" yelled a man in the hall.

Ali cringed, and Connor tightened his grip on her elbow.

"Aye . . . Aye." The words repeated over and over again until Ali thought it would never end.

She heard Rory's deep voice rumble over the gathered crowd. "I canna' do it. I'm marryin' Lady Aileanna."

Ali closed her eyes and slowly released the breath

she hadn't realized she held. Aside from the fact he'd just announced they would marry, and didn't seem too concerned she had told him they wouldn't, she was relieved. Happy he hadn't allowed his men to force him into a union with Moira MacLean.

Silence met his announcement until someone shouted in disgust, "Ye risk our lives to wed a thief."

Grumbles of discontent followed.

Trembling with anger, Ali stepped carefully off the bottom stair. How dare they question him after all he'd done for them? The man spent every waking hour seeing to their needs, their well-being.

She caught a glimpse of Rory in his plaid, towering above them on the dais. The man took her breath away. He was magnificent, and she couldn't help but wonder if it was true that highlanders wore nothing beneath their kilts. Watching him standing there, powerful and in command, she knew she wanted to find out.

Aidan, Fergus, and Iain stood with him. Rory laid a hand on his brother's arm to stop him from the protest he appeared ready to deliver. With a brief shake of his head, Rory looked down at the crowd. "Lady Aileanna is no thief. She thought to protect the flag from the MacLeans is all. Misguided she may have been, but nothing more. You condemn her, Donald, but I seem to recall you'd no' have yer leg if no' fer her."

"Aye, and 'tis on account of the magik she wields as a witch that she heals as she does," someone shouted from the back of the hall. Several more chimed in, their *ayes* reverberating off the stone walls.

Connor tugged on her arm. "Mayhap it would be best if ye went back to yer room, my lady."

Ali shook her head. It was difficult to hear what they said, but she needed to know how the clan felt about her. She edged closer to the entrance of the hall. Rory must have sensed her presence and their eyes met across the room.

He held her gaze with his and said, "I willna' have Lady Aileanna's name besmirched. She will soon be the lady of Dunvegan, and will be treated as such, or you'll answer to me."

"But . . . but what does she bring to us?"

She saw the glint in his eyes and the slight curve of his sensual lips. "'Tis no' what she brings to the clan, but what she brings to me that I'm thinkin' on."

Ribald laughter greeted his remark and some of the tension in the hall dissipated. Ali rolled her eyes and he winked at her, causing a heated flutter in her belly. Then he drew his gaze from hers and returned his attention to his men. A part of her wanted to believe what they shared would one day take precedence over all else, but she knew with a man like Rory, it would never happen.

"Connor, if you don't mind I'd like to go down by the loch." She kept her voice low so no one would realize she'd been there, but she needn't have bothered. Already talk of the upcoming battle drew their attention.

"Aye, we can try to manage it if ye'd like, my lady."

Rory swung his legs over the ledge of boulders onto the stone beach of the loch, fighting a smile when he spotted Aileanna. Like a sea nymph washed up on shore, the sunbeams danced in the waves of her long hair. She leaned against a rock with her gown hiked to her knees, her feet in the water.

"I'm certain I told Mrs. Mac to keep you in yer bed fer the day," he grumbled as he came to stand over her.

Her eyes fluttered open and a slight smile curved her lips. "You did, but you should know by now I don't follow orders very well."

"Aye, I see that." Rory crouched beside her and took her injured foot in his hand. "It doesna' look as bad as it did." With a light touch, he traced the bruises.

"The water's cold. It helps with the swelling." She squirmed when he trailed his fingers farther up her long leg, and a soft sound of pleasure escaped her parted lips. Lowering her foot, he came to sit at her side and bent his head to claim her mouth. She curled her fingers around his neck, deepening their kiss. The scent of her sun-warmed skin and the feel of her lush curves enveloped him. Cupping her face with his hand, he tilted her head and delved deeper with his tongue, tasting her sweetness. He wanted to devour her, to take her away and never let her go, just the two of them—no battle looming over their heads, no clan who depended on him for their every need. But just the thought of those demands was enough to make him pull away from her.

He rested his forehead against hers. "If yer no' careful I'll have you on yer back down here by the loch."

Her long fingers stroked him beneath his plaid. His cock, as stiff and hard as the rock at her back, jerked at her delicate touch.

"Grass . . . in the grass would be better," she said in a husky voice.

"Aye, and to be sure it would give the clan somethin' more to talk aboot."

"Right . . . I . . . uh . . . forgot."

He groaned as she released him, then nibbled at her neck. "Why doona' I take you to yer room and we can continue this there?"

"Is that your subtle way of getting me to stay in bed?"

"Aye, would it work?" He brushed the hair from her beautiful, flushed face.

"It would," she said, running the pad of her thumb over his

mouth. "But could we stay here for a little while longer? It seems a shame to miss out on such a beautiful day."

"Aye. The loch brings out the best in you, lass. Yer in a much better mood. Mayhap we should set you up down here."

Aileanna pulled a face. "Very funny. Almost as funny as what you did in the hall."

Rory grinned. "What did I do in the hall?"

She rolled her eyes. "Oh, I don't know—maybe your little announcement that we were getting married, even though I told you we weren't." She tapped his chest.

Laughing, Rory brought her finger to his lips. "You ken you want to marry me, mo chridhe, yer just too stubborn to admit it."

"Stubborn? This has nothing to do with me being stubborn. I won't marry you, Rory. I don't want a husband who married me because he felt he had no choice, who felt he was responsible for me." She shook her head. "What kind of marriage would that be?"

"Better than most," he commented dryly. Rory looked out over the shimmering waters of the loch before he turned to her. "You want me to wed Moira then, is that what yer tellin' me?"

She averted her eyes. With his finger beneath her chin he brought her gaze back to his. "Answer me, Aileanna."

"No . . . no, I don't want you to marry her. There, are you happy now?"

He brushed his mouth over hers. "Aye. The banns will be read, and we'll marry after we've met the MacDonald on the field."

"I didn't say yes, Rory."

"You will."

She shook her head, arms folded across her chest. "You know, I have a hard time understanding this feud with the MacDonalds. Why can't you meet face-to-face and try to work it out?"

He raised a brow and looked into her stormy eyes. "We've had this discussion before, Aileanna. You doona' understand."

"That's right, I forgot—I'm just a woman. But I'm the same woman who will be looking after all of you when you drag yourselves half-dead from the battlefield," she sputtered at him.

"We'll no' be half-dead," he muttered.

"You nearly died the last time, Rory." She blinked, and he saw moisture gather on her lashes. "The next time you might not be so lucky and I don't think I—" The last of her words came out on a choked sob.

He buried his face in her hair, wishing he could take away her worries, wishing he could make her understand that in his time, this was the way of it. Nothing else to be done but stand up for what was right, and fight for what was yours. "Shh. I'll come home to you in one piece, mo chridhe, I promise."

Aileanna slapped a hand to his chest. "You can't make promises like that." She frowned when he stood up. "Where do you think you're going? You can't just walk away from me when we're having a fight."

Rory bit back a smile and shook his head. "I didna' think we were havin' a fight, mo chridhe, but someone approaches. Here, let me help you." He reached for her hand.

"What are you talking about? There isn't—" She rolled her eyes when Iain called out to him.

Rory laughed at her disgruntled expression. Wrapping an arm around her waist, he tucked her to his side. "We'll continue our talk later, in yer room."

"Talk?" She raised a perfectly arched brow. "I'm sure we will."

"Aye, for a wee while we will." He nuzzled her neck.

"Ouch." She grimaced, running a finger along the stubble on his jaw. "You're rough."

"I'll see to it before I come to you." Their wee chat was putting Rory in the mood for more than talking, and he drew her in front of him to conceal the evidence as his brother came toward them.

"Yer all right, Ali?" Iain asked, grinning at them both. "My brother hasna' been browbeatin' you into givin' him an answer?"

"An answer?" She frowned.

Iain looked from Aileanna to him. "He asked you to marry him didna' he?"

With an unladylike snort, she said, "No. He *told* me I was marrying him."

Iain gave a shout of laughter. "Wait until I tell Aidan this one—but I'm certain he'll no' be surprised. Mayhap we should have a wee chat after the evenin' meal, and we'll explain to you how it's done, Rory."

"I think I ken how it's done, little brother."

Aileanna leaned her head against his shoulder and looked up at him. "I don't know, Rory. I think it might be a good idea." She patted his thigh, and from the look in her eyes he could tell she knew why she stood in front of him.

"Thanks fer the offer, but I have plans fer this evenin'." He tightened his hold on her. "Is there a reason you've come lookin' for me, Iain?"

"Aye, and you'll no' be pleased. Cyril's back. Says he must speak to you. He's no' lookin' too well."

Rory cursed under his breath. "Iain, help Aileanna get back to the keep fer me and I'll see to the mon." He kissed the top of her head. "And I'll see to *you*, later."

"Promises, promises." She grinned at him as he walked away.

"Aye, 'tis," he said over his shoulder. Anxious to be rid of MacLean so he could return to Aileanna, he sprinted along the path. As Rory neared the courtyard, he noted several of his men gathered at the doors to the keep.

Cyril, in the middle of the crowd holding court, looked up at his approach. "Ah, here he is now. I'm certain 'tis a misunderstandin' that can be quickly put to rights."

"Cyril, I doona' recall sendin' fer you," Rory said as his men parted to let him through, most unwilling to look him in the eye.

"I had word the MacDonald is on the move and kent you'd be anxious to sign the papers, so I—"

"Bloody hell, what happened to you, mon?" Rory asked upon getting a closer look at Cyril. Three deep gouges slashed open the left side of his face.

Cyril raised a hand to his cheek, his face flushed. "I . . . ah . . . a branch. I was ridin' and no' payin' attention to where I was goin'. Now enough aboot me—we must see to the contract."

"Mayhap we should continue this in my study," Rory suggested, nudging the man forward, ignoring the grumbling at his back.

"Ye may wish to set the men at ease first, Rory. They have taken a strange notion into their heads that yer plannin' on marryin' that . . . that woman." He gave a dramatic shudder. "Where on earth they got such an idea, I canna' imagine. You, marryin' an accused thief." He gave a delicate snort and brought his handkerchief to his lips.

"She's no thief, Cyril, and Lady Aileanna will be my wife."

"Ye canna' be serious. She stole from ye, and I've heard whispers she'd be a witch."

He narrowed his gaze on the man. "Tread carefully, Cyril. The woman you slander is the future Lady of Dunvegan. All charges against her have been proven false, to my satisfaction."

"But what of my sister? What am I to tell her?" The man had a panicked look on his face and a death grip on Rory's arm.

"'Twas no' a good match fer either of us."

"No' a good match! Ye need us, mon, ye need us," the man shouted, looking wild-eyed. He pointed across the courtyard to where Iain assisted Aileanna across the cobblestones, screaming, "'Tis her! She has ye bewitched. 'Twas the MacDonald's plan all along. She'll be the death of the MacLeods, mark my words. She'll be the death of all of ye."

Chapter 19

Gripped by an urge to choke the raving lunatic in the center of an ever-growing circle of onlookers, Rory clenched and unclenched his fists. He shoved open the doors of the keep and bellowed, "Aidan!"

Grabbing Cyril by the collar, Rory hauled him up the steps. "You'll shut yer mouth or I'll shut it fer you," he growled.

Cyril struggled, his mouth opening and closing like an overgrown mackerel. Rory pushed him toward Aidan, who stood in the entranceway, brow quirked. "What's he doin' here?"

Rory didn't answer. He sought out Aileanna over the heads of his men. She listened to something his brother was telling her, but it was obvious she took no reassurance from his words. "Give him some ale, then see him on his way."

"I think I can manage that. Looks like he lit a fire under that lot," Aidan said before he led a sniveling Cyril away.

Rory released a weary sigh and turned to face his men. "You listen to that mon, but mayhap you should consider why he's so anxious fer this match. And doona' think fer one moment he's concerned fer the clan's well-being. He needs my coin is all, and if any of you question me on this matter I'll no' have you at my side in battle. Go to the MacLeans and see if you enjoy ridin' under that mon. Now see to yer families. We leave four days hence."

None too happy, the men dispersed. Rory knew some of what he said would eventually sink in, at least with some of them. It was not his way to denigrate another, but Cyril left him no choice, and Rory spoke the truth. The MacLeans were in desperate need of his coin, thanks to Cyril's penchant for gambling.

He strode across the courtyard to Aileanna's side. His belly clenched at the look in her eyes. Unconcerned his affection for her would be witnessed, he wrapped her in his arms. "You willna' listen to him, mo chridhe. The mon's mad."

He met his brother's concerned gaze above her head. "Mayhap you can make her understand 'tis no' her fault," Iain said.

She leaned back to look Rory in the eye. "The man is as crazy as his sister, and I'm glad you won't be married to her, Rory. But you have to see, the clan will hold me to blame if you lose this battle." She loosened his hold on her and attempted to walk away, cursing when inadvertently she put weight on her injured foot.

Rory swung her up and into his arms. "Yer a stubborn wench, Aileanna Graham, and you have a mouth as wicked as a mon."

Her slight smile turned into a frown when she looked toward Dunvegan. "I don't want to go inside, not if he's there."

"I'll no' let him bother you, and he'll no' be here fer long."

Iain squeezed her arm. "Doona' fret. I'll go in and distract him."

"Iain," Rory called after his brother, "I'll see Aileanna settled and then meet with you, Aidan, Callum, and Fergus. We have much to discuss."

"When do you leave?" she asked, plucking at the laces of his shirt.

"In four days. We'll make our stand at Skeabost."

"How long will you be gone?"

Rory entered the keep with an eye out for Cyril. He tightened his hold on Aileanna when he heard the man ranting in the hall. "I canna' say," he said, looking into her troubled eyes as he made his way up the stairs.

"Could you not at least try to speak to the MacDonald?"

"Aileanna, there's no talkin' to the mon. He's a stubborn old fool who willna' listen to reason. He disputes our claim to Trotternish. 'Tis a long-standing feud that only ended when Brianna and I married and he used it as part of her dowry, but it was no' his to begin with. Now he means to have it back." He shook his head—the man was as mad as the one seated in his hall.

"How much property do you need? Aren't the lives of your men more important than a useless stretch of land?" she muttered as he opened the door to her chambers.

Laying her on the bed, he set a hand on either side of her head and lowered his face to hers. "Do you no' think if there was a way out of this I wouldna' have found it? You doona' ken me if you believe I'd put anythin' above the lives of my clan."

"I know you don't," she whispered. "Not even me."

He narrowed his gaze on her. "Aileanna . . . *What?*" he bellowed at whoever was rapping on the chamber door. Aidan entered the room with a surreptitious glance at Aileanna. "Sorry to disturb ye, cousin, but I think ye should come to the hall."

Rory rubbed his hand along his jaw. "Aye, I'll come." He hesitated before leaving Aileanna, troubled by her words. He wanted to make her understand why he did what he did, but he was needed elsewhere. Touching her cheek, he said, "Rest."

"How's yer lady?" Aidan asked when Rory joined him in the corridor outside her room.

"No' verra happy with me. She thinks I should find a way to make peace with the MacDonald."

Aidan shook his head. "Women, they doona' ken the way of it."

"Aye." And Aileanna less than most. But how could she understand when she was not from their time? Rory feared she never would. "What's goin' on in the hall?"

"I doona' think we're goin' to get rid of MacLean so easily. The mon's terrified to face his sister, and I wouldna' be surprised to learn 'twas her who marked him."

Rory frowned. "I didna' consider that."

"I ken the mark a woman leaves, and it has the look of it."

"Familiar with it, are you?" He grinned. His cousin's exploits with the ladies were legendary.

Aidan's gray eyes glinted with humor. "Aye, but of a different kind—on the back, ye ken."

Rory ignored his cousin's quip, wondering how he'd been blind to what Moira MacLean had become. He shuddered to think he'd almost married her. But then again, she'd been a means to an end, a way for him to protect his clan. Now with the match out of the question, it was up to him to find a way to win the battle with the least amount of lives lost. "I'm thinkin' I'm well rid of that one."

"Aye, I ken ye are, especially considerin' the woman yer replacin' her with."

Ali sat on her bed and wrapped the strips of linen around her foot, wincing when she pulled too tight. She was determined to get to know the people of Dunvegan, and it wasn't going to happen if she stayed shut up in her room. She had to go out amongst the people and somehow gain their trust.

Ignoring the age-old fear of rejection that knotted her

stomach, she prepared for a visit with Maureen Chisholm and anyone else who would let her see to them. Considering Cyril MacLean's ranting on the front step of the keep yesterday, she doubted there would be many. She brushed the thought aside, wishing she'd asked Mari when she'd brought her breakfast if Cyril remained at Dunvegan.

Ali looked up when the door to her chambers creaked open to see Rory standing there. He looked tired, and the dark shadow on his jaw heightened his dangerous good looks. She shivered. He was dangerous—not someone you'd want to cross—but she didn't fear him. He wouldn't hurt her physically, at least not intentionally, but he could break her heart.

"You're tired," she said, watching as he prowled toward her. The white shirt he wore contrasted with his deeply tanned skin, accentuating his powerful broad shoulders and the corded muscles beneath.

He sat beside her. "Aye, 'twas a long night and promises to be a longer day. I'm sorry I wasna' able to come to you last eve. 'Twas late, and I didna' wish to disturb yer sleep." His heavy hand came to rest on her thigh.

She'd missed him, and tried not to resent the time he spent away from her. "That's all right. I don't expect you to spend all of your time with me. I know you're busy." Her voice sounded petulant, even though she hadn't meant it to. Ali didn't add *playing at your war games,* however tempted she was. It wasn't the time. This was no game, and she couldn't make light of it.

His reaction was fierce and swift. He had her backed against her pillows before she had time to blink. "Do you no' think I'd rather be with you?" He speared his long fingers through her hair, trapping her with his body. His muscles rippled beneath the fine fabric of his shirt.

"Rory, I—" He crushed her protest with a demanding kiss. Heat spiraled through her, pooling between her thighs.

His tongue probed between her lips, dueling with hers for supremacy. Her breathing quickened, and she clutched at his shoulders.

Rory lifted his mouth from hers. "I want you now, mo chridhe, but this time I willna' be rushed." He chuckled when she moaned in frustration, giving her a hard, fast kiss. "This night I'll love you long and well."

She brought her palm to his roughened jaw. "I'll hold you to that."

He gave her a lecherous grin before his gaze went to her wrapped foot. "Mayhap 'twould be best if you stayed abed, Aileanna."

"Why, is Cyril still here?"

"Aye. The mon is no' in a hurry to take his leave."

"I can't say I blame him. But I don't want him here, Rory. There's enough bad feelings over me without him adding to it."

He sighed. "You doona' understand, lass. I canna' just toss him out. 'Tis no' a highlander's way. I'll keep an eye on him and you'll take Callum and Connor with you if you'll no' stay in yer room."

"Is it so bad I have to take both of them?"

"Fer now, but 'twill pass." His gaze softened as though he sensed how difficult it was for her to have so many of his people despise her.

"No, it won't, Rory, not if you lose men in the battle. It'll just get worse, and I don't think I'll be able to . . ." He didn't understand how hard it was for her to know she would be held to blame, distrusted and disliked. He couldn't know the painful memories it resurrected.

"Aileanna, we go nowhere with this, and I willna' discuss the battle with you."

"Because you won't listen, you—" Once more he silenced her with a hard kiss.

"Nay, I won't, so save yer breath. I have much to do and willna' see you until later this eve."

"Busy planning your war strategies, are you?" As soon as Ali said it she knew she shouldn't have, but his easy dismissal of her made her angry.

"Aileanna." His voice was rough, tempered steel.

"Well, maybe I'll be busy, too. If I'm not in my room . . ." Her tone was flippant, and she raised a shoulder to make her point. "I'll see you tomorrow."

Before she could stop him, he had his hand beneath her gown. She gasped when he shoved aside the heavy layers of fabric. "What do you think you're doing?" she sputtered, but it didn't take the heated look in his eyes to tell her what he meant to do, and still, her struggles were half-hearted. Her anger melted along with the rest of her as his fingers caressed the inside of her thigh, grazing her where she was swollen and throbbing for his touch.

He teased her. Over and over again, he stroked her slick folds only to trail his fingers back down her thighs. Groaning in frustration, she fisted her hands in the sheets, tilting her hips toward him, her body begging for more.

He watched her through heavy-lidded eyes. "Nay, mo chridhe, you'll be here waitin' fer me, of that I'm certain." His deep voice caressed her ear, and he twirled his tongue in the delicate whorls. When he plunged his strong fingers deep inside, her hips rose from the bed. "Yer so hot, and wet." His words brought her to the brink as much as his touch.

She bucked against his hand as he increased the tempo of his stroke. "Come fer me, mo chridhe," he rasped against her ear, putting pressure on her swollen nub. Under his passion-filled gaze she shattered, and he swallowed her moans of pleasure.

"Aye, I think you'll be here, doona' you?" he murmured against her lips before he rose from the bed.

Ali's face heated. "You're such a conceited ass, do you know that?"

Rory grinned as he headed for the door. "I doona' think you've called me that one before." He ducked when she flung a pillow at him.

Callum and Connor trailed behind Ali while she hobbled along the narrow path, leaning on the stick they had provided for her when she insisted on walking instead of riding Bessie. Even with a sprained ankle she was faster than the horse; not that it mattered. It wasn't like she had any pressing engagements, unless she counted Rory and his promise to love her long and hard tonight. Muscles low in her stomach tightened at the thought, and no matter how much she denied it, she knew she wouldn't make him wait. It wouldn't be fair—to her.

Connor took the lead and Callum brought up the rear. Lost in thoughts of Rory, Ali hadn't noticed the three men blocking the path until Connor stopped short and she slammed into him. She fought back the urge to run. She wouldn't get very far, and she'd be damned if she'd let Cyril MacLean think he frightened her. Callum and Connor wouldn't let him near her, but the man didn't need to physically touch her to hurt her. His words did enough damage on their own.

"Stand aside and let us pass," Callum growled.

Cyril rolled his eyes and flicked a handkerchief at his two men. They moved off the path. The cold, condescending look he gave Ali was full of malice, his upper lip curled in a sneer. His companions leered at her, and she quickly averted her gaze. One was almost as tall as Callum, but without the muscles. He looked like he hadn't bathed in weeks; his shaggy, light brown hair fell well past his shoulders, and his teeth when he smiled at her were rotten. His sidekick's head was misshapen, and he barely met his friend's shoulder. The man licked his lips and palmed his crotch when Ali walked by. She held her breath, afraid their rancid smell would cause her to lose her breakfast.

"Lady Aileanna," Cyril MacLean's high-pitched voice called after them. "Are ye off fer a wee walk?"

Ali gave a curt nod without looking at him.

"Best have a care then. The woods can be a verra dangerous place and I'm certain Laird MacLeod wouldna' want anythin' to happen to ye."

Her attention diverted, she tripped on a raised tree root and one of his men snickered. She heard Callum's heavy footfalls and turned to see him step in front of them. His hand rested on the hilt of his sword.

Cyril raised his hands defensively. "'Twas a friendly warnin' is all."

"Take yerself back to the keep and bring yer companions with ye."

"Now, see here." Cyril puffed out his chest.

"Laird MacLeod's hospitality to ye extends only so far, and if ye doona' want him to send ye packin', then I'd suggest ye do as I say."

Cyril blanched. Motioning for the two men to follow him, he headed in the direction of Dunvegan with a mincing step.

Callum snorted. "The mon is a bloody peacock."

"Who were the other two men with him, Callum?" Ali asked, uncomfortable with how they made her feel.

Callum frowned. "I doona' ken, but I mean to find out once we get back to the keep. I didna' like the looks of them."

Ali shuddered. "Me neither."

"And I didna' like the smell of them," Connor quipped.

They walked on in companionable silence. Weak sunlight filtered through the heavy shadows of the pines and the birds flitted happily overhead. Not far from the Chisholms',

Callum laid a heavy hand on Ali's shoulder. When she looked back at him, he put a finger to his lips and jerked his chin toward Connor. Ali tapped Connor on the shoulder and nodded to Callum.

A loud crack rent the air and Connor dove for Ali, pulling her to the ground. She held up her injured foot, her bottom taking the brunt of her fall.

"Halt," Callum called out, placing himself in front of her and Connor. She heard him curse before he said, "Jamie Cameron, ye get yerself out here now."

Dragging his feet, the little boy emerged from behind a tree.

Ali released a relieved sigh, allowing Connor to help her to her feet.

"Sorry, my lady. I didna' hurt ye, did I?" Connor asked, his ears pink.

"No, not at all." She didn't want him to feel worse than he obviously did and refrained from rubbing her bruised behind.

"Get yerself over here, lad. Ye'll remain with us until I can take ye to yer mam," Callum bellowed at Jamie.

The boy kicked a stone. "But I doona' want to."

"And I doona' care. I'm thinkin' 'tis time yer mother tanned yer wee arse, and mayhap I'll be offerin' to do it fer her."

Jamie's eyes widened.

"Callum, I'll be awhile. Why don't you take him to Janet?" she suggested quietly, feeling sorry for the little boy. "Connor and I will be fine. You sent Cyril back to Dunvegan, and I think he's too afraid Rory will send him home to Moira to be much of a threat."

The big man looked unconvinced. Ali lowered her voice. "It might help if you spent some time with Jamie, Callum. I'm sure Janet would appreciate it."

"I doona' ken, my lady. The laird will be none too happy if I leave ye on yer own."

"I'm not on my own. I have Connor. Don't worry, I'll deal with Lord MacLeod."

When Callum hesitated, she said, "The biggest threat to my safety is Cyril, and since you sent him back to Dunvegan it might be best if that's where you were so you can keep an eye on him."

Callum looked at Connor, who shrugged his shoulders.

"Go," Ali said, giving him a light push in Jamie's direction.

"Aye, I'll go, but have a care."

Ali smiled. "Don't worry about us. We'll be fine."

"Thank ye, my lady," Jamie called out to her, waving happily as he hurried after Callum.

Upon their approach to the Chisholms' thatched cottage, Ali pointed out a tree standing off from the stand of firs to Connor. "I won't be too long. Why don't you have a rest, and I'll ask Maureen for a tankard of ale for you."

"Thank ye, my lady." Connor grinned.

Ali spent an enjoyable hour with Maureen Chisholm and the baby. In their short time together she came to the conclusion women were no different in the sixteenth century than they were in the twenty-first. The important things remained the same: love, family, and friendship. And Ali felt as though she and Maureen were going to be good friends. It left her hopeful that other members of the clan would soon warm to her.

When Maureen tried to stifle a yawn, Ali decided it was time to leave. With a promise to visit again soon, she headed out the door. She expected to find Connor napping under the tree, but he was nowhere to be found.

"Connor," she called out, scanning the area. Leaning on the stick, she limped to where she'd last seen him.

"Connor, where—" A big hand clamped over her mouth.

"Doona' make a sound or the lad dies."

Chapter 20

Gasping for air, Ali struggled to pull the dirt-encrusted hand from her mouth.

"Did ye no' hear me?" He jerked her head back. "The lad gets it if ye doona' do as I say." Her captor ripped the walking stick from her hand and flung it against a tree. One half of it rolled on the pine-needled forest floor to where Connor lay bound and gagged.

The man with the misshapen head stood above him, dagger in hand. "Let's stick him, Gordie. He's of no use to us."

Ali struggled, whimpering beneath her captor's hand. Her stomach roiled at his stench and her fear for Connor. "No . . . no." Her cries were muffled beneath his sweaty palm.

"Nay, I'm thinkin' he'll make this wee piece behave."

The man guarding Connor licked his thick lips. "Give 'er to me. I'll make 'er behave."

"Nay, Mungo. Himself says the MacDonald will pay fer her return, and I'll no' risk his anger by returnin' her to him sullied by the likes of ye."

Ali swallowed the bile that rose in her throat. The man that held her pushed her forward and she stumbled. A sharp pain arched up her leg. Her knees buckled, and

Gordie sent her sprawling to the ground. She crawled to Connor, touching his pale face. He was unconscious and the hair at the back of his head was matted with blood.

"What did you do to him?" she demanded, anger overcoming her fear.

"Ah, Gordie, just a wee taste is all I want." Mungo groped at his crotch, leering at her.

"Shut yer mouth, Mungo, and ye, too." He jerked Ali's hands behind her. The rope he bound her with cut into her wrists. He planted his foot on the small of her back and shoved her, face first, into the ground, tying her ankles together. He stuffed a dirty rag into her mouth and hauled her to her feet. "Put him on yer horse and I'll take her."

"Nay, I'll take her." Mungo lurched toward Ali.

His tongue flicked out and he licked her cheek. Ali shuddered, turning her face. He grabbed her breasts and squeezed, but Gordie slapped his hands away.

"Cut it out, Mungo. Yer wastin' time. Himself said to make fer Portree. 'Tis the direction the MacDonald was last seen headed fer. If we ride hard we can get us our coin before morn." Gordie shoved him back.

"I doona' ken why ye won't let me have a bit of fun with 'er," the man muttered, glaring at his friend.

"I'm savin' yer neck, ye fool. Both the MacLeod and the MacDonald will have yer head if ye touch her."

A sense of hopelessness smothered Ali. She couldn't do anything to put Connor in danger. They'd kill him if she didn't do as they said. Her only chance was to cooperate, and to stay as far away from Mungo as she could.

"Help me," Mungo groaned as he tried to lift Connor.

"Doona' move," Gordie ordered as he strode toward his companion. Together they tossed Connor over the back of the shaggy brown horse.

Ali's gaze darted through the shadows of the forest, but there was no one in sight. They wouldn't be looking for her, not for a long time yet. Rory, Fergus, and Iain were too busy preparing for battle—battle with a man who would in all likelihood hold her as his prisoner. A pawn to be used against the MacLeods. What would Rory do if the MacDonald offered her in exchange for the rights to the land? Ali blinked back tears, certain she knew the answer.

Gordie dragged her along behind him. Her foot throbbed as she tried unsuccessfully to keep her weight off it. She bounced when he threw her onto the horse. The saddle dug into her stomach, and the breath she sucked in pulled the cloth deeper into her mouth. Panicked, Ali worked on it with her tongue, determined not to die. If she did, Connor didn't stand a chance, and she couldn't let that happen. It was because of her he'd gotten caught up in this mess.

With each jarring movement, her stomach was pummeled by the stiff saddle. *Rory,* she cried inwardly. She needed him and his powerful arms wrapped around her to give her strength. How could she live without him?

Keep sucking that cloth into your throat and you won't have to worry about it. That thought alone was enough to make her try again. She pushed, prodded, and then breathed out as hard as she could until a small edge of the cloth dangled from her mouth. Ali turned her head into the saddle and caught the rag on a jagged piece of leather. She wrenched her head in one direction and then the other. The cloth fell to the ground and she sucked in deep gulps of air.

Tilting her head back, she filled her lungs, ready to let loose a cry for help, until she remembered Connor. The scream died in her throat. She couldn't risk his life in the hopes someone would hear her pitiful cries. The towers of Dunvegan had already faded in the distance.

Blood pooled in her head, and she felt like she faded in and out of consciousness. She was unaware of where they were, or the landscape that sped by. All she saw were the horse's hooves as they pounded on, the ground blurring beneath them. Gravel and dust kicked up behind them. For the most part she kept her eyes closed, overwhelmed with dizziness when she didn't.

"Mungo," Gordie called to the man who followed behind them. "The horses need to be watered and rested. We'll stop at that copse of trees over yonder. I ken there's a loch nearby and we'll be well hidden."

Ali almost groaned with relief, but her relief was quickly replaced by dread when she realized her captors would see she was no longer gagged.

They reined in the horses and Gordie dragged her from the saddle. He tried to stand her upright, but she sank to her knees. Her muscles cramped. She had never felt such pain in so many places. Her ankles and wrists were chafed by the ropes. "Untie me. I won't run away. I wouldn't leave Connor," she croaked.

Gordie swept his unkempt hair from his face and glared down at her. "When did ye get rid of the gag?"

"What does it matter? I didn't scream, did I?"

"Nay, ye didna'." He narrowed his gaze on her.

With what little strength she had, she jerked her head to her hands. "If you want coin from the MacDonald, I'd suggest you don't bring me to him like this." There was no way they could escape, not with Connor wounded. She'd come to realize her only hope lay with Rory's enemy.

Gordie drew a wicked-looking blade from his boot and laughed at what must have been the look of terror on her face. "If I was goin' to stick ye, I would've done it back there." He sawed through the rope that bound her ankles and wrists. She bit her bottom lip to keep from crying out. The fibers burned, cutting into her already abraded skin.

"Why have ye let her go?" Mungo slid from his horse, pulling Connor down after him, letting him drop to the ground like a sack of potatoes.

Finally free, Ali rose unsteadily to her feet. Gordie grabbed her arm. "I didna' say ye could go anywheres."

"I have to check on Connor. He works for the MacDonald, too. He's . . . he's his nephew."

Gordie dropped her arm, staring at Connor. "MacLean didna' say anythin' aboot that."

Ali snorted. "Why would he? All he cared about was getting rid of me." The knowledge Cyril was behind her abduction didn't surprise her. She only wished she'd suspected just how far he would go to get rid of her. Had she known, she would've stayed in her room like Rory had wanted her to. Waited for him to come to her, to hold her, to make love to her. Fresh tears clouded her vision as she stumbled toward Connor. "Untie him," she demanded. "His uncle will have your head if he's harmed."

"Why did ye no' say somethin' before?" Gordie asked, taking the knife to Connor's ropes.

"It's a little hard to speak when you have a rag stuffed down your throat."

He didn't say another word. Ali knelt at Connor's side, checking for a pulse. She felt Mungo watching her and suppressed a shudder.

"She lies," Mungo said. Coming up behind her, he tangled his fingers in her hair and jerked her head back. Her pained cry choked off when he pressed the tip of his dagger to her throat. "Why did she fight us afore?"

Ali swallowed carefully. "I . . . I thought you were going to kill us. I didn't know where you were taking us." Her heart hammered in her chest, the beat pounding in her head.

"Let her go. Do ye no' want the coin?" Gordie yelled at the man.

Ali cried out when the dagger pierced her skin. A drop of blood glistened on the steel point.

Gordie grabbed his arm. "Ye crazy bastard, get away from her. Are ye mad? 'Twill all be for naught if ye kill her."

Mungo turned on Gordie, pointing the blade at her. "Fer now she lives, but ye'll no' tell me what I should or should-na' do. If I want 'er. I'll take 'er. She's a spy. What could the old mon say if I did?"

"Think of the coin, mon."

Mungo lowered the dagger. "Aye," he grunted, but he didn't take his eyes off Ali.

"Water the horses. 'Twill no' be long before night falls." The big man watched his friend reluctantly follow his orders, grumbling under his breath as he did. "See to the lad," Gordie told her. Without a backward glance, he followed Mungo.

"Connor . . . Connor, please wake up," she cried, patting his colorless cheek.

He moaned weakly, but at least he'd made a sound. She gently turned his head to examine him. A knot the size of an egg formed at the site of the wound. Although he'd bled quite a bit, it didn't look as bad as she first thought. She expelled a shaky breath. Connor would be okay. If they could survive Mungo and his threats, they would be all right. At least until they had to face the MacDonald.

Ali heard a horse whinny and looked up to see Gordie approach. He led both horses back with him. He stopped and withdrew a piece of linen from the pack attached to his saddle. Wiping his hands, his gaze met Ali's. "He'll no' threaten ye again."

Her eyes widened. Streaks of crimson stained the cloth. Staggering to her feet, she limped through the low brush and emptied her stomach.

"'Tis time to be on our way," Gordie said from behind her.

She nodded, and brought the hem of her gown to her mouth. A tremor rocked her body. Mungo was dead. Mur-dered. She reminded herself it could've just as easily been her or Connor. Gathering what little strength she had left, she followed Gordie.

"The lad will be riding with me. Doona' get any ideas."

Ali gave a nervous nod, clutching the reins when he helped her onto the saddle. He carefully placed Connor on the front of his mount, then swung up behind him. They rode in silence over hills covered in heather, past meandering streams. Her mind a whirlpool of emotions, Ali didn't see the beauty that surrounded them.

She jerked her attention to Gordie when he called out to her, "The lad's awake." Ali tapped her heels against the horse's flanks, urging her mount forward. She had to get to Connor before he gave them away. Coming alongside of them, she took Connor's hand in hers. He turned to her, a dazed look in his eyes. "Lady Aileanna, what happened?"

She held his gaze, trying to convey everything she couldn't say out loud. "It's all right, Connor. Gordie's taking us to your uncle, Lord MacDonald. It will be all right." She squeezed his hand, her nails biting into his palm.

His eyes widened. "Aye . . . aye," he mumbled.

She looked up at Gordie. "Is it much farther?"

"Nay, but we'll no' have much light left. We should set up camp fer the night."

"No." She shook her head. "No, let's keep going." If they stopped, Ali didn't think she'd be able to get back on the horse. There wasn't an inch of her that didn't ache. And her fear of facing Lord MacDonald would only intensify, the more time she had to dwell on the meeting.

Hours later, Ali questioned her decision. They could barely see ten feet in front of them. But just as she was about to suggest they go no farther, she saw balls of light glowing in the distance. "Gordie, what's that?" she called out to him.

"'Tis the MacDonald's camp."

Dread tied her stomach in knots. As they drew closer the campfires were clearly visible. Men dotted the landscape like ants at a picnic. Dread unraveled into a full-fledged panic attack, and she gulped in the damp night air.

"The MacLeods doona' stand a chance," Gordie muttered, shaking his head.

Ali squeezed her eyes shut as an image of Rory, wounded and bleeding, came to her, just like that first night. She wanted to find the MacDonald and get down on her hands and knees to beg him to end the battle before it began.

"Halt." Two men strode through the shadows toward them, swords drawn. "State yer business."

"I'm returnin' the MacDonald's nephew and his spy to him," Gordie said in a tone that suggested he expected to be held in some esteem for what he'd done.

Ali knew better.

The men looked at one another and appeared ready to send them on their way. It was then Ali brought her horse alongside Gordie. The older man's jaw dropped, and his companion gasped, falling to one knee. "Lady MacDonald."

Gordie looked at her, eyes popping out of his head.

"Will you bring us to Lord MacDonald, please." She added a soft lilt to her voice, surprised it came as naturally as it did. She couldn't afford to be turned away. If she was, Gordie would probably kill them both for her lies. And Rory, Iain, and Fergus, men that she loved, didn't stand a chance against an army this size.

Both men reached up to help her from her mount. Gordie was quick to dismount and ease Connor to the ground. Ali thanked the men, coming around to Connor's side. "Do ye ken what yer aboot, Lady Aileanna?" he whispered.

"Aye." Her eyes met his, and he grinned.

They passed small clusters of men gathered around the campfires. Their conversations ended the moment they saw Ali. They looked at her as though they'd seen a ghost. She was, at least to them—the ghost of Brianna MacDonald.

As they approached a large tent, one of the men rushed

forward. "My laird . . . Laird MacDonald." He tapped on the canvas.

"What are ye disturbin' me fer now?" The flap flipped open and a gray-haired man unfolded his large frame. Piercing blue eyes set in a handsome, aristocratic face stared back at her. The man let out an anguished cry and fell to his knees, clutching his chest. "Brianna."

Chapter 21

Rory glanced up from the battle plans he, Aidan, Iain, and Fergus charted. "Mrs. Mac, sorry we've missed the evenin' meal havena'—?" The anxious look in her eyes brought him up short. He laid his quill on the desk. "What is it?"

She twisted her apron in her hands. "'Tis Lady Aileanna. She's no' in her room. I havena' seen her all day."

A smile lifted the corner of his mouth as he thought of Aileanna's earlier threat. "She'll no' stay away much longer. Daylight's fadin' fast. Doona' fret, Mrs. Mac, Callum and Connor are with her. Mayhap she spent the day with Maureen."

The older woman gave him an odd look, obviously wondering at his lack of concern. "Nay, I asked Robert and he says she was with Maureen early this morn and has no' been seen since. And she sent Callum back with wee Jamie, told him to keep an eye on the MacLean, she did."

Rory tried to ignore the knot of unease in his gut. "We've been at this long enough." He pushed back his chair. "The three of you get somethin' to eat and I'll look fer Aileanna." And when he found her, she'd learn he was none too happy with her wee game.

"Nay, I'm goin' with you," his brother said, a look of

concern in his eyes. "She shouldna' be roamin' around on that foot of hers."

"Aye, I ken that, but she'd no' listen. She's a stubborn wench." He sounded defensive, but his brother seemed to suggest Rory didn't concern himself enough with Aileanna's welfare.

Aidan clapped him on the shoulder. "I think I'll keep ye company. The lass is always good fer a laugh."

Rory didn't have to wait for Fergus to offer his assistance. The man was already out the door, muttering as how he'd warm her arse if she'd gotten herself in a fix. If Rory's worries weren't getting the better of him, he'd have laughed.

He combed the area around the loch while the others searched the keep and questioned anyone they came upon. When they met back in the courtyard the sun had set, dusk closing in on them. The three men shook their heads at the question in his eyes and he saw his own growing fear reflected in his brother's.

Mrs. Mac and Mari waited anxiously for them on the steps to the keep. "You didna' find them?"

"Nay." He turned to the men at his back. "Gather as many as you can and we'll search the woods around the Chisholms'. It was the last place anyone had seen them. We'll need the torches," he said, scanning familiar shadows that now seemed sinister. He struggled to slow the pounding in his chest and gather his control before the others realized the panic that all but consumed him. *Where are you, Aileanna?* he silently asked, as though their bond was strong enough no words needed to be spoken. She would hear him, and lead him to her side. He could sense her before she came into a room, aware of her presence from a distance. Why then did he not feel her now? He would not let himself consider the reason.

"What's happened?" Callum joined him as Fergus, Iain, and Aidan arrived with torches and more men.

"'Tis Aileanna. She's missin'," Rory said tightly. His anger at the man for leaving her with only Connor was tempered by his knowledge of Aileanna and how difficult she could be when her mind was made up.

Callum bellowed a curse. "I shouldna' have listened to her. I didna' want to leave her, but she seemed more concerned I keep watch over the MacLean after we crossed paths."

"Crossed paths? Did he do somethin' to make her feel he was a danger to her?" He heard Fergus and Iain muttering at his back.

"Nay, a few words is all, but his companions were unsavory, to say the least."

"Bring MacLean to me," Rory yelled over his shoulder.

"The man is in his cups. Best we look fer yer lady now and have someone see to him while we're aboot it," his cousin suggested.

Aileanna's and Connor's names echoed in the stillness of the damp night air. As they approached the Chisholms', there was still no sign of them, no answering response. Callum and Aidan accompanied Rory to question Maureen and Robert.

"Doona' tell me she's yet to be found?" Maureen placed a hand to her mouth, eyes wide with worry.

Rory shook his head, watching as spheres of light danced in the small copse of trees to the left of the cottage. "Did she say where she was headed, Maureen?"

"Nay, I told her she'd be wastin' her time seein' to the others. A bunch of fools if ye ask me, and if one of them has done her harm . . . I'll . . ." Her soft brown eyes filled with tears.

Robert wrapped an arm around his wife and kissed the top of her head. "She's verra fond of yer lady."

"I ken she values yer friendship as well, Maureen, and I

thank you fer givin' it to her." He heard his brother call out to him and cut his questioning short.

"Please tell us as soon as ye have word," Maureen called after him as he ran toward the woods.

"'Tis the wee stick we made fer her," Callum said as they approached Fergus and Iain, who held the piece of carved pine in his hand.

Rory's heart pounded in a panicked rhythm at the grim expressions on the two men's faces. "What is it?"

"Blood." Fergus led them to the spot, shining his torch over the forest floor.

Rory crouched by the patch of moss. He cut it away with his dagger and brought it to his nose to sniff, cursing when he smelt the all-too-familiar coppery scent.

"Anything else?" Dread crept into his soul and his voice.

Fergus lay a heavy hand on his shoulder. "Aye, lad, there's signs of a struggle." He waved his torch to a place deeper in the woods. "There were at least four of them. I'm thinkin' Aileanna and Connor and two others. The ones who took them had horses."

Terror for what might have happened to her nearly brought Rory to his knees until rage melted the icy tentacles of fear and exploded inside of him. He would find Aileanna, and whoever had stolen her from him—was dead. Wound so tight he thought he would explode, Rory slammed his fist into a nearby tree.

"Ali's strong, and verra canny. She'll get away from whoever has her. She escaped the tower, didna' she?" His brother tried to ease his worry, but beneath his encouraging words Rory sensed his fear as easily as he sensed his own.

"Fight, mo chridhe. Fight and I will find you," Rory murmured. He gave a curt nod to Iain, unable to say anything. If he gave his rage free rein he would be no good to Aileanna.

* * *

Callum and Aidan brought Cyril to the hall as Rory requested. Sitting in a chair, the man's head lolled. Rory planted his foot on the edge of the seat and kicked it over.

"Sweet Jesu', brother," Iain gasped.

Rory ignored him and fisted a hand in the front of Cyril's tunic. Lifting him from the floor, he dangled him in the air. "Who has her?" he grated between clenched teeth.

Cyril struggled to breathe, his face purple. "Please . . . doona' kill me." He gave a strangled cry.

Rory shook him. "Tell me and mayhap you'll live."

"The MacDonald. I sent her to the MacDonald. She . . . she's his spy. 'Tis where she belongs."

He released his grip on the sniveling bastard's tunic, and Cyril dropped with a thud into a crumpled heap on the floor. "Get him out of my sight."

Aidan and Callum grabbed Cyril none-too-gently by the arms. "'Tis yer own fault. Ye left me no choice, Rory MacLeod. Ye were to wed my sister. I wouldna' had to go to such lengths if ye had stuck to the agreement," Cyril cried as he was dragged unceremoniously from the hall.

"Get him out of here!" Rory bellowed.

Fergus eyed him. "I ken what yer thinkin', but you'll do neither the lass nor the clan any good if yer dead, and that's what you'll be if you go after her on yer own. You have to think this through, lad. The MacDonald will no' harm her and well you ken it. She has the look of Brianna, remember that. She'll have him eatin' out of the palm of her hand in no time. Mayhap she'll harangue him to death with her opinions on the feud."

Rory allowed himself a tight smile. The MacDonald wouldn't give in to her pleas for a truce, of that he was certain, but Rory had no doubt she'd try. She was as stubborn as the old fool. Mayhap the MacDonald would get so tired of her harassing him he'd send her back to Rory without any demands. He gave a derisive snort. It wouldn't take much for his enemy to recognize the leverage he now held. How he would use her was the question.

Ali dropped to her knees beside Lord MacDonald and loosened the laces of his shirt. "Breathe, slow and easy now—there you go, that's it." She rubbed his broad back, ashamed she'd knowingly caused him pain. He might be Rory's enemy, but the man had lost his daughter, and it was obvious he grieved for her still. "I'm sorry. I should've said something. Given you some warning."

"Who are ye, lass?" His bright blue eyes drank her in.

"I'm Ali Graham. Cyril MacLean had this man kidnap me and Connor from Dunvegan." She pointed to Gordie, who stood shifting from one foot to the other behind her. "Cyril thinks I'm your spy, but all he really wanted to do was get rid of me so Rory will marry his sister Moira," she rambled.

Lord MacDonald touched her hair and a tear slid down his weathered face. Ali gently wiped away the moisture from his cheek, inexplicably drawn to the man. She felt guilty because of it, knowing he was the cause of Rory and his clan's suffering, but Lord MacDonald suffered, too, and she'd made it worse.

Gordie took a step closer. "I doona' ken what she's talkin' aboot. All I ken is Laird MacLean said ye'd give me coin fer bringin' her to ye."

Lord MacDonald slowly drew his gaze to Gordie. The tender look Ali had seen in his eyes turned deadly. If Ali thought Rory looked dangerous, he had nothing on this man, and she prayed he would not skewer her with the same look he now skewered Gordie with. Her captor was quaking in his boots.

Drawing himself to his full height, Lord MacDonald's gaze raked over Ali. "Did he harm ye, lass?"

"Nay . . . no." Ali shook her head. She wouldn't have Gordie's death on her conscience. And if she said yes, she was certain Lord MacDonald would not hesitate to cut him down where he stood.

"I'll see yer compensated on the morrow. Take him." He jerked his chin at his waiting men. They led Gordie away with Connor staring after them. "Is the lad with ye?"

"Aye . . . yes, Connor was guarding me."

The older man raised a silver brow as though to say he didn't do a very good job of it, and Ali felt the need to come to Connor's defense. "There were two of them. Gordie killed Mungo when he threatened me." Without thinking, Ali's hand went to the spot on her throat where he'd pierced her with his blade. Eyes wide, Connor's jaw dropped.

"Good. No mon should harm a woman, no matter what the provocation. Come, yer shiverin'. We'll set ye by the fire. Are ye hungry, lass?" He guided her carefully to the open flame, handling her as though she were a fragile piece of glass. In a language Ali didn't understand, but had heard often at Dunvegan, he ordered his men about. Within minutes she had a steaming bowl of stew in one hand and a chunk of bread in the other. A swath of plaid was draped over her shoulders. Ali was relieved to see that Connor, too, was being treated as a guest.

"So tell me—how did ye come to be at Dunvegan in the first place?"

Ali related the story Fergus had concocted, then went on to tell him about Moira and Cyril MacLean and their accusations she was a spy, embellishing details as she went along. She left out the part about the fairy flag, but told him how Rory sided with the MacLeans and locked her in the tower. She peeked through her lashes at Connor as she told the story. He didn't bat an eye, just kept on eating, but Ali thought she saw his mouth twitch.

She didn't know why she babbled on. For some reason Lord MacDonald made her feel she could confide all her worries and her fears to him. "He locked ye in the tower, of all the . . ." he roared, and Ali jumped.

"It's all right," she reassured him. "I escaped. It's how I hurt my ankle." She lifted the edge of her gown to show him her wrapped foot. The once white linens were now as filthy as the rest of her.

The older man slapped his thigh and hooted with laughter. Wiping his eyes, he said, "Ye escaped from the tower, did ye? Well, yer as brave as ye are bonny, my pet."

Ali smiled to see the twinkle of amusement in his eyes, glad to take away at least some of the sadness she'd put there earlier.

"And what did the young fool do then?"

"He believed me and brought me back to Dunvegan." She flushed under his scrutiny as though he knew exactly what happened next.

He stroked his mustache, his voice subdued. "Are ye in love with the mon?"

She hesitated. Rory had been his daughter's husband and Ali didn't know how he'd react, but she felt a need to be honest with him and figured she'd already given herself away. "Aye . . . yes, I am."

He shook his head slowly. "'Twas the same with my Brianna. I didna' want the match, ye ken, but she wanted no other. No matter how many lads I paraded before her, she always went back to him."

Ali tried to ignore the pinch in her heart. It never got any easier to hear about the love Rory and Brianna had shared. Although she knew he loved her, too, no one wanted to be second best, and for her, Rory would always be her one true love.

She cleared her throat. "Why didn't you want her to marry him?"

"The MacLeods and the MacDonalds were always feudin' over one thing or another. Ye must ken that, lass."

"But the feud ended with their marriage. Surely you must have come to like Rory?"

The man looked beyond the fire and his answer came slowly. "Fer the most part. He wears the mantle of responsibility well fer all that it was forced upon him at a young age. Mayhap 'tis why he puts his clan above all else. Brianna thought it was so. She never felt she truly came first in his heart. The day my daughter died the truce between our clans ended."

Ali's heart slammed into her throat. Brianna had suffered the same doubts she did. Her hope that one day Rory would be able to put her ahead of his clan diminished with each word the man at her side uttered. But she felt a need to defend Rory, and thought maybe she could ease some of Brianna's father's sorrow at the same time. "You mustn't doubt he loved your daughter, Lord MacDonald. I know he did—very much."

His jaw hardened. "If no' fer him my daughter would be alive."

"What are you saying? Rory would never have hurt his wife, not intentionally. He tried to do whatever he could to save her." She touched his big hand. "Her death and the baby's still affect him. I saw it not long ago when I helped a woman with her delivery. He hasn't gotten over it, Lord MacDonald. He still feels guilty."

"Aye, and so he should. My daughter was no' strong from birth. 'Twas her sister who was the strong one." A gentle smile curved his lips, fading when he continued. "He shouldna' have forced her to have a bairn. Him and his godforsaken clan wanted a babe to carry on the MacLeod name. He could've left it to his brother."

Heat rushed to Ali's face. She didn't want to have this conversation with Brianna's father, but no matter how uncomfortable it made her, she would. If there was even the slightest chance she could change the course of the feud, she'd take it. "Have you ever stopped to consider that your daughter knew her time was short and wanted to give Rory something to remember her by?"

He turned away from her, his voice gruff when he asked, "Why would ye think that?"

"I'm a healer, Lord MacDonald, and it's been my experience that sometimes people have a sense of their impending death. I don't know all there is to know about your daughter's medical history, but if this was a condition she had since birth, then you were blessed to have her as long as you did. You must have taken wonderful care of her."

He swiped at his eyes. "When I lost her mother and her wee sister she was all I had left."

"She was very lucky to have you. I envy her that." She gave him a watery smile.

"We're a pair, aren't we?" He squeezed her hand. "Ye bed down in my tent and we'll talk on the morrow."

"Lord MacDonald, would you send a message to Rory and tell him I'm safe here with you?"

"Aye, at first light. Ye ken I'll no use ye in the feud, lass. I'll no' have ye suffer. But . . ." He hesitated, watching her closely. "Ye'd be welcomed at Armadale by me and my clan if after the battle ye wish to return home with me."

"Thank you. Is it because I remind you of your daughter?" she asked quietly. It was ridiculous, but she hoped not. Ever since coming to Dunvegan she'd been compared to Brianna, and grew weary of being wanted only because she so closely resembled someone they had all once loved.

"Aye, ye do remind me of her. Although I ken yer no' like her, ye've lightened my heart this night and I thank ye fer that. Ye canna' blame an old man fer wantin' to keep ye around, now ken ye?"

"If you and the MacLeods weren't feuding, maybe we could visit one another."

He quirked a brow. "I knew where ye were headed all along, lass. I just didna' ken how long it would take ye to get there. In that yer like my wife. She hated the constant feudin'. 'Tis why I think she left me that night, takin' my other daughter and runnin' off. If Brianna wasna' so sickly as a bairn, I'm certain she would've taken her as well."

"You never found them?"

"Nay. Searched for years until I realized 'twas hurtin' Brianna."

"I'm sorry." She squeezed his hand.

"Sleep well, my pet. On the morrow we'll talk." He laughed when she gave him a hopeful smile.

"I'm no' makin' any promises."

Chapter 22

Rory sagged with relief in his chair, handing the parchment across the desk to his brother. "He has Aileanna, says she's well, but he will return her only when he's satisfied she's rested." She was coming back to him. Rory didn't know when he'd ever been happier. Without her it was like the light had gone from his life.

He had lain in her bed, breathing in her scent. Sleep had eluded him as he battled his demons. Torn by the needs of his clan, he had feared what demands the MacDonald would make of him for her safe return, only to find there were none. Rory was certain the reason the old goat backed off was that Aileanna reminded him of his daughter.

"Sounds like the MacDonald has taken a special interest in yer lady." His cousin grinned. "Ye best be careful he doesna' steal her away from ye. The ladies are all atwitter when he's at court. Consider him to be a handsome old bugger, they do."

He scowled at Aidan. "She has the look of his daughter, 'tis all it is."

"Do we hold off readyin' the men?" Iain interrupted.

"Aye, we hold. I want to be here when Aileanna is returned."

"Fergus, Iain, are ye no' surprised Himself wants to be here to greet his lady? Imagine, the great warrior would rather keep the home fires burnin' and see to his woman than lead his men into battle. We'd best be certain the men doona' get wind of this," Aidan quipped. His laughter faded when he met Rory's gaze. "I'm teasin', cousin. I fer one would think yer daft if ye went ridin' off without seein' to her first." Aidan shook his head. Placing his two hands on the desk, he leaned toward Rory. "Can ye no' let it go, cousin? Yer no' yer father. There's no better laird than ye, but ye deserve a life and doona' ye dare let that lass suffer because of yer foolish notions." Aidan slammed his fist against the polished wood, then left the study.

"He's right, Rory. I ken yer worries. Doona' ferget, I lived them, too. I doona' carry the weight of yer responsibilities, but I do understand, and mayhap you will let me shoulder some of the load. I may no' be the man you are, but I am a man," his brother said quietly, walking away before Rory could think of something to say.

"Bloody hell, what just happened here?" Rory grumbled. Leaning back in his chair, he rubbed the stubble along his jaw.

"We all desire the same thing, lad. We want to see you happy, truly happy, and we ken Aileanna is the one to do that fer you. We doona' want you to mess it up is all."

Rory rolled his eyes. "I canna' mess it up. I love her. She kens that."

Fergus grinned. "She does, does she? How are yer weddin' plans comin' along?"

"Go tell Mrs. Mac and Mari the good news," he muttered, waving his friend from the study.

Ali crawled from the tent and met a grinning Lord Mac-Donald. He crouched at her side. "Are ye havin' a bit of trouble, lass?"

"I feel like I've been run over by a car . . . cart," she quickly amended.

"Here, let me help ye." He looped a strong arm around her waist and pulled her to her feet. "I'll bring ye down to the loch and ye can clean up a bit." He held up the bundle he carried in his other arm. "I have everythin' ye need. I'm certain ye have no wish to get back into yer own things."

Ali shook her head and smiled. "Definitely not." She looked out over the campsite to the men milling about. "Where's Connor?"

"Over with some of the other lads. Doona' fret. I told him to have a care fer a day or two. He has quite the bump on his noggin."

"He does. Is Gordie gone?"

"Aye, hightailed it out of here at first light, along with the messenger. Now here's some linens and soap. No one will bother ye, lass." He unsheathed his sword with a smile. "I'd no' allow it. I'll be over there." He pointed out a large boulder just beyond the edge of the loch.

"Thank you." Ali hobbled along the black sand beach until she found a secluded spot behind a cluster of rocks and low shrubbery. She shrugged out of her filthy gown and underclothes, leaving them in a heap in the brush. The cool, clear water lapped gently over her, taking some of the ache along with it. Her thoughts went to Rory and she wished he was with her, holding her in his arms. She missed him, more than she thought possible. The knowledge she would soon be back with him was heartening, but only if she didn't think of how little time they'd have together before he left her for the battle. Closing her eyes, she tried to block out the gory images that haunted her.

"Ye havena' drowned on me, have ye, lass?" Lord MacDonald's deep voice jolted her from her musings.

"Nay . . . no, I'll be right there." Ali paddled to shore. She quickly dried off and began to dress. She pulled the crisp white shirt over her head—it fell to her knees. She wrapped the red, green, and blue plaid around her as though it were a sari, quite pleased with herself until she walked toward Lord MacDonald and saw the look in his eyes. "Is something wrong?"

"Nay." He patted her cheek. "The resemblance is un-canny is all."

She sighed. "To Brianna?"

"Nay, to my wife. Come, I . . ." He looked down at her feet encased in the light suede boots. "I forgot to bring ye some linens to wrap yer wee foot."

"I'm fine. The boots are a little snug, but it does the same as wrapping it would."

"I wonder what the lad will think when he gets a look at ye dressed in the MacDonald colors?" A wide grin split his handsome face.

Ali arched a brow. "I have a feeling you'd like to see that for yourself."

"Aye, I might just."

"You'd take me back—yourself?" Ali couldn't suppress her joy at the thought she could bring the two men together and find some way to avoid the battle, to save Rory and his clan, and maybe the man at her side.

"Now, doona' be gettin' yer hopes up. We'll no' be leavin' till the morrow. Ye had a rough go of it. I'll make my decision then."

Although Ali was disappointed she'd have to wait another day to see Rory, her backside was relieved. She wouldn't be bouncing on a horse for one more day, and what better way to use her time than working on Lord MacDonald?

Ali fidgeted on the horse she shared with Alasdair MacDonald. "'Tis no' much farther, my pet. Would ye like us to stop and give ye a wee rest?"

Connor let out an exasperated sigh as he rode beside them with one of the men-at-arms, and she bit back a grin. She didn't blame him. Lord MacDonald insisted they stop every few miles for Ali's benefit, and she was sure they'd doubled the length of time it took to get to Dunvegan because of it.

"No, I'm fine, Alasdair. You don't have to worry about me," she said, calling him by his name—something he had insisted upon the night before as they sat by the fire sharing stories, Ali weaving her own experiences growing up with a made-up childhood along the borders.

In two short days together they'd grown close. It was as though they'd known each other forever and adopted each other: Ali a substitute daughter for the one he had lost, and he a substitute father for the one she had never known.

Because of the bond that had developed between them, Ali knew he would try to come to some sort of truce with Rory, although no promises had been made. But he didn't rule it out either. For Ali it was a start. If she could just get the two men in the same room, some good had to come of it. It couldn't get any worse, and she'd be damned if she'd let the two of them kill each other over a stupid piece of land.

"I ken yer gettin' yer hopes up, lass, but he's a stubborn one," Alasdair said, as though he could read her mind.

Ali snorted. "That's what he says about you."

"Harrumph. Are ye certain ye wouldna' rather come to Armadale with me?"

Out of the corner of her eye, she saw Connor stiffen. "I told you, Alasdair, I'm happy at Dunvegan. I've made friends, people I care about. The others will have to warm up to me sooner or later."

"Good—I doona' like to think of ye bein' unhappy."

"I won't be." She patted his hand and smiled back at him. "And if Rory makes me mad, I'll just come visit you."

Alasdair chuckled. "I'm certain that will please him to

no end. Ye do ken, my pet, 'twill no' be easy. The lad was verra young when he was forced to become laird, no older than this one." He jerked his chin at Connor.

"I didn't know. That couldn't have been easy for him."

"Nay, I ken it wasna', but he had no choice. His father was mad with grief over the loss of his wife. I ken how he felt. I lost my wife and daughter, but ye have to go on fer those left behind, those who depend on ye, and he couldna' do it. He took his own life. 'Tis said 'twas Rory who found him. Bad enough that, and on top of it his father had left them in dire straits. They were practically starvin'."

Ali's heart ached for Rory. No one should have to go through what he did. But she welcomed the insight, and in some ways she thought the trials he had faced created the very characteristics that drew her to him, made her love him as much as she did.

"Sounds to me like you admire the man."

Alasdair gently tugged her hair. "Minx. And ye'll no' be usin' that against me."

"I can see by the end of it I might be knocking your two stubborn heads together to make you both see reason."

Alasdair's amused laughter brought a smile to his man-at-arms's face. It was obvious his men were fond of their laird and glad to see him happy.

Over the next rise, Ali spotted the towers of Dunvegan. Bathed in gold, they gleamed as the sun set behind them. Excitement tingled from the tips of her toes to the top of her head and she wanted to urge the horses to pick up their pace.

"Hoist the flag, Gilbert," Alasdair directed the man Connor rode with.

Ali nudged him. "I don't think that's really necessary, do you?"

"Aye, my pet, I do. Look to the men linin' the walls."

She looked to where he pointed and swallowed hard.

Bows were aimed in their direction. "No, there must be some mistake. Rory would never allow it."

Rory walked the parapet. Aidan, Iain, and Fergus followed in his wake. Even though Aileanna and Connor rode with the MacDonalds, a show of force was necessary. As the contingent broke through the line of trees he couldn't help but smile. In a short time he would have her in his arms again. But his smile quickly faded when he saw who rode at her back—Alasdair MacDonald, and the old goat had dressed her in his colors.

"Yer lady looks as bonny as ever. His plaid suits her," Aidan said, a hint of laughter in his voice.

Rory shot him a quelling look over his shoulder. "Lower yer bows," Rory commanded down the line. The show was over. He wouldn't allow Aileanna to be wounded by an archer with a twitchy finger.

"Do ye think his presence means he's amenable to negotiations?"

"With Aileanna, anythin's possible, but doona' get yer hopes up, Aidan. He's a stubborn old goat."

Aidan chuckled as they crossed the courtyard. "I'm thinkin' ye may have to give as well, cousin, or yer lady may no' be as welcomin' as ye hoped."

Fergus, Iain, and his cousin shared a laugh, but all fell silent as the drawbridge lowered and the sound of the horses' hooves clattering on the wood heralded their arrival.

Before Rory could reach Aileanna, the MacDonald had her off the horse, her hand tucked beneath his arm, and they shared a smile. Rory clenched his hands into fists at his side.

"Easy, lad," Fergus murmured.

His anger was forgotten the moment Aileanna turned

her brilliant blue gaze upon him and smiled a smile that he knew was meant for him alone.

When he reached her side, he brought a hand to her cheek. "Yer well, mo chridhe?" he asked quietly, fighting the urge to take her in his arms, knowing it would be in poor taste considering the man at her back was his former father-by-marriage.

She pressed her cheek to his palm. "I am. I missed you," she said shyly, keeping her voice as low as his.

"I missed you, too, and later I'll show you how much," he said before he raised his eyes to Alasdair MacDonald and his men. "I thank you fer seein' to Aileanna's well-bein' and bringin' her home."

An emotion that Rory didn't recognize flickered in the man's cerulean gaze, but quickly disappeared. "'Twas my pleasure."

They hadn't seen each other since they'd laid Brianna to rest at Armadale—an allowance Rory had made to the other man's grief. The MacDonald was thinner than he remembered, but there was a lightness about him now, and Rory hoped he had found peace.

No matter that they might soon face each other on the battlefield, he didn't begrudge him that. The man had lost more than most, and Rory owed him for not using Aileanna as a pawn. Alasdair MacDonald was an honorable man, and although he'd never let the old goat know it, he had a great deal of respect for him.

"Will you sup with us before you leave?"

Aileanna frowned. She took Alasdair's hand and tugged him to her side. "He's not leaving, Rory. Not until this ridiculous feud is settled."

Chapter 23

The old goat had the nerve to grin at Aileanna's pronouncement, and Rory was forced to follow in their wake like a minion in their service. He stifled a growl as his brother and Fergus took her in their arms as he longed to, and cooled his heels while Mrs. Mac and Mari happily welcomed her home.

Their greeting of the MacDonald was more subdued, but politely made. All except Fergus, who genuinely liked the man. The two had developed something of a friendship upon Rory's marriage to Brianna, and it was obvious it still endured as they clapped each other on the back on the way into the keep.

Rory nudged his cousin, who'd been watching the proceedings with an amused eye. "It looks like ye'll be doin' some negotiatin' after all." Aidan grinned.

"Aye, and it would be best if I kent just what Aileanna's been sayin' before sittin' down with the mon. I ken he's no' anxious to let her out of his sight so I'll need yer help. Challenge him to a game of chess. He'll no' be able to resist and 'twill give me time to speak to Aileanna alone."

Aidan raised a brow. "Aye, I'll do it fer ye, cousin, to give ye and yer lady a chance to *talk*."

The small contingent that accompanied the MacDonald had entered the hall before Rory caught up to Aileanna and Alasdair. "Why doona' we retire to the upper salon, Alasdair, and yer men can take their leisure in the hall. We'll rejoin them at the evenin' meal."

"I'm in the mood fer a game of chess. Would anyone care to join me?" his cousin asked.

Alasdair's gaze flickered over Rory, and then back to Aileanna. A slight smile caused his mustache to twitch. "I'd be up fer a game. Fergus?"

"Aye, I ken the last time we played you beat me, so 'tis time for a rematch." As soon as the words were out of Fergus's mouth, Rory knew he regretted them. The last time they'd played it was a means to distract themselves on the long days leading up to Brianna's death.

"Will ye be joinin' us, my pet?" Alasdair asked Aileanna, his gaze softening.

"If you don't mind, I'd like to freshen up first."

"Aye." He patted her cheek. "And have a wee rest while yer at it. A ride like that takes a lot out of a person, especially one as delicate as yerself."

Rory managed to stifle his shout of laughter, but Iain, Aidan, and Fergus were not as successful. Aileanna glared at them before she reached up to give the old goat a kiss on the cheek. "Make sure you beat them, Alasdair, for me. I'll see you at dinner."

"Aye, my pet, I will. Rory, will you no' be joinin' us?" Alasdair gave him an intent look.

Rory clenched his teeth. The arrogant old fool would be the death of him, especially if he continued to fawn over Aileanna as though he had the right. "Aye, but first I have a couple of matters that require my attention. Aileanna." He offered her his arm. "I'll see you to yer chambers."

She took his arm, making an obvious effort not to smile.

"Am I one of those matters you have to see to?" she asked when they were well out of earshot at the top of the stairs.

"Aye, the only matter I wish to see to," he growled. Tugging her into his arms, he lowered his mouth to hers. Desire flared within him as once more he held her lush curves next to him. At her eager response, he deepened the kiss. She moaned, parting her lips to allow his tongue to tangle with hers. Her arms wound around his neck, and he gripped the round firmness of her behind. Lifting her off her feet, he backed her against the wall. He ground his cock into the soft curve of her belly.

At the sound of footfalls on the staircase, Rory cursed under his breath and broke their kiss.

Mrs. Mac approached with a handful of fresh linens. "Och, there you are. I was wonderin' where you'd be wantin' me to put his lordship."

Rory swept Aileanna into his arms, turning his back to Mrs. Mac so she wouldn't see his raging cock-stand or Aileanna's flushed face and passion-filled eyes. Just as he was about to tell her exactly where he wanted Alasdair, the woman in his arms took hold of his shoulder and pulled herself up to say, "Why don't you put him in Brianna's room, Mrs. Mac? It might be nice for him to be surrounded by some of his daughter's things."

"'Tis a wonderful idea, my lady."

"Wonderful, just bloody wonderful," Rory muttered as he strode along the corridor toward Aileanna's room.

She frowned at him. "What's wrong with putting him in Brianna's room?"

"What's wrong is by doin' that"—he shoved open the door to her room—"yer puttin' him in the room next to mine."

She rolled her eyes. "Rory, it's not like you're sleeping in the same room with the man. You have a door between the two of you."

272   *Debbie Mazzuca*

He set her down on the edge of the bed. "Aye, there is, but the mon will ken when I'm comin' and goin'."

"What does that have to do with anything?"

He shook his head, carefully removing the boots from her feet. "Think on it, Aileanna. He'll ken when I creep back to my bed after bein' with you."

"He'll just think you had business to take care of."

He snorted. "The mon's no fool."

"Funny, you keep saying he is."

Rory sat back on his haunches and looked into her beautiful face. "Are you tryin' to make me daft, mo chridhe?" he asked, stroking her smooth, bare legs beneath the plaid.

"No." She gave him a slow, sensual smile before she ran the tip of her pale pink tongue along her full lower lip.

"I ken what I wear under my plaid, but what do you wear?" His voice was low and gruff as he smoothed his palms along the warm, satiny skin of her inner thighs.

"Nothing," she whispered. Her eyelids fluttered closed, her legs parting ever so slightly. He bunched the fabric to her thighs and tangled his finger in her silky curls, stroking her slick, wet folds. She leaned back on her hands, her hips arched, and he knew he wanted her naked and on the bed beneath him—now.

Kissing her knee, he rose to his feet. "I think I'll have you dress in a plaid more often, mo chridhe, but it will be MacLeod plaid, no' MacDonald. But right now, I need you out of this so I can show you just how much I missed you." He tugged the swath of fabric from her shoulder.

She slapped his hands away. "You're too rough. You'll rip it."

He shrugged, watching as she carefully unraveled the plaid. "I doona' care—you'll no' be wearin' it again."

"Yes, I will. I like the colors. They're pretty."

"They may be pretty, but they're the MacDonalds' colors no' the MacLeods'."

She laid the plaid on the end of her bed, standing before him in only a sheer linen tunic. Her nipples puckered beneath the fabric, ripe for his attention. "I'm not a MacLeod, Rory, and I can wear whatever I want," she countered with a stubborn jut to her chin.

"Yer mine, and you *will* be a MacLeod." He held her in his arms and lifted her off the floor. "Do you ken yer mine, mo chridhe? That I'll never let you go?" Through the light-weight fabric he suckled her taut nipple.

"Yes . . . yes, I know I'm yours," she groaned, wrapping her legs around his waist.

He could feel her warm, wet core through the fabric of his tunic and his cock throbbed. She pressed her breasts tight to his mouth. He fought with his trews while he held her with one hand, needing to be inside her.

A sharp rap on the door stayed his hand, and he cursed when he recognized the deep voice calling through her door. "Lass, can I have a moment of yer time?"

A look of panic came upon Aileanna's face and she struggled to get out of his arms. "Put me down . . . put me down," she whispered fervently.

"Mayhap I would if you'd unwind yer legs from my waist," he whispered back, his voice laden with sarcasm.

She glared at him, then cleared her throat. "Give me a minute, Alasdair. I'm not quite decent."

"That's the truth," Rory muttered.

She grabbed the plaid from the end of her bed and hastily tried to wrap herself in it. "Hide," she hissed at him.

"I'm no' hidin' in my own keep," he grumbled, crossing his arms over his chest.

"He was your wife's father, and I'm not going to flaunt that we're together like . . . like this." She waved an arm at the bed before her gaze frantically searched the room. "Bed . . . under the bed."

"Coming, Alasdair," she called out sweetly as she

shoved him toward the bed and tugged at the plaid to cover the wet spot on her tunic.

"You would've and so would've I," he muttered to himself as he crawled beneath the bed.

"Shh!"

He heard her pad across the floor and the door creak open. He couldn't believe he was hiding from Alasdair MacDonald like a wee lad, but Aileanna was right. He'd not rub the mon's nose in their relationship.

"Sorry fer disturbin' ye, my pet, but there's somethin' been weighin' on my mind since we arrived."

"Come in." Rory heard the door close and Alasdair's heavy footfalls as he came into the room.

"Has someone said anything to make you feel unwelcome, because if they—"

Rory rolled his eyes. Now she protected his enemy.

"Nay . . . nay, 'tis no' to do with the MacLeods. Get into yer bed. Ye must rest yer wee foot."

The bed creaked and the toes of Alasdair's boots stared Rory in the face. He barely resisted the urge to hit them.

"Alasdair, I'm fine," he heard Aileanna laughingly protest. Rory's fist came within an inch of the old man's foot. "Now tell me what's bothering you. You look upset."

"Ye ken when I first saw ye I was no' myself and ye introduced yerself as Ali Graham." She must have nodded because Alasdair continued. "But upon our arrival I heard Rory refer to ye as Aileanna. Why is that?"

"That's my name. Ali is short for Aileanna. Alasdair . . . Alasdair, what is it?"

The man staggered and Aileanna must have made him sit down because the bed dipped, and Rory now faced the heels of Alasdair's boots.

"Ye remember how I told ye Brianna had a sister, a twin? Her name was Aileanna. Nay, doona' look at me like that. Ye ken well enough how much ye look like Brianna, but even more ye have the look of my wife. Ye have her ways, too, and yer name—'tis too much to be only a coincidence."

Rory sucked in a pained breath and nearly choked on the dust beneath the bed. He brought his hand to his mouth. Alasdair MacDonald had his faults, but he'd lost much and handled it better than most. Rory didn't wish him to suffer further, and he knew how difficult it would be on Aileanna. But she wouldn't lie to the man, even if it was to ease his pain. She was honest and compassionate, and somehow he knew Aileanna would find a way to relieve Alasdair's disappointment.

"Alasdair, you have to believe me when I tell you there is nothing I'd like more than to be your daughter, but I'm afraid I'm not." She paused, and Rory could almost hear the wheels turning in her head as she planned out her wee story. It was not as if she could tell him the fairies had stolen her from her own time. "I told you I never met my father, and that's the truth, but my mother spoke of him often. She said he was from . . . from England, and he had . . . red hair . . . red like an apple, and . . ."

Bloody hell, Rory thought. *She's rambling again.*

"I'm sorry to disappoint you, Alasdair." Rory heard the raw emotion in her voice and he thought she was just as disappointed as Alasdair, even though she'd know there was no way the old man could be her father. Rory had sensed when she spoke to him about her life that she'd missed out on having a family, and it had left her deeply scarred. It was something he hoped to rectify by making her his wife, part of his clan.

"Nay, 'twas only the hopes of an old man. I'm sorry, Aileanna. Ye get some rest now, lass, and I'll see ye later."

He heard Aileanna sniff, and groaned inwardly. There was nothing he hated more than when she cried.

"Now, I didna' mean to make ye weep. Dry yer eyes—

there ye go. Doona' worry, my pet, I'll be fine. I'll see myself out."

At the sound of the door closing, Rory began dragging himself from beneath the bed. When it slowly creaked open again, he cursed inwardly and scrambled back to his hiding place, cracking his head on the rail as he did.

"Aileanna?"

"Yes?" She sniffed.

"I'm thinkin' yer in need of a father, seein' as how yer tangled up with the MacLeods. And since ye have the look and name of one of my own, I'm goin' to be lookin' to ye as though ye are. If that'd be all right with ye."

"Yes . . . yes, that would be wonderful."

No . . . no, it won't! Rory silently banged his head on the floor.

"Good, 'tis settled then. And, Aileanna, tell the lad I ken he's under the bed and I expect to see him in the salon momentarily." With that said, the old meddler slammed the door.

Rory stood, rubbing his head. "What do you think yer doin' tellin' him he can stand in fer yer father? Do ye no' ken what that mon will put me through?"

She shrugged. "It made him happy, and I think it will be nice to have someone stand up for me."

He snorted. "As if you canna' stand up fer yerself. And if you couldna', Fergus, Iain, and Mrs. Mac would be quick to do so."

"I know, and now I have Alasdair, too. It won't be so bad, Rory. Can't you humor him, just a little?"

He looked at Aileanna, her bonny eyes shining, and thought if it pleased her, the least he could do was try. If she could bring a little joy to the MacDonald's life, so be it. "I'll no' make any promises, but fer now we'll let it be, as long as you remember yer no' a MacDonald, yer a MacLeod."

"Not yet I'm not." She grinned.

"Aye. Yer mine, and well you ken it." He threaded his fingers through her hair and took her lips in a deep, slow kiss, savoring the taste of her.

"Rory," she said against his mouth. He pulled back to look at her. "I don't think Alasdair . . . my father will be too happy if you don't join him in the salon." He heard the laughter in her voice, saw the mischievous light in her eyes.

He gave her one last hard kiss. "Yer as stubborn as he is. I shouldna' be surprised if you truly are his kin."

"Rory," she called to him as he strode to the door. "I'm glad to be home."

Her words touched Rory deeply, and it made him more determined than ever to make her his wife. "No more than I am, mo chridhe."

Ali took her place on the dais between Rory and Alasdair, saying hello to Aidan, Fergus, and Iain, who looked like they shared a good joke no one else was privy to. She narrowed her gaze on them, and looked to the two men on either side of her. "Is there something I should know?"

"Nay . . . nay, my pet, everythin's fine. Shall I fix yer plate fer ye?"

Rory scrubbed his hands over his face and the other three men laughed into their mugs. Ali patted Alasdair's hand. "I can manage, but thank you for the offer." She nudged Rory and he raised a brow, looking down his nose at her.

Fergus said something to Alasdair and drew his attention from her.

She leaned into Rory and asked, "What's put you in such a bad mood?"

He took a deep swallow of his ale before he answered. "You'll find out soon enough, and you have only yerself to blame."

"What are you talking about? Blame for what?"

"Aileanna, eat before yer meal grows cold," Alasdair chided.

"But I—"

"Nay, eat, and then we'll talk," Alasdair said firmly, tapping his spoon against her plate.

She heard Rory's low chuckle and turned to him. He shrugged. "'Tis yer own fault."

After her third mouthful, Ali couldn't take it anymore. "Is someone going to tell me if you came to an agreement or not?"

Alasdair leaned around her to look at Rory. "Will ye tell her, or shall I?"

Rory tipped his mug at the man at her side. "By all means, do the honors."

"Aileanna, we've agreed to a truce."

"Oh, thank God." She blinked back tears, placing a hand over her heart. A deep sense of relief flooded through her.

"You might no' want to thank him just yet," Rory muttered.

"Aye, I've signed Trotternish over to ye, Aileanna, as part of yer dowry when ye wed Rory."

Chapter 24

"But . . . I'm not . . ." *Oh, dear Lord, what has Alasdair done?*

"Here." Rory wrapped her hand around a goblet of ale. "Drink."

She took a deep swallow and turned to him. "I don't understand why you're not happier about this. I thought it's what you wanted."

"Aye, I want to wed you, but no' like this. I'll no' have you forced."

"Oh." Relief loosened her tense muscles—he still wanted her. For a minute there, she'd thought he'd changed his mind. And now, Alasdair had put her in a position where her decision would affect the lives of Rory's clan—again. It would be so easy just to agree to the marriage. She loved Rory, more than she'd thought possible, but she didn't want to always wonder if he felt forced into the marriage, obligated to offer her his name and his protection because of the fairies. And now the matter had been complicated further. If Rory didn't marry her, they would battle over Trotternish, risking the lives of him and his clan. But if she did marry him, how would she ever know for certain what truly was in his heart?

Ali pushed her chair from the table. "Alasdair, I need to have a word with you."

"Aye." He rose slowly and took Ali by the elbow, a look of confusion in his bright blue eyes.

"Use my study," Rory suggested, watching her closely.

"Aileanna," Alasdair said as they left the hall, "I thought 'twould make ye happy."

She squeezed his hand, opening the door to Rory's study. "I know, and it was a lovely gesture, but—" She sighed. "If I tell you something, will you promise not to say a word to Rory?"

"Aye, on my honor." They entered the study and he took the chair opposite her.

"I love Rory," she said, then grimaced. "I'm sorry, he was married to Brianna and—"

He patted her hand. "Doona' worry aboot it, my pet. Say what ye will."

"I know he loves me, but when he spoke of marrying me he didn't say anything about love, only obligation and responsibility."

"That doesna' sound so bad to me, lass."

She blew out a frustrated breath. Were all highlanders the same? "Maybe not, but I need more. I don't want to be just another responsibility to him . . . like his clan. Remember how you said Brianna felt Rory would never be able to put her first? Well, that's how I feel, and it's not good enough."

Alasdair grinned. "Yer more like my wife than I first suspected. I made matters worse, didna' I?"

"A little," she admitted.

"Tell me this—when ye feel certain of the lad's commitment to ye, and he comes around to askin' in the manner ye hoped, will ye say aye?"

Ali snorted. "He didn't ask me, he told me." She narrowed her gaze at the glimmer of amusement in his eyes.

"Don't you dare laugh, but the answer to your question is yes. He's the only man I'll ever want."

"All right then, here's what we'll do. I'm goin' to gift Trotternish to ye, and ye can do with it what ye will. I ken I shouldna' have revoked Brianna's dowry. 'Twas no' right, and she wouldna' be happy with me fer doin' it, but you canna' tell the lad."

"No, I won't tell him," Ali said, rising to her feet at the same time he did. "And I was about to refuse your gift as too generous, but seeing as how you're using me to save face, I won't." She tapped her finger on his broad chest.

"Yer as canny as ye are bonny, my pet. Truly a frightenin' combination in a woman. I almost feel sorry fer the lad." He chuckled, taking her by the arm. "Shall we share the news with the clans?"

She reached up on tiptoe and kissed his cheek. "Thank you."

"Nay, 'tis I who should thank ye," Alasdair said as they left the study and returned to the hall.

Alasdair carefully settled her into the chair beside Rory, but remained standing. Rory frowned, looking to Ali as though she had the answer.

The older man banged his goblet on the trestle table. "If yer laird will permit me, I have an announcement to make." Rory gave a brief nod and waved him on. "As ye all must be aware, yer laird and I have been tryin' to come to an agreement over Trotternish as a means to avoid further bloodshed between our clans. I am pleased to tell ye, there will be no feud." Cheers broke out through the hall. It was pandemonium. Both men and women wept, and Ali took the handkerchief Rory offered her, sniffing her thanks. "I no longer hold Trotternish. It belongs to Lady Aileanna."

Table after table fell into stunned silence. Alasdair nudged her, and she realized he expected her to say something. She rose uncomfortably to her feet. "I'd like to propose a toast to

Alasdair MacDonald for gifting me with Trotternish. I'm honored." If not for the men on the dais taking up her toast, Ali thought it would have died a slow and painful death—just like her.

Once the crowd quieted, she turned to Rory. "And, for my part, I'd like to gift Trotternish to the MacLeods. To you, Rory," she said softly.

This time the celebratory cheers were so loud they shook the timbers of the hall. Rory stood and took her hands in his. "Are you certain?"

She nodded. "Aye."

Rory grinned, his goblet held high. "To the verra bonny Lady Aileanna, soon to be Lady of Dunvegan."

He laughed when he heard her mutter to Alasdair, "You see."

Rory watched as Fergus, Iain, and Aidan took turns sweeping her into their arms. The clan, not about to miss out on the opportunity to honor her, swarmed the dais.

Over their heads he raised a silent toast to Alasdair. The man held his goblet aloft and tilted it toward Rory. He looked as if he was about to say something to him when Callum swung Aileanna into his arms. Alasdair banged his goblet on the table. "Now see here, mind her wee foot."

Tables were pushed up against the walls, and several men took up their fiddles. Rory lost sight of Aileanna in the chaotic swirl of activity. His gaze scanned the hall for a second time, coming to rest on her sitting on a bench with Janet, Maureen, and old lady Cameron. She held a babe in her arms. His chest swelled. One day it would be their bairn she held. As soon as the thought entered his head, he panicked. He reminded himself she was strong, a healer, but still, a part of him rebelled at the thought of getting her with child. Then he remembered, she had yet to agree to marry him.

Content to watch the clan pay homage to Aileanna, he settled back in his chair.

"Ye love her, doona' ye?" Alasdair asked.

Rory nodded. He didn't know what he could say without hurting the man, without taking away from his union with Alasdair's daughter.

"Ye doona' have to worry, lad. I ken 'tis different with her. Ye doona' have to feel bad. What ye had with my Brianna was still better than most. I doona' fault ye in that."

Rory was taken aback. It was no secret Alasdair had held him to blame for Brianna's death. He hadn't resented the fact. How could he fault her father when he himself wondered the same? Before he could respond, Alasdair pushed back his chair. "I have a long ride on the morrow, and I'm no' as young as I used to be. If you'll excuse me, I'll be retirin' now."

Rory extended his hand and Alasdair took it in a firm grip. "Thank you," Rory said, and he meant it, more than the man would ever know.

"Ye may wish to hold yer thanks. I mean to have a say where it concerns Aileanna."

Rory groaned and Alasdair laughed, clapping him on the shoulder. "'Twill no' be that bad."

Aye, it will, Rory thought. He'd never be rid of the old goat.

"It seems ye get yerself a new wife, only to keep yer old father-by-marriage—an interestin' turn of events," his cousin said as together they watched Alasdair weave his way toward Aileanna.

"Interestin' is no' the word I'd choose," Rory grunted.

They were sitting in companionable silence when Aidan shot from his chair, sending it crashing to the floor.

The ale Rory had been drinking spilled from his mug onto his lap. "Bloody hell, Aidan, what is it?"

"My men," his cousin said, jerking his head at the two men-at-arms who stood in the entrance to the hall. "Lewis must be under attack."

Together they fought their way through the crowd.

Fergus and Iain, obviously noting their hasty retreat, were soon at their sides.

"They've come, Laird Aidan. The adventurers attacked, setting fire to the village on the south side of the island."

As Rory listened to Aidan question his men, he felt a gentle tug on his sleeve. "Rory, what's happened?"

He drew Aileanna aside. "Lewis has been attacked. The adventurers burnt down a village."

"Oh, no," she cried, and Rory saw the moment the realization of exactly what that meant hit her. Color drained from her face. "You're going, aren't you? No, don't say anything." She tugged her arm from his grasp. "There's nothing you can say to make me understand." Turning away from him, she lifted her skirts and fled from the hall as fast as her injured foot could carry her.

"Give her time, Rory. She'll come to understand."

"Do you think so, brother? Because I doona'," he said wearily as he watched her leave.

"She's frightened is all. Afraid somethin' will happen to you."

"I ken that, but right now I doona' have time to alleviate her fears. We head out on the morrow with Aidan. Fergus, ready the men." Once his cousin's men left, Rory approached him.

Aidan scrubbed his hand over his shadowed jaw. "I saw yer lady. She didna' seem verra happy."

"Nay, but 'tis the way of it, somethin' she will have to get used to."

"I'm sorry ye'll no' be spendin' much time with her. I wish I didna' need yer help in this, Rory, but I do."

He waved his cousin's concerns aside. "'Tis a good thin' we settled with the MacDonald, is all. How's Lan?"

"I didna' think it would happen this soon or I wouldna' have left my brother on his own. He's too young for the responsibility."

"He's got Dougal and Torquil with him, doesna' he?"

"Aye, he does, and fer all that he's young, he's canny and strong as well."

Rory threw an arm over Aidan's shoulder. "He'll be fine. We'll be by his side before long. Doona' fash yerself."

By the time Rory had assured himself all was at the ready the hour had grown late. He paused before entering Aileanna's darkened chambers. The fire had died down, and a lone candle flickered by her bed.

"I know it's you," she said, her voice husky.

He sat on the edge of the bed and brushed the hair from her face, kissing her tear-swollen eyes.

"Why do you have to go?" she asked.

"Aileanna, do you think if it wasna' necessary for me to be there that I would be goin'?"

"Yes. I've seen you, Rory MacLeod, playing with your men. You love the fight, the thrill of the battle."

At one time she would've been right, but no longer. He would give anything to stay at Dunvegan with her, but he couldn't abandon his cousin. "Would you have me leave Aidan and Lachlan to battle the adventurers on their own? They doona' have the men, and the ones they do have are no' trained as well as mine."

"It's not fair, Rory. I thought . . . I thought with the truce signed there wouldn't be this threat hanging over us. The ink is barely dry, yet you're off to fight another battle."

"We doona' face an enemy like the MacDonald, mo chridhe. 'Twill no' be the bloodbath that would've been."

"But you're still going to fight, and let me guess—no one even tried to negotiate with these men."

"'Twas sanctioned by King James. There will be no talks. The MacLeods of Lewis have held the island for centuries, yet the king means to depose them. Do you see the fairness in that, Aileanna? Would you no' fight if you were in their place?"

"Can't they go to the king?"

"They did, and it did them no good. There's no other way but to fight for what is theirs. I'm obligated to assist, and I will."

"There has to be—"

"Nay, stop. I willna' battle you as well." His words were terse, angry at her stubborn refusal to understand. "Will you no' let it go?"

"No." She shook her head. "I can't. If you would just try, I'm—"

He held up his hand. "Nay, you refuse to see reason. You doona' trust that I ken what is necessary and what is no', and I willna' spend my last night with you battlin' over this. Good night, Aileanna. I leave at dawn. I will see you on my return." He scanned her face for some sign she'd relent. Finding none, he took his leave, even though he wanted nothing more than to take her in his arms.

Ali's eyes widened at the sound of the closing door, stunned Rory had walked away without a backward glance. He was furious with her, but she didn't think he would leave without one last kiss. What if he didn't come back to her? As soon as the thought entered her head she shoved it aside.

A night that had been filled with joy and hope had turned into a nightmare. With her presentation of Trotternish to Rory she felt she'd made some progress with the clan. At least they no longer looked at her with suspicion—well, most of them didn't. She might not have gained total acceptance, but it was a start.

Was Rory right to insinuate she was too stubborn to understand, unwilling to see how things really were? Why didn't he try to see it from her viewpoint? She was a doctor. How was she supposed to come to terms with the taking of human life for the sake of pride, for the thrill of the fight?

Ali squeezed her eyes shut. What was wrong with her? Knowing Rory as she did, how could she for even one minute think that's why he fought? He was one of the most honorable, caring men she'd ever met. And even though she'd only been at Dunvegan for a short time, if the MacLeods were threatened, she would leap to their defense. Ali thought of the burnt-out village, the look of anguish on Aidan's face when his men reported the incident to him. *Incident,* she scoffed inwardly. *It was murder.*

Swallowing her pride, she slipped from the warm cocoon of her bed and left in search of Rory. The torches cast an eerie glow along the corridor. Ali wrapped her arms around herself, warding off the damp chill and a heavy sense of foreboding. The keep was quiet, and she hesitated outside of Alasdair's door, tiptoeing past as best she could with her injured ankle. Rory was right. She should never have suggested they put Alasdair in the room next to his.

The door to Rory's chambers creaked when she turned the handle. Closing her eyes, she waited for Alasdair to fly into the hall. But there was no sound coming from his room. She slipped inside Rory's chambers, quietly shutting the door behind her.

Shadows cast by the fire danced on the wall, and on the man in the bed. Rory lay with an arm behind his head. He watched her hesitant approach with a wary eye.

"Do you need somethin', Aileanna?" His tone was abrupt. The expression on his beautiful face was hard and unyielding.

"You," she answered honestly.

A slow smile curved his full lips. He held the covers back for her to climb in beside him, revealing his powerful, naked body.

Ali laid her head on his chest, listening to the strong, steady beat of his heart. "I'm sorry," she murmured, his chest hairs tickling her lips.

"What was that? I couldna' hear you, mo chridhe."

There was a hint of laughter in his deep voice and she scooted up, bringing her face level with his. "I know you heard me, but I'm not too proud to say it again. I'm sorry." She brushed her lips over his. "You were right. I didn't try to see it from your perspective. I don't know, maybe it's because I've never had anything worth fighting for. And I'm scared, Rory. I can't bear the thought of you being hurt, or anyone else for that matter." She rested her head against his shoulder and ran her fingers over the hard, muscular planes of his chest.

"I ken that, Aileanna." He kissed the top of her head, wrapping her in the warmth of his arms. "'Tis no' a question of a desire to do battle, but an obligation to one's clan and at times to one's country."

"Rory?" Ali didn't want to talk anymore. She needed to forget what he would face on Lewis and lose her worries and fears in him. Tracing ever-widening circles on his chest, she trailed her fingers lower to give him a hint of just what it was she wanted.

"Hmm." His voice rumbled deep in his chest.

"Do you . . . well, don't you want to make love to me before you leave?"

"I thought we'd just hold each other, lass, like this." His muscles rippled as he held her firmly in his embrace.

She tilted her head and narrowed her gaze on him, but before she could respond he had her on her back, his warm breath caressing her ear. "I want to love you, mo chridhe, but I'm no' certain you can be quiet. Yer a verra noisy woman. And thanks to you, we have a meddlin' old goat as a neighbor, and he'd be none too pleased that I have you in my bed."

She lightly slapped his chest. "I am not *that* noisy."

"Aye, you are." His hand skimmed over her leg until his fingers lingered at her throbbing core. "When I touch you here." He lowered his head and took her pebbled nipple deep into his hot, wet mouth, suckling her through the fabric of her shift. "Or here," he said as he thrust two fingers deep inside her. He smothered her gasp of pleasure with his mouth. Lifting his lips from hers, he said, "I'm glad you came to me, mo chridhe. If I could, I wouldna' spend even one night away from you."

She pressed her palm to his roughened jaw and held his emerald green gaze with hers. "I wish you didn't have to, but I do understand, Rory. I love you."

He covered her hand with his. "I love you, too, mo chridhe. And the moment I come back from Lewis I intend on makin' you my wife. Even if I have to drag you kickin' and screamin' to the altar."

"You can't—" Her protest ended on a moan as he swept her away on a tide of passion and desire.

"You canna' be mopin' already, my lady. He's no' been gone but a few hours." Mrs. Mac gave a shake of her head as Ali knelt at the edge of the fragrant garden, carefully pulling at the herbs and dropping them into her basket.

"I'm not," she said, but she was. Rory had promised to love her long and hard, and made good on his promise ten times over. The fullness between her legs, the dull ache that matched the one in her heart, were lasting reminders of what had passed between them. She had slept the sleep of the dead, missing the chance to tell him good-bye, and she was sure he'd done it on purpose.

"I wish someone would have woken me before Rory and Alasdair left," she groused, sweeping her hair over her shoulder.

"Och, well, the laird didna' want you to be disturbed. As for Laird MacDonald, we did try to wake you, but it did us no good. He said he'd be checkin' in on you in a day or so, on the trek back to Armadale."

"Good, I—" She turned her head at the sound of someone yelling off in the distance. As the shouts grew louder, she heard the panic in their voices and dread coiled in the pit of her stomach. Ali came quickly to her feet and hurried after Mrs. Mac to the far side of the keep. Cook, the girls from the kitchen, and several of the men Rory had left behind, raced in the direction of the loch.

"What's goin' on?" Mrs. Mac yelled to them.

"'Tis wee Jamie. He's fallin' into the loch."

"Always into mischief that one is," Mrs. Mac grumbled as they quickened their pace.

A woman's anguished cry rent the air and an icy chill slithered down Ali's spine. Standing on the rocky ledge above the loch she saw Janet Cameron being held back by two men while old lady Cameron and members of the clan formed a protective ring around the hysterical woman. A dark-haired man Ali didn't recognize waded to shore with the lifeless body of the little boy in his arms. She scrambled down the bank and shouldered her way through the throng of people, young and old alike.

A gnarled hand grabbed her by the arm. "There's nothin' ye can do, my lady. He's gone." A heavy sadness quaked in the old man's voice.

Janet Cameron collapsed, screaming, tearing at her glossy black curls.

Pushing aside her personal feelings, Ali shook off the man's hand. She had to reach Jamie. Once she did, she quickly placed her lips to the little boy's blue-tinged mouth and puffed in a rescue breath. Ignoring the gasps of horror at her back, Ali wrenched the unconscious child from the man and lowered him to the ground.

She rolled Jamie onto his stomach. Gently turning his head, she pressed firmly on his back several times and watched in relief as water gushed from his mouth. Turning him on his back, she checked for his pulse. Not finding one, she tried to remain calm and began CPR. Between breaths, she yelled, "Bring me a blanket! We have to get him out of these clothes." Janet was quickly at her side. With trembling hands she removed her son's sodden shirt and pants.

After what seemed like hours to Ali, but was in reality only minutes, Jamie's slight body arched and he threw up. His lids fluttered open and he let out a soft moan.

Ali wrapped him in a blanket and motioned for one of the men. "We have to get him to the keep." When the man simply stared at her open-mouthed, she shouted, *"Now."* Jamie was alive, but she didn't want to lose him to hypothermia.

His mother sobbed, and Ali tugged her to her feet, wrapping an arm around her. "He's going to be all right, Janet. I promise," she murmured as the man lifted Jamie into his arms. Ali prayed it was a promise she could keep.

"Thank ye, my lady, thank ye," Janet repeated over and over while the crowd stood motionless in stunned disbelief.

Connor reached for Ali and helped her and Janet up the rocky embankment. Behind her she could hear voices rise in excited whispers. "He's alive, wee Jamie lives."

And then the ominous word echoed in her ear. "Witch."

Chapter 25

Not more than a mile from Dunvegan, the threatening skies Mrs. Mac promised would amount to nothing, opened up. Ali pulled the MacLeod plaid over her head, and scowled at the woman who rode beside her through the teeming rain.

Mrs. Mac chuckled. "Och, well, a little water never hurt a body. Besides, yer a highlander now—best you get used to it."

The older woman's words warmed Ali's heart, but didn't do much for her frozen fingers clutching Bessie's reins. She wished the rest of the clan felt the same way, but saving Jamie had destroyed what progress she thought she'd made. At least the little boy was well on the road to recovery and, in the end, that was all that mattered.

Mari, riding ahead with Connor, glanced over her shoulder. "Do ye wish to return to the keep, my lady?"

Ali forced a smile, determined not to put a damper on Mari's excitement at visiting her family. And the last place Ali wanted to be right now was wandering the halls of Dunvegan, missing Rory. "Och, well, a wee bit of rain never hurt a body," she mimicked.

Connor's snort of amusement was lost in a loud rumble

of thunder. Ali pulled back on Bessie's reins, realizing it wasn't thunder after all, but the pounding of horses' hooves that caused the sound, and the ground to tremble. Four men on horseback tore up the narrow path, and she dug her heels in Bessie's side to get her to move before they were bowled over.

The man in the lead brought his mount to an abrupt halt, and his big bay whinnied in protest.

"'Tis the sheriff," Mrs. Mac muttered.

The auburn-haired man with the full beard, the one Mrs. Mac identified as the sheriff, gave his full attention to Ali. She tried to ignore the heaviness in the pit of her stomach at the suspicious look in his pale blue eyes.

"Are ye Lady Aileanna Graham?" His aggressive tone scraped her nerves raw.

Out of the corner of her eye she saw Connor attempt to bring his mount to her side, but two men who rode with the sheriff blocked his progress. Grabbing him roughly by the arms they held him back.

Her heart sped up. A shiver of dread ran down her spine. "I am. Is there something I can do for you?"

"Ye'll have to come with me. A charge of witchcraft has been brought against ye, and yer to stand trial on the morrow." He leaned over and jerked Bessie's reins from Ali's hands. The strip of leather bit into her numb fingers.

"Nay . . . nay!" Mrs. Mac and Mari cried.

A roar as loud as the pounding surf filled Ali's head, and she clutched Bessie's mane to hold herself steady. "Who . . . who brings these charges against me?"

"Ye'll meet yer accusers soon enough." He shot a menacing look over his shoulder as Connor struggled to break free of the men. "Try that again, lad, and ye'll regret it."

Ali saw a flash of steel and screamed. "Connor, no, please, please, do as he says," she begged him.

Connor's shoulders bowed as he raised his hands in surrender. Ali released a shuddering breath when the sheriff resheathed his sword.

"Let them go. It's me you want. They have nothing to do with this." She swallowed her fear long enough to control the tremor in her voice.

"Nay, I'll no' leave you, my lady." Mrs. Mac clung to her hand.

Ali squeezed, then withdrew her hand. "Please, Mrs. Mac, go home." With her eyes she pleaded with the older woman, tilting her head in Mari's direction.

Mrs. Mac gave a quick nod, indicating she understood what Ali tried to tell her. If the priest was behind this, and Ali was almost certain he was, she didn't want Mari anywhere near these men.

She met the sheriff's implacable stare. "Please, let them go."

"Aye, but doona' attempt anythin' foolish, my lady, or yer companions will suffer the consequences."

Ali choked back a hysterical laugh. What did he think she could do against four heavily armed men? The sheriff must truly believe the charges against her held merit.

Mrs. Mac leaned over and gave her a fierce hug. "Doona' fear, my lady. We'll be there on the morrow to see justice is served." She drew away from Ali and turned on the sheriff. "Ye would do well to remember 'tis Laird MacLeod's lady ye bring these charges against."

A spark of emotion flared in the man's eyes, and his jaw clenched. "She will receive a fair trial no matter who she is."

"Will I be given an opportunity to defend myself?" Ali barely got the words past the tight knot in her throat.

He gave her a long, considering look, as though he knew there was no one else who would come to her defense. "Aye, my lady. Now 'tis time to be on our way."

Mrs. Mac moved her horse aside to allow Mari a chance to say good-bye. Ali held on to Bessie's mane with one hand, reaching over to put an arm around her sobbing maid with the other. She whispered in her ear, "Mari, I don't want you at the trial. Promise me you won't come."

A hot tear rolled down Mari's cheek to splash on the back of Ali's hand. "I'll pray fer ye, my lady. I'll pray our laird comes back in time to save ye."

Oh, God, she couldn't think about Rory, not now. Ali nodded, unable to speak, her vision blurred.

Connor, free of his guards, reached for her hands. "Doona' worry, my lady. I'll find him. He'll come fer ye. Ye ken he will and we'll send word to Laird MacDonald at Portree."

Ali covered her mouth to keep a sob from escaping. Her chest ached from trying to hold back her emotions.

"Enough. All of ye take yer leave before I change my mind," the sheriff said impatiently.

Raising a hand to her brow, Ali squinted in the dull, midday sun, her eyes unaccustomed to even the dimmest of light after a night spent in the windowless cell beneath the squat building she now exited. The guard shoved her down the rickety wooden staircase, and she fell to her knees.

"On yer feet," he growled.

Using the bottom step for leverage, Ali hauled herself up, her legs trembling. She wiped her damp palms on her thighs. Her beautiful sky blue gown was torn and streaked with dirt. She heard the din of excited voices, and self-consciously touched the tangled mess of her hair, lowering her hand at the sound of the man's derisive laughter.

He grabbed her arm, his grimy fingers biting into the flesh of her upper arm. He dragged her around the corner of the building—the marketplace was jammed with people. They lined the walls of the surrounding buildings ten deep.

"There's the witch! There she is!"

A rock whizzed by her ear and struck the wall behind her. Ali fought against the same sense of defeat that had all but consumed her during the long, cold night on the mud-packed floor without blankets or food. Her resilience, her strength to face whatever they might do to her, had slipped from her then.

As she did in her cell, she called on her memories of Rory, and her love for him, to give her the strength to fight. She had too much to live for to give up now. Ali lifted her chin and walked defiantly into the center of the square.

Someone shouted out her name, and Ali searched the angry faces of the crowd. Her gaze froze on the wooden stake just beyond the fringe. She forced herself to look away, then spotted Mrs. Mac, Cook, Janet, Maureen, and several of the girls from the kitchen, relieved to see Mari was not among them. Their kind, caring faces blurred before her, and she swallowed past the lump in her throat.

The guard jerked her arm and hauled her in front of the sheriff, who sat behind a small wooden table. He kept his eyes glued to the piece of parchment on the desk. "We await yer accusers."

One by one the onlookers' heads turned and Ali looked to see what drew their attention. A small contingent pushed their way through the curious spectators, and Ali's mouth dropped when she saw who led the way—Moira MacLean. But of course, what did she expect? The priest, the one who'd accused Mari and Ali once before, followed close behind.

The sheriff rose to his feet with a smile of welcome and assisted Moira to her seat on the narrow bench. She thanked him, batting her eyes at the man. He looked be-mused as he walked back to his stool, and Ali groaned.

Moira shot her a haughty look. "Yer circumstances have changed much since last we met, *Lady* Aileanna." Brushing a dainty hand over her magenta gown, Moira's upper lip curled in a sneer she made certain only Ali would witness.

Out of the corner of her eye, Ali saw Cook and Janet hold Mrs. Mac back. Ali knew how her friend felt. Her own fingers itched to wrap around the little witch's neck. Anger battled with fear, and won.

"The truth will win out, Moira, and I'll be anxious to see how you explain your part in this to Rory."

The other woman's composure slipped, but was quickly replaced with a disdainful smile. "I'm certain he'll understand given the evidence. In all good conscience, I had to come forth."

The sheriff cleared his throat. "Lady Graham, yer brought here on charges of witchcraft. How do ye plead?"

She held his gaze until he lowered his. "Not guilty, and as all are innocent until proven guilty, I ask you, Sheriff, what is your proof?"

The sheriff blinked and looked from Moira to the priest. His voluminous gray robe swirling, the little man jumped to his feet. "She struck me down in defense of a witch."

"Those charges were addressed by Lord MacLeod and all were dismissed." Ali didn't look at the priest, giving her full attention to the sheriff instead.

He stroked his beard. "Is this true?" Although he had brought her there to stand trial, Ali was beginning to think the man at least would be fair. A glimmer of hope flickered to life inside her. All she had to do was stay strong and hold her ground.

"Aye, but the trial wasna' fair."

"Ye had yer chance, Priest. The only reason ye bring charges against Lady Aileanna is because she shamed ye in front of the people fer stonin' an innocent child," Janet Cameron cried out.

"Aye . . . aye." Several of the others from Dunvegan agreed loudly.

"Quiet! Did ye stone a child?" the sheriff asked.

"She was no' innocent with her red hair and eyes of two colors. 'Tis the sign of a witch."

"The sheriff has red hair. Are you accusing him of being a witch?"

The priest glared at Ali. "Ye see, 'tis what she does. She twists the truth. 'Twas the same at Dunvegan."

The sheriff blew out an impatient breath. "Sit down, Priest."

Moira patted the distraught man's hand and rose to her feet. "Although it pains me to say, Sheriff, there is no doubt this woman is a witch. I've seen it with my own eyes." Her hand fluttered to her chest, and crocodile tears slid down her flushed cheeks. "I was to be married to Laird MacLeod, and this woman, she bewitched him. Cast her wicked spells on him, she did. I was a witness to it all."

"No, Moira, what happened is Rory finally came to his senses and saw you for who you really are. You're more of a witch than I'll ever be."

For a brief moment all the hate Moira MacLean felt for Ali shone in her eyes, but she was quick to conceal it. "I have other witnesses, Sheriff, if you'll allow them to speak." Not waiting for the man's response, she motioned to someone in the crowd behind her. Two men and a woman stepped forward, unwilling to meet Ali's eyes, and her heart sank. They were gaunt, their legs thin and bowed with obvious signs of starvation, and Ali knew they would do anything for money.

"Say yer piece." The sheriff waved his hand and ordered, "Speak up."

"I . . . I saw 'er dance naked under the moon with the devil himself."

There were gasps of outrage, and Ali would have laughed if not for the fact they appeared to believe the woman.

"Aye, 'twas what I saw as well," one of the woman's companions said. "And 'twas after that my cow dropped dead."

"Aye, and the water in the well turned blood red."

"Do ye have anythin' to say fer yerself, Lady Aileanna?" the sheriff asked, his expression grim.

"I'd like to question the witnesses."

Moira and the priest looked at each other in obvious distress.

The sheriff scratched his head. "'Tis an unusual request, but I'll no' have Laird MacLeod sayin' ye were no' given a fair trial."

"Thank you." Ali turned to her accusers. "You do realize when you give evidence at a trial you're swearing to God to tell the truth?" She paused to let her words sink in.

The priest once again jumped to his feet. "What right does she have to invoke the name of the Lord?"

"I wasn't. I'm simply stating a fact, is that not true, Sheriff?"

"Aye." He gave her a tight nod. "Ye may go on."

"Did Lady MacLean offer you money for your test . . . to speak against me?"

"Nay," the oldest of the three was quick to say.

The other two bowed their heads.

"Tell him," Moira shrieked. "Ye tell them I gave ye no money or—"

The sheriff came to his feet and shot an angry look at Moira and the priest. "I doona' like to be played fer a fool. 'Tis my findin' that Lady Aileanna Graham is inn—"

"Nay . . . nay." A young dark-haired man pushed his way through the crowd. "I saw it with my own eyes. She brought a wee lad back from the dead. He'd drowned in the loch."

Ali closed her eyes. Now how was she supposed to explain that?

"She's no witch. She's an angel. Saved my son, she did." Janet Cameron's cries were drowned out by the sound of horses' hooves pounding on the hard-packed earth. The ground shook beneath Ali's feet. Dust billowed and choked the onlookers.

When the cloud cleared, she looked up to see Alasdair MacDonald. Like an avenging angel, he urged his white steed forward. The people fell over themselves to get out of his way. At least a hundred men rode with him—fierce, angry men.

"Are ye all right, my pet?" he asked.

Ali nodded. Bemused relief washed over her.

"What is it ye charge my daughter with?"

"Yer daughter? I didna' ken she was yer daughter, Laird MacDonald."

"Speak, mon! What are the charges?"

"Wi . . . witchcraft, my lord."

"Yer chargin' *my* daughter with witchcraft?" he bellowed, bringing his horse within snorting distance.

"Nay . . . nay, they are." The sheriff stumbled backward, pointing to Moira and the priest. "But . . . but I was just about to declare her innocence when this lad says she brought a child back to life."

"Aileanna?" Alasdair raised a brow.

She gave a frantic shake of her head. "He wasn't dead. He swallowed a lot of water and the loch brought his body temperature down too low, that's all."

"I saw her. She blew into his mouth."

"Yes, of course I did. I had to replace the air he'd been deprived of. I've seen it done before."

"My daughter is a healer. She's no witch, and if I hear another spout lies against her, they'll answer to me." He reached for Aileanna's hand and pulled her onto the back of his horse. "Do ye declare my daughter innocent?"

The sheriff's Adam's apple bobbed in his throat. "Aye, my lord, aye."

Alasdair brought his horse around to face Moira and

the priest. "I warn ye, doona' ever threaten my daughter again or ye'll be verra sorry ye did." Color drained from their faces. "Fire the stake," Alasdair roared. "And make certain I see no other raised in its place."

Those that had come from Dunvegan cheered, rushing toward Ali. "We'll see you at the keep then, my lady," Mrs. Mac said with tears in her eyes.

After returning their happy smiles and good wishes, Ali slumped against Alasdair's broad back, too weary to do anything but. "Yer safe, my pet, yer safe." He patted her leg.

Rory leapt from the boat, leaving the men that accompanied him to pull it onto the rocky shore. Soaked through to his skin from rain and sweat, but he barely noticed, too intent on rescuing Aileanna. They'd crossed The Minch in the middle of the night, thankful for the winds at their back.

Racing along the path to the courtyard, Rory called out to the men on the parapet. "I need four of you to accompany me to the village."

If his men were surprised to see him, they didn't show it. Cedric shot him a sympathetic look. "We willna' make it, my laird. The trial is already underway."

"Nay, I will make it on time. There's a chance she'll be proven innocent."

Byron shook his head. "It doesna' look good, my lord. I ken she's innocent, but after Jamie's accident . . ." The man gave a helpless shrug of his shoulders.

"What . . . what happened?" Connor had been so exhausted on his arrival at Lewis that Rory had been unable to get more than a few words from him.

"The lad drowned in the loch. He was dead, my lord, I swear it, and yet she brought him back to life."

Rory had never felt more helpless than he did at that moment. He raged inwardly at his inability to save her, to protect her. With evidence such as that, there was no question in his mind she'd be found guilty. Heart pounding, he raced for the keep before it was too late. He knew what had to be done. There were no other options available to him. He couldn't allow her to die.

Rory threw the door to his study open and pulled the books from the shelf to get at the secret compartment behind them. His hand shook as he withdrew the fairy flag. Closing his eyes, he clenched the piece of silk in his fist and slammed it into the wall. The books from the shelf above crashed at his feet.

Rory took the stairs to the tower two at a time, knowing he had no choice but to use the clan's last wish. All he could think of was Aileanna. He had to save her. His chest grew so tight he thought it would explode. His throat ached from choking back the emotion, the pain of losing her.

A rush of cold air whipped at the flag as he raised it. "Good-bye, mo chridhe, my love."

Rory strode from the keep. "Back to the boat," he barked at the men who awaited his command in the courtyard. As they prepared to set sail for Lewis, Rory took one last look at Dunvegan and the fairy flag on the tower fluttering in the wind. She was lost to him forever, and he cursed the fairy flag and the superstitious fools who had forced his hand.

Haunted by images of Aileanna—her beautiful face, her laughter and her strength—he wanted to be as far away from everything that meant anything to him as he could get. He'd lost the only woman he truly loved. And not even Dunvegan or thoughts of his clan offered him peace.

Chapter 26

As the distance between Ali and the village grew, the tension inside her eased. Exhausted, she clung to Alasdair.

"'Twill no' be long, lass, and I'll have ye back at the keep."

Ali smiled, raising her head as the tower of Dunvegan beckoned in the distance. A cream colored piece of fabric fluttered at the very top. Ali gasped. *No, it can't be!* She rubbed her eyes, praying she was mistaken. She held her breath as once more she raised her gaze to the tower. Her heart shattered. Rory had raised the fairy flag.

Her breath came in short panicked gasps and spots dotted her vision. A prickly heat flooded her limbs and she clutched at Alasdair's shirt to keep from falling off the horse. How could he do this to her? How could he send her back to a place she no longer called home, to no one, to nothing?

Alasdair, as though sensing her distress, twisted in the saddle to look back at her. "Aileanna, what is it? What's wrong?"

"Take me to Armadale with you, Alasdair. Please," she choked out on an anguished sob.

"Aye, my pet, whatever ye wish." He took one last look at her before he waved his men on. "We ride fer Armadale."

The men cheered. The raw beauty of the landscape

blurred before her eyes. Ali didn't know how long it would take for the fairy magic to work, but she couldn't be at Dunvegan when it did. To spend whatever time she had left surrounded by the people she loved, only to disappear, would be unbearable. They were lost to her forever.

"Wake up, lass, we're home. There sits Armadale." Alasdair pointed proudly to the fairy-tale castle perched on a sloping hill with a loch below.

Ali shook off the last remnants of sleep, glancing at her hands and the landscape to reassure herself the flag's magic hadn't worked—at least not yet. "It's beautiful," she finally managed to croak.

The horses clomped across the cobblestoned courtyard. Servants rushed to greet them. Noting Ali's presence, they held back, their jaws dropping in open astonishment. A lovely looking woman, her auburn hair lightly streaked with gray, stepped through the massive oak doors with a warm smile on her face. Catching sight of Ali, she clapped a hand to her mouth. Her cry of dismay brought several servants to her side.

Alasdair sighed. "That would be Fiona, my wife's sister. After Anna left with the babe she remained to care for Brianna."

Ali's eyes widened. "Your wife's name was Anna?"

Helping her from the horse, his brow furrowed. "Aye."

"My . . . my mother's name was Anna."

Alasdair stared at her. Grabbing her by the shoulders, he gave her a little shake. "Do ye see it now, lass? 'Tis the truth—ye are my daughter."

Ali shook her head. "No, it's a coincidence, Alasdair, that's all. I can't tell you why I'm so sure, but I am." If she told him the truth, he'd think she'd lost her mind. Unable to escape on the long journey to Alasdair's home, she had to find a way to leave Armadale without raising his suspicions, or he'd find a way to stop her. She didn't know where she'd go to wait until the magic sent her back, but she couldn't be with Alasdair when it did. The man had suffered enough.

"Ye'll tell me, Aileanna. I must ken, or 'twill eat at me until the day I die. Can ye no' understand, my pet? I need to ken."

"Aileanna? Alasdair, is it truly she?" The woman stood plucking at his sleeve. Luminous brown eyes brimmed with tears, and Aileanna felt a fleeting sense of recognition.

"'Tis. Whether she will admit to it, or no'," he said, his voice tight with anger.

"Alasdair, I don't mean to hurt you, but I can't pretend to be your daughter when I know I'm not. No matter how much both of us wish it was true."

He shook off the woman's hand and dragged Ali after him. "I ken 'tis true, and I'll show ye why."

"Alasdair, can this no' wait? The child is obviously exhausted."

"Nay, I've waited over twenty-seven years to find her, and I'll no' wait a moment longer."

Ali stumbled after him, past the gaping servants. He led her up the curved stone staircase and opened a door to a long, narrow room lined with portraits. "There." He pointed. "Now, tell me yer no' my daughter."

"Alasdair, I know I look like Brianna. I've seen her portrait be—"

"Nay, that one." He held her by the shoulders and directed her gaze to the portrait on the right of Brianna's.

Ali stared at the painted image of a woman with the topaz eyes and hair the color of spun gold. Her breath quickened, and her heart stuttered in her chest. Faded memories rushed at her in a swirling torrent. The room spun, and her knees buckled. She was so terrified it was the fairy magic she could barely breathe. But it wasn't—it was shock, the shock of looking at her mother's beautiful face.

She clutched Alasdair's arm. "How . . . how can it be? I'm not from . . ." Her voice trailed off, unable to tell him the truth.

Fiona dragged over a chair. "Here, sit, my dear. There, there." She patted Aileanna's shoulder. "Ye should ken better, ye old goat. The child is dead on her feet."

Alasdair scowled at the woman. "I need to ken once and fer all. Ye of anyone should understand, Fiona."

"Aye, I do." Her voice was gentle as she knelt at Ali's side. "I ken ye've had a rough time of it, and I doona' want to add to yer troubles, but when yer mo—when my sister had the babies she sent fer me. I helped with the bairns, until . . . until." She let out a shuddering breath. "If ye allow me, I can tell ye fer certain whether or no' yer Aileanna MacDonald."

"But I can't be . . . you don't understand."

Alasdair shot Ali a ferocious glare before he turned to the other woman. "What are ye sayin', Fiona? How would ye ken?"

"The bairn had a birthmark, Alasdair, a wee crescent moon just below the hairline at the back of her neck."

Before Ali could respond, Alasdair lifted her hair. She heard Fiona gasp, and let out a weary sigh. "I'm sorry, Alasdair. I tried to tell you."

He pressed his big palm to her cheek and turned her to face him. His sky blue eyes were bright with unshed tears. "The wee moon is there, my pet. There is no doubt, ye are my daughter."

Ali stared at him in shocked disbelief. She shook her head. Heart racing, she managed to say, "But I can't be. I'm not from—"

"Tell me, Aileanna. Tell me why ye canna' believe 'tis true."

"I can't." She bowed her head. Ali understood his frustration when so much of the evidence seemed to validate his claim that she was his daughter: the portrait of a woman who looked like her mother, had the same name, and now to learn she bore the identical birthmark as the daughter he had lost all those years ago. Good Lord, she'd almost believe it herself if not for the fact she was from the twenty-first century.

He moved to stand in front of her, arms crossed over his broad chest. "Aye, ye will." Jaw set, he skewered her with an unbending stare.

Seeing the glimmer of moisture in Alasdair's eyes, Ali couldn't keep the truth from him any longer. To try to help him understand why there was no way she could be his daughter was the least she could do. She didn't want him to suffer more than he already had, and she knew he'd keep her secret. He'd never allow anyone or anything to hurt her.

"All right, I'll tell you, but I think you had better sit down and close the door."

He frowned, but did as she asked. Once he and Fiona had brought their chairs round to sit in front of her, she began her story. She told them everything she remembered of her mother and life growing up without her, without anyone.

At times she depended on the memories of the old neighbor she'd tracked down on one of her many searches for her family, to fill in the blanks. It was how Ali learned about the man her mother married when Ali was too young to remember, a husband who had been abusive, and abandoned them less than a year after the marriage. Her mother had cleaned houses, barely managing to eke out a living. But most painful of all was the memory of the car accident that had taken Anna's life and left Ali an orphan.

Alasdair sat stiffly in his chair, the expression on his face unreadable. Absently he handed Fiona his handkerchief.

Her aunt sniffed as she asked, "How is it ye came to be a Graham, Aileanna?"

Ali closed her eyes before answering. "After the accident I was put in foster care. Just before my seventh birthday, I was adopted. The family's name was Graham."

"But ye didna' remain with them?"

Ali shook her head, determined not to cry. She'd buried that particular hurt a long time ago. "No, Mrs. Graham died eighteen months after I was adopted, and Mr. Graham sent me back to foster care. He . . . he said he couldn't manage to care for another child, especially as I wasn't his own. He hadn't wanted me in the first place."

"My poor wee poppet," Fiona cried.

Ali cleared her throat and told the rest of the story, about the fairy magic, and how she came to be at Dunvegan. She hesitated before she said to Alasdair, "Rory raised the fairy flag the day you took me from the trial. That's why I asked you to bring me to Armadale. I couldn't bear to be there waiting for the magic to take me away. And now when it does, I . . . I'm going to cause you more pain, and you don't deserve that."

"Nay, no one will take ye away from me again," he said fiercely.

Ali gave him a sad smile. "I don't think there's any way to stop it, Alasdair. But now, despite all the coincidences, can you see how it's just not possible that I'm your daughter?"

"They aren't coincidences, my dear. Ye are Aileanna Mac-Donald. Think on what ye've told us. What Duncan Macintosh told ye that day at Dunvegan. The MacLeods raised the fairy flag in fifteen seventy and defeated the MacDonalds." Fiona held her gaze with a gentle confidence.

"They won because yer mother and ye went missin', Aileanna. I was too busy searchin' fer ye to lead my men into battle."

"'Twas over twenty-seven years ago, Aileanna. How old are ye?" Fiona asked.

"Twenty . . . I'll be twenty-eight on my birthday."

Alasdair pulled her from the chair and folded her into his warm, protective embrace. "Aileanna, ye can doubt it no longer. I'll no' let you go, my pet. They'll no' take ye from me."

Fiona and Alasdair were right. There was no denying the facts. The MacLeods' fairy flag had stolen Ali and her mother from their home over twenty-seven years ago, only to return Ali on the day Iain raised the flag to save Rory. It was true, all of it. She had a father, a family, and she didn't know what she'd do if the fairy magic took her away from them again.

"I don't want to leave, Alasdair. I can't tell you how much I want to stay. How can I go back when everyone I love is here?" *Dear God, please don't let them take me. I don't think I could bear it.*

He cupped her face between his hands and gently wiped her tears away with his thumbs. "Shh, yer no' goin' anywhere, and ye'll call me Alasdair no more. Ye'll call me father from now on, or da, whichever ye prefer."

Fiona gave an unladylike snort, swiping at her own tears. "And at times ye'll call him an old goat like I do."

Ali laughed, then hiccupped. "That's what Rory calls him."

A wave of intense pain arched through her body at the thought of Rory. She wanted nothing more than to go to him, but didn't have the strength to be ripped from his arms. It hadn't taken her long to come to the realization Rory raised the flag to save her. And she wouldn't make him suffer with the knowledge there'd been no need for him to do so.

She'd managed to save herself. Although in the end, her father's presence had swayed the sheriff more than she ever could. In his attempt to save her life, Rory had destroyed their one chance for happiness.

"That one has a lot to answer fer, and the first question will be what possessed him to raise the bloody flag in the first place. A man who professes to love ye then sends ye away to be lost to him forever," Alasdair growled, tightening his hold on her.

"'Tis because he loves her, Alasdair. Mayhap he thought 'twas the only way to save her. Did ye no' say it was the last wish, Aileanna, and he'd no' send ye back because it was all his clan had left?" Fiona went on, not giving Ali a chance to respond. "I'd say the mon loves yer daughter above all else, wouldna' ye, Alasdair?"

He muttered something under his breath before he kissed Ali on the forehead. "Yer aunt will show ye to yer chambers. Ye need yer rest, fer this night we celebrate my daughter's return." His eyes welled, and Ali's heart ached as she tried to imagine how he felt. He might have her back, but he'd lost his wife, and now, after finding Ali, he could turn around and she'd be gone again. But for now, she'd put the thought from her mind, and let them both enjoy what little time they had left together.

Rory stood in the grand hall at Lewis and begrudgingly accepted the mug of ale his brother offered him, but refused to take a seat with them by the fire.

Aidan released a weary sigh. "I ken yer in a bad way, cousin, but ye canna' solve anythin' by stayin' here and fightin' like a mon possessed."

"I'm no' in a bad way, and I thought by fightin' the adventurers I was helpin' you save yer home." Rory scowled at him.

"Brother, 'tis time fer us to leave. Aidan and Lachlan can handle those that survived, without our help. The men are anxious to return to Dunvegan and their families." Iain eyed him warily. "I miss her too, Rory. I ken no' as much as you, but I do miss her," he finished quietly.

Rory glared at Iain, angry he talked of her. Since the day he had returned to Lewis after raising the fairy flag, he had allowed no mention of her in his presence. The pain hadn't subsided. If anything, it grew worse. Like a piece of him was being cut away each and every day, and soon there would be nothing left of him. The last place he wanted to be was Dunvegan, where the memories of her were bound to taunt and torture him.

His cousin Lachlan watched him carefully. Chewing on his bottom lip, he shot his brother Aidan a worried glance. The lad was the youngest of the MacLeods, but one day he would surpass them all in height and strength. "Rory, did ye think mayhap there was a way to contact the fairies and ask them to return yer lady to ye?"

With barely contained rage, Aidan glared at his brother. "Are ye daft, Lan? The fairy flag was passed to the MacLeods centuries ago. 'Tis a myth, is all."

"'Tis no myth. The fairies exist," the lad mumbled, shifting uncomfortably on the bench.

"Have ye gone mad, brother?" Aidan was angrier than Rory had ever seen him and he laid a hand on his cousin's shoulder to calm him. Although he knew better than anyone that the flag was no myth, he had a hard time believing the fairies still existed in this time. But he wouldn't hurt the lad's feelings by saying so. For a fleeting moment he wanted to hold on to Lan's belief, but was quick to brush it aside as foolishness. The only magick that existed was in the flag, and without another wish, he had nothing.

Lan flushed crimson. "I ken they do. I've heard them."

"When, Lan? When did you hear them?" Rory heard the desperation in his own voice, a slippery thread of excitement that vanished as soon as he saw the look of disbelief in the eyes of Fergus, Aidan, and Iain.

"When I was a bairn I heard them. They came to me in my dreams." Lan flushed to the roots of his fair hair. His forehead beaded with sweat. Rory felt sorry for the lad. The only reason his cousin had made mention of the fairies was to offer Rory some hope, risking ridicule to do so.

Aidan slammed his hand on the arm of his chair. "'Tis the old crone that looked after ye when ye were a bairn that turned yer head. No more talk of fairies, brother, or I'll lock ye away."

"You send fer me if he does, Lan, and I'll bring you back to Dunvegan with me. I appreciate yer tellin' me aboot the fairies. If you hear them again, be sure to make mention of . . ." He hesitated, not certain he could say her name aloud without unleashing the emotions he'd locked away. He swallowed hard. "Aileanna." He ruffled his young cousin's hair when he nodded shyly.

Rory looked at Fergus. "Tell the men we leave on the morrow."

Rory bowed his head as the boats approached the shores of Dunvegan, unable to look upon the flag that fluttered on top of the tower. Emotions warred within him, and he battled an urge to set sail in the opposite direction, but he couldn't—not yet.

The excited chatter of his men grew the closer they got to Dunvegan. Rory felt a twinge of guilt for keeping them away as long as he had. It hadn't been warranted. They could've returned weeks ago, and he should've sent Fergus and Iain back to Dunvegan with the men. But they refused to leave him, too afraid he'd go too far in battle, risk too much. Maybe they were right. Maybe he would have.

"Are you all right, brother?" Iain asked from where he sat in the boat behind Rory.

Both Iain and Fergus had cut him a wide berth on the way back. He didn't blame them. He wasn't fit for company.

A sorry lot they must have looked as they left the boats on shore and walked along the path to the keep. Lord knew they should be bellowing out their triumph. They'd pushed the adventurers back to lick their wounds, and the MacLeods had lost no one to the enemy's swords.

"I'll be fine, Iain, but I'm thinkin' of goin' to court fer a time. Mayhap I can do some good there fer Aidan and Lachlan, and it would no' hurt our cause either."

"Aye . . . aye, if that's what you need to do."

Out of the corner of his eye he saw the look his brother shared with Fergus. He ignored them. The emotional turmoil of coming home was taking its toll, and he was anxious for his bed.

He looked up to see Mrs. Mac cross the courtyard to greet them. She was flanked by Janet, Maureen, Mari, and old lady Cameron. The women looked none too happy. Rory sighed. It would be awhile before he saw his bed.

He glanced at Fergus and Iain. "Bloody hell, what have we come home to?"

"I doona' ken, but they look plenty fashed at you, lad," Fergus said, watching as the women drew near.

"Ladies, is there a problem?" They crossed their arms and glared at him. "Since I've just come home, I doona' ken what I coulda' done wrong."

"Why did you no' bring our lady home?"

Rory blanched, a tight pressure building in his chest. "I'm sorry, Mrs. Mac. I didna' make it back in time."

"Och, and what does that have to do with it? All this time her bein' at Armadale and no' with us. 'Tis no' right. Get yer horse and go and get her."

The emotion was so thick in his throat he could barely

get the words out. "Mrs. Mac, she's no' at Armadale." He pulled her aside and lowered his voice. "Did you no' see the fairy flag? I had to send her back. I was too late to save her. There was no other way."

Mrs. Mac ducked her head. "'Twas no' the fairy flag you raised."

Chapter 27

Ali sat up in bed, clamping a hand over her mouth. "Not again," she groaned into her palm. The wave of nausea passed, and she flopped onto the down-filled pillows. A long, drawn-out creak drew her attention, and she cracked one eye open to see her aunt peek around the door.

"Oh, poppet, yer ill again this morn." Fiona swept into the room. Her royal blue silk skirts swished over the stone floor as she made her way to Ali's bedside, a look of concern in her kind eyes. "Mayhap we should have someone see to ye. I havena' said a word to yer father. I didna' want to worry him, ye ken, and ye always perk up by midday, but really, my pet, this has gone on too long." The bed dipped when she sat to stroke the hair from Ali's clammy forehead.

"Aunt Fiona, I think you've forgotten I am a doctor. I'm quite capable of seeing to my own care, more competent than most of the heal . . . oh, good Lord." Maybe not so competent after all. Ali felt like giving herself a couple of knocks on the head, but didn't, afraid it wouldn't have the desired effect. Instead of knocking some sense into her, she'd probably throw up—again.

How stupid could she be? Pregnant. She was pregnant. It certainly explained why she'd been so tired of late. A symptom she'd ascribed to lack of sleep when she'd been too afraid to close her eyes in case the fairies stole her away. Missing her period and her overwrought emotions, she'd put down to stress—stress and missing Rory.

"What is it, Aileanna? Is it serious, poppet?" Her aunt's eyes filled and she twisted her hands in her lap.

Ali drew Fiona into a reassuring hug. In the few short weeks she'd been at Armadale her aunt had loved and cared for her like a mother. "No, it's nothing. I mean, it's not nothing, it's just that, well, I'm pregnant." Ali grimaced, not sure how her aunt would take the news.

Lying back, Ali rested her hand on her still flat stomach. She smiled, filled with an excited bubble of wonder and joy. She was having a baby—Rory's baby. A man she hadn't seen in weeks. A tiny bit of her happiness dissipated. He hadn't responded to her letters and the little niggling of doubt was getting harder to ignore.

Fiona's mouth dropped. "A bairn . . . yer havin' a bairn?"

Ali chewed on her bottom lip. "Umhmm. Rory's baby."

"Laird MacLeod. Of course—good, that's good." Her aunt's brow furrowed and she tapped a finger on her lightly-lined cheek. "Well, there's no time to waste, then," she said after a moment of silence, flipping the covers off Ali.

Ali arched a brow. "If you don't mind, Auntie, it might be best if I lie here for a little longer."

"Oh, of course, I didna' think. I'm sorry, poppet." She patted the coverlet into place and resumed her seat. "Now, 'tis most important we get in touch with Laird MacLeod."

Ali sighed. "I tried. As soon as I knew the fairies' magic wasn't going to work I sent him a letter—more than one actually. He hasn't responded, and it's been a couple of weeks now." Trying to ignore the sinking feeling in the pit of her stomach, Ali plucked at the satin comforter.

Fiona's brow furrowed. "I didna' ken ye sent a letter. Did yer father?"

Ali nodded. "I didn't know how to send it without his help." And Alasdair had fought her tooth and nail, until the tears. When Ali had begun to cry, he gave in.

Her usually mild-mannered aunt cursed under her breath. "That mon, sometimes I'd like to shake him. Aileanna, I doubt verra much yer father sent yer missive. He's no' relented aboot yer seein' the MacLeod, no matter what he's led ye to believe. 'Tis what the gatherin' this night is aboot. There are plenty of potential suitors on the guest list."

Ali groaned. "Aunt Fiona, you have to make him stop. The only man I want is Rory, and that's not going to change, especially now." She patted her stomach to make her point.

"I've tried, but he's a stubborn old goat. 'Tis like talkin' to a wall—a big, thick one." Her aunt gestured just how thick with her hands. "Mayhap 'twould be best if ye doona' mention the bairn."

"I didn't plan on telling either the father or the grandfather, at least not for a while."

"I understand ye no' tellin' yer father. He's liable to call the lad out, but why would ye no' be tellin' Laird MacLeod?"

Ali rolled her eyes. "Thanks for that comforting thought, Auntie. As for Rory, I refuse to let him marry me just because I'm having his baby. And as soon as he finds out, that's exactly what he'll expect. Not that there's much chance he'll find out anytime soon." She sat up and hugged her knees to her chest. "He must know I'm here, Aunt Fiona. I'm worried he's having second thoughts about us, that he regrets using the clan's last wish, especially since it didn't work." There was something else, something she herself had a difficult time thinking about. How would Rory feel when he found out he was in love with his late wife's sister?

Her aunt smoothed Ali's hair over her shoulder. "That's

nonsense, and ye ken it as well as I do. From what ye've told me, the lad loves ye, and I ken ye love him. Which leaves me to wonder why ye'd no' want him to marry ye even if it was on account of the bairn."

Ali released a frustrated breath. "Auntie, I've told you before. I'll not have Rory MacLeod marry me out of a sense of duty. I want him to marry me because he loves me, because he doesn't want to live without me. And I won't have him bully me into it, which is exactly what he'd do if he found out I was pregnant."

Fiona chuckled and patted her knee. "Well, poppet, I'd say we have our work cut out fer us."

Ali blinked back tears at the sight of her father and aunt waiting for her at the bottom of the stairs. The look of love and the pride in their eyes made her heart swell. In the short time she'd been with them, she'd come to love them both dearly.

"There is no' a woman in Scotland who can hold a candle to ye, my pet." Her father beamed as she reached the bottom step. He looped Ali's arm through his, and kissed the top of her head.

Ali reached up to kiss his grizzled cheek. "Thank you, and thank you for the gorgeous gown." She lifted the crimson velvet skirt. "I feel like a princess. You spoil me." He had. The wardrobe in Ali's room was overstuffed with gowns of every color in sumptuous fabrics—silks, satins, and velvets. "But this . . . this is too much." She touched the heavy, jewel-encrusted necklace with a large ruby at its center.

Her aunt wiped a tear from her eyes. "Nonsense. Yer the image of yer mother, poppet. She would've been as proud of ye this night as we are."

Ali swiped the moisture from her cheek, and squeezed

her aunt's hand. "Thank you," she murmured past the knot in her throat.

Her father groaned. "Look at the two of ye, greetin' away when we've guests awaitin' us."

Ali's eyes widened as he led her into the grand hall. The massive room overflowed with richly dressed men and women. Gilded torches graced the oak-paneled walls. Thick forest-green velvet draperies hung at the windows. The tables groaned with food and a small group of musicians stood by the massive stone fireplace.

Someone had gone to a great deal of effort to make this evening special, and Ali imagined that's why she'd been unable to pin her father down for their much-needed chat. But she couldn't put it off any longer. She had to see Rory, and if he wouldn't come to her, she'd swallow her pride and go to him.

"Here she is," her father announced to a group of men congregated in the center of the room. "Come, my pet. I have some gentlemen who are verra anxious to meet ye."

Good God, her aunt hadn't been exaggerating.

Fiona leaned toward her. "See, what did I tell ye?"

Before Ali could comment, her father whisked her away from her aunt to introduce her to the men. Although later that evening he did deign to introduce her to more than just the eligible bachelors, of which there seemed to be an inordinate number.

Ali sipped her water and smiled politely, but after another hour passed, her smile felt as though it was frozen in place. Each face blurred into the other. Their inane chatter faded to an annoying buzz that left her light-headed. Ali tugged on her father's sleeve.

He lowered his ear to her, and she said, "I need to talk to you. It's important." Without further ado, Ali dragged her father unceremoniously to an unoccupied corner of the overheated room, as far from the blazing hearth as she could manage.

"Aileanna, 'tis rude to leave our guests in such a manner. I ken ye may no' do things the same way in yer time, my pet, but—"

"I'm sorry, but I've been trying to speak to you all day and I can't wait any longer." She crossed her arms over her chest and narrowed her gaze on him. "Did you send my letters to Rory? And I expect you to tell me the truth."

"Nay." He crossed his arms over his broad chest, a defiant set to his chin. "And I willna' do it, even if ye beg me. The lad is no' fer ye. There are some fine gentlemen over there, just waitin' fer the opportunity to court ye. If ye would give them half a chance, my pet, I'm certain—"

Hands on her hips, she glared at him. "No, and if you won't send my letters, I'll go to Dunvegan on my own."

"Ye'll no' set foot from Armadale, Aileanna MacDonald. Besides, the MacLeod is no' at Dunvegan. He's on the Isle of Lewis."

"But it's been weeks. I thought the battle would be over by now." Ali's hand went to her throat. "He isn't hurt, is he? Please tell me he's all right."

"Aye, the lad's well, more's the pity. They've beaten the adventurers back. No need for them to remain, but they do. It appears the lad is in no hurry to return to Dunvegan, and I'm certain I ken why. Ye should've listened to me, Aileanna. He'll no' be able to live with himself fer riskin' his clan on account of ye."

Her aunt, who must have been keeping an eye on them, chose that moment to appear at Ali's side. "Alasdair MacDonald, shame on ye fer sayin' such a thing to yer daughter. Come, poppet, ye look a mite overheated." She shushed Alasdair and led Ali from the room.

Ali threw up her arms. "He's so stubborn, he's maddening. He's—"

Her aunt chuckled. "Doona' worry, we'll figure somethin' out. Mayhap ye should take a stroll in the gardens, poppet. Yer father had the torches lit and I'm thinkin' a wee breath of air is just what ye need. Take yer mantle with ye, though. 'Tis a mite chilly out."

Rory's hands tightened on Lucifer's reins. "I'll no' say it again, Reggie. I've come fer Lady Aileanna Graham," he roared at the MacDonald's man-at-arms, a warrior he'd faced often in battle.

"And I told ye, MacLeod, there's no Lady Aileanna Graham here. And the laird doesna' want ye on his lands." In the shadows, Rory saw the slash of white as the idiot grinned.

"Open the bloody gates. Lady Aileanna is my betrothed and no' you or the MacDonald will keep me from her."

"Is that so? Do ye hear that, lads? MacLeod here thinks Lady Aileanna is his betrothed." The man guffawed with his companions on the parapet.

One of the other men laughed. "I doona' think the young bucks in there vyin' fer her hand would be too pleased to hear that, do ye, Reggie?"

Reggie rested a foot on the stone ledge and leaned over, tugging on his fiery red beard. "Like I said, MacLeod, we have only one Lady Aileanna here, and she's a *MacDonald*. The gates are closed to ye so ye'd best head back to Dunvegan. Have a nice ride."

Rory cursed roundly. He was getting nowhere with the fools, and if MacDonald thought he could keep him from Aileanna, he'd best think again.

He brought Lucifer around and headed back the way he'd come. Raucous laughter followed him on a blustery wind. The stallion snorted puffs of white frost. Rory patted Lucifer's thickly muscled neck. "Doona worry, boy, we're no' goin' far." Once they were out of the laughing men's line of sight, he changed direction, making a wide circle of Armadale to the woods at the back.

Rory's gut boiled. Anger and frustration steamed from his pores. MacDonald had gone mad. It was the only reason Rory could come up with to explain the man claiming Aileanna as his daughter, and worse, trying to marry her off. Like hell he would. She was his. Rory brought Lucifer alongside the back wall. Since MacDonald was at peace with most of the clans at the moment, including Rory's, he would have no men guarding the isolated area.

"Hold, boy." He stood unsteadily on the saddle, his legs weak from his long trek. The muscles in his arms strained and burned as he clung to the top of the stone ledge. Finding purchase with his foot in a crack in the wall, he heaved himself over.

The momentum sent him to the top, and he lowered himself to the ground. With a soft thud he landed in the frozen earth behind a tree. He dragged himself to his feet and pushed aside the branches.

Aileanna. Rory sucked in a ragged breath, his chest so tight it hurt. Her head tipped back, moonlight kissed a profile so perfect it looked as though it was carved in marble. Her pale hair gleamed in soft waves down her back. Awestruck by her beauty, he stumbled from the shadows of the tree.

Aileanna slowly turned. Her lips parted. "Rory," she whispered. "Oh, Rory." Laughing and crying, she ran down the narrow path to throw herself in his arms.

He clung to her as though his life depended on it, on her. She showered his face with soft kisses, and Rory choked back a sob. He speared his fingers through her hair and looked into her emotion-filled eyes before he crushed her lips with his. His kiss fierce and demanding, hot and wet, he devoured her, inhaled her sweet, familiar scent.

Only when he felt her tremble did he reluctantly ease back, his breathing harsh, hers the same. "Yer cold."

Her eyes searched his face as though memorizing every detail. He winced, realizing what he must look like, what he must smell like.

"I'm sorry, mo chridhe. We'd just returned from Lewis and I rode straight to Armadale. I ken I doona' smell particularly fine at the moment."

She grinned and wrinkled her nose. He laughed and kissed the turned-up tip before he ran his hands down her arms and held her out from him. "I'm goin' to ruin yer bonny gown." Aileanna slid her arms around his neck, closing the space between them to bury her face in his chest.

"I don't care. My God, Rory, I thought I'd never see you again." Her lips brushed his chilled skin, and then her shoulders shook, her tears dampening the front of his tunic.

"Shh, love, doona' cry," he crooned, stroking her silken tresses. "I'm here now. I'll never leave you again."

She tipped her chin and gazed up at him. He wiped her tears away with his thumbs and smiled down at her. "I thought I'd lost you forever, Aileanna. It wasn't until I came back from Lewis that I learned you were here, that the magick didna' work."

Fresh tears trickled down her cheeks. "I was so scared, Rory. I kept waiting for the magic to happen, waiting for it to take me away from you, from everyone."

The look of anguish in her face tore at every fiber of his being. "You have to believe me, mo chridhe, I never would have raised the flag if I'd thought there was any other way. I couldn't let you die. I—"

She shook her head and pressed two fingers to his mouth. "I know." Her lips curved in a gentle smile. "I know you felt you had no other choice. I understood what the decision cost you. How difficult it was for you to use the clan's last wish, and I loved you for that."

He gave her a fierce kiss. "I couldna' do anythin' but. I love you, Aileanna, ye must ken that."

She touched his cheek. "I do. I love you, too." A shadow darkened her luminous blue eyes. "But I don't understand why I'm still here. Why the magic didn't work."

He gave her a wry grin, and brushed a strand of hair from her face. "Mrs. Mac. She didna' want to risk you findin' the flag and leavin' us. She switched the silk. It was no' the real flag I raised that day."

Aileanna sagged against him. "I wish I had known."

He cradled her head against his chest. "You and me both, my love," he murmured.

She threaded her fingers through his hair and brought his mouth back to hers. Her kiss was achingly sweet.

"Get yer filthy paws off my daughter, MacLeod." Mac-Donald's angry words crackled in the stillness of the night.

Rory's head whipped up. Lost in Aileanna, he had no warning of the other man's presence, and he cursed his inattention.

Aileanna groaned. She squeezed Rory's hand. "Let me handle this."

He shook his head, looking past her to the older man who stood on the garden path. "Nay, this is between me and MacDonald." He gently placed her out of harm's way, ignoring her protests.

In four angry strides, MacDonald closed the distance between them. "Yer no' welcome here. Get off my lands, MacLeod."

"'Twill be my pleasure, but I willna' leave without Aileanna."

"Over my dead body. I'll no' give ye another of my daughters after what ye did to the last."

Rory heard Aileanna gasp.

"I did everything in my power to save Brianna and you bloody well ken it. As fer Aileanna—"

"Ye'll no' have her," the man bellowed. "Ye godforsaken MacLeods and yer bloody flag took her from me the first time. Ye'll no' be takin' her from me again." He thumped Rory in the chest with his fist.

Anger hazed his vision and Rory thumped him back, going toe-to-toe with the raving lunatic before him. "She's mine, and no' you or anyone else will keep her from me."

"She's no' yers, she's mine, and I'll no' see her wed to ye. I've got men inside, good men, better than the likes of ye, beggin' fer her hand."

Heat blasted through Rory. He fisted his hands, the temptation to hit the man overwhelming. "Ye canna' promise her to another. We're as good as wed. She's been in my bed."

Aileanna's outraged gasp pierced his temper and he cursed, turning to apologize to her.

Smack.

The MacDonald's powerful fist glanced off Rory's cheek, hitting him square in the eye. Rory stumbled. His battle-honed reflexes took over and he planted his fist in the MacDonald's eye.

With a bellow of rage, the older man charged him, and the two of them landed in a prickly bush. Pummeling each other, they rolled off the bush and onto the hard ground.

"Stop it, stop it!" Aileanna's pained cry froze their fists in midair. Rory lowered his hand and rolled onto his back, as did the MacDonald. The two of them stared wide-eyed at the glorious angel who looked down at them—a very angry angel. Her stormy blue eyes flashed, and Rory winced at the string of curse words coming out of her innocent-looking mouth.

"Aileanna!" came the MacDonald's shocked response.

"Doona' Aileanna me. Bloodthirsty highlanders, the two of ye. Doona' think either of ye have a say over me. I'll decide who and when I wed. And ye can wipe that silly grin off yer face, MacLeod. I didna' say I was marryin' ye."

When the MacDonald chortled gleefully, she shook her finger at him. "And ye, paradin' yer merry band of suitors before me. I'll no' wed any of them, and I can tell ye they'll no' want to wed me, a woman who carries the MacLeod's bairn."

She cursed. Pivoting on her heel, she stormed from the gardens, leaving them lying in stunned silence on the frozen ground.

Chapter 28

The sure-footed old goat managed to get to his feet before Rory did. But Rory imagined it had less to do with agility, and more to do with the fact that he still reeled from the emotions Aileanna's sharp tongue elicited.

Despite her anger, the memory of her thick brogue brought a smile to his face. The knowledge he was to be a father warmed his heart with a depth of emotion he'd thought only Aileanna could cause him to feel. But her stubborn unwillingness to wed him was a punch to his gut more debilitating than the one the MacDonald had delivered.

Once Rory managed to get to his feet, he rushed to catch up to the old man. They reached the door to the keep at the same time, jostling each other for entry. Their shoulders squeezed together as they tried to get through the door. Rory grunted, took a step back and shoved the old goat inside. Following him through the dimly lit corridor, he matched the MacDonald stride for stride when he saw Aileanna speaking to an older woman at the foot of the stairs.

Bathed in the warm glow of torchlight, she took his breath away. She no longer wore her mantle and Rory drew his gaze from where the large ruby glinted between the generous hollow of her creamy white breasts. If he hadn't, the evidence of how much he wanted her would be visible to anyone who cared to look.

"Aileanna, we need to talk." Rory barely managed to keep his frustration in check.

"Aileanna, ye and I have much to discuss," the MacDonald said pointedly, giving Rory a little shove.

She regarded them with a haughty stare. "I'm not in the mood." She tossed her hair and headed up the stairs. The delectable sway of her backside left Rory fighting the urge to throw her over his shoulder and make off with her into the night.

"Poppet, 'tis best fer all if this matter is settled."

Rory heard her sigh, then she turned to meet the older woman's beseeching gaze. "All right, Auntie, we'll meet in the salon."

Auntie? Rory narrowed his gaze on Aileanna. What the bloody hell was she playin' at?

"Nay, we have guests, Fiona. 'Twould be best if we left this until the morrow, and I'll no' have this mon anywhere near my daughter."

Rory thrust his fingers through his hair. "Are you daft, mon? She's as much yer daughter as I am yer son."

Aileanna held up her hand. "Father, not another word out of you until we have some privacy." She tipped her head toward the entrance of the grand hall where a small crowd gathered.

"Aileanna, you doona' understand. He'll make our lives a livin' hell if you continue to let him believe yer his daughter. Doona' pander to the mon, love."

Alasdair gave a snort of self-satisfied laughter and clapped Rory a staggering blow to his shoulder. "Welcome to hell, my boy."

The older woman intervened before Rory could respond. "Alasdair, see to yer guests while—" She stopped midsentence, her lips pursed. "After ye've put yerself to rights, that is. Laird MacLeod, I'll see ye to yer rooms and mayhap a bath would be in order." She wrinkled her nose, a twinkle in her eyes.

They were mad, the lot of them. Including the bonny mother of his child, whose soft giggle hadn't escaped his notice. Remembering his manners, Rory brought the woman's hand to his lips. "'Tis a pleasure to meet ye, Lady Fiona."

Ali looked up from where she sat, legs curled beneath her on the overstuffed armchair. Her father and Rory, with a matching purple hue surrounding their left eyes, entered the salon together. If the expression on their faces was anything to go by, it was not by choice.

When her eyes met Rory's, her breath caught in her throat. His damp hair, pushed back from the chiseled lines of his gorgeous face, brushed the snowy white linen that encased his broad shoulders. The tan suede pants he wore heightened the allure of his narrow waist and long, muscular legs.

As though he sensed the direction of her thoughts, his beautiful mouth curved in a sensual smile. That and the promise in his eyes caused Ali's stomach to do a slow roll.

A commotion behind the men drew her attention. Fiona, followed by two young serving girls carrying platters, entered the room.

"I thought mayhap ye could use some sustenance, Laird MacLeod." Fiona smiled at Rory, motioning for the platters to be placed on the table behind her.

Ali groaned when the smell of roasted meat wafted past her nostrils.

Rory strode to her side, a look of concern in his emerald eyes. "Are you all right, mo chridhe?" His long, warm fingers tipped her chin. She nodded, the intensity of his gaze making it difficult for her to speak.

Rory stroked her cheek with the back of his knuckles. "Good." He crouched beside her, bringing her hand to his lips. "I'm sorry if my words in the garden hurt you, love. 'Twas no' my intention."

Her father's loud grumbling was becoming difficult to ignore. When Fiona elbowed him, he glared at her. "What was that fer? Ye canna' expect me to stand quietly by while he . . . he tries to seduce my daughter."

Rory shot to his feet, rounding on her father. "Ye canna' possibly believe that Aileanna is yer daughter."

Ali's nails dug into her palms, afraid of Rory's reaction when he found out she was a MacDonald, Brianna's sister.

"Laird MacLeod, please sit." Her aunt nudged him into a chair opposite Ali. "Alasdair, you, too." She pointed to a chair a good distance from Rory. "I think 'twould be best if he hears it from ye, poppet."

"Aileanna, what's goin' on here?" Rory's voice was harsh, edged with steel.

Ali swallowed hard. "He's my father, Rory. No." She held up a hand to stop his angry protest, then proceeded to tell him all she had learned since the day he had raised what he thought was the fairy flag.

Rory shook his head slowly. His mouth opened and closed.

Her father leaned back in his chair, a wide grin splitting his handsome face. "At a loss fer words, lad? 'Tis a welcome change." Alasdair chortled.

Ali was tempted to smack him.

Rory took a deep swallow from the goblet of whiskey her aunt had pressed into his hands midway through Ali's halting explanation. He lifted his gaze to hers. "So, yer Brianna's twin, then?"

Ali nodded. She looked down at her hands, the crimson velvet twisted through her fingers. She couldn't bring herself to meet his eyes, too afraid of what she'd see there.

"Aye, and now yer free of any guilt ye may have had fer takin' Aileanna from her time. In truth, ye brought her back to us, and we must thank ye fer that," her aunt said in an obvious attempt to relieve the tension in the room.

Ali held her breath when her father began to mutter about it being because of the MacLeods she'd been stolen away in the first place. But it didn't appear as if Rory even heard him. He sat, deep in thought. As the silence dragged on, the knots in Ali's stomach twisted.

"Alasdair," Fiona said, jerking her chin at Rory, a determined look in her eyes.

Her father left his seat to pace in front of the hearth. Coming to an abrupt halt near Rory's chair, he shot Fiona a disgruntled look. "It appears, MacLeod, that I have no choice but to give ye my daughter's hand in marriage. If no' fer the bairn she carries, I can tell ye I'd no' let ye near her. I've arranged fer the priest to be here on the morrow."

Rory scrubbed his hands over his face, shaking his head. "Ye ken as well as I do, Alasdair, I canna' marry Brianna's sister."

Ali's heart squeezed. She couldn't breathe, her worst fears confirmed. Now that he knew who she was, Rory didn't want her. She choked back a sob. Tears streamed unchecked down her face.

"Aileanna, what is it?" Rory came to her side and gently wiped the moisture from her cheeks.

"You don . . . don't want to mar . . . marry me anymore," she sobbed.

With a tender smile, he took her hands in his. "You doona' understand, mo chridhe. 'Tis no'—"

"It's because I'm Brianna's sister." She hiccupped. "You can't love me because . . . because I'm her sister." Heartbroken, Ali cried all the harder.

"Shh, yer goin' to make yerself sick, love. Look at me." He cupped her face between his roughened palms. "There is nothin' in this world that would make me stop lovin' you, mo chridhe. You misunderstood me. 'Twas marryin' you before a priest that I was speakin' aboot."

Ali swiped at her tears. He loved her. The knots in her stomach loosened ever so slightly. "You don't want a priest to marry us?"

He arched a brow. His deep chuckle rumbled over her. "As I remember it, you were no' plannin' on marryin' me in the first place." He tilted his head to look at her. "Are you tellin' me you've changed yer mind?"

She sniffed, then nodded. The thought of losing Rory overrode any of her silly sensibilities, and they *were* silly when she considered how much she loved this man.

He stood and pulled her up along with him. Wrapping her in his arms, he held her close. "Then we're as good as wed," he proclaimed with a grin.

"What?" she squeaked, easing out of his arms.

"Aileanna, because yer Brianna's sister, a priest willna' marry us until I get dispensation from the pope. If 'tis important to you, I will, but 'twill take some time. I ken this may sound odd to you, but all it takes for us to be legally wed is fer us to agree that we are. We have witnesses." He nodded toward her father and her aunt. "Although even that is no' necessary. This one, here"—he flattened his palm to her stomach, a heated look in his eyes—"is the only one we truly need."

Ali drew her gaze to Alasdair and Fiona, who stood together a few feet away. "Is this true?"

Her aunt gave her a watery smile. "Aye, 'tis how many are wed in the highlands, poppet. 'Tis legal."

Her father's mouth opened as though he planned to argue the point, grunting when Fiona elbowed him. He turned on her aunt. "Woman, what has gotten into ye?" He rubbed his stomach then looked at Ali, his expression softening. "Aye, my pet, yer now wed to . . . to *him*."

"Oh." She looked up at Rory. "We're married?"

Rory laughed. "Aye." He turned to her father and aunt. "And if ye doona' mind, I'm takin' my wife to her chambers. She needs her rest." With that said, he swung Ali into his arms and strode from the salon, leaving her aunt chuckling and her father sputtering behind them.

"I have a feelin' I'll pay fer that on the morrow," Rory said wryly. "Where's yer chambers, love?"

"In the East Wing, fourth door on the left." Ali waved her hand in the direction of her room. Wrapping her arms around his neck, she snuggled closer.

Rory groaned.

She lifted her head. "Am I too heavy?"

He snorted. "Nay, yer room is too far." He quieted her response with a hard kiss that had her squirming in his arms.

Breaking their kiss at the sound of feminine giggles, Rory growled at the two young maids. The girls squealed and ran in the opposite direction.

Ali laughed. "You're fierce, Lord MacLeod."

"Aye, and you best remember it. Now, please, tell me this is yer room."

She looked up. "It is."

"Thank God. You'll have to open the door. My hands are full at the moment."

Ali rolled her eyes and lifted the latch. Once they were inside, Rory kicked the door closed. He laid her on the bed, stretching out beside her. His eyes drifted shut, and he released a contented sigh.

Ali raised herself up on her elbow and pressed her palm to the dark shadow that lined his jaw. "You're exhausted."

He brought her hand to his lips. "Aye." Rolling onto his side, he nudged her onto her back. "But I'd have to be dead no' to be able to show you how much I missed you."

She trailed the tips of her fingers along his cheek. "I think you should let me take care of you, Lord MacLeod. After all, I am the doctor in the family, and I know just what you need."

Rory grinned. "You do, do you?" His expression turned serious. "Aileanna, yer all I'll ever need. I love you." He slid his lips back and forth over hers, then kissed her thoroughly, deeply, in a slow and possessive kiss. He cradled her head with one hand while the other traced along the edge of her necklace.

Ali sucked in a ragged breath when feather-light fingers dipped beneath the neckline of her gown, stroking her breasts. He lifted his mouth from hers. "I think 'tis time to rid you of some clothes." His voice was deep and husky.

Placing a palm on his chest, Ali pushed him onto his back. Coming up on her knees, she knelt beside him. "Funny, that's exactly what I was thinking."

Ali leaned over and tugged the soft leather boots from his feet, tossing them beside the bed. She ran her hand up his leg, over his hip, stroking him beneath the waistband of his pants. The hard muscles of his stomach rippled. Ali pushed his shirt aside, dipping her head to trail her tongue over his lightly bronzed skin.

Rory sucked in a harsh breath. "Doona' tease me, love. I've been too long without you."

He didn't look amused when Ali chuckled. "Patience, my lord," she said as she tugged his pants over his hips, raising a brow at his lack of underwear.

Seeing her expression, Rory shrugged. "'Twas bad enough I had to borrow his trews and tunic. I bloody well wasna' goin' to borrow the old goat's braies."

Ali fought back a smile. "Rory, that's my father you're referring to."

"Aye, doona' remind me," he grumbled, raising his hips so Ali could relieve him of his pants while he shrugged out of his shirt. His powerful, naked body, golden skin stretched tight over rippling muscles, was a feast for the eyes. A feast she was only too happy to partake of. Ali ran the tip of her finger along his jutting erection. His long, thick shaft twitched, and he groaned. "The priest was right—yer a witch," he growled.

"Hey." She twined her fingers in his chest hair and tugged lightly.

"Rough, too, but I like it." Rory grinned. Reaching for her, he hauled her within easy reach of his nimble fingers and unclasped her necklace, tossing it on the bedside table. He worked at the hooks of her gown. Seconds later, he had her bared to the waist. "You must have had a lot of practice to be able to get me out . . . ah." She moaned when he reached up to cup her breasts, sucking one nipple and then the other into his hot, wet mouth.

She let out a startled cry when he tossed her onto her back. He lifted his head and winced. "I'm sorry, did I hurt you, love?"

Ali slowly shook her head from side to side, as anxious for him to be rid of her clothes as he was. Rory tugged her gown over her hips, then froze. Searching her face, he shoved his fingers through his hair. "I'm sorry, Aileanna—the bairn, I forgot."

He caressed her belly, then dipped his head to drop a soft kiss there. The muscles in her stomach contracted. Her core grew slick and hot with need. With one last gentle pat to her belly, he dropped onto his back, an arm over his eyes, his breathing ragged.

Ali struggled out of the rest of her clothes and came onto her knees beside him. She lifted his arm from his eyes. He cracked one eye open. "You can't be serious?" she muttered.

"I doona' want to hurt you or the bairn. We can't . . ." He waved his hand at their naked bodies.

His eyes widened when Ali straddled him. She brought her face within inches of his. "Rory MacLeod, I am strong and healthy. So is our baby. Trust me—not making love to me at this moment is much more harmful to my health, and that is definitely not good for the baby."

His eyes searched hers. A slow smile curved his full lips. "We canna' have that, now can we?" He threaded his fingers through her hair and brought her mouth to his. "Yer certain?"

"Positive," she murmured before she nibbled the corner of his mouth, sweeping the tip of her tongue over his lips, tasting the smooth, rich flavor of whiskey. She delved inside the moist heat to thrust and parry with his tongue. With her kiss, she showed him how much she loved him, how much she needed him.

Rory groaned and wrapped her in his arms. "You canna' ken how much I've missed you, missed this."

Ali blinked back tears. She didn't want to cry, not now. Raw emotions simmered too close to the surface, and she could only nod her agreement.

She eased out of his arms. "Now it's my turn to take care of you." Her voice deepened with desire.

Rory's eyes darkened. "Whatever you say, my love."

His long, hard erection jerked against her. Ali leaned forward with her hands pressed to his broad chest and slid up and down his shaft.

"Ride me." His thick brogue grew more pronounced.

Ali wrapped her hand around his pulsating shaft and guided it to where she was throbbing and needy. She lowered herself slowly. Taking him inside her, her sheath embraced him. He arched his hips, filling her to the hilt.

She rode him, panting, groaning when he kneaded her breasts with his big, rough hands. He pulled her down to him, drawing her nipple into his mouth. He suckled hard.

She opened her eyes. He devoured her with his, her love and passion reflected back at her.

"Come fer me, Aileanna." His voice was thick with desire.

She leaned back, her fingers digging into his strong, muscular thighs. He plunged in and out of her, stroking her nub with his talented fingers. He seared her with his touch, branding her as his. Ali felt the intensity building at the center of her core and shuddered as the sensations washed over her. She shattered at the same time as Rory let out a low, guttural groan and came inside her.

Later, lying spent in Rory's arms, she brushed the pad of her thumb across the full bottom lip of a mouth that had brought her to unbelievable heights only moments before.

He smiled and dropped a kiss on her forehead. He tugged a silver band from his baby finger and brought her left hand to his mouth. Rory kissed the tip of each of her fingers before sliding the ring onto her fourth one.

"It's beautiful," she said, admiring the intricate markings on the thick silver band. "Was . . . was it Brianna's?" The words were out of her mouth before she could stop them. She wished it didn't matter to her, but it did. "What are you doing?" she protested when he slipped the ring from her finger.

"I had the ring made before I went to Lewis, Aileanna. Can you see the etchin' on the inside of the band?" His voice was gruff. He held the ring so it gleamed in the moonlight, tilting the band so she could see the engraving.

She squinted. "I can't read it."

"It says, 'you and no other'." He slid the ring back on her finger. "There is no other fer me, Aileanna, but you. Yer sister and I married, as most do in my time, fer the betterment of the clan. I did love her. But no' like I love you. At one time it scared me how strong my love fer you was, but no longer. I ken I'm no' my father."

"I'm sorry, Rory. I don't mean to be jealous." She

brushed her lips along the underside of his jaw. "Maybe it's time to let go of our ghosts and concentrate on our life together, our love for one another."

He pressed his lips to her forehead. "Aye, on us and the little one."

She entwined her fingers with his. "Are you happy about the baby?"

He smiled. Leaning over her, he nuzzled her stomach before he lifted his eyes back to hers. "In truth, I've never been happier than I am now. You and the bairn will want fer nothin'."

"If we have you, we won't need anything else."

"You have me, Aileanna, all of me—heart, body, and soul."

Epilogue

Ali eased her son's flailing arm through the sleeve of the long, white, lacy gown and kissed his little rosebud mouth before he let out a lusty wail.

She glanced over to Rory as he closed the door to their room. He released a long-suffering sigh, a tortured look on his gorgeous face. She bit back a grin.

"Doona' you laugh, yer no' the one who has to put up with him. Please tell me he's leavin' after the bairns' christenin'."

Ali heard the rustling in the cradle and said, "Bring me Jamie, Rory. Alex is ready." She held the baby up for his father's inspection.

"Aye, he looks charmin' in his wee gown." Rory shook his head while he fingered the lace. He pressed his lips to Alex's inky black curls, then gave Ali a mind-numbing kiss until the baby squawked in protest. Rory grinned. "Ye have the look of me, laddie, but ye have the temper of the old goat down below, and yer mother."

He gave Ali a playful slap on the behind as he walked over to the cradle and lifted Jamie into his arms. "And yer as bonny as yer mother with yer father's easygoing temperament." He kissed his son's cheek and laid him on the bed beside his brother.

Ali rolled her eyes, then began to dress Jamie.

"Hurry up now. If we're quick with the celebratin' we'll have them on their way while it's still light," Rory urged impatiently.

"That's not very nice. He's my father."

"Aileanna, I'm no' jokin'. The man will make me daft if he's here much longer. And you ken I love yer aunt, but she's always flittin' aboot and I'm no' gettin' enough time alone with you."

Ali arched a brow. "I seem to recall last night we had quite a bit of time alone."

He stood behind her and wrapped his arms around her waist. "Aye." His voice was deep and husky. "But I'm a verra greedy mon, with an insatiable appetite fer my bonny wife."

"Just like your sons." She hummed in pleasure when he nuzzled her neck.

"Please, mo chridhe, promise me you'll send them home." His heated breath caressed her ear.

"I'll—" Ali didn't get a chance to finish what she was about to say. Her father barged into the room followed by her aunt, Mrs. Mac, Fergus, and Iain.

"Can ye no' leave my daughter alone long enough to get the bairns ready?"

"Aileanna," Rory growled in her ear.

"The boys are ready. Look at them—aren't they adorable?" Mrs. Mac and her aunt all but shoved her aside to get to the babies, oohing and aahing over them. Before Ali could get out another word, the two women made off with Alex and Jamie. The three men followed close behind and ordered the women to have a care, instructing them on how they should be holding the babies.

Ali turned in her husband's arms. Threading her fingers through his thick, black hair, she tugged his mouth down to hers. "See, there are some benefits to keeping them around," she said against his lips.

ABOUT THE AUTHOR

Debbie Mazzuca thinks she has the best job in the world.
She spends her days cavorting through the wilds of
seventeenth-century Scotland with her sexy highland
heroes and her equally fabulous heroines.

Back in the twenty-first century you can find her living
in Ottawa, Ontario with her husband, two of their three
children, and a yappy Yorkie. You can visit Debbie on the
Web at www.debbiemazzuca.com.